I0601043

Twin Worlds

Flight of the Raven, Book One

F. J. Talley

Thank you for reading If you enjoy this book, please leave a review or connect with the author.

All rights reserved. Aside from brief quotations for media coverage and reviews, no part of this book may be reproduced or distributed in any form with the author's permission. Thank you for supporting authors and a diverse, creative culture by purchasing this book and complying with copyright laws.

Acknowledgements

Thanks to my family -- Ellen, Mark and Rosa -- for their patience and support during the production (and endless editing and gnashing of teeth) of Twin Worlds: you are the best!

Also thanks to Twin Worlds' awesome launch team!

Ann Backus
Roy Backus
Ashantee Barnwell
Joanna Colvin
Nancy Danganan
Cody Dorsey
Mary Dorsey
Gene Edwards
Jasmyne Heitmeyer
Jordan Parker
Morgan Smith
Ellen Servetnick
Rosa Talley-Servetnick
Aryana Ware

Chapter One

Beta Quadrant Space, Star Alliance Vessel SAV/ Endeavor *Ready Room*

"All hands, all personnel. All hands, all personnel. Docking at Quadrant Headquarters in one hour. Return to base stations for final inspection. All hands, all..." The speaker seemed particularly loud.

Commander Stuart looked to his captain and friend. "Are you sure you're ready for this, Tucker?"

His captain smiled. "As ready as I can be, I imagine," Captain McLeod said, as he finished securing his uniform jacket, his bronze hands dancing over the buttons.

"I did notice the dress uniform. Too afraid to go with your 'bats?'"

"Not exactly," McLeod said. He turned to his friend. "Though I *do* remember the reception I got during my last review -- about half of them weren't happy with me, so...."

Commander Stuart turned serious. "Tucker, are you still stuck on this diplomatic thing?" he asked his commanding officer. You have to be in line for the *Valiant*. I can't think of anyone better qualified to command the quadrant's flagship. How can you turn her down?"

"As serious as I can be, Andy," said McLeod. "I'm still energized by the team we have, by our mission, even by some of the less than pleasant tasks we have to perform. I just think there must be a better way to fulfill our mission than defaulting to torpedoes and phase weapons."

Commander Stuart was quick to respond. "And you know you're going to hear the same argument I've heard for the last twelve years, right?"

McLeod laughed. "I've heard it for longer, and yes, I know what they'll say. My job is to show them that what's happened in the last twelve years is the norm and not a fluke." McLeod lowered his head for a moment. Stuart's apprehension about McLeod's abrupt career change would be duplicated at his board of review, he was sure. While he didn't doubt the direction he wanted his career to take, he did question his preparedness. Could he convert from a career military officer to the diplomatic corps, especially when rising conflicts between several organizations were testing the ability of the Alliance to ensure peace even in its strongholds?

McLeod shook his head to return to the present. "Which reminds me, did you find out if the *Cidney* is coming in for refit and a new crew?"

"Far as I know."

"Good. I'll work on that."

Stuart smirked, adding "And that's the end of the story?"

McLeod was thoughtful. "I've put together a comprehensive list of promotion recommendations. The first is for your first command, if I have anything to say about it. I have a thought for Anjer Alba as well: the XO slot here on the *Endeavor*. She's gone far enough as a Tactical Officer. She'll make a great XO."

Stuart was silent for a while. "Anjer's certainly going to miss you, Tucker."

"It's mutual, believe me. I can almost guarantee that she'll be tapped for an XO slot somewhere in the quadrant. Having her on the *Endeavor* will make everyone's lives easier. Plus, if I do decide against my better judgement to take on the *Valiant*, there are others who are ahead of her for the XO position: I couldn't guarantee that her selection would be approved."

Stuart chuckled. "You mean, the great 'Captain Thunder' didn't make them an offer they couldn't refuse?" he asked.

"'Captain Thunder' is just about out of rain clouds, my friend," McLeod countered. "Besides, Anjer wants *Endeavor*, and the base crew trusts her. Enough of them will remain that her selection would maintain *Endeavor's* fighting edge, especially here in Beta Quadrant."

"But *I'm* hoping you'll have your hands full in your new assignment," McLeod said, confidently. He placed his hand on his friend's shoulder. "Now, are *you* ready?"

Stuart looked into his friend's eyes. "I've learned from the best, so yes." He checked the time. "We need to head to the bridge."

* * *

McLeod and Stuart climbed to the primary bridge and into their positions. McLeod sat and faced Lt. Commander Anjer Alba.

"Anjer, report from sections." Anjer looked briefly at her panel, then turned to her captain and friend.

"All sections reporting in line as scheduled. All personnel in base positions and prepared for final docking."

McLeod turned to face the helm. "Marty, position and ETA?"

"We are within one click of Beta Central, Sir." He looked up. "We'll be in the clamps within 30, Captain."

"Thank you, Marty."

McLeod turned toward Communications. "All-Com, Goldy," McLeod directed. His communications officer nodded. McLeod cleared his throat.

"Ladies and Gentlemen of the *Endeavor*, we've had a tremendous run. One of the many duties of ship captains' since long before the founding of the Star Alliance some 129 standard years ago is the formal ending of our missions. In doing so, we have the privilege of acknowledging the superior efforts of our crew, including both

NCOs and officers." He paused. "We have prevailed in many conflicts throughout the quadrant and beyond, supporting both the Star Alliance and other worlds, repelling tyranny and conquest, and keeping worlds within the Star Alliance safe. We have done well, and in my formal report to our review board, I will ensure that they know the good work you have all done. But this work has not been without sacrifice, so I ask that we all observe a moment of silence as our Executive Officer, Commander Stuart, reads the names of our fallen." He nodded toward Stuart, who began. After each name, a single bell was sounded.

> Enlisted Chief Second Class Paul Anderson
> Sergeant Jennifer Bell
> Senior Specialist Robert Haines

As the bells sounded, McLeod took the time to look around the bridge at the faces of his crew. They have worked incredibly hard, he thought. How lucky I've been to command them. He smiled slightly at each in turn, trying silently to communicate his gratitude.

> Lt. Commander Stef Peters
> Lt. Ranalon Tate
> Altern Angela Winn

"Ladies and Gentlemen," McLeod continued. "Please remember their sacrifice, and their selflessness. For that, we are forever grateful." He turned to the helm.

"Helm, prepare to dock."

"Yours Aye, Captain."

McLeod turned to Lt. Commander Alba. "Anjer, what's your plan? Will you be able to see your brother during first liberty?"

Commander Alba smiled and spoke quietly. "That's the plan, Tucker," she said. "So, will we be hearing about a new captain for the *Valiant*?"

"That's to be seen, Anjer," he said. "As for who it's going to be, well that part may be a surprise." His look softened. "I'm going to miss you, Anjer. We've had so many years together, though it really is time, isn't it?"

Anjer touched his arm. "It is," she said. "We've helped each other through tough times, Tucker, and I think we're both ready."

McLeod nodded. "Then let be what will be," he said.

* * *

Outside Primary Board Room, Star Alliance Beta Quadrant Headquarters

The hallway to the primary board room seemed longer to McLeod than in past cycles: perhaps the nature of his meeting was the reason. McLeod nodded to those he knew, or who seemed to know him. While more nervous than usual, he was prepared, and he greeted the review board aide cordially. The aide rose as McLeod approached.

"Sr. Captain McLeod," she began. "Welcome, sir."

"Thank you, Altern." He smiled. "Anything I need to know about the board?" Something in his manner relaxed the young officer. "And, let's sit, shall we?"

The Altern sat and began, "Well, sir, they've completed the review of SAV/ *Spirit*, so I think they'll be in a good mood." She looked at him like a co-conspirator.

"And given the *Endeavor's* record, Captain, you should be going in with a lot more swagger than you have right now." They heard the door open quietly. McLeod leaned toward her and whispered, "Well, we'll find out soon, won't we?" She smiled as McLeod rose and turned toward the door. He broke into a smile when he saw an old colleague.

"Captain Ausfel," McLeod said, extending his hand.

Ausfel returned the smile. "Good to see you, Tucker," Ausfel said. "So, are you ready for this?"

"Done it before, happy to do it again," McLeod said. He tilted his head toward the conference room. "Let's go." Both men ambled through the door, looking toward the conference table and screen. Seated at the middle of the table was Senior Admiral Tripathy, the board of review chair, who rose to greet McLeod.

"Captain. Welcome," he said. "Before you sit, shall we perform our introductions?" He nodded toward the first member to his right. The member rose and McLeod approached him.

"General Hawthorne, Captain. Welcome." He was followed by a man in simple civilian dress.

"Captain," he began. "I am Councilor Elias Trent of the Beta Intercouncil." Trent smiled. "Some civilian's got to be here to keep you military types in line." McLeod acknowledged him with a smile and nod.

"Councilor," he said.

The final member of the board rose and approached McLeod. "It's been too long, Tucker," said the Federation Fleet Captain.

McLeod smiled. "*That* is an understatement, Ben. And it's good to see you, too."

Sr. Admiral Tripathy smiled and waved all to their seats.

"Shall we get to it, then?" he asked. "Captain McLeod, you've been here before and know the process. We are already agreed after careful review of records that in terms of the operations of the *Endeavor* and mission reports that the tour has been successful and fruitful in support of the mission and goals of the Star Alliance. In fact, and in line with your request, Fleet Captain Burkhart of the Central Federation is a member of this board and is in general agreement with our assessment of the success of *Endeavor*'s last tour." He turned toward Captain Burkhart. "That is correct, is it not, Captain?"

Ben Burkhart nodded. "It is, Admiral."

The Sr. Admiral continued, "So, our purpose today is to hear more about specific operations so that we may determine future actions in the Beta Quadrant areas patrolled and serviced by *Endeavor*, hear additional formal information about your crew, including your recommendations for promotions and reassignments, and any other questions or requests any of us may have." He looked around the entire table. He nodded again, then turned to McLeod.

"Captain," the Sr. Admiral began. "Can you provide your general summary of the *Endeavor's* last tour, paying particular attention to the conflict against the Shan Confederacy near the M'Lonian system?" McLeod nodded. He had provided such reviews on many occasions in the past, and had little difficulty recalling his previous battles, or providing useful summaries and analyses for his superiors. He took a deep breath and began by recalling the initial tasks taken on by the *Endeavor* following her last refit.

"Gentlemen," McLeod began. "Our first challenging encounter after embarkation was at Ansonia Prime, where...." McLeod continued his detailed recounting of specific events and activities during his tour. While he maintained his composure during his presentation, he felt pangs of guilt whenever he spoke about the losses of crew members under his command, even pausing once to clear his throat. He suspected that the board members knew why he was pausing and didn't call attention to his feelings so as not to embarrass him, for which he was grateful. One of the situations he glossed over was an encounter involving two independent planets within the Camerac system which were engaging in escalating skirmishes. He had just moved on to discuss his recommendations for promotion when Councilor Trent addressed Sr. Admiral Tripathy.

"Admiral, if I may?" Trent asked.

Tripathy nodded. "Go ahead, please Councilor."

"Thank you," Trent said. Turning to McLeod, he continued. "Captain, you have spoken about a number of encounters during *Endeavor's* tour that involved conflicts on or near unaffiliated worlds, such as the Camerac system. What do you think is the role of a Star Alliance officer, particularly a commanding officer in conflicts like that?"

McLeod thought for just a moment. "Councilor, I honestly was focusing on the formal role of the Alliance when we arrived in system. We stopped there for a short bit of R&R for our crew and to spread general goodwill on the part of the Alliance, and the tension on both planets was palpable. I'm innately curious, so after consulting with my senior officers, I requested formal audiences with the leaders of both planets. My object was to see what I could do, and not exactly to forge a formal agreement for the planets. As I mentioned, I believe the fact that the leaders and governing councils of the planets set up formal meetings as we were departing was a positive development for us, and generated goodwill for the Alliance. We simply acted based on our gut feeling that additional dialogue would help the system, not so much because that was our formal role as a starship." McLeod leaned forward. "And to be honest with you, a number of my crew told me that they felt something could have exploded within that system while we were there, so self-preservations was certainly part of our thinking as well."

Trent nodded his head as McLeod finished. "Thank you, Captain." Turning to Tripathy, he added, "That's all, Admiral."

Pausing briefly, McLeod thought, I wonder where that question came from? Then he continued with his promotion recommendations.

* * *

Sr. Admiral Tripathy looked at each of his colleagues on the review board before speaking. "Gentlemen," he said. "We've heard the formal recounting of *Endeavor's* last tour in addition to recommendations made for promotion by its commanding officer, Sr. Captain Tucker McLeod. Are there any further questions for

Captain McLeod regarding *Endeavor*?" No one spoke, and Tripathy turned again to McLeod.

"Tucker," he began. "You have made a formal request to be considered for a formal transfer to the diplomatic corps, is that correct?"

"Yes, sir," said McLeod.

Tripathy exhaled, saying, "Well, as you know, that request has gone to the personnel center and consideration of that request is not the purview of this board." He smiled again at McLeod, "But I have to ask Tucker as someone who's known you for years, and with all due respect for Councilor Trent, just what are thinking?" The other board members -- including Trent -- all laughed. "Tucker, we all know you as a fine officer and a valuable asset for the Alliance, and also for the Federation given your career path. And it certainly shouldn't surprise you that given your career, you are the first person on the list to take command of the quadrant's flagship." Becoming more formal now, Tripathy added, "Can you share with us your reasoning for this proposed change?"

Calmly, McLeod replied. "Of course, Admiral, and let me first assure all of you that this is not an unconsidered decision on my part." He exhaled. On three occasions over the last twelve years," he continued, "I've seen both Alliance and Federation captains make the decision to attack long before they should. I briefly mentioned my conversation with Capt. Porren of FV/ *Stator* over her conflict with ships associated with the Shan Confederacy." He chuckled. "Now, we all have issues with how the Shan insert themselves between the Alliance and Federation and our affiliated worlds, but to be honest, they are more an annoyance and negative influence than an actual opposing force. I believe Capt. Porren's decision to take them on militarily was ill-advised and unnecessary and I told her so." McLeod sat back slightly. "It doesn't matter that *Stator* had little chance of failure against the Shan -- that wasn't the point. The point is that when we have the opportunity to talk or negotiate our way toward our desired end, we ought to do that." He shook his head. "Let me rephrase that." He thought briefly before continuing. "We already know that negotiation is preferred over armed conflict.

The problem is that too few of our officers know how to do that, and to some degree our military training makes suppressing the urge to strike very difficult."

"I agree with you, Tucker," Captain Ausfel said. "While we are all trained in avoiding armed conflict, and truly understand and support that ideal, training in negotiation is short in comparison to tactics and strategies during armed conflict -- perhaps we just don't have sufficient practice in negotiation." McLeod nodded. "But to me, that just indicates that we need you and your perspective *within* the Alliance military force, including as commander of the quadrant flagship."

"I agree," said Burkhart. "There may have been a time when you were seen as trigger happy, Tucker, and we'll get to that today too." He looked to Admiral Tripathy, who nodded. "But as a more seasoned and highly respected leader, the command chair is an excellent forum from which you can lead by example." He smiled. "After all," he continued, "You've shown an incredible aptitude for commanding a starship."

McLeod allowed himself a small smile until Ausfel spoke again. "But of course, we *know* you, yet there are those within the Federation and the Alliance who don't, yet have heard some version of the story of 'Captain Thunder,' so tell us how you would reconcile that nickname and the events surrounding it with this transfer request, and also tell us how you think people might view you in that purely diplomatic role given *all* of your background."

McLeod paused then said "Certainly, Captain, and if this sounds rehearsed, I can only say that it *is* given how many times I've told this story." McLeod smiled. "But," he added, "I also know the importance of telling the story again now." "This was in Stardate 2447.1 and SV/ *Valiant* had been patrolling near the Andoran system, when we were hailed because a number of rogue vessels had been disrupting shipping near the system. While Andora Prime is a Federation world, *Valiant* was the closest starship of any size to their system. Now to give you an idea, the rogues in that sector of space had become increasingly aggressive about piracy, such as intercepting supplies, disrupting commerce and that sort of thing, which had been taxing the ability of individual worlds to defend themselves. Other worlds, such as two in the Petrov system had asked for emergency assistance from the Alliance at around the same time, so we were already at a heightened alert level."

"Well," McLeod continued, "By the time we arrived in system, the rogues had made a critical decision: two of the ships had sent landing parties to the surface of Andora Prime and managed to take the governing council hostage. It was very tense." He shook himself, reliving the memory. "As we arrived, Captain Standing hailed the rogue ships, offering Alliance assistance to help defuse the situation. We couldn't gauge what the rogues on planet were thinking, but we weren't getting anywhere with the two rogue ships in front of us. That's when one of the ships opened fire on *Valiant*. We performed a brief evasive maneuver, and it just so happened that our captain had been moving on the bridge and lost his balance, falling and hitting his head. Since it wasn't the time to ask a lot of questions, certainly not with a rogue ship firing on us, as executive officer, I took command." He looked at the board, adding, "I should emphasize that I did not *formally* invoke Article 84 -- especially since I knew it would be temporary." McLeod turned his gaze to Councilor Trent. "Councilor, Article 84 allows for the formal transfer of command in situations where the commanding officer is infirm or unable to perform his or her duties effectively. What I did was to invoke them *informally* simply by acting, which happens in similar situations." Trent nodded his understanding and McLeod continued.

"While dealing with the occasional fire from the rogue ship, we received a vid transmission from the governing council on which they told us they had been moved to the power plant control room for the capitol city on Andora Prime. The leader of the council said that the rogues, who we could see in the background, demanded that *Valiant* leave the system or risk an explosion at the power plant that would devastate the city." McLeod paused again. "It seemed clear to me and the other senior officers on *Valiant* that the rogues had gotten in way over their heads and were hoping for some kind of solution. So we -- that is I -- decided to call their bluff, and activated the self-destruct sequence for *Valiant*." At this, members of the board stiffened slightly. "We also repositioned the ship so that our destruction would take out both rogue ships as well as cause significant issues on Andora Prime. Now, at some time during our exchange with the rogues I said something like 'they didn't want to mess with someone who could rain thunder down on them with a single command,' and less than a minute later, one rogue ship changed its orientation and departed." He looked to the board members with a smile adding, "I guess I have a flair for phrases like that. Anyway, minutes later, the rogues on-planet surrendered to Andoran authorities and we ended the self-destruct." McLeod chuckled. "According to the ship's log, the entire time from the beginning of self-destruct to ending it took just seven minutes, yet 'Captain Thunder' has become an unwelcome nickname even to people who have no idea what happened at Andora Prime."

"So to answer your original question, Captain, I imagine there are those who might think that the Alliance had lost its collective minds by reassigning me to diplomatic, and I understand that. At Andora Prime, I made what many people still view as an impulsive and reckless order which seems to default to firepower rather than negotiation, and they might be less than inclined to see me as a diplomat even over twelve years later. I have felt the weight of that decision myself. I have a good friend within the Federation who is Andoran, and my actions at her homeworld drove a wedge between us for years." McLeod smiled again. "But I believe she would also say that I am not the younger executive officer I was twelve years ago, and I've demonstrated a more mature and creative way of problem solving without weapons since that time."

The board was silent for a while until Tripathy spoke. "Reflect on that a bit more, Tucker if you would," he said. "How would you have acted differently in that situation?"

"Well," McLeod began. "While I would still have taken command informally, I might have implied the self-destruct without activating it, and tried to pit one ship against the other. I could also have simply ordered lethal strikes against the rogue ship that wasn't firing, because it's likely they already had cold feet. In fact, that was the ship that left the system. It was probably their leaving that showed the rogues on-planet that they really didn't have much support to rely on from their own ships." McLeod noticed nods of approval and understanding among all the officers on the review panel, and he wasn't sure he should continue, but felt the need to be above board and honest.

"Having said all of that gentlemen," he continued. "I'm not sure that as a younger officer with the experience and understanding I had at that time, that I would have been able to make those decisions. They have come with the seasoning that no young officer could ever hope to have. So, I stand by my original decision as being about the best I could have done at that time, while acknowledging that there are several better ways I *could* have resolved the situation, had I been a forty three year old Sr. Captain, which of course, I was not then." He smiled. "By the way, that's *exactly* the feedback I received from Capt. Standing once he regained consciousness, and I've taken it to heart over the last twelve years."

Admiral Tripathy looked around the room at the board members, none of whom seemed to have any questions. "Fair enough, Tucker," he said.

Chapter Two

Star Alliance Beta Quadrant Headquarters

On the morning following his board of review, McLeod rose early and went to the recreational area of his wing to exercise. After lifting weights and a short aerobic exercise, he donned light gloves and began punching and kicking a heavy bag. Within minutes, he recognized the tension that he had been ignoring for weeks, and slowly allowed the tension to leave him. He found that he valued the opportunity to completely remove himself from the upcoming questionings and re-questionings about his career aspirations. Frankly, he wasn't looking forward to the next "inquisition." But, he thought, at least I have a few days to do what I enjoy.

Following his workout, he visited with the *Endeavor's* base crew and lunched with them in the NCO quarters before returning to the south wing of Beta Quadrant Headquarters for the regularly scheduled briefing on activity within the Beta Quadrant. There was little new in the briefing, and McLeod found his mind wandering toward the end. It was as he was leaving the conference room that he turned and bumped into one of his former XOs.

"Tucker!" the man called. "I thought you were still distant with the *Endeavor* until next month." He embraced his former captain.

McLeod returned the gesture. "Things change, Lace," he began. "We arrived two days ago, and I completed board of review yesterday." He looked at his friend with a sly grin. "And have you been taking care of my ship?"

"Ha! *Pegasus* doesn't even remember anybody named McLeod, I'll have you know." He paused. "Tour was good. We were lucky -- very few casualties."

McLeod humphed. "Lace, I've read the reports. Luck wasn't involved. You made some great calls. I'm glad you were in command." He gestured toward the speaker. "Coffee afterwards?"

"Can't today, Tucker," Lacey replied. "But are you up for a workout tomorrow?"

McLeod smirked. "Do you really have to ask that? When shall we meet?"

"How about 0800?"

"Works for me," McLeod replied. "I've got things to do later as well."

Lacey laughed. "Don't tell me you're going to hit that dive you used to always talk about. Sector 9, was it?"

"Well -- yes," said McLeod. "I think of it as more of a pilgrimage."

Lacey shook his head. "You will just never change, will you?"

"I'm told its part of my charm"

"Right," said Lacey with a smile. He glanced to his right, adding, "Oh, I need to see my XO, Tucker, so, 0800? Officer's Gym?"

"Yep," said McLeod. "See you then.

After shaking Lacey's Hand, McLeod returned to his quarters.

* * *

Thor Cantina, Sector 9 Beta Quadrant Headquarters Central City

As he walked the last few blocks to the cantina, McLeod noted that little had changed in the three years since he had last visited: the smells, the bit of haze in the air, and the sounds of workers and families throughout the district all seemed the same. He smiled to himself as he realized that he was quite a student of the human condition. Some would look at the people in this district shake their heads and think 'what a shame.' Yet, I see the joy, the energy and the spirit and know they have great lives, he thought. Well, to each his own. He squared his shoulders, suppressed a grin, then opened the cantina doors.

Immediately, he was assaulted by even more earthy smells and the familiar sounds of the cantina. I've missed this, he thought to himself. Walking toward the bar to his right, he glanced up and noticed something he had honestly forgotten about: a portrait of himself in formal dress uniform directly over the bar, among other captains of Saranite heritage. He moved to the bar and noticed a relatively young bartender watching him as he approached. He smiled at her.

"Henowing," he said as he nodded, in a common Saranite greeting." The young bartender returned the greeting.

"How can I help you, sir?" she asked.

"I would say my usual," he began, "but we haven't met before. What I would like is a Curando." The bartender's eyes widened and she looked very nervous. "You know, the common Saranite welcome cocktail," McLeod prodded.

The bartender looked up. "Yes, I know, it's just that I haven't made it before."

McLeod smiled. "That," he began, "will not be a problem." He moved toward the side of bar and joined the bartender behind it. "Do you have everything to make it?"

"Um, I think so, but I don't think…."

McLeod waved her away playfully. "It will be alright." He pointed toward his portrait. "I'm a part-owner."

The bartender looked up to the portrait and back to McLeod. She frowned. "I thought those were ship's captains."

"And I thought I hired a pretty young bartender last week, rather than a freeloading Terran," a voice boomed. The voice came from a man, fully two meters tall who filled the doorway to the kitchen. McLeod looked at him and smiled.

"Marty."

"Tucker. It's been a while."

McLeod glanced toward his portrait. "Long enough that I'd forgotten all about *that*."

Marty harrumphed. "Hell, I tried to take it down, but some of my patrons complained."

"Not sure I believe that, Marty."

"Well, two of them complained, but one might be one of your distant cousins." He moved closer to the bar and looked at McLeod.

"Good to see you."

"It's mutual," McLeod said. He glanced at the young bartender. "I was just showing…" he paused looking at her.

"Anna." The young woman said.

"…Anna how to make a Curando." McLeod looked up again at the cantina owner. You do have everything, don't you?"

Marty nodded before responding. "Since I knew the *Endeavor* had docked, I made sure of it." The owner sat at the bar. "What took you so long?"

McLeod shrugged. "It was the end of my tour, so lots of things, like the final assessment of the *Endeavor*, promotion recommendations, that sort of thing."

"You're Captain *McLeod*?" Anna asked.

McLeod turned to her. "You say it like it's a bad thing."

"No, I just know that you're famous."

McLeod and Martin both chuckled.

"Maybe in his own mind," said Marty.

"Yeah, fame leaves a lot to be desired," McLeod said. Then he turned toward the bartender with his palms raised in surrender.

"Hey, I'm just a farm kid from the plains," McLeod said.

Martin chuckled. "And apparently, also a bartender."

"Do you mind?" McLeod asked.

"No. As I recall, you're pretty good at exotics. Can you make me that brewed drink both of your parents liked?"

"The Stratos," McLeod said. "Sure. Do you have dried pepper leaves?"

Marty nodded. "Right next to the steeper," Marty said, as he pointed to the glass jar.

"Great," McLeod said. "One Stratos coming right up." He turned to Anna. "You'll want to watch this. These drinks are very popular in the fancier establishments."

"Oh, please," Marty said. Turning to Anna, he added, "Though I have to admit, he's very good at this, so learn what you can, okay?" Marty smiled at the young woman, who relaxed and returned the smile.

McLeod glanced around the bar, and quickly took out bitters, a dark almost black wine, cocopan oil and Yumi fruit.

"I need to scrape off some of this rind," he said to Anna. "Where is your peeler?' Wordlessly, Anna pointed to the peeler.

"Thanks," McLeod said. He turned behind him and took a bottle of aqua liquor off the shelf, and one of Kazaki whiskey. Then, he noticed the jar of yellowish syrup next to the dried pepper leaves, brought it over to his work space and began assembling the cocktails. As he started the steeper to brew the pepper tea, he looked up at his portrait.

"You'll have to change that now. *Endeavor* is ready for its new captain."

"And the old one apparently not ready to take on the quadrant flagship," Marty countered.

McLeod smiled. "Now Marty," McLeod said. "Don't believe everything you hear out there."

"You think I *do*?" He paused as he watched McLeod add the wine to a large shaker, then cut the Yumi fruit and add its juice to the wine. "Seriously, Tucker, what's the downside with taking on the *Valiant*? I thought you've wanted that for years?"

McLeod paused before answering. "Do you remember the conversation we had on my last leave about getting a little tired of battle?"

"Well yes, but I thought you were just annoyed at how I mixed your drink," Marty said. McLeod measured out the Kazaki whiskey into a small glass.

"Well, yes, that too," McLeod said. "But it's true -- I am a bit weary." He looked up at Marty again. There is certainly still a chance I will take on the *Valiant*; I've heard about some of the potential crew assignments and I know it would be a superb crew, maybe even better than the *Endeavor,* though that seems hard to believe." He looked up wistfully, "Anyway, I've got a lot to think about."

"Huh!" said Marty. "The word here for over a month is that the *Valiant* is yours -- nobody else has the right background, especially with the growing Federation presence." McLeod poured the steeped pepper tea into a large cocktail glass, then added the Kazaki whiskey and a small bit of syrup. Adding the top, he quickly shook it, then placed the drink on the bar. Finally, he added a generous layer of the aqua liquor on top before handing it to his friend.

Your Stratos, Sir," McLeod said with a bow. Marty took the drink, raised it in thanks and took a sip. He smiled.

"Damned if that doesn't taste the same as the last time you made it for me," Marty complained. "I can never get it right."

McLeod shrugged his shoulders. "I used to make it for my folks all the time, so I've had more practice." McLeod returned to his Curando, adding in a dash of bitters, then stirring the drink slowly. He then added the cocopan oil on top and set it aflame. He doused it after a few seconds, then grated the Yumi fruit zest on top. He acknowledged Marty with a tip of his head then raised the glass slightly before taking a sip.

"For you, Mom," he said. He turned back to Marty. "What can you suggest for dinner that won't make me sick?"

Marty scowled. "If I didn't like you, and know why you said that, I could get pretty angry." His eyes darted up briefly. "We have a mild roast of Cantrou beast that we have plenty of. You could combine that with an ale and ground sprouts."

McLeod nodded. "That does sound good. I'm going to sit awhile. Could I have it in thirty minutes?"

Marty rose and went behind the bar toward the kitchen. "Sure. Just take a seat."

McLeod turned toward Anna. "Nice to meet you, Anna." As Anna and Marty returned to work, McLeod went back to his seat at the bar to enjoy his Curando, a traditional Saranite drink he always consumed in honor of his mother. Checking the time, he noticed it was still shy of 1800 hours, so he turned to watch the other patrons. He lost himself in developing stories about the individuals and groups, so much so that he didn't notice a visitor until he cleared his throat.

"Captain," said Councilor Trent. McLeod started, and began to rise.

"Please do not rise, Captain," Trent said. "May I join you?"

"Of course, Councilor." Then reverting to his usual banter, continued, "Something tells me you didn't come here for the ambience."

Councilor Trent looked around. "Actually, no. I came specifically to see you."

McLeod rose. "Would you prefer a table?"

"That would be better. Yes." They moved to a table not far from the door, and McLeod sat with an open stance, waiting."

"Captain," the Councilor began. "I was curious to know more about what you hope to accomplish by your rather abrupt career change. Wait, let me start again." He looked more directly at McLeod.

"I guess what I really want to know is what you're willing to do to prove that a shift to the diplomatic corps would be a wise one either for you or for the Star Alliance."

McLeod shifted in his seat. "I'm not exactly sure what you mean, Councilor." The councilor relaxed, confident in now being in charge of the meeting.

"Exactly what I said, Captain." He sat forward even more. "What would you be willing to do, where would you be willing to go, how willing are you to start not at the top, but closer to…" he gestured with his palm facing the table "… the middle?" The Councilor sat back.

McLeod pondered. "Councilor," McLeod began cautiously, "I am quite willing to start in the place where I might be most useful, and where I might learn the most." He continued. "And as for hurdles or benchmarks, and certainly for travel, I'm rather open. I have traveled throughout all four quadrants." He chuckled. "There isn't much that is legal or moral that I wouldn't do."

The Councilor studied McLeod's face for a moment, then relaxed again. He smiled and nodded. "Thank you, Captain. I thought that was the case." He looked briefly around the cantina, then returned his gaze to McLeod.

"I have some … thoughts and possibilities that may work out for you."

McLeod interrupted. "Such as?"

"Well, I do still need to confirm with other people before this can be made more formal but I wanted to determine your willingness before proceeding. In short, it involves an observer assignment that would expose you to a diplomatic initiative for which you might have particularly apt preparation."

"I understand, Councilor. And our follow up conversation…?" The Councilor rose and extended his hand. McLeod grasped it as he rose in turn.

"I hope we can discuss that tomorrow at another location." Trent handed McLeod a card.

"If we were to meet at the Central Hub, B wing after lunch, say 1400 hours?"

McLeod nodded. "Of course, Councilor. You have certainly piqued my interest."

"I hope so, Captain," Trent said. "I hope so."

Chapter Three

Star Alliance Beta Quadrant Headquarters Officer's Gym

As he opened the door to the Officer's Gym, McLeod remembered the last time he worked out with Isaiah Lacey, and his bruised ribs as well. He shook off the memory, and found his friend had just left the front desk screen and was moving toward one of the private studios.

"Lace," he called. His friend looked up and smiled.

"Hey, Tuck," he said. "Ready?"

"I will be," McLeod said. "Had a light breakfast so I shouldn't be too loaded down." He placed his bag down on the bench. "Have you been able to work out lately?"

"Short answer -- not as much as I would like."

McLeod nodded. "Amen, brother." He looked around. "I see the heavy bag; are there pads somewhere in here?"

"Yep," Lacey said. "There's a closet over there," he pointed toward a distant corner. "I think that's where they are."

Each of the men dressed in his preferred gear; McLeod in the heavy dark pants of Ryanjin Kenpo, his primary style, and Lacey in the lighter gray of a heavy wrestler, as he was a master at grappling. The two men began warming up, speaking when necessary, silent when it suited them. The comfort and affability was evident in how easily they shifted from one activity to another. Following a rigorous regimentation and calisthenics, they rested briefly and hydrated.

"So," Lacey began, "What do you think this meeting is going to be about?"

McLeod shrugged. "Damned if I know," McLeod answered. "Councilor Trent said it would be something worth my while and a good learning experience, but I don't have any details other than it has something to do with a diplomatic assignment as an observer."

Lacey shook his head and smiled. "Well, I hope the whole thing just fizzles out, and you get your ass into *Valiant*. She's been waiting for you for years."

McLeod smiled. "Thanks for the vote of confidence." He stood. "But at least I'll get to spend some time in that fancy wing of the Central Hub."

Lacey nodded. "Yeah, that will be nice. Let me know how the rich people work, will ya'?" He stood to join his friend. "How about some forms?" Fighting forms, in essence pantomimed multiple attacker fights, were McLeod's favorite.

"Works for me," McLeod said. Both men moved back to the center of the room, and Lacey called out:

"Hunsuki!" Both men faced the back wall side by side, about six feet apart, and began the form, smiling all the while. As they continued their movements, the smiles were replaced by intense gazes that flitted back and forth to the many attackers they were fighting during the form. While not deliberate, their movements were almost perfectly synchronized. They completed the form, bowed toward the wall, then relaxed.

McLeod thought for a moment, then said,

"Razor!" Lacey chuckled, then bowed. The friends went through thirteen forms from various martial arts styles, which served to warm them up even farther. Each form required strikes, blocks, kicks and evasive maneuvers that ran the gamut of their wide range of techniques.

McLeod smiled to himself as he realized which forms they had chosen; some favorites, some forms that had bedeviled them both for years, but still important in one of their many martial arts styles.

Lacey held Master rank in seven martial art styles; McLeod in five. And while Lacey was clearly the more accomplished on the mat and as an instructor, it was McLeod who had used the styles in close order combat more frequently; he was the more experienced fighter.

Their self-defense work was challenging. Since many of the techniques lead to take downs, flips, and submission holds, the aggressor was frequently thrown to the floor. And just as frequently, he would break out into laughter as soon as he hit the mat. This would cause the defender to do the same. McLeod thought to himself, "this is the fun we have in martial arts: it's not all about breaking boards and hurting people."

Their sparring time was predictable as well. Lacey tended to prefer his powerful and fluid kicks and sweeps, while McLeod favored hand techniques. They both enjoyed their time together immensely, and fortunately, neither of them suffered a visible or serious injury.

After promising to meet again prior to their next assignments, McLeod and Lacey shared a healthy lunch before going their separate ways. It was a subdued, yet relaxed McLeod who later left his quarters to travel to the Central Hub and the Councilor's office to meet with Councilor Trent.

Chapter Four

Star Alliance Beta Quadrant Headquarters, Central Hub, B Wing

Though unfamiliar with the more formal and ornate areas of the headquarters city, McLeod made his way easily to the Council rooms in the Central Hub. He entered the B Wing, called up the office location for the Councilor, and made his way to the Councilor's Office. As he entered the vestibule, a young assistant rose and greeted him.

"Captain McLeod," she said. "Good afternoon. May I get you coffee?"

"Yes, please. Black," he replied as she left. McLeod surveyed the room. "Nice," he thought. This was certainly more plush than even a senior officer's quarters or the common areas. He rose when she returned with his coffee.

"Councilor Trent is ready for you now, Captain. This way." She turned on her heel and led him down a short hallway into a modest office. It seemed in stark contrast with the opulence of its surroundings. Councilor Trent seemed to read his mind. He extended his hand warmly.

"Good morning, Captain," the Councilor began. "And yes, it *is* something of a letdown after the beauty of the outer office."

"That *was* going through my head," McLeod smiled as he replied.

"Well, those big areas are more for show," Trent said. "Working offices and conference areas have what they need without a lot of extras. Shall we sit?" He gestured toward his small conference table. As they got comfortable, Councilor Trent looked at McLeod, smiled slightly, then began.

"Captain, what do you know about the Twin Worlds of Hemod and Herai?" McLeod briefly looked up briefly, then back at Councilor Trent.

"As I recall, they are rather far from Alliance or Federation affiliated planets near a number of independents. The planets have also had a strong relationship for centuries, though with some strains." He learned forward. "I remember them being very different internally. Hemod has fewer natural resources but a stronger economy." He gained momentum. "Wasn't there some talk about formal affiliation with the Caprists on Hemod?"

Councilor Trent nodded in agreement. Correct, Captain," he said. "The strong orientation toward commerce that is so central to life on Hemod is very akin to the Caprist's laissez-faire attitude. Were Hemod operating alone, there is little doubt that they would formally affiliate with the Caprists."
"Which would be very inconvenient considering the Unionist factions on Herai," McLeod replied. "I can just imagine how the labor organizers on Herai would react to formal affiliation of Hemod with the Caprists." He chuckled. "I've always wondered how they could get along so well with such different political orientations."
"That's the problem, Captain. They don't." McLeod looked at the Councilor expectantly.

Councilor Trent sighed. "While the coordinating council and governing councils on each planet believes the two planets need to work more closely together, as you probably know, they haven't always resolved their problems peacefully."

McLeod shook his head and replied, "That's never made any sense to me."

Trent laughed. "Spoken like a true problem solver. What I think you see Captain, is two worlds, that despite their differences also have remarkable similarities. But they've never been able to make the leap to greater collaboration for the benefit of both worlds." McLeod nodded in understanding and the Councilor continued.

"And that would make perfect sense if the internal issues on both planets were the same. There is as you note, a strong desire on the part of some on Hemod to seek formal affiliation with the Caprists, yet there is also a strong faction which wants to remain independent.

You already commented on the Unionists' hold within the professional and working classes on Herai." Suddenly, the Councilor had a thought.

"Were you aware of the contact with the Federation over quite a few years on Herai?"

McLeod nodded. "Yes. That's why I know so much about it. When I served on the *Xian*, we were invited to Herai to participate in a conference on ecological damage. We were there for over a week, and…" He chuckled. "I've always been known to spend ground time exploring people and cultures. I recall encountering a lot of strong Unionist sentiment on Herai, which I didn't see being shared with the few Hemodians I spoke with."

"And that's one good reason to consider you for this project," the Councilor said. "Going back to the state between the two worlds, the coordinating council and the governing councils of Herai and Hemod are acknowledging -- finally -- the need for greater cooperation, and to help promote that, the Twin Worlds' Cooperation Council has brokered requests from the planet governing councils to ask for formal assistance in negotiations from the Federation, and for both planets to be considered for Federation membership."

"Wow," McLeod began, "that's something of a surprise." He sat up straighter. "Mind you, they've never seemed to have problems with the Federation, but much preferred them at a distance, if you know what I mean."

"Exactly," Councilor Trent said. "Their belief now is that Federation assistance would help them develop better communications structures, some greater formality of relationship, reduce or eliminate the potential for war, and so on."

"I agree."

"Of course," Trent continued, "another wrinkle in this is that the Shan Confederacy has been present in that system for a while, and they have bristled at the idea of Federation membership spreading in that sector. The Shan generally oppose any kind of centrally organized governmental structures, and they oppose both the Federation and the Alliance there because they believe affiliation with either body would make one-on-one negotiations with either Herai or Hemod more difficult." McLeod rolled his eyes and sighed. Councilor Trent acknowledged McLeod's response.

"I agree, Captain. The Confederacy seems hell bent on containing the Alliance and the Federation, and that is particularly unfortunate on two worlds where the expertise and maturity of the Alliance or the Federation could be so valuable."

Trent paused and looked at McLeod. "So, that's the landscape of the problem: Twin Worlds that need some internal and inter-world work and are being pulled and pushed by three separate powers none of which are particularly enamored of the Central Federation or the Star Alliance."

McLeod squinted. "But, what's the Alliance angle on this? Have they requested membership in the Alliance as well? That's not been uncommon for the last ten years or so."

Councilor Trent shook his head. "No, but the Federation has requested a team from the Alliance because of our mutual interests, for which I am certainly grateful."

McLeod nodded in agreement. "That does make sense, and given that there are two worlds involved, it might speed up or at least facilitate the process." He smiled. "Of course, this is the perspective of a ship's captain, rather than a diplomat." Councilor Trent laughed and smiled at McLeod.

"Maybe you should have been a politician."

McLeod laughed. "That was never my intent," McLeod said.

"Understood," said Trent.

McLeod leaned toward Trent. "So, what is this idea you have for Hemod and Herai that involves me?" It was hard to contain his sense of excitement, but the Councilor didn't comment on it.

"Well," Trent began, "we are assembling several teams from both the Alliance and Federation." He sat up straighter, almost like a teacher. "In these types of situations, and depending upon the assessment done by the Alliance or the Federation, we usually include sub groups on economic cooperation, policy and trade, natural resources, military cooperation, cultural and scientific exchange -- you get the idea."

"Understood," said McLeod.

Councilor Trent continued. "I've spoken with the head of the negotiating team for the Alliance, and have her preliminary approval for you to participate in the negotiations -- purely as an observer, mind you. But I felt it would be valuable for you, and perhaps for the team to have you there." He paused. "Perhaps the hardest part of this for you is that you would have no actual role in the proceedings, but are simply an observer -- certainly a change for a man of action such as yourself." McLeod wondered if he sensed something in the statement, but chose to ignore it.

"The point is, you'd be able to see exactly how diplomatic negotiating teams operate, and how different they are from starships. Whether what you see excites you or you find it completely unappealing; in either case, you'd be learning something valuable." Trent leaned back in his chair. "Thoughts?"

McLeod chose his words carefully. "Certainly an interesting proposal, Councilor. If you don't mind me asking, what's in it for you? Or maybe put more delicately, is there a reason you've brokered this offer for me?"

The Councilor grinned at McLeod. "See? You're already forming words more like a diplomat than a ship's captain." The Councilor chuckled. "And it's a good question. My reason to broker the offer as you put it is that I'm not sure a ship's captain of your caliber is best suited for the diplomatic corps, and you in particular, not because you may not have the right skills, but for two other reasons: first, that your skills as a ship's captain are best used on a starship. Secondly, I believe that someone with your kind of military background would be bored out of his mind by the pace and compromises you have to make in the diplomatic corps. Quite honestly, my hope is that after this assignment you come back and lead *Valiant*." He paused before continuing. "But if you truly choose to pursue the diplomatic corps, I want you to make that decision with your eyes wide open. Then you can bring the same dedication to diplomatic that you have to the military." He sat back. "In essence, there are no downsides here for either you or the Alliance."

"It does seem that way," McLeod acknowledged. "How might we go about making this happen?"

Councilor Trent leaned forward again, showing his energy. "I think you're making a wise decision, Captain. As I mentioned, I've already spoken with the head of the Alliance negotiating team, and she plans to speak with the Federation negotiating team head since they are the primary facilitators of the negotiations. She does not believe it will be a problem, particularly because of your Federation credentials."

"Who is the Alliance team leader?" McLeod asked.

"Demeter Long, the Interstellar Minister from the Ketchuan System." McLeod smiled and Councilor Trent continued. "I believe her proximity to the Twin Worlds is one reason she was chosen."

"In addition to the fact that one of the major language groups within the Twin Worlds is Ketchuan."

"Which is why you were smiling?" Trent asked.

"Which is why I was smiling; I speak it too," McLeod replied.

"Do you know Minister Long?" The Councilor asked.

"Only by reputation," McLeod said. "My understanding is that she is highly regarded among the worlds in that sector, even though Ketchua is the closest Alliance world to the Twin Worlds as I recall."

Councilor Trent nodded in acknowledgement. "That's correct. When the Federation called the council for assistance, they specifically asked for Minister Long."

"I think that's a wise choice," McLeod said.

Trent noticed the smile on McLeod's face. "I take it your interest is strong enough to pursue this through Minister Long to the head of the Federation negotiating team?"

McLeod looked resolute. "Yes, Councilor," he said. "As you said, this is a no-lose situation." Thinking again, he asked, "Do you know who is heading the Federation team?"

"I do not, though Minister Long does." He grinned slightly. "I believe she knows you -- by reputation, of course, and I don't believe Minister Long would support your participation as an observer if she didn't believe she could convince the Federation team head to allow it."

McLeod chuckled. "I know little of Minister Long, Councilor, except that she is known for speaking her mind and being a very skilled negotiator."

Councilor Trent laughed in turn as he rose. He extended his hand. "I'll contact Minister Long and get back to you, Captain."

McLeod shook the Councilor's hand firmly.

"Thank you, Councilor," he said. "I appreciate the opportunity-- assuming it works out."

Councilor Trent chuckled again. "I hope you can say that while you're sitting through boring meetings on the Twin Worlds, Captain."

"Understood," said McLeod. "And thank you again."

Chapter Five

Central Federation Beta Quadrant Headquarters Command Staff Conference Room

Central Federation Commander Raina Wolfe was surprisingly nervous as she sat waiting for her Executive Officer's review. Having experienced reviews of many types in the past, in both the Central Federation and Star Alliance, she couldn't pinpoint what made this review different from the others -- with the possible exception that today she may finally learn if her expected promotion to Su-Captain would finally happen. Wolfe was a career Federation officer, widely seen as the finest pilot in the Beta Quadrant if not the entire Federation, and she had served with distinction through several challenging assignments. Yet, the captain's chair had eluded her.

Wolfe was third generation in the Central Federation. She had graduated first in her class at the Academy, despite the fact that she made several complaints regarding unfair treatment by her fellow cadets. In addition, she never held a command position within the corps of cadets despite consistently superior performance. Her father was her advanced training officer following graduation. She smiled as she recalled their dinner table conversations after the completion of her training.

Following her advanced training she made the perhaps fateful decision to work closely with the Star Alliance, including serving two complete tours on Alliance vessels. While she did not regret her service within the Alliance, nor the connections she made with Alliance personnel during her tours, it is widely understood that the Central Federation does not count service within the Star Alliance as time in rank for Federation officers, or NCOs; thus, her twenty three years of service as a Federation officer was generally counted as only sixteen. She had been surpassed in rank by several officers with far less stellar records -- which is perhaps why this junction was so important to her. "If I'm not advanced in rank this time, might it be time to retire?" she asked herself. So more than usual hung on the decision of this particular review board. She was lost in thought as a voice from behind roused her.

"Commander Wolfe," said a burly Federation Captain. "We are ready for you."

He smiled as Raina rose and took his outstretched hand. She followed him into the board room, where she saw two other people, a Fleet Admiral and a man in civilian dress, who while she didn't know him, seemed vaguely familiar. While Wolfe stood at attention, the Federation Captain performed the introductions.

"Fleet Marshall Masters, Fleet Marshal Su'Kho, this is Commander Raina Wolfe, now former Executive Officer of our Beta Quadrant Flagship, the *Courageous*." Raina suppressed a reaction when she heard Masters' name: while technically still on active duty, Masters had become one of the most prominent negotiators within Federation worlds. As she recalled, Masters was deputy head of the diplomatic corps within the Beta Quadrant, which certainly confused her since diplomats seldom spent a great deal of time with line officers on Federation vessels. Why in the world would he be part of this review?

The captain turned to Wolfe. "Commander, I'm Captain Adam Andreason, former captain of FV/ *Spectrum* within the Gamma Quadrant -- which is probably why we haven't encountered each other before." Wolfe nodded, then turned again to -- which of the two other people? She chose to look respectfully at Fleet Marshall Su'Kho, and realized she made the proper choice as he said,

"Please be seated, Commander." His voice was low and quiet, but had a very melodious tone, Wolfe thought.

"I realize, Commander," began Su'Kho, that this is a somewhat unusual format for the final review and report for a Central Federation Executive Officer. And Fleet Marshall Masters' presence is deliberate." Su'Kho looked at her more directly and smiled. "Also, rest assured, we are not here to pick apart your Executive Officer's report. We've reviewed it, and while we have a few questions, there is nothing in there that presents to us any concerns."

Wolfe nodded.

"So, Fleet Marshall Su-Kho continued, "would you be so kind as to tells us about your encounter with the Molandran Protectorate near the Tabard System?"

Wolfe took a deep breath. "Well sir," she began, "that was actually a very challenging encounter." Wolfe continued by recounting the last few months on *Courageous*, and their rescue of two Alliance Lunar class vessels and their XL fighters that were threatened by rogues and the Molandran Protectorate forces near the Tabard System. The sector borders on Molandran space, and several loosely organized groups of rogues were launching attacks on transports from the Protectorate. The Protectorate guards its assets fiercely, and they returned attacks with little regard for the Alliance ships in the area. FV/ *Courageous* had just arrived in system when they became aware of the situation.

As Wolfe related the story, she explained how the Mollies refused to hold off their attack on the rogues, fearing that the rogues would simply double back and outflank them. The captain of FV/ *Courageous* decided to launch his own strike to contain the Mollies and rogues until the XLs could return to their ships, and the ships could clear Molandran space.

"And this was easier said than done," Wolfe said. "The Lunar class ships were engaged in training exercises with several of their XL fighters -- simple maneuvers. The conflict between the Mollies and rogues broke out totally without warning: the Alliance ships didn't know what hit them." She shuddered slightly as she remembered. "And some of the pilots were relatively new -- which is why they were training in what should have been easy-to-navigate safe space."

 "And as XO, you certainly couldn't lead the squadron yourself," Andreason said.

"Correct, sir," Wolfe replied, "though that part wasn't as tough as I thought it would be." She smiled to herself. "Once we deployed the squad -- about five fighters -- the captain turned to me and said, 'take care of this, Commander,' so, I did. And it didn't take me long to realize that our squadron leader -- who is normally quite capable -- wasn't experienced enough with adjusting to some of the creative ways rogues tend to attack and maneuver. So I took over, directing the formation and at the same time, directing the movements of the XLs on the Alliance side, since my captain had already cleared that." She paused. "We lost one of the XLs and one of the Lunar class vessels sustained significant damage, but I think we came out okay." She sighed. "Of course, the squadron leader from *Courageous* was annoyed that I took over his role from our bridge. When we submitted the formal request for the squadron's recognition for the rescue, he finally backed off." She smiled. "Hey, I already have that medal."

Andreason laughed in agreement. "And just about every other one, as I recall."

Su'Kho scanned the faces of his fellow board members, then turned again to Wolfe. "Just how long have you held the grade of commander?" Wolfe was startled, but regained her composure quickly.

"Four years, sir."

Su'Kho nodded. "Not too long, then," he said, then quickly added, "Yet there are those who graduated from the Academy with you who have held command for seven years -- or more." Wolfe was silent. Su'Kho's voice softened.

"Commander, this is not an inquisition. I have looked at your record -- your entire record, as have Captain Andreason and Fleet Marshall Masters, and we see you as an exceptional officer, one we are proud to have within the Federation."

"Thank you, sir."

"And I wonder -- would you care to share, why you believe your advancement in rank has been slower than some of your peers?" He waited while Wolfe took a few deep breaths.

"Sir, I cannot comment on the performance of other officers unless they served with or under me during my career," Wolfe said. "Therefore, to be able to say that they should have advanced slower or more rapidly than me is something I am unable to do." She spoke confidently, knowing that talking like a politician is something often expected of senior officers. Su'Kho chuckled and pointed a thumb at Masters.

"You know, Commander," Su'Kho began, "if I wanted a political answer, I would have asked my former school classmate Paulo, here."

Masters chuckled as well. "However, Commander," Masters said, "if you were looking to provide an answer that showed political sensitivity, yours was the correct one." He turned more serious. "On the other hand, as someone who has operated within our military establishment for years, I would venture to say that your rank has been slowed because of the antiquated way that *some* in our military -- present company obviously excepted -- treat service by Central Federation personnel on Star Alliance vessels." Wolfe realized quickly that Masters knew what he was talking about. "Let me ask you more directly, Commander, knowing that service on Alliance vessels might slow your progress -- or perhaps you didn't know that -- why did you choose to serve on them? What was the benefit as you saw it of service within the Star Alliance?"

Wolfe smiled. "Well, Sir, I can't always say I've made these decisions with all the information at my disposal." She paused, then continued. "To be honest, I may not have been aware of any impact on my career of serving on Alliance vessels when I was asked to serve on the *Endeavor*. And perhaps the impact wasn't seen until a few years later." She looked up again.

"Having said that, gentlemen, I have valued my service with the Star Alliance and believe it has helped make me a better Federation officer, and to be able to serve our common goals within the galaxy. My progress through ranks -- if I may be frank -- is something of a concern, but not one to change my view of my past decisions." Wolfe surprised herself. After thinking of retiring if she wasn't advanced in rank to being almost defiant about her choices -- what *did* she really believe?

"Humpf. And *still* she can speak like a politician," said Su-Kho. He laughed then looked to his former schoolmate. "She sounds more like a diplomatic officer with every answer, Paulo." Masters only responded by opening his palms face up and shrugging his shoulders. Su-Kho tuned again to face Wolfe.

"Commander, I have a confession to make," he said. "Our true purpose today was to accomplish two specific things." Su'Kho rose, and out of long habit, Wolfe rose as well.

"Commander, I have been authorized to present you with formal notification of your advancement in rank to Su-Captain effective immediately." He paused. "And let me tell you that this is long overdue, and I am honored to be able to advance you in rank."

Wolfe was momentarily speechless, before she said, with a clear voice, "Thank you, Sir." She allowed herself a small smile and exhaled.

Su'Kho got her attention again. "Furthermore," Wolfe wondered what else he could have to tell her. "You are also hereby notified as these written orders will attest that you are to report to FV/ *Axon* at 0700 hours, Stardate 2461.4 as its new commander." He smiled as he held out the orders. Wolfe was stunned. *Axon*? That's a …

"And to answer your thoughts, Captain, yes, *Axon is* a Densen Class battle cruiser. The promotion and assignment board felt that your first command deserved nothing less than Densen class, and may I say, I am equally proud to give you your orders for *Axon*." He shook Wolfe's hand.

"Continue to make us proud, Captain."

"Sir," Wolfe said.

* * *

Following Wolfe's review, Fleet Marshall Masters waved her to a table, and ordered tea for them, a blend that Wolfe was particularly fond of. When she commented on this, he waved her comment aside.

"Don't be impressed, Captain," Masters said. "Senior officers like Alak Su'Kho make it a point to know what our important military officers prefer, as do I." Wolfe's eyes widened. "You'd be surprised what we know about you and many, many other well-regarded officers within the Federation." He smiled. "Feels a little different being called 'Captain,' doesn't' it?"

Wolfe smiled in response. "It does," she said. "My parents will be thrilled when I tell them." Their tea arrived, and they prepared their own before Wolfe looked up at the Fleet Marshall.

"I must say, Fleet Marshall," Wolfe began, "That your presence on the review board was something of a shock."

Masters chuckled. "I have that effect on people," he said.

Wolfe was feeling confident, so she continued. "So, I have the feeling we're not just here for tea." She trailed off, asking Masters silently to complete the sentence.

Instead, Masters looked up. "What do you know of the Twin Worlds of Hemod and Herai, Captain?" Masters asked.

Wolfe frowned. "I don't know much about them at all," she said, "though I seem to remember something about them seeking Federation membership." Her eyes traced the ceiling. "I believe they're located in sector 9, near a number of unaffiliated and independent worlds."

Masters nodded. "That's correct on both counts, Captain. In fact, the Twin Worlds Cooperation Council has made two requests of the Federation: first, that a Federation team come to the Twin Worlds and help them resolve some interplanetary disputes that are making cooperation difficult, and second, a formal request for Federation membership." Masters looked up. "We are, for the most part, positively disposed to their membership. Frankly, I believe affiliation would serve their needs and be positive for the Federation."

Wolfe nodded expectantly. "Yet," Masters continued, "The significant differences between the Twin Worlds themselves are enough to slow or stifle Federation membership. Therefore, the team that travels to the Twin Worlds to help them resolve these differences will be key in helping them gain Federation membership." He looked up at Wolfe again. "And that's where I come in and perhaps you."

Wolfe frowned again. "Me?" she said, then she leaned forward saying playfully, "I'm just a ship's captain." Masters laughed out loud.

"Touché," he said. "Yet you are also a ship's captain who is a weapons expert and who has extensive experience with military cooperation between forces; perhaps you can help us bring the Twin Worlds together regarding weapons and military cooperation."

Wolfe sat up straighter. "Tell me more," she said.

Chapter Six

Star Alliance Beta Quadrant Headquarters Temporary Officer's Quarters A6

McLeod heard the door chime in his quarters, and verified his visitor. He smiled.

"Come!" The door slid to the side and Anjer Alba walked in. She smiled and opened her arms for a hug.

McLeod hugged her and brought her deeper into his quarters. "Right on time," he said.

"Are you ready? I'm hungry."

"Not quite." He quickly calculated how much he had to do. "Five minutes?"

She looked at his luggage and frowned. "Uh.., how long did you say you'd be gone?" she asked.

"About three weeks standard."

Her eyes widened. "Three weeks!? I've never seen you carry this much for three weeks."

"Well," McLeod began, "I do have to bring both uniforms *and* civs for this trip, and I wasn't sure about the civs."

Alba snorted at him. "Neither am I," she said. "And I've seen what you wear sometimes." She shook her head. "You probably need a fashion consultant -- but that's not my thing either." She sat on the nearest chair and looked at her friend.

"I have good news: my promotion and assignment to the *Endeavor* were approved."

McLeod smiled. "Was that ever in doubt?" he asked.

Alba shook her head. "Not really, but I didn't want to assume anything until it was done. And you were right, they have assigned Campbell as CO; that's a relief."

"Cherry is the best," he said. "She's a great choice for *Endeavor* and the base team."

Alba nodded in agreement. "We all agree." She turned again to McLeod. "Oh, and I got a look at the larger promotion list."

"I hope you're going to tell me about Andy," McLeod said.

Alba rolled her eyes. "Well, of course," she said. "But I wanted to tell you about Raina Wolfe."

McLeod perked up. "You mean, the Federation has finally given her her bars?"

Alba nodded. "Yep, and they've given her command of the *Axon*."

McLeod squinted in response for a moment before breaking out in laughter. "*Axon*?" He turned to Alba. "Well, sometimes good things *do* come to those who wait."

Alba's eyebrows furrowed in confusion.

"*Axon* is a Densen-Class Battle Cruiser, Anjer," McLeod said. "I know for a fact that no Federation captain has *ever* had a Densen-Class vessel as a first command." He continued to nod. "Good for her. I'll have to contact her sometime soon to congratulate her."

Alba smiled. "I knew you'd want to know about her."

"You were right," he said. "Just as I wanted to know about you and the *Endeavor* -- and Cherry."

"By the way, Tucker, Campbell thinks you're a fool for turning down the *Valiant*."

McLeod let out a sigh. "I haven't turned down the *Valiant*, Anjer. I'm just weighing my options."

Alba snickered.

"And before you say anything else," McLeod continued. "Center *and* the Admiral gave me the maximum time to make my decision." He grinned. "This is kind of like a camping trip -- you know, go out and see the world?"

"You've never camped in a dress uniform in your life, Tucker."

"True." He looked up. "Ready?"

"Yes." She stood. "What's your food pleasure?"

"I'm supposed to ask *you* that," he said as he rose and stretched his back.

"Where is that Terran buffet place you used to always talk about?" Alba asked.

McLeod laughed. "Boy, we've been together a long time, haven't we?"

"Yep."

McLeod and Anjer Alba walked a short distance to a land transport then walked the few blocks to a small bistro offering Terran specialties. McLeod had always been impressed with the number and variety of restaurants on station. As they entered the restaurant, McLeod reminded Anjer of his favorites, and they took a brief tour of the buffet table before returning to their table. After round one, they paused to sip their coffee (McLeod) or tea (Anjer).

Alba broke the ice.

"So, leaving tomorrow?" she asked.

McLeod nodded. "Yes. It's around two standard days to the junction, Beta Gamma 4 I think, then two more to the Twin Worlds."

"Umm. Who did you say is the head of the Alliance team?"

"Minister Long of the Ketchuan System."

Alba squinted, thinking. "Demeter Long, right? Silver hair, very tall?"

"That's her."

Anjer smiled. "And you think she's ready for you?"

"That's my hope." McLeod said. He sipped his coffee. "It's really exciting. I know I have a lot to learn, and this is a great way to do it."

Alba's smile grew wistful. "I don't want you to waste your talent, Tucker."

McLeod shook his head. "Never a waste, Anjer. Never," he said. He pointed with his head toward the buffet.

"And you haven't tried the waffles yet." They returned to the buffet for a second round of food, and sat back in their chairs to enjoy their time together. As they sat, McLeod noticed Alba becoming sadder and sadder, and he thought he knew why.

"I'm looking at a very sad face." He took her hand. "Steel?" She nodded, tears forming at the corners of her eyes.

"Anjer, I…" she raised her hand to stop him.

"Don't. You don't have to. No one's been as supportive as you've been. When I lost Steel, I lost a part of myself." She wiped her eyes. "I can't bring him back, and you're the one who helped me realize that. I just began to understand that you and I won't be together anymore. It's a little tough saying goodbye to your 'big brother.'" She shook her head and looked up. "But," she began, "That doesn't mean we won't be connected forever, does it?"

McLeod smiled. "You're right," he answered. "It doesn't. And it also doesn't mean we won't talk just because you're the big, tough XO of the *Endeavor*."

Alba laughed. "Which reminds me Tucker, who is on this team from the Alliance?" McLeod pulled his hand back to sip his coffee.

"I know very few of them, and we aren't even arriving together. Several members are already in sector, including Minister Long. Councilor Trent is on the team for cultural and scientific exchange, and the InterStellar Minister from Yemane is chairing a team, too. Plus, a number of staff people who do this for a living, but who are lower level administrators serve as staff for each team. A lot of the work is hammered out behind the scenes by them as I understand it. It's very well organized."

"You do sound very excited about this."

"I am," said McLeod. "Perhaps a little apprehensive, but excited. And," he added, "I promise you if I don't enjoy the trip or don't feel I should make the shift to diplomatic, I will take the *Valiant*. Someone's got to show Campbell how to run an Andromeda class starship." They both laughed.

"Deal," she said.

Chapter Seven

Star Alliance Beta Quadrant Headquarters Docking Area Two

The lights in the docking area were brighter than usual, McLeod thought. He had arrived a half hour earlier than required -- a long standing habit -- went through the screen, and placed his luggage in the intake area. Soon afterwards, other people in the delegation arrived, such as Councilor Trent, two bureaucrats from the InterStellar Ministry who McLeod had met on a few occasions, and others. He smiled to himself as he saw the size of the clothing bags everyone else was taking. Despite taking far more than he usually would for a three week assignment, he noticed that all of the civilians took more. He'd make sure to slide that little bit of information to Anjer when he communicated with her again.

Out of another long standing habit, he asked about the starship in which they would be traveling, which was a Luwen Class Federation vessel. Then he mentally calculated the number and type of fighters assigned to it and contained within the hangar. With his experience to guide him, it seemed like an adequate vessel for this purpose. He had previously been told that the ship would travel to the junction point, then continue to the space station near Hemod and Herai, each leg of the trip taking two days. He also knew that this speed would present something of a strain to the smaller Luwen Class ship, though not an insurmountable one.

McLeod smiled as Councilor Trent completed his security screen. He approached with his hand extended.

"Councilor."

"Captain," said the Councilor. "I see you're ready. What's that phrase -- If you're early, you're on time…"

McLeod smiled. "And if you're on time, you're late. I heard that from my mother more times than I care to count." He looked at Trent's companions. "I don't believe we've met before,…"

Councilor Trent intervened to help McLeod. "These are my colleagues, Captain," Trent began. "They were assigned directly through Minister Long. Let me introduce you." Trent turned toward the man to his left, who McLeod noticed was small but powerfully built.

"Captain McLeod, Director Vaughn Allen." The two men shook hands.

"Captain," Allen said. "Your reputation precedes you."

McLeod chuckled. "I hope not too much. Good to meet you, Director."

"Director Allen is an expert in natural resources negotiations, which will be very important on the Twin Worlds," Trent continued. McLeod nodded his understanding. Trent then turned toward the woman, who McLeod noticed had the slightly bluish skin tint of a T'Gowan. "This is Consul Thora Wu," Trent said. "She is a specialist in cultural and scientific exchange." McLeod extended his left hand to Wu, and as she grasped it, placed his right hand lightly on her wrist. She returned the gesture and smiled.

"It's nice that someone serving as an observer with this team has your understanding of different species and cultures, Captain," she paused, "You are part Saranite, are you not?"

McLeod nodded. "Yes, half Terran and half Saranite," McLeod began, "and whatever I've learned about other cultures has been a gift, Consul. It's good to meet you."

McLeod turned again toward Councilor Trent. "So," he addressed the Councilor. "You said that Director Allen and Consul Wu were assigned not by you, but by Minister Long."

"Yes." Trent looked around. "If we can board, why don't we do so and talk there?" The group walked toward the nearest access point, and once inside agreed to meet in the port conference area at 1600 hours. They were each told their assigned quarters for the journey and led to their quarters by junior staff members. McLeod was embarrassed when he received his quarters assignment. He cringed slightly when he was told he would be in 7A Port, and was about to object when the sergeant making the assignments called asked a corporal to escort McLeod to his quarters. As they approached the lift on the opposite side of the ship from his companions, McLeod addressed the corporal.

"So," he began, "Where is your XO?"

The corporal seemed slightly startled, then answered. "Groundside, Sir. I believe he has a family emergency, and won't be accompanying us." He looked up. "Our Chief Engineer is serving as XO for this assignment, which is why you have the XO's quarters."

"Understood," McLeod said. They entered the lift and continued to face the opposite door. The corporal keyed in the proper deck.

He looked up again at McLeod. "The captain made it clear that no former Federation XO would be sharing quarters with anybody else, sir." McLeod conceded the point, given his experience within the Federation. He addressed the corporal.

"And your captain would be...?"

"Commander Jax, Sir. Aranova Jax."

McLeod smiled. "Well, you may feel free to let the Commander know that I appreciate her hospitality." He chuckled. "And you can also let her know that she still owes me from our last encounter, and getting the XO's quarters doesn't quite pay the debt." The young corporal suddenly looked nervous. McLeod shook his head slightly as he noticed the corporal's unease.

"I'll take care of it, Corporal." The young man relaxed.

"Thank you, sir." The lift opened, and McLeod instinctively turned to the left toward his quarters, walking side by side with the corporal. They arrived at the door to his quarters and McLeod waited for the corporal to enter the code, then placed his hand on the plate to be scanned. They heard a simple click, and the door opened. McLeod entered and noticed an area that had obviously been cleared for his use.

He looked over his shoulder. "I hope you didn't have to move too much, corporal."

The Corporal shook his head. "No, Sir. Our XO travels light, plus he has extra storage space. You should have plenty of room, sir."

"I agree," McLeod replied. "Though I have to tell you I feel a little bad about getting the XOs quarters -- I don't know where my colleagues are being assigned, and doubt they will be as comfortable as me."

"I do believe Councilor Trent has taken the guest quarters," the corporal answered. "We usually do that for dignitaries. I don't know about the others. In any case sir, Commander Jax said you would always have been assigned quarters such as this."

McLeod shook his head slightly. "Good old 'Nova."

"Sir?"

"Old nickname, Corporal." He turned to the young man. "Is your CO available for a visit?" The corporal nodded, but before he could speak, they heard a voice from the entrance.

"Available for some; not so sure about you, Tucker."

McLeod's smile widened as he approached the ship's captain. "Nova," he said, as he embraced her. He looked at her conspiratorially. "Please don't let anybody else see my quarters. I'll never be able to live this down."

Nova Jax smiled. "Tucker, you worry too much," she said, "but I won't say anything unless you do. Besides, it is protocol for a former Federation XO."

"Well, thank you. It is appreciated," McLeod said, as he looked around the quarters.

Jax stepped back and gestured toward the door with her head.

"Time for a coffee break?"

"Absolutely," he responded.

McLeod and Jax left the XO's quarters, then walked down the hallway toward the lift. Jax punched in the code, and the lift slowly rose to the primary deck. As they traveled, McLeod reflected on his first encounter with Aranova Jax. While a Prolate, Aranova Jax had served as Tactical Officer aboard FV/ *Xian* while McLeod served as the ship's Executive Officer. Having served previously as Tactical Officer on another Federation vessel, FV/ *Andros*, McLeod was well suited to work with Jax and help her in her transition. They had become fast friends, even with the differences in their ranks. He looked at Jax and smiled.

"Been a long time, Nova."

Jax nodded. "You might say that. But this whole *command* thing," -- she swept her arm around the lift -- "It's all because of you. So, in all honesty, you're never that far from me." She shook her head slightly. "And you really need to tell me what you're doing on this mission."

McLeod chuckled. "Coffee first."

"Agreed."

They exited the lift and Jax immediately ran into two lieutenants who had questions for her. McLeod stood aside and watched her interact effectively and respectfully with her subordinates. He smiled to himself as he recalled seeing the same qualities when she was a young prolate on the *Xian* and he knew she had all the raw talent for command. "That was one of my best recommendations as XO of the *Xian*," he thought.

As she completed her conversations, Jax turned to her friend and nodded her head toward her ready room. They walked the short distance and entered after Jax was scanned. She called for coffee and waved McLeod toward her lounge. McLeod sat, looking around and getting a feel for the ready room.

"I can see things are going well on the *Kuron*, Nova. Captain Ozaki knew what he was doing when he turned her over to you."

Jax smiled appreciatively. "Thank you, Tucker. I'm happy to be here, and my crew is excellent." Their coffee arrived, and she poured for her friend. "I must say, Tucker, I'm surprised to see you here. So, what's the story?"

McLeod briefly explained his current thinking, his consideration of a major career change and the offer to serve as an observer on the mission to the Twin Worlds. She listened politely and asked questions for clarification on two occasions: she clearly gave him her full attention. She noted the energy with which he talked about the assignment and what he hoped to learn as well as how he was preparing for the negotiations. Once he finished, Jax smiled and said,

"If I hadn't spoken to you, Tucker, I never would have understood why you're doing this." She paused. "The more you talk, the more this assignment seems like the right thing to do. I mean, it does seem like everyone wins with this. And even if you decide it isn't for you, you said they'd keep the *Valiant* for you?"

"That's what they seem to be saying," McLeod began, "but I'm trying not to think I have a failsafe: I have to commit myself to this assignment as though it's all I have…"

"Or else you'll pull back the minute something goes wrong?" Jax interrupted, and laughed. "Who does that sound like?"

"Ozaki" they said together, and both laughed.

"So, do you have any meetings tonight?" Jax asked her friend.

McLeod checked his chron. "It's 1520 now," McLeod began. "We're going to meet at 1600 to orient ourselves to the negotiations. Councilor Trent hasn't said anything about a meal."

"Well, while I would much prefer to dine with just you, I've already sent the Councilor an invitation for dinner in my quarters at 1900 hours." Jax smirked. "We had already planned on a few specialties from Herai for dinner tonight: I don't know how that's going to go over, but I'm sure you'll like it."

McLeod laughed. "Why, because I eat so much?"

"No, because you've always been very adventurous when it comes to food." She sat up. "And whatever we're having, you've probably had it before anyway."

McLeod nodded. "I'll look forward to it. Have you assigned us a conference room?"

"Um hmm. The Aft NCO lounge."

"Good choice." Rising, he said, "I should probably get back to my quarters then head to the lounge."

Jax rose, saying, "I understand. We'll have plenty of time over the next few days to get together."

They began walking slowly toward the lift and to the XO's quarters. When they finally arrived, McLeod briefly embraced her, saying, "Are you sure you want your crew to see you hugging an Alliance officer?"

Jax snickered. "You're not just *any* Alliance officer, Tucker," she said. "Plus, they all *know* you or know of you. I doubt you could do anything to surprise them."

"Got it," McLeod said. "Breakfast tomorrow?"

"That would be nice," Jax replied. "How about 0700 at my quarters? Then if you don't have any meetings directly afterwards, we can tour the ship."

"Great. Thanks," McLeod said. "Until then."

Chapter Eight

*Central Federation Beta Quadrant Headquarters Temporary
Officers Quarters*

Raina Wolfe looked through her packed clothing and gear, and
sighed. This was a lot harder than it looked, she thought. What *does*
a career military officer wear on a purely diplomatic assignment?
She only hoped her instincts were correct, or if not, that she would
be able to find alternatives on the Twin Worlds, though that seemed
at best challenging, and at worst, impossible. Perhaps, she thought,
if she were to dress in Twin Worlds clothing it might help the
Federation cause? She smiled and tossed her head.

She had truly enjoyed her conversation with her new Executive
Officer. Parker Scott was Andoran on her father's side, so Wolfe
believed they would have something in common. And Scott's
service on FV/ *Suran* was stellar: Wolfe was pleased when she saw
Scott's name on the short list for XO. She had decided to assert
herself once she received her orders to ask about the status of
selection for Executive Officer. She needn't have worried: Fleet
Marshall Su-Kho had already arranged for her to review the
promotion documents and recommendations at the Military
Personnel Center and had told the quadrant command that Wolfe
would need at least a few days to review the documents. He had
become quite the advocate, Wolfe thought. A pity I didn't come to
his attention ten years ago.

Wolfe and Scott had discussed the tasks before them, both in terms
of refit and crew selection, and Wolfe asked Scott to ensure that refit
was organized according to Federation standard Y-6, which while
not the newest standard, was the one Wolfe understood and
supported the most. She was pleased to find Scott held the same
opinion. After agreeing that she would visit *Axon* as soon as her
temporary assignment to the Twin Worlds was complete, Wolfe
signed off, a very satisfied ship's captain.

Is that what she was, finally -- a ship's captain? She allowed herself
the satisfaction of the title temporarily, before then reflecting on the

importance of being successful in her first, and perhaps only, ship's command.

"Better make this good," she thought. Her door chimed.

"Come." The door slid to the side and Fleet Marshall Masters appeared. He greeted her first.

"Hello, Captain," he said "Are you ready?"

She beckoned the Fleet Marshall in. "About as ready as I'll ever be," she said, then turned to her luggage. "I'm still trying to make sure I bring the right things." She looked up at him. "This is a little harder than I thought it would be."

"What did you pack in terms of uniforms?"

Wolfe sighed. "Well, I have three dress and two field uniforms, in addition to some civilian clothing -- not sure when we should in fact be in civs rather than uniforms."

Masters nodded. "I think what you have packed is fine," he said. "We have little use for formal 'reds' except on the first night -- but it's not necessary." His eyes twinkled. "Were you able to have your uniforms altered to reflect your rank?"

Wolfe chuckled. "Yes, and it cost me a great deal to have them altered; the remainder will wait until I return. I'm certainly hoping my raise in pay will cover it."

"That and your bonus," Masters said. "Most of us simply assume the bonus is to cover either new uniforms or alterations."

"I'd forgotten about that," Wolfe said. "And I'll use that to cover new formal reds, too. It certainly doesn't make sense to try to alter my current one."

"I agree," said Masters.

Wolfe took a quick look through her clothing and gear, and closed the luggage. "How will we be traveling to the Twin Worlds?"

"We'll be on FV/ *Polaris*. We'll reach the first junction in about one day, then travel two additional days to the Twin Worlds."

Wolfe nodded and asked. "Luwen class?"

"Yes," Masters said, laughing. "Is there anything you *don't* know about this assignment so you can tell *me*?"

Wolfe laughed at his remark. "No, sir. Not at all." Then she got a mischievous look in her eyes. "Unless you want to know that the first junction will probably be Beta Delta 4, and the junction nearest the Twin Worlds is Beta Gamma 9."

"Right. That's what I thought," Masters said. "Now, will you be able to fly there without being in command?"

"Well," she began, "that is still new to me."

"But it won't be for long," Masters said. "You'll be great."

Wolfe looked directly at him. "Thank you for these opportunities, sir" she said.

Masters chuckled as he shook his head. "Hey, I wasn't chair of the review board who actually gave you your promotion and command assignment."

Wolfe shrugged. "Good enough for now," she conceded. But she still felt there was much more to Masters' involvement in her career than the assignment to the Twin Worlds.

"Besides," Masters continued, "It's we who should be thanking you for your service as well as for this work on the Twin Worlds: we need a person with your understanding and expertise."

"Who is actually on this team?" Wolfe asked.

"Actually, the team is being organized and overseen by the Federation and Star Alliance team heads: Demeter Long, Interstellar Minister from the Ketchuan system and Vice Chancellor Pel Noregan of the Federation Beta Council. Our team will be co-chaired by Susan Redstar and me. She is a former Lands NCO within the Alliance. She currently serves on the military outreach council for Gamma Quadrant. She's particularly skilled at interspecies negotiation and weapons negotiations. Susan's sharp, and very confident, but then again, most Lands NCOs are."

Wolfe laughed. "Goes without saying, sir, though with her experience, why do you need me?"

"Because you are a currently serving officer; Susan's got the credibility as a negotiator, but she's not in the trenches anymore." Masters said. Wolfe nodded in understanding, then looked at her luggage. She looked back up at Masters.

"Well, I'm ready," she said.

"So am I. Let's head out."

Chapter Nine

Federation Vessel FV/ Kuron, *Executive Officer's Quarters*

McLeod returned to his quarters the following morning surprisingly tired having only attended one two and a half hour meeting. And besides being fatigued, he was also a little miffed. During the meeting, Consul Thora Wu seemed bound and determined to put him in his place repeatedly. As the meeting began, it was clear that the three professionals were impressed with the depth of McLeod's preparation. In truth, only about half of the preparation took place immediately before the trip; the remainder of McLeod's knowledge about the Twin Worlds, language, internal challenges and other issues, came from his personal knowledge as a Star Alliance officer and generally well-traveled person. He was particularly annoyed at Consul Wu since she seemed like such a positive person when they met.

Consul Wu *was* impressive, as were Trent and Allen. Councilor Trent began the meeting by outlining in greater detail some of the issues that were likely to be addressing during the negotiations, and asking what general information both Director Allen and Consul Wu could provide. Trent proved himself a master at asking probing questions, and McLeod continued to be impressed with him. And both Allen and Wu seemed quite up to the task: each provided concise, clear answers that addressed both the letter of Trent's questions, and their understanding of his intent.

However, whenever McLeod asked a question, more for his information than to challenge an assumption or conclusion of the professionals, he found their reactions generally negative, as if they were annoyed having to explain something so simple to an amateur. On one occasion, McLeod carefully challenged an assumption by Consul Wu regarding the status of women on Herai, the world where he had had the most contact. He was unconvinced that the status of women on that planet was as subservient as Wu thought, based on his personal experience and the evaluation of women at several rungs of that society whom he had encountered in universities throughout the galaxy. The response of Consul Wu was typical of her attitude that morning:

"Captain," she said with clenched teeth. "These many issues we are talking about are not so simple as they appear to an amateur. In fact, they are quite complex and probably beyond anyone's ability to comprehend without *significantly* more study." She looked pointedly at McLeod, then at Trent before continuing. "I was under the impression that observing meant simply that: observing and learning, rather than participating in fields where your knowledge is severely limited."

The table became quiet, then McLeod casually pointed his hand at Trent, conceding the floor, so the Councilor could continue the meeting. While he continued to be respectful during the meeting, and did ask Councilor Trent a question (a good one, given the discussion that ensued and the response he eventually received from Trent), he decided to remain quiet and try to build a stronger picture in his mind of the issues. McLeod made a point of staying after the meeting to chat casually with Councilor Trent and to interact with them all as if he wasn't annoyed, then declined Councilor Trent's invitation to lunch, saying that he had a previous engagement with the ship's captain. In truth, he had a standing invitation with Jax, but he could have cancelled it easily. His objective now was to get some alone time, re-center himself, and spend the remainder of the afternoon until their after-dinner meeting doubling down on his preparation. He smiled to himself and thought, "Well, I did say I had a lot to learn, and I was willing to do it."

McLeod returned to his quarters where he spent a half hour meditating. Afterwards, he was able to come back to his work quite refreshed. He studied for a little over an hour when he heard the door chime.

"Come!" he said. McLeod looked up as a member of the mess staff entered with a food tray. McLeod was surprised, because he realized he hadn't requested anything from the galley, yet he was hungry. The steward cleared a place at the dining table, then stood and smiled. McLeod returned the smile, then went to the table and lifted the lid. He then leaned down and sniffed. Lifting his eyebrow, he asked,

"Is this blood soup?"

The steward nodded, and added, "Compliments of Commander Jax, sir." The corporal lifted the second lid and declared, "Along with fresh Cassom bread. The commander said it was one of your favorites."

McLeod sat down, exclaiming,

"Especially with blood soup! Thank you, Corporal." He picked up a spoon, then raised his left hand. "Hold on a minute," he said, then he tasted a spoonful of the soup. He smiled broadly.

"This is excellent, Corporal. Please give my compliments to the chef."

The corporal returned the smile. "That would be me, sir." McLeod rose and extended his hand.

"Thank you, Corporal," he said. "This is a nice reminder of home."

"Thank you, sir." Standing square, he added, "Will there be anything else, sir?"

"No, Corporal -- I'll give my thanks to Commander Jax for her thoughtfulness later." The Corporal nodded, backed up, then turned and left the quarters.

McLeod had been honest with the young NCO: the soup was excellent, and it was at least as good as his mother's. The soup and traditional bread gave him a wonderful feeling, and he returned to his study renewed and with a far better attitude.

McLeod made a point to speak briefly with Commander Jax after his meal to thank her. He also filled her in on the nature of the meeting with the three bureaucrats. Jax was understanding, yet confirmed his conclusion that the meeting simply pointed out how much he had to learn. So, she was supportive, yet still holding up the mirror as if to say "If this is what you want…." Still, McLeod appreciated her support, and arranged for them to work out the following day prior to his morning briefing.

McLeod completed studying at 1700 hours, and had a snack in his quarters. Afterwards, he returned to the Aft NCO lounge to meet with his three colleagues. He entered the lounge smiling and affable, yet noticed Trent, Allen and Wu seemed wary. He sat down, opened his materials, and turned his attention to Councilor Trent, who, after a few minutes, started the briefing.

"Now," Trent began, "Vaughn, it is not clear to me how deeply the Shan Confederacy is embroiled in the internal politics of either Hemod or Herai. What can you tell us about that?"

"Councilor," said Allen, "The Confederacy has been a presence in the system for several years though at present they seem to be focused primarily on defending the sovereignty of Herai, which we believe is tied to their significant abundance of natural resources." Trent nodded for Allen to continue.

"Now, we understand that they have been openly working with forces on Hemod as well, all focused we believe, on ensuring that any worlds loosely affiliated with them have primary access to the resources of Herai and the technological prowess of Hemod."

Trent looked around the table as Allen continued. "Their emphasis is on blocking the Alliance and the Federation from greater or preferred access to the Twin Worlds. And we further believe that they are fueling some of the anti-Federation forces on Herai among some independents." As Vaughn Allen spoke, McLeod wondered what information Allen had access to that led him to these conclusions. Apparently, McLeod was unable to assume a blank affect while Allen spoke. The young staffer looked to McLeod, saying,

"You seem to have another idea about the confederacy in the system, Captain?" It was an obvious challenge, and McLeod knew it. So, were Allen and Wu both trying to put him in his place before arriving at the Twin Worlds? The thought annoyed him, but he consciously kept his face neutral.

"Not at all, Director," McLeod said. "I'm listening and trying to gain a greater understanding as you speak. I'm sorry if I gave you the wrong impression." McLeod smiled calmly at his colleague, allowing Allen to break the gaze first.

Allen looked first to Trent, then continued. "To continue, the Shan seem to have strengthened their stronghold in the Twin Worlds, enough so that they are demanding the opportunity to work with the competing parties to develop an internal solution separate from any action the Alliance or the Federation might promote."

Trent nodded. "Vaughn, I can't help wondering if representatives of the Shan aren't somehow more connected with the governments on Herai and Hemod than anyone cares to admit," said Trent.

The whole conversation was something of a mystery to McLeod since the Shan generally aren't so well organized as to promote this level of unrest unless someone is directly threatening a world on which they are dominant. Their whole reason for being is to prevent the creation of super powerful organizations like the Alliance or the Federation, yet they are seldom as actively and openly involved as they seem to be on Herai and Hemod. Trent asked a few more questions of Allen to gain a better understanding of some of the points of view that would be important during the negotiations, then asked other and equally challenging questions to Wu.

McLeod was pleased to learn that because of his increased study, he understood more of the discussion than before. Fortunately, or unfortunately, his greater understanding also forced him to work even harder at preventing his facial expressions to reveal his doubts about the conclusions of Allen and Wu, and occasionally, Trent himself. It occurred to him that perhaps his broad general experience in so many areas of the galaxy and particularly in the Beta quadrant, was an asset he could still provide to the negotiations -- if only he could get someone to listen to him.

While somewhat fatigued by the end, McLeod was still energized by the conversation, and his slowly increasing ability to understand, and perhaps to contribute. As he left the briefing room to return to his quarters, he found Councilor Trent waiting for him at the lift.

"Can we talk for a while, Captain?" he asked.

"Of course, Councilor," McLeod replied. The Councilor gestured to indicate a small alcove in the hallway, and McLeod followed.

"Captain, I appreciate your willingness to learn during these discussions. It confirms my sense that you have the strength to know when you're the expert and when you're not, which is admirable." He paused and looked directly at McLeod.

"On the other hand, I sensed that you might have objected to a number of the conclusions we came to this evening. Would that be accurate?"

McLeod smiled slightly before continuing carefully. "Councilor, I have committed myself to intense study since you offered me this opportunity. And, I have certainly seen time and time again when a conclusion I may have reached was clearly inaccurate because of information I didn't have access to that the three of you because of your backgrounds, find to be common knowledge." He looked again, more confidently, at Councilor Trent. "So, if you're suggesting that perhaps I should be more assertive in my comments or questions, I can assure you that when the time comes, I can do that."

Councilor Trent nodded, then smiled slightly. "I know both Allen and Wu can be -- challenging -- at times," Trent said. "I probably would have invited them anyway, but in this case, their being chosen by Minister Long seems to have given them a sense of superiority over even me in these discussions." He chuckled, then added, "Of course, I know I have deeper knowledge and experience than they do, so I don't allow it to deter me." He looked again at McLeod.

"So, don't let it deter *you* either. I wouldn't have suggested you for this assignment if I didn't believe you could contribute perspectives and experiences that none of us who haven't spent significant time in that sector could ever hope to duplicate. We certainly can't do so based solely on heavily sanitized and filtered reports written by people who aren't any more experienced in the system than we are." Trent paused and smiled at McLeod.

"So again, Captain, please let us have your thoughtful contributions so we can be as well prepared as possible when we arrive at the Twin Worlds."

"Understood Councilor," McLeod said.

"Very well, Captain. Have a good evening." Councilor Trent turned from the alcove and walked toward the aft lift, while McLeod continued down the hallway to the forward lift.

McLeod returned to his quarters, and finally acknowledged his fatigue from the day. Since he wanted to sleep soon, yet still wanted coffee, he made low-coffee, then meditated for a brief while before going to sleep.

* * *

McLeod exercised the following morning in the officer's rec area before joining Commander Jax in her quarters for breakfast. As he entered the captain's quarters, Jax studied her friend. He seemed generally relaxed, a change from a day or so prior.

McLeod noticed her. "What?" he asked."

Jax smiled.

"Nothing. Just seeing if those bureaucrats are still getting on your nerves."

McLeod chuckled. "They are," he began, "But I seem to have found the formula to turn the tables." Jax's eyebrows rose in question.

"I'm not actually *doing* anything, Nova."

Jax looked doubtful.

"Okay, okay," McLeod conceded, "All I've been doing is studying enough so that I really understand what's going on and what they're talking about. And I think they realize that I know more and can reach conclusions about what's going on as well as they can, yet I'm not sharing it. They're making themselves crazy waiting for me to say something so they can attack it, and I'm not obliging them." Jax shook her head.

"It's only partly deliberate, Nova," McLeod said. "I certainly don't want to make a fool of myself, and I find if I listen three or four times longer than I might normally be inclined to, that many times, I can see that my original conclusions might be wrong." He looked up. "My sense is that Allen and Wu see my thought process and they're worried I'm going to come up with something profound and put them in their place. But honestly, I don't really care -- I am learning some things I didn't know before, which I think is the point. And when I have something to say that I believe will contribute, I'll say it -- and defend it."

"Well, that certainly sounds like you," Jaz quipped."

"Guess you're right, Nova." He surveyed the table. "This is a very nice breakfast, by the way."

Jax nodded in agreement. "The mess staff is incredible on this ship. The officer's rec is the busiest I've ever seen and for obvious reasons." She checked her chron. "I think we have about two hours until the junction."

"Is anyone joining us there?" he asked.

"Not to my knowledge, and I doubt it will change at this late date. The plan is to enter the junction at around 1100 hours, confirm course, then accelerate toward the Twin Worlds." She smiled as she turned to face McLeod more directly. "Do you think your companions are prepared for the acceleration, especially on a smaller federation vessel?"

McLeod smiled. "That remains to be seen," he said, "though I believe Councilor Trent knows what to expect, since he postponed our morning briefing to late afternoon. To be honest, I'm not inclined to give any warning to Allen or Wu given the circumstances."

Jax shook her head again. "Fine. Tucker, I swear, you're never going to stop being the jokester who sits in the corner snickering. In any case, why don't you come to the bridge with me when we hit the junction?"

McLeod smiled broadly. "You don't have to ask me twice. Thanks, Nova." The two friends finished their breakfast, then separated, McLeod returning to his quarters, and Jax to the bridge. McLeod decided to don his Class A uniform so he wouldn't be out of place on the bridge. At 1030 hours, he chimed at the access to the bridge, identifying himself. As the door slid open, he turned to Commander Jax.

"Permission to enter, Ma'am," he asked.

Commander Jax rose and faced McLeod. "Granted," she said, then she added to the assembled crew "Captain on the bridge!"

While not strictly protocol, the acknowledgement was welcome. McLeod entered the bridge, formally greeted his friend, and asked rather than directed that she please "carry on."

Jax introduced McLeod to the personnel on the bridge, including the Chief Engineer/ Temporary XO, Helmsman, Communications Officer, Astrogator and Tactical Officer. He watched with interest as the Astrogator confidently went about her work, calculating direction and feeding headings directly to the Helmsman, while waiting to arrive at the junction. Junctions throughout the galaxy were areas of relative "quiet" where star winds and other phenomena which complicate astrogation are absent. This permits very precise astrogation to areas extremely distant from the junctions. Also, courses between junctions are relatively simple to calculate. The course between this junction, Beta Gamma 4, and the junction closest to the Twin Worlds, Beta Gamma 9 was quite easy to confirm and lock into the helm. McLeod knew from experience that the Astrogator would breathe a sigh of relief in a few moments.

"Helm. Time to junction," said Commander Jax. When McLeod heard this, he returned his attention to his friend.

"Estimate 12 standard minutes, Ma'am," came the reply from the helmsman.

"Thank you, Jack." Jax turned to her Astrogator. "Prepared to confirm course, Sal?"

"Yes, Ma'am." She smiled. "This is a familiar junction, Ma'am."

"Understood. Thank you Sal."

"Aye, Ma'am." McLeod continued touring the bridge and listening to the precise yet cordial communications between the personnel and smiled. The bridge of a starship was the place where he was perhaps most comfortable, yet he seemed determined to give it up. On the other hand, diplomats have to travel by starship all the time: he certainly wouldn't and couldn't leave space travel in any case. He allowed his mind to wander, until he heard the Helmsman.

"Approaching junction, Ma'am." The helmsman looked at his captain. "Suggest secure positions, Ma'am." Jax nodded toward her Chief Engineer, who opened the intercom channel.

"All hands, all personnel," he began. "We are approaching Junction Beta Gamma 4. All hands and all personnel are to move to secure positions. All hands, all...." he repeated the warning, ending with "All decks, acknowledge." McLeod sat at the second officer station then heard several decks reporting in, and calculated when all had reported. At the same time, the Chief engineer looked to his captain. "All hands, all personnel secure, Ma'am."

"Acknowledged," Jax said. "Sal, course confirmed?"

"Aye, Ma'am."

"Helm. Course laid in?"

"Laid in and ready, Ma'am."

Jax nodded. "Good. We've got liberty on Hemod when we arrive," she smiled, "and I for one don't want to waste any time." Turning again to her Helmsman, she said,

"Engage, Mr. Pullem," and McLeod felt the slow then forceful engagement of the ship's engines as the *Kuron* propelled herself toward her final destination and a very new adventure for him.

Chapter Ten

Twin Worlds Space Station Alpha, Plenary Room

McLeod, resplendent in his dress uniform, continued to mingle comfortably with the assembled diplomats, bureaucrats and staff for both the Alliance and the Federation, in addition to the many diplomats, staff and dignitaries from both Hemod and Herai. He had originally thought he might be more awkward during the introductions and reception, but he recalled how frequently he had attended inaugurations, coronations and other significant ceremonies throughout the galaxy. This proceeding didn't differ very much from them.

McLeod also realized how much he knew about Twin world culture and internal politics even prior to his briefings on the *Kuron*. He greeted the Finance Minister from Hemod, and after shaking hands, leaned in to touch her cheek with his and seemed to surprise the minister. And when being introduced to a Herain officer of superior rank, he shook his hand, then saluted by placing his hand over his heart. It was only as he left some of these encounters that he realized other members of the team from the Alliance and Federation hadn't done the same.

The beginning of the reception was a tedious series of introductions by the Twin Worlds Coordinating Council, and the governing councils of both Hemod and Herai, both of which introduced the members of their negotiating teams. This was followed by the equally drawn out introduction of the Head of the Central Federation Negotiating Team, Vice Chancellor Pel Noregan of the Federation Beta Council, and the Head of the Alliance Delegation, each of whom then introduced the members of their delegations, after which everyone talked about how excited and committed they were to positive solutions for all concerned. McLeod certainly agreed with the sentiment, but thought that someone should teach these career politicians better ways to start a meeting. But then again, he needed to see and experience this program if he were ever to make the jump to diplomatic.

The only surprise -- and a pleasant one -- was the introduction of a long term colleague as a member of the Federation negotiating team. He smiled broadly when she was introduced, and acknowledged her with a wink, which was returned. They signaled each other that they would speak later, and following the introductions, they mingled separately with members of other delegations. McLeod decided he would make a point of seeing her directly after the meal rather than interrupt her mingling. She must have made the same decision, as he didn't see her again for almost an hour. A tap on his shoulder broke his concentration.

"I certainly didn't expect to find you here," said Raina Wolfe.

McLeod smiled and looked furtively around the room. "Just to be safe, I'm not going to hug you, but that's coming." Instead, he took her left hand in his right and squeezed. "You are definitely the finest surprise of this gathering."

"Flatterer," she said. She quickly glanced at McLeod's black wavy hair, which was just starting to include wisps of gray. "You're looking good, Tucker, though seeing you here is certainly unexpected. So, the first thing you have to tell me is: what in the world are you doing here and why?"

McLeod shook his head. "Uh-uh. First thing is for me to congratulate the Captain-designate of FV/ *Axon* -- and the first ever captain in the Central Federation whose first command is a Densen-Class Battlecruiser."

Wolfe shook her head in amazement and laughed. "Tucker, no one could ever say you don't do your homework. When did you find out about my promotion?"

"A few days ago. Anjer -- you remember Anjer Alba?" Wolfe nodded. "Well, Anjer saw the Federation promotion and assignment list when she received her promotion and assignment as XO for the *Endeavor*"

"She deserves that slot," Wolfe said.

"And you deserve this one," McLeod said. "Raina, this is long overdue. I know it's been a long time coming, but you deserve it."

Wolfe nodded. "Thank you, Tucker. That means a lot." She looked at him sternly. "Now, why here; what are you doing; and why would you ever think of turning down the *Valiant*?"

"Talk about having a network of spies," McLeod said. "Why here is -- well -- because they offered me the opportunity to serve as an observer because," he paused and leaned forward, "I've asked to be transferred to diplomatic."

Wolfe frowned and said, "I'd heard that, too." She looked around the reception. "And we certainly don't have the time to explore that now, but we will and soon."

"Agreed." McLeod frowned. "And what are you doing here? Don't you have some refits to supervise on the *Axon*?"

"I do," she said, "but my plan is to return to the space yards following the negotiations. I've been assigned to staff the committee looking at military cooperation and weapons agreements." She squinted slightly, "How about you?"

McLeod shook his head. "Oh no. I'm only assigned here as an observer." He smiled. "I still have a lot to learn about diplomacy, but I have to tell you, I've already learned a lot: maybe I'll be able to contribute at some time during the negotiations."

Wolfe shook her head in annoyance. "They don't know enough about you, Tucker," she said. "Few people understand more about military cooperation and weapons than you do, in either the Federation or the Alliance." She frowned slightly. "And if they don't want you to do anything, why would they assign you in the first place?"

"Not so sure about that," McLeod said. "Councilor Trent from Beta Council suggested it to Minister Long, and she consented to the assignment." He stood slightly straighter. " It doesn't really bother me, since I really came here to learn more than to throw my weight around. Though serving as a staff member on that committee might be interesting."

"Shall I suggest it to my delegation head?"

McLeod started. "No," he said quickly, "Don't do that. The last thing I want to be accused of is trying to direct things I know *so little about.*" Wolfe frowned before he continued, "and I'll fill you in on some of those dynamics later. What's your sense of the schedule for our gatherings? Councilor Trent suggested that we might have a brief meeting of the Alliance team after dinner."

"I'd heard that, too," Wolfe said. "And it actually may be a larger meeting with both delegations. I think Vice Chancellor Noregan wants to set the tone early for what he wants to accomplish." She looked up. "Apparently, he and Minister Long have worked together on teams like this for years, sometimes with him in the lead and sometimes with her leading. They won't have any trouble keeping the Federation and Alliance teams together."

McLeod looked around the room, then nodded in agreement. "Well, if we don't have time to talk after that briefing, we'll have to schedule some time tomorrow." He smiled. "It's really good to see you, Raina: this is going to be a much better assignment with you here."

The two friends departed, and rejoined the larger group as they began to be seated for the meal. After a few more introductory remarks of welcome, the meal, consisting of several Twin world specialties, was served. Toward the end of the meal, several toasts were proposed by the leaders of the delegations, and members of the combined Alliance and Federation team were reminded of their brief meeting in the general hall immediately following the meal. While not exactly excited, McLeod listened attentively to the words of welcome, and to the tone being set by the delegation leaders. Instinctively, he began getting a sense of each individual's priorities and points of view, then cautioned himself that perhaps he should reserve his conclusions until he'd had more time to reflect. As McLeod rose from his seat, he noticed Raina smiling at him slyly. She signaled at him to wait for her, and McLeod was frowning slightly, trying to find out what she wanted to talk about, when his thoughts were interrupted.

"Sr. Captain McLeod," came the warm tones of his delegation head. Demeter Long extended her hand to McLeod who took it while standing at attention.

"Minister Long," he said, then added, "How may I help you, Ma'am?"

She looked around and smiled slightly. Continuing in a softer voice she said, "Well, for one thing, please don't make me feel older than I am by being so deferential." Her eyes brightened. "Actually, I wanted to chat with you briefly prior to this meeting. Can we...."

"Absolutely," McLeod said. "Lead the way." Minister Long walked to the side of the head table and took a seat toward the end, motioning McLeod to the adjacent seat. Even while seated, McLeod noticed, Demeter Long had a commanding yet approachable presence, which he concluded might make her an excellent negotiator. Once settled, she addressed him again.

"Captain, I was happy to accommodate you within this delegation on the request of Councilor Elias Trent. When he explained your exploration of a career change in service to the Star Alliance, I was interested in helping you get this inside glimpse of the inner workings of an important negotiation." She smiled. "And I remain confident that not only can you learn from this experience, but that we can benefit from your expertise as well."

"Thank you, Ma'am," McLeod said. "I would be happy to serve in any way possible."

"I know you would, Captain," Long said. "So, Vice Chancellor Noregan and I would like you to serve as the Star Alliance staff member on the committee on military cooperation and weapons." Minister Long continued, but for a moment, McLeod's mind was wandering. Had Raina asked Minister Long or Vice Chancellor Noregan for this assignment, and if so, how did he feel about that? Fortunately, he turned his attention back to Minister Long.

"So, Captain, as I said, your experience in several informal
negotiations among warring worlds regarding weapons and conflicts
is too valuable to waste by having you go from meeting to meeting
solely as an observer. Do you agree?"

"I do, Ma'am, and I am appreciative of this offer." He hesitated. "Is
this something Councilor Trent is aware of as yet?"

Long nodded. "Yes, Captain. Councilor Trent and I spoke about
this earlier today just prior to the reception. He is in full agreement.
And while the original proposal for you to serve as staff for the
committee was mine, please be assured that Vice Chancellor
Noregan is also in full agreement." She smiled again. "I wanted
you to be aware of this assignment prior to the upcoming meeting,
because we are announcing several shifts and new assignments now,
and I didn't want you to be surprised."

Something in her manner caused McLeod to ask, "Did someone tell
you I didn't like surprises?"

Minister Long rose and smiled as she checked her chron. "I'll see
you in the general hall in twenty minutes, Captain." With that, she
left. McLeod rose to follow her, and turned to face Raina Wolfe,
who laughed, her violet eyes dancing. Before he could speak, she
raised her palm toward him.

"Not my doing," Wolfe said, "But I did see the staffing lists from the
Vice Chancellor right before the reception and knew about your
assignment. That's why I was so surprised when you said you were
only an observer."

McLeod smiled.

"Who is chairing the meeting for the Alliance and the Federation?"
he asked.

She frowned at him. "Didn't Long tell you?" she asked.

McLeod looked down sheepishly. "Probably, right after she told me about the assignment. But I was so stunned I wasn't listening for a short while." He looked up defensively. "But I did listen at the right time to accept the assignment, I'll have you know."

"Fine," she said, smiling. "The head of the negotiating team for military cooperation and weapons is Fleet Marshall Masters. He was Fleet Admiral in Gamma Quadrant when we served on the *Andros*." McLeod nodded his head. Wolfe added, "He's the one who recruited me for this assignment."

"I remember him," he began, "From when he did an inspection tour of the *Andros*."

"Right," she said. "He's a good man and easy to work with." She looked toward the general hall.

"Meet you inside in ten?

"Yep."

After taking a brief break, McLeod and Wolfe met in the general hall for the briefing.

Vice Chancellor Pel Noregan strode to the front of the room. "Ladies and Gentlemen," he began. "Welcome to this first general session, really, an orientation to our work and what we hope to accomplish. Those of us from the Central Federation and the Star Alliance are here at the invitation of the Twin Worlds in hopes that we can help them build stronger ties between the two planets, ensure sustained economic development, and provide for their mutual defense. As it has been explained to me and my colleague," he indicated Minister Demeter Long," potential membership in the Central Federation is only a secondary consideration of these negotiations. Of course, Minister Long has told me on more than one occasion that membership in the Star Alliance is even more suited to Hemod and Herai, but since we're friends, I know she didn't really mean that." Polite chuckling followed Noregan's joke. As representatives of the Central Federation and Star Alliance, we share the responsibility to facilitate lively and full discussions within our committees, and this is truly our greatest challenge: for we must challenge assumptions, ask clarifying questions and dig through some of the rhetoric to help the Twin Worlds committee members get to real and sustainable solutions."

As he listened, McLeod was alternatively excited and intrigued by the Vice Chancellor's words and tone. He understood the intent, he thought, but also imagined maintaining the proper decorum during committee meetings would take some work. Vice Chancellor Noregan then turned to Minister Long. "Demeter?" Demeter Long rose and smiled at Noregan before facing the negotiating team. "What Pel has mentioned to you is important," she began, "but at the same time, you should understand that what you may see as political rhetoric or posturing may very well be misunderstandings or genuine ignorance of the other side's point of view." She smiled and shook her head slightly. "When you've been working on these teams as long as Pel and I have, you come to understand that you may reach in your minds accurate conclusions or potential points of agreement very quickly. But if that happens, stop and think before you direct the conversation to that conclusion. The people on these negotiating teams all have perspectives that have been honed by years or decades or lifetimes of bias. They're not evil or devious; they're just like the rest of us. Try to ask them the questions they need to consider to make good collaborative decisions, and gently challenge their assumptions in ways that make them think rather than resist.

Long smiled and relaxed. "Now one more thing," she continued. "We have made two changes in staffing for our committees. The first is that we have reassigned Ungel Spear to the committee on economic cooperation." Ungel, a slight bald man with a bright smile, nodded his understanding. "The second is that we have changed Captain Tucker McLeod's role on the committee on military cooperation from that of an observer to official staff." Those are the only changes people," Minister Long said.

McLeod smiled in much the same way as had Spear, and while he failed to notice the scowl on the face of Thora Wu, Wolfe caught it and frowned.

"So," Long continued. "If there is nothing else for tonight, get a good night's sleep -- we have a lot of work ahead of us."

Chapter Eleven

Twin Worlds Space Station Alpha, Casual Dining Area

Wolfe arrived for breakfast before McLeod in one of the private dining areas of the headquarters. On the walk from her quarters, she marveled at the view out of the ports. She could see in the distance to her right and left the Twin Worlds themselves and could even make out the more desert-like appearance of Hemod as opposed to the deeper color of lush Herai. She had chosen again to braid her hair and wear one of her standard uniforms, and was pleased that she hadn't yet purchased the very ornate full dress captain's uniform. She had marveled at how easily McLeod wore his the night before, but she thought, he's had a bit more practice at this than I have. Her standard uniform felt much better. She was still quite surprised by McLeod's intended career change, and agreed with many others that McLeod was one of the finest officers with whom she had ever served, and she still couldn't see him too far from a starship. Wolfe had a flash of memory to the time when both she and McLeod had been Sub-Commanders, and served on FV/ *Andros,* McLeod's first tour on a Federation starship. The *Andros* had been warned away by ships for an independent planet for traveling into "their" space, and *Andros'* captain had been inclined to simply leave, neither showing fear nor escalating an unnecessary conflict he knew he'd win. It was McLeod who'd persuaded the captain to both send and accept a landing party from the planet to talk about a formal agreement between the Federation and the planet. She chuckled, remembering that McLeod had said "Hey, we're already *here*," when the executive officer objected to McLeod's plan. But the captain decided it was worth the time, and in the end, tensions were reduced and the Federation had a new connection in that area of space. Wolfe had to admit that McLeod had a certain flair for finding creative solutions to problems. She looked up and saw her friend enter the dining area. He smiled as he saw her. He waved her to stay in her seat, and he leaned down giving her a brief hug.

"That was overdue," he said. Looking at the table, he asked "Have you ordered yet?"

"No," she said, "Waiting for you." He looked her over and Wolfe frowned at his obvious inspection.

"What?" she asked.

"You know," he began, "I think I've been waiting to see you in the captain's braid almost as long as you have."

She shook her head. "Not hardly, brother," she said. She looked up and saw a staff person approach the table with a menu. She and McLeod both ordered common Twin world dishes. Both dishes had the characteristic yellow and blue colors of Hemodian and Heraian fruit. Once they ordered, Wolfe turned serious first leaning forward as though telling him a secret. "But the first thing I want to know, is what's up between you and those two civilians from Beta Quadrant HQ? I thought their eyes were going to bore holes through you when Minister Long announced your assignment." Have you been showing your true colors to people again?" she added playfully.

McLeod protested. "Not deliberately," he said. "During our trip here, Wu and Allen spent a lot of time putting me in my place. I was, after all, the rank amateur, while they were the consummate professionals. Councilor Trent took me aside once and encouraged me to speak up more and not be intimidated by them." He paused and squinted. "As a matter of fact, I wonder if the whole experience with Consul Wu and Director Allen was a test to see if I could work in a very different environment in which I wasn't the expert anymore."

"And?" Wolfe prompted, "how did that go?"

McLeod smiled. "I think pretty well; I pulled back enough to really listen to what was going on and learned a lot more as a result. It was a good but somewhat humbling experience."

Wolfe looked at her friend, trying to discern his mood. Finally, she said, "You did, didn't you?"

"Did what?"

"Learn a lot," Wolfe replied. "And apparently didn't mind being humbled, either."

McLeod shrugged his eyebrows. "I guess I didn't exactly think about it that way until just now. But I guess you're right, he said. "That can't be bad."

"Not at all," said Wolfe. "I'm just getting a better understanding of why you're here -- it's good."

"Good," McLeod said. "Can we eat now?"

Just then, their breakfasts arrived. After ordering more coffee for him and tea for her, they settled into their meal. After a short while McLeod looked up at Wolfe. "So, do you really know what happens at these sessions?"

Wolfe swallowed a sip of tea. "My understanding is that there is a lot of posturing between opposing forces, then some of the staff and key players behind the scenes get together and try to hammer out compromises and agreements that reflect where the competing sides are really willing to go. So, we'll probably be meeting after the formal negotiations with their staff to see what we can come up with."

"To be honest," McLeod said, "I don't recall meeting the staff members from either of the Twin Worlds at the reception last night. Did they attend?"

Wolfe raised her eyebrows. "Probably," she said. "But I don't remember: I certainly didn't speak with them. Something tells me if they were at the reception, that they're accustomed to staying in the background. These receptions seem to be more for the politicians than the regular grunts like us."

McLeod sipped his coffee and nodded. "I agree," he said. "Why don't we see how the first meeting goes, then we can decide on how we want to approach them. Plus, we may be receiving assignments from the chair every evening to work on, so I suppose we should remain flexible."

"Good point," she said. McLeod placed his coffee cup on the table and looked at Raina again.

"Raina," he paused to get her full attention. "Is your father still mad at me?"

Wolfe laughed. "Tucker, my father will *always* be mad at you, and that's hardly a surprise. The possible loss of a homeworld does that to a guy." She frowned. "What brought that on?"

He sighed. "It's the old 'reputation precedes you' stuff: that does follow you everywhere doesn't it?"

Wolfe sat lower. "It does, Tucker, and when it comes to Andora Prime, we all know why."

"But you…"

"No, I don't still hold it against you. On the other hand, I have the benefit of having worked with you for half my career." She looked serious again. "You also know how I felt right after Andora Prime, and how difficult it was for us. But unlike other people, I know who you are *and* your motivations." She tapped his hand. "No, my friend, I don't hold anything against you. I know that you did what you thought was right and for all the right reasons, whether I agree with it or not. And to be perfectly honest, if I could probe my father's mind I would probably find that he agrees with me, but he'll never admit it."

McLeod smiled. "Understood," he said. "Now, you still haven't told me about your review board after serving on *Courageous*." He leaned forward expectantly. "How did it go?"

With that, Wolfe smiled and sat forward herself. "I suppose whirlwind would describe it, Tucker," she said. "We had successfully completed our tour on *Courageous*, even getting through a tough encounter with the Mollies in the Tabard System."

McLeod nodded his head. "I read about that; sounds like it was incredibly tough."

"It was," said Wolfe. "Anyway, that was clearly the event uppermost in the minds of the audit board when we completed our tour. Still, I was surprised when our captain returned from the review board, and told me they wanted to see me. I suppose my reaction concerned him., because he assured me 'No reprimands, Raina; it's all good.' So, I headed to the board room. I even brought my XO log in case they needed to review something." She smiled and paused.

"And..." McLeod prodded and gestured with his hand.

"And, the meeting wasn't much of one. They simply reiterated their positive evaluation of *Courageous'* actions throughout our tour and mentioned that they appreciated my actions in the Tabard system. Then, out of the blue, they told me that I got my promotion and first command. That's when Fleet Marshall Masters asked me to accompany him on this assignment." She looked up. "And, here I am."

"Meaning," McLeod said, "that they had already approved both the promotion and assignment that quickly?"

"Yes and no," she said. "My captain submitted the promotion and command recommendation right after Tabard. He had planned to submit both anyway; this was just the spark that made him submit it early, though the approval was still rather swift." She laughed. "Obviously, I said yes, and they directed me to the Military Personnel office to review the files of available officers." She chuckled. "I wasn't really ready to do it, and only spent a short time there learning what to do and how to access information until I returned to *Courageous* and the captain. Only then did I contact my family." She shook her head as she smiled. "As I said it was all a whirlwind, and now that I think about it, did you already know all this?"

"Well yes," McLeod said, "But I wanted you to tell me. It was much more entertaining this way."

Chapter Twelve

Twin Worlds Space Station Alpha, Conference Room C

The conference room for the Committee on Military Cooperation seemed cold to Raina as she entered it. After leaving breakfast with McLeod, she had briefly returned to her quarters for her materials. She was as excited as McLeod about what she might learn during the proceedings, but equally guarded given the issues that needed to be addressed. She also didn't know how she would get along with the staff members from Hemod and Herai. As she pondered these questions, she heard the distinct sounds of footsteps, and moved toward the table off to the side of the large conference table, where she assumed she would be sitting.

First to enter to her surprise was Vice Chancellor Noregan, followed closely by the Vice Chair of the Twin Worlds Coordinating Council. She recalled his name to be Griffin Patt'son, and her first impression of him wasn't particularly positive: he seemed to have a bluster about him that was off-putting. Patt'son was followed by Fleet Marshall Masters, who smiled as he saw her. He broke from his colleagues, and went straight to her. His approach was more friendly than official, and instead of preparing to salute, she smiled and took his hand as he offered it.

"Good morning, Captain," he said. "Always good to see you."

"Thank you Fleet Marshall," she said. Then turning, she added, "should we sit at any particular spot at the kid's table?"

Masters laughed. "Yes, that is the staff table," he leaned forward. "And it may be a lot nicer place to be once we begin the tough discussions. Which reminds me, I'm pleased that both you and Captain McLeod will be staffing this for the Federation and the Alliance: your backgrounds and experience are going to be invaluable here, particularly since the staff members for both Hemod and Herai have little military experience."

Wolfe nodded, then asked quietly, "Why is the Vice Chancellor here?"

"Kind of a fail-safe: the first committee meetings will be started by either the Vice Chancellor or Minister Long. It's a good idea: they'll be able to set the tone for the negotiations. My remarks will follow afterwards."

"That's a good plan. The Vice Chancellor and Minister have a flair for this."

"And how about you?" he asked. "Are you thinking of making a shift like Tucker?"

She shook her head. "Fleet Marshall, I am very happy to be in Federation uniform, even with or maybe particularly because of the weight of the braid," she said, smiling. Fleet Marshall Masters returned the smile, then left Wolfe to greet other members of the committee. Wolfe remembered meeting the chief Alliance negotiator, Susan Redstar, before. McLeod knew her as well, and said she was highly respected in both military and civilian circles. He thought she might be in line for an even higher level diplomatic post at Alliance Central Headquarters.

McLeod entered after Redstar, acknowledged Wolfe, then turned his attention to the others clustering around the door. Wolfe squared her shoulders and moved toward the center of the room to participate in the brief welcoming and mingling prior to the start of the meeting. The first person she encountered was the Heraian director of management and budget, whom she had met previously. Wolfe was puzzled to see her at this meeting. They hadn't spoken of their committee assignments the previous night, and Wolfe would have assumed she would be a better fit for the committee on economic cooperation.

The woman saw Wolfe approach and smiled at her. "Captain Wolfe, right?"

"Yes. And you're Director Oberon?"

The woman smiled in response. "I am. I've been assigned here to serve as staff for the committee representing the Heraian governing council."

Wolfe made sure to maintain her neutral expression. "I see," she said. "You may remember that I'm staffing the committee for the Central Federation. My colleague, Captain McLeod," she indicated Tucker with her hand, "is serving in the same capacity on behalf of the Star Alliance." Looking back at Oberon, she added, "Captain McLeod and I have been friends and colleagues for many years."

Oberon's eyebrows furrowed and she nodded her head slowly. "I've," she paused, "heard a lot about him."

Wolfe sought to lighten the mood. "Many people have, Director. But few know him as well as I do." She chuckled. "And, some of what you've heard is the stuff of legend rather than reality. He's a good man." Oberon seemed unconvinced, but nodded nonetheless. They both turned their attention to the man approaching them.

Oberon performed the introductions. "Captain Wolfe, this is Director Ed'ards -- Owen."

Wolfe and Ed'ards shook hands. "Good to meet you, Director," Wolfe said. "And, by the way, I am perfectly happy to go by first names: mine is Raina."

Ed'ards smiled. "Raina, it is then." Ed'ards said.

Oberon stepped in to face Wolfe. "I'm Lane," she said.

"And he," Wolfe tilted her head indicating McLeod, "is Tucker, and I know him well enough to know that he prefers first names as well."

"Great," said Ed'ards. He looked toward the smaller table. "I take it that's ours?"

Wolfe raised her eyebrows and smiled. "Yep. I think it will be fun." They began to hear more sounds indicating that the meeting would soon be convened. McLeod made his way to the table, placed his briefing materials next to Wolfe's and went to greet his fellow staff members. Wolfe performed the introductions and they sat just as Vice Chancellor Noregan called the meeting to order.

"Ladies and Gentlemen," he said. "Please be seated." All sat and the room grew quiet in anticipation. "I am going to beg your indulgence for a few minutes before we hear from Fleet Marshall Masters and Ambassador Redstar, then your full committee meeting can begin." He surveyed the room. "Minister Long and I have committed ourselves to open all of the committee meetings of these negotiations so there is a common understanding of our collective tasks and how we wish to approach them."

"In essence, we in the Central Federation and Star Alliance are here at the request of the Hemodian Governing Council, the Heraian Governing Council and the Twin Worlds' Coordinating Council to discuss -- in their words -- 'ways to increase economic and security cooperation between both planets and to improve the quality of life on the Twin Worlds.' In addition, the Governing Councils and Coordinating Council have submitted a formal request for membership in the Central Federation."

Noregan looked up. "I don't think I've put words in anyone's mouth with that statement." A quick survey of the room revealed no one objecting to his statement. "Since we are here at the invitation of the Governing Councils and Coordinating Council, I must emphasize that these negotiations rest primarily on the shoulders of the people of the Twin Worlds: if they ask us to leave, we will do so. This also means that any positive result from these negotiations, regardless of the tremendous talent in this room and the other conference rooms, will be a result -- ultimately -- of the efforts of the people and members on this committee from the Twin Worlds. No one in the Central Federation or Star Alliance need or will seek any aggrandizement for our collective success. And I know," he added, "that we in the Federation and Alliance will do all we can to facilitate your success here during these negotiations." With the general agreement around the room, the Vice Chancellor turned to Fleet Marshall Masters and Ambassador Redstar.

The Vice Chancellor sat and Masters rose. "Thank you, Vice Chancellor," Masters said. He faced the committee members. "And indeed we in the Federation and Alliance are committed to being part of positive solutions, yet those solutions will be those you as citizens of the Twin Worlds will ultimately develop and approve." He raised his arm to indicate the staff table. "The staff members of the committee who will help research and provide background to our discussions are all particularly skilled," and here he chuckled, "and may find themselves spending more time together than those of us officially on the committee." Everyone laughed, and he turned to Ambassador Redstar, who rose as he sat. Redstar briefly surveyed the group before speaking.

"So, we've had the opportunity to hear from our delegation head at our opening reception, which laid out many of the tasks we have to face on this committee. However, now that we are formally here, we should understand in more detail the perspectives and objectives of the committee members." Turning to the her right, she nodded toward a man of medium height. "Griffin, would you be so kind as to begin?

The man rose and began.

"I am Griffin Patt'son, currently serving as Vice Chair of the Twin Worlds Coordinating Council. We in the Coordinating Council believe first in developing closer ties between our two worlds, and believe that the Central Federation can help us to do that. What role we may choose to have within the Central Federation after these discussions is in question, but my focus is truly on our Twin Worlds." He looked toward Ambassador Redstar. "This is not to give offense to the Star Alliance, Madam Ambassador." Redstar nodded cordially. "In any case, thank you, and welcome to the Twin Worlds." As he sat, Wolfe thought he sounded like a tourist advertisement. She looked over at McLeod, and noticing his smirk, was sure he felt the same way. As Vice Chair Patt'son sat, the woman seated to his right rose, which she did with some difficulty. The woman was of average height, with deep blue hair, and a clear military bearing. Wolfe knew she was a retired Admiral.

"I am Zara Nereze, retired Admiral of the Hemodian Navy, and Commandant of our Naval Training Academy. I've had the chance to see -- in action -- both our navy and that of Herai, and believe that if we could cooperate more fully, that would help our worlds tremendously." She looked up. "And by the enthusiastic nod of my colleague," here she pointed across the room to a powerful looking man in uniform, "I know I am not alone."

The Heraian captain rose. "I do agree, Admiral…"

The Admiral interrupted him. "You've called me Zara for three years now Brad, don't get all formal on me now," said the Admiral to laughter around the table.

The Heraian captain smiled. "I stand corrected, Zara." He looked up and faced the rest of the committee members. "I'm Captain Bradwyn Malvo of the Heraian Defense Forces, and what Zara did not tell you is that at one point we were engaged in battle against each other." He paused. "That didn't make sense to me then and it doesn't make sense to me now, and that's why I'm here." He sat to general agreement around the table. The final general committee member, a young woman of below average height, stood up. She seemed to Wolfe to be a very precise person.

"Good morning. I am Tora Kayne, the Home Secretary for the Heraian Governing Council. How our military works and how much we invest in the military, from either of the Twin Worlds, is something I think we should discuss as we look toward greater cooperation." She looked toward the head of the table. "And how we respond to the Central Federation, I believe should also be on the table." Her tone suggested that she would welcome a response from Fleet Marshall Masters, but he was far too skilled to oblige her.

"Thank you, Madam Secretary," said the Fleet Marshall. "And thank you all." He spread his arms to encompass the entire gathering. "Our first task, as we see it," indicating Susan Redstar, "is to begin by visioning, meaning discussing what an ideal Twin Worlds community would look like in terms of military cooperation. Now, we don't want to suggest that this will be easy for us, in fact, it will be particularly challenging. Our objective is to help us identify both differences and agreements early, so we can more carefully outline the work we have to do." He looked around the table, resolutely.

"So, are we ready to get started?"

Chapter Thirteen

Twin Worlds Space Station Alpha, Captain T. McLeod's Quarters

Wolfe entered McLeod's quarters quickly.

"Shut the door!" she said. McLeod, following her, creased his brow, but closed the door quickly. As the door latched, Wolfe turned to him and burst out laughing. Seeing the humor, McLeod laughed as well.

"So *those* are the people you want to hang out with, Mr. Diplomat?" Wolfe had a hard time getting her words out through her laughter.

"Well," McLeod said, "Not necessarily *those* people. Why? Did you have a problem with them?" He continued to chuckle.

"Oh, Tucker, you are in for a very unpleasant career," she said. Trying to become serious again, she said, "Okay. Okay. I have to get serious for a moment." Then she burst out laughing again and sat on a chair.

"Tea?" McLeod said. She nodded. McLeod moved to the galley, and began brewing tea and coffee. "So," he began, "maybe not the most enjoyable first meeting, huh?"

Wolfe slowed her laughing and nodded in agreement.

"Will you *please* quit laughing?" McLeod cried. "At least through these negotiations; you're in this, too!"

Wolfe shrugged, and moved to the galley. "Oh," she said, holding her belly. She sighed. "You're right. You're right. I do have to deal with these people for the next -- what -- fifteen days?" McLeod sighed and nodded. "Okay," Wolfe continued. "We need to work out some kind of signal so one of us can escape to punch a wall when it gets too tough to keep from smacking one of those people. Whoever signals first gets to escape."

McLeod smiled. "Agreed," he said. McLeod and Wolfe continued chatting amiably for a while as they waited for the coffee and tea to finish brewing. Once he served their drinks, McLeod checked his chron.

"We did tell them 1400, right?"

"Yep -- to give us time to eat and to decompress -- only they don't *know* that we're decompressing."

"That's about right," McLeod said. "And we may need to hit the rec area every night just to work some of this out. Though it just occurred to me, that we should probably speak to Ambassador Redstar and Fleet Marshall Masters soon." He shook his head. "Some of these people just don't have a clue about military cooperation and we need to run some of our concerns by the Ambassador and Fleet Marshall sooner rather than later."

Wolfe agreed. "That does make sense; we are supposed to be staffing this committee on their behalf." She checked her chron. "Do you think we should meet with them briefly before 1400?"

"Yes, since that's probably what Owen and Lane are doing." McLeod frowned slightly. "I still can't figure them out, though I've only had one long session with them."

"I agree," said Raina. "Though again one session isn't everything." She got up. "Let me contact Fleet Marshall Masters." She scanned the quarters, found the com link, and entered the code for Masters.

"Sir?" she asked, "Captain Wolfe here." She listened. "Sir." She looked towards McLeod. "Captain McLeod and I would like to speak with you and Ambassador Redstar soon. We apologize for the short notice." She smiled and nodded. "Yes, exactly that. Certainly, Sir. In the conference room at 1315? Yes, Sir. See you then."

She turned to McLeod. "You heard?"

"Enough. Sounds like he was expecting our call."

"He was, and he laughed when I proposed it. He was having lunch with Ambassador Redstar." McLeod looked at her quizzically,

"What do you know about her?" He asked. Wolfe's eyebrows furrowed. "I mean, I know of her," continued McLeod, "but she worked primarily in the Gamma Quadrant. I've worked there, but served much more in Beta. She's just a name and reputation to me, and even then I only know the skeleton."

Wolfe considered. "Well, as I think about it, she kind of reminds me of you. She has a lot of experience in interspecies negotiation throughout all four quadrants, I believe. And she is an expert on weapons issues. Since she was a Land, I think her background on the ground is more extensive. And her overall knowledge base is incredibly extensive."

McLeod nodded at her assessment of Redstar. "I could see and feel much of that during the meeting. I could see her body language make subtle shifts as some of the people talked about weapons and cooperative agreements; she just knew they were stretching the truth."

"No," Wolfe countered. "They were out and out *lying*, Tucker."

"Agreed," he said, " but these negotiations are less about truth and more about what you can negotiate."

Wolfe shook her head in annoyance. "I've heard that, too. In any case, I think she will be the one to poke holes in people's arguments or at least point out what she knows that challenges them; probably the Fleet Marshall will be the nicer of the two…"

"I agree," said McLeod, interrupting, "And he is the one with greater military credibility."

"Except for you and me, of course, but we're on the staff."

"If we're going to meet them so soon, we should get something to eat." The two went on the commercial deck for a light lunch before returning to the conference room.

* * *

"With the obvious exceptions of Admiral Nereze and Captain Malvo, the remainder don't seem to understand the military or military cooperation at all," said Redstar. "That's going to make your jobs harder. And while we can assist you in most ways, you will have to determine how and when to push your colleagues in your private meetings."

"I agree, Susan," said Masters. He turned his attention more deliberately to the two captains. "I know you are aware of your support functions as staff for this committee -- working on hammering out compromises behind the scenes, as well as providing information to us as the Co-Chairs. What you may *not* understand is that there will be times during which you will need to push your staff colleagues pretty hard to get them to take our challenges and our questions back to their people to help move them from their entrenched positions: that's the only way to move these proceedings forward. The trick, of course, is knowing when your pushing will provide results rather than even more entrenchment." He paused and looked up, then he smiled. "Is this what you two signed up for?"

McLeod smiled. "It sounds like this won't be a walk in the park, but I was given to understand something of the sort, though perhaps not so much challenging and pushing so hard behind the scenes."

"I agree," said Wolfe. "What you describe seems like more of the entire negotiating process, and not caring so much about saving face. Would you describe it that way as well?"

Redstar jumped in. "I think you've summarized it well Captain, but please don't feel that we're leaving the entire process to you; we're not." Redstar stopped and smiled again. "Our objective is for us to keep the formal negotiations reasonably positive, while using our staff time to work through the differences. We have to ensure that anything we come up with is a public win-win: bickering among the formal committee members compromises that."

"Understood, Ambassador," said Wolfe. McLeod also indicated his approval.

Ambassador Redstar checked her chron.

"Then, I guess you're on," she said.

Chapter Fourteen

Twin Worlds Space Station Alpha, Conference Room C

McLeod and Wolfe walked the short corridor to the conference room to meet with the two committee staffers for the Hemodian and Heraian Governing Councils. They were a bit more sober after their meeting with the Fleet Marshall and the Ambassador, but facing tough or unique situations is something they'd accomplished successfully before. They just weren't sure they wanted to tackle them with these particular colleagues.

They arranged the seating around the conference table, and looked up as Lane Oberon and Owen Ed'ards entered. During their first brief meeting, it was clear to McLeod that Ed'ards had serious concerns about natural resources on Hemod and the impact an increasingly active military would have on them. McLeod couldn't be sure, but it seemed to him that Ed'ards was more concerned about how to pay for the military than what the military should be doing, which seemed to McLeod to be backwards.

Lane Oberon had a similar concern about money, and it occurred to McLeod that this one thing they agreed on may make it challenging to secure Federation membership. While taxation and fees aren't the only feature of Federation membership, the population of the Twin Worlds, even when taken separately, would require both worlds to provide military personnel to the Federation. That, combined with the actual monetary investment had been enough in negotiations on other worlds to scuttle affiliation with either the Alliance or the Federation.

As Oberon and Ed'ards entered, they greeted McLeod and Wolfe cordially, chatted for a brief while, then sat at the table.

Ed'ards spoke first. "Tucker, Raina." He nodded to each of them in turn. "Both Lane and I are new at this from the interplanetary standpoint except when dealing with some of our own colleagues world to world. We assume the two of you are more experienced in looking at things from a larger distance." Wolfe and McLeod glanced briefly at each other before agreeing.

"So," Ed'ards continued, "We thought it might be helpful for us to review the basic issues we'll be dealing with so at least we know where we already agree, and where we have a long way to go."

"That's our plan as well," said McLeod. "It's always better to start with agreements, because we may find we're not as far apart as we think we are." Oberon smiled, but the smile held no warmth.

"You can't be discouraged so early, Lane," McLeod said with a smile.

Oberon looked up and exhaled slowly. "No. No, you're right," Oberon said, "That's not the way to start our discussion. I only meant to point out that our differences may be large enough that we'll be working on them for quite a while."

McLeod smiled. "Well, we can always send out for sandwiches." He looked up. "Shall we begin?"

Ed'ards began, providing his own summary of the issues facing them. McLeod thought his presentation was quite lucid. "There is just some concern certainly on Hemod about the level of taxation. In fact there are many who believe we ought to be shrinking the size of our military given that we are basically at peace with our nearest neighbor. That makes the whole idea of joining another larger force completely unacceptable."

"I agree," said Oberon. She chuckled "Of course, as a director of management and budget, I'll always object to costs, but it goes deeper than that. Many of us support greater cooperation, we just aren't sure that joining the Federation would give us the return on investment we want."

"Reflecting on our meeting with the full committee before lunch," McLeod said. "I'd really like us to focus on issues of concern from each of the planets, and what cooperation might look like to you.

Focusing on the Federation however valuable membership would be isn't going to get us anywhere."

Wolfe nodded her head in agreement. "Exactly," she said. "I'm not here to advance the Federation. I'm really here to help you make some decisions about military cooperation. Federation membership, if it comes at all, can come much later."

"So, if the only goal of our discussion is military cooperation, what are the roadblocks you each see on your sides?" Ed'ards and Oberon continued laying out their understanding of the concerns on their individual planets, and McLeod was struck that there was little discussion of weapons limits, particularly since limits on phase weapons was specifically noted in the briefs both he and Wolfe had read. Whether their omission was deliberate or a result of Oberon and Ed'ards knowing little about weapons was unclear. What was clear to McLeod was the need for both he and Wolfe to educate Oberon and Ed'ards without seeming too aggressive.

Chapter Fifteen

Twin Worlds Space Station Alpha, Conference Room C

"This may sound like a silly question," began Oberon. "And I'm aware of the difference in support for phase weapons, but all I know about them is that they use radiation." She looked to McLeod and Wolfe. "Can you just tell me exactly what they do so I really understand them?"

"Happy to, Lane," offered Wolfe. "When a force uses a phase weapon, usually a cannon or torpedo, it's the radiation within the weapon that disrupts the molecular structure of the target. Think about it like this," she continued. "If you were to shoot particles of sand at a piece of wood or something else soft really fast, eventually the sand would start to poke tiny holes in the wood, right?"

"That makes sense," Oberon replied.

"Well, a phase weapon does the same thing, only it can do it to metal, rock, composites, pretty much everything. It doesn't so much blow the metal apart, but it weakens it into a mesh that can't stay together."

"That's the easy part," said McLeod. "The tough thing about phase weapons is that the radiation used to make the mesh if you will, lingers in space and can weaken the hulls of ships flying in that area of space. In other words, it can damage things that you weren't intending to target in the first place."

"Then why would anyone want to use them?" Oberon asked. "It seems incredibly destructive."

"It is," said Wolfe. "But that isn't the whole story. I was looking this morning at the view of both planets from the cafe, and the contrast in terms of landscape is pretty clear."

"Not to say that Hemod isn't beautiful in its own right, Owen," McLeod said quickly. "But your resources are very different than those on Herai." Ed'ards raised his hand indicating he understood.

"Exactly, Wolfe said. "When you look at the natural resources, such as the metals and fossil fuels used to make composites, there is much less on Hemod. They use phase weapons because they have a lot more radioactive ore than they have metal."

"Simply put," McLeod said, "when you're building weapons for your military you use the materials you have, not the materials you don't. But we also know that Herai is asking for a reduction in phase weapons because of the damage or contamination of space around both Twin Worlds, and I think that's going to be a big sticking point for our committee to deal with.

Both Oberon and Ed'ards looked defeated.

"Hey," Wolfe continued. "That's a big issue, but that doesn't mean we can't help the committee make progress addressing it.

"Exactly," McLeod added. "Our objective is for us to determine how we can come closer together." He turned to Oberon and Ed'ards. What do you think?"

Ed'ards was the first to answer. "So many things come down to money, or other resources for us," he said. "Vice Chair Patt'son is a fierce budget watcher, and he is very concerned about adding to our budget problems." Ed'ards paused briefly, then smiled. "Not to say we actually have budgetary problems on Hemod, mind you." His colleagues laughed.

"We're behind closed doors, Owen," Wolfe said. "Doesn't mean we won't listen and remember, though."

"I echo those monetary concerns," said Oberon. "Moving toward Federation membership, to say nothing of joining the Alliance," here she looked briefly at McLeod, "would really put a strain on our military spending."

McLeod turned briefly to his long-time colleague before replying. "Federation membership is something both Raina and I strongly support, but it's not the only goal of our discussions." He laughed, adding "and it could be said that if you already agree on money issues, that's one less thing to fight about."

"I do understand that, Tucker, said Ed'ards, "However, I am at least partially channeling the concerns of our Vice Chair, and of many on Hemod who want to know the benefit of spending more on what they believe is already being done by our military and governing council."

"These are reasonable concerns, Owen, which we may be able to get to at some point," said McLeod. "But one of the things I think we should get back to now is how the Hemodian and Heraian military function: could they be combined into a single force? Are the structures similar enough and the cultures similar enough to allow that? And the larger question that we may want to address at some time: does it make sense to maintain the current strength of either force if the Twin Worlds continued to pursue Federation membership?"

As the other staff members considered this, Wolfe spoke up. "We know that is a big 'if,'" she said. "Though we also believe it should be on the table."

"And how do we ensure our sovereignty if we give up so much to the Federation to protect us?" asked Oberon. Her inflection indicated rising annoyance.

Wolfe countered her calmly. "And that's why I call it a big if, perhaps a really big if," said Wolfe, adding quickly, "But let's get back to Tucker's question: there are many who see greater cooperation between the two military forces as essential to a stronger relationship, yet there is resistance to moving toward a single force. What are those concerns? And when does working closer and closer together for the common good as separate forces become more difficult than creating and sustaining a single force with the proper mission?"

The question seemed a good one to Wolfe, and she knew McLeod enough to know that he would agree with her. The question seemed to stop both Ed'ards and Oberon in their tracks. McLeod allowed the question to linger before breaking the silence.

"And we don't expect you to have the answers right now," said McLeod. "This question is different though: what do you need to know or understand to be able to answer those questions?" He turned to Oberon and Ed'ards. "Your committee members include two career military officers, and two government people -- probably the right people to be there. On the other hand, you are both behind-the-scenes government people. What can we tell you, or answer for you that will help you get the information you need from your committee members so we can determine our areas of agreement and move toward closer cooperation, in whatever form it should take?" Oberon had listened to McLeod carefully, but her expression suggested she was miffed.

"I believe we do know those concerns and differences," Oberon began, "and I don't think we need to be schooled in military terminology or tactics to do so." McLeod only nodded, keeping his expression slightly more positive than neutral.

Oberon continued, her mood not changing.

"Closer cooperation is fine, and we don't see any problem doing that, either in terms of the budget or in terms of ships."

"And in terms of phase weapons?" McLeod interrupted. Oberon was silent for a while, then she allowed herself a small smile.

"Well *that* might be a problem," she said.

"Lane," McLeod continued, "we're not trying to start arguments, and we're certainly not trying to insult your intelligence, or yours, Owen." He briefly faced Ed'ards. "I ask those questions because military cooperation and weapons is what Raina and I have done our entire careers, yet these negotiations have to be civilian-led and directed. We just want to be sure that as the civilians make the decisions only they can make, that they have the information they need at their disposal." Oberon and Ed'ards nodded.

Wolfe quickly added to McLeod's statement, feeling that additional explanation was necessary.

"And if any of us gets a little passionate about something, this" she gestured at the conference table, "is supposed to be where that happens, not in the committee meetings." She smiled, then added, "and if any of us gets a little testy, we could just say that we were channeling one of our committee members."

"I don't think that will be a problem for me," said McLeod. "So far as I know, Ambassador Redstar can do her own channeling, thank you very much."

Everyone laughed, with Ed'ards adding, "Same could be said for Vice Chair Patt'son."

McLeod smiled again before continuing. "Then, why don't we take a brief break, get some coffee and tea, and continue?" he asked. He quickly gathered and took their orders to the galley, then returned to the conference room.

McLeod decided it would be best to approach Oberon during this brief break. "I don't know your experience in these sorts of discussions, Lane" McLeod said, "but it's new in many ways for both Raina and me." He looked at her cordially, "Is this something you volunteered for, or were you assigned by the council?" Sensing that he was asking out of genuine curiosity, Oberon relaxed.

"A little of both, actually," she said. "Most of us on the staff of the Governing Council have been assigned to various committees. This is the committee I was asked to staff, I believe because our concerns regarding the military tend to revolve around finances."

McLeod nodded and chuckled at this. "Well, in that regard, you're in clear agreement with the Hemodians."

"We are," Oberon answered. "And I know that based on several meetings with them over the years." She looked more directly at McLeod. "One thing that interested me with these negotiations was the opportunity to work on this committee with you. I mean, it seems as if you've been doing this for a long time, particularly in the way you ask questions," she said. "They seem very pointed and designed to elicit responses -- thoughtful responses, I would say. Is that something you've become used to doing as a ship's captain?" Sensing his hesitation, she added, "I don't mean offense by it; I was just curious."

McLeod smiled to acknowledge Oberon's tone, then took a brief moment before responding. "I would say that being in a command or leadership position has required me to ask questions all the time, primarily to understand the complexities of the situations facing the ship and its crew. I also ask open ended questions that require more global responses, because I found that if I ask more specific questions, I would get answers, but not necessarily the complete answer, if you know what I mean." McLeod looked at Oberon, who seemed to be following him. He continued. "The open ended questions give the crew the opportunity to give me the entire picture of the situation, and since they are the experts in their areas, such as engineering or astrogation, that's usually the best way to get complete and helpful information." He looked up again at Oberon. "To be honest, it's hard to turn that off even when I'm in a different context. My sense -- knowing Raina -- is that she does it the same way I do and for the same reasons."

"You've worked together before, I take it?"

"Raina? We've worked together for about half our careers."

Oberon was shocked; she hadn't expected this. "But, you're in the Star Alliance, and she serves in the Central Federation, isn't that right?" asked Oberon.

"True," McLeod began, "But the Federation and Alliance are on very friendly terms, and have been for decades."

Oberon nodded, beginning to understand. "I believe I knew that."

"There is also a program for officers and NCOs within the Alliance or the Federation to serve on the vessels of the others, either for full tours or shorter more focused stays. It is also not uncommon for us to train together at many different academies."

"I see."

"Yes. Raina and I served together on SAV/ *Endeavor* as junior officers together, and served together on FV/ *Andros*. We were also in the same class at the Alliance/ Federation War College. After completing our tour at the War College, we served on different Federation vessels in the same sector, so we still had a great deal of contact."

Oberon was still surprised. "I didn't know such a program existed. So, they really promote that kind of understanding between the two large organizations?"

"Yes, though some people take more advantage of that opportunity than others," McLeod said. Then he added, "There are hundreds of people who have served for brief tours on the ships of the Alliance or the Federation, but only fifty or so have completed full multi-year tours. I also know for a fact that only nine of those people are still on active duty: Raina and I are two of them." McLeod grew more animated as he spoke. "And two other pieces of information: no Federation officer has served longer on Alliance vessels than Raina Wolfe, and the same can be said of me with Federation vessels -- and it isn't even close, to be honest. I also served as the only Alliance Executive Officer ever on a Federation ship, FV/ *Xian*. Raina is also the only person in history to have been awarded the Distinguished Flying Cross by both the Alliance and the Federation."

Oberon responded more to his tone than his words.

"You seem proud of her."

This made McLeod think for a moment. As he responded, he noticed he was smiling slightly. "I suppose I am," he said. "There are few people I've ever encountered who I trust more than her -- a trust we've both earned, believe me." He looked up and glanced at Raina who was speaking with Ed'ards. "And I would say she's one of my best friends."

Returning his gaze to Oberon, he said, "Well, shall we get back to our discussion?"

McLeod and Oberon returned to the table, and all four sipped their drinks before returning to their meeting. The informal discussion during their break relaxed them enough to return to the questions originally posed by McLeod and Wolfe. McLeod in particular, noticed that both Oberon and Ed'ards were open to learning more about how the military operates, and the challenges of combining forces with slightly different goals, traditions and operations.

At one point Ed'ards creased his brow. "It sounds like you two believe military cooperation between our two worlds might be as difficult as simply cooperating with the Federation might be," Ed'ards posed. McLeod and Wolfe were silent -- looking somewhat wistful.

Finally, Wolfe responded. "In a way, that's true," she said. "The purpose or mission of the forces, the way people are trained, the structure of the organizations, how people are taught -- all of these elements impact how they can work with other organizations with perhaps different missions, training methods, etc." Wolfe looked to McLeod. "Speaking for myself, I believe the Federation and Alliance have worked together well for decades: we've trained together, gone on cooperative missions, and have missions that are very similar in scope and content." She paused, glancing briefly at McLeod again. "Yet, to be honest we've both been in several conflicts over the years where one force didn't have a clue what the other was doing."

McLeod exhaled quietly, but couldn't help nodding in agreement before speaking. "And we've been doing this for many, many years, and have been working collaboratively for decades," McLeod said. "Effective military cooperation is much harder to achieve than you might think -- even with forces that already share some of the same history and space." It was a sobering thought.

"But," Wolfe added, "Let's not focus on the negative. If you believe forces on Hemod and Herai are really focused on military operation and working closely together, it can be done. And we can certainly help you explore the methods for that kind of cooperation, not so much for the Admiral and Captain, but for Vice Chair Patt'son and Secretary Kayne."

"Yes, they may be the ones we have to convince," Oberon said, chuckling. She turned to look at Raina and McLeod,

"So, how do we get started?"

Chapter Sixteen

Space Station Alpha Twin Worlds Guest Wing, Captain R. Wolfe's Quarters

"Something tells me we may never move the Hemodians off their desires for more phase weapons," said McLeod, rubbing his eyes. He was more tired than he thought he should be, but perhaps spending so much time in intellectual gaming rather than burning off some energy through pure physical activity was a difference he would need to get used to.

Wolfe tried, but couldn't stop herself from yawning. "I agree," she said, "But then again, I wonder how important that's really going to be in the long run."

"Meaning?"

She paused before answering. "Meaning I don't know how far we're going to be able to go regarding Federation membership with these negotiations; so focusing on phase weapons is only driving a wedge, however small, between Owen and Lane."

"Umm," was all McLeod could muster. Their discussions with their staff colleagues, while cordial and very open had begun to degenerate toward the end as Ed'ards and Oberon continually repeated their positions. When it seemed that the group had gone as far as they could go, Wolfe suggested a break for the night. Ed'ards protested, but the others suggested that it would be better to continue after rest and perhaps consultation with their committee members. Both McLeod and Wolfe wondered what instructions they would all be receiving.

McLeod's mind began to wander before he looked up to Wolfe and asked. "When should we contact Ambassador Redstar and Fleet Marshall Masters?"

"I think probably soon, and while I would prefer to have dinner first, I think it would be better to see them while everything is fresh in our minds."

"Agreed. I'll put in the call."

As Wolfe contacted their superiors, McLeod tried to organize his thoughts so their meeting would be productive. By force of habit, he immediately thought of areas of agreement that he saw between the two parties, only thinking about an area or areas of disagreement toward the end. He was so wrapped up in his thoughts that Wolfe had to nudge his shoulder to get his attention.

"Tucker? Did you hear me?"

McLeod sat up and looked at her. "What?"

"I was saying that we can meet with the Ambassador and Fleet Marshall in about a half hour. Do we have any notes we need to organize before we see them?"

McLeod thought before answering. "Actually, no," he said. "The way we work, we can probably do it without any prompting. Why don't you start with context and areas of agreement, then I'll continue with areas of concern and disagreement?"

Wolfe smiled at him. "I was thinking *I* would do the disagreements but that structure is what I would have suggested."

McLeod shrugged, weary from the day's work. "Doesn't matter to me -- so long as I have a coffee before heading down." He raised his eyebrow and asked. "Conference room?"

"Yep."

Twenty minutes later, they found themselves entering the conference room followed shortly by Fleet Marshall Masters and Ambassador Redstar. When the Fleet Marshall saw Wolfe inside the conference room, he checked his chron, then laughed.

"Ten minutes early," Master's said. "I guess we never get rid of that habit, do we?" McLeod and Wolfe laughed in response. Masters waved them all to chairs.

"So, Captains," Master's began. "What can you share with us about your first staff meeting. Was it as contentious as we led you to believe?"

Wolfe shrugged. "In some ways, yes, in other ways, no." She briefly consulted her notes. "Let me give you the context, or at least the way it was explained by Ed'ards and Oberon, then some of the significant areas of agreement, before Tucker outlines our challenges." She looked briefly at McLeod. "I think all four of us would identify the same things, wouldn't you, Tucker?"

"I would," he said.

"Good. Proceed, Captain," said Redstar. Wolfe outlined very carefully the positions as explained by her Hemodian and Heraian colleagues, in addition to what she saw as some of the personal or underlying biases each of them had. McLeod agreed with everything she said, even those assessments she made that they had not discussed together. Wolfe also noted where she felt there was agreement, being careful not to suggest total agreement on what greater cooperation between the two militaries would look like. She also spent time discussing the fact that the two staff members from the Twin Worlds had no military experience, or knowledge whatsoever.

On that point, Ambassador Redstar felt the need to interject. "That's unfortunately not uncommon, Captain," she said. "We try to educate them as best we can, and in all honesty, we don't want a committee or staff members made up solely of military personnel, but some knowledge or experience, such as my few years as an NCO, or a family member within the service is always helpful." She paused briefly. "Here's a question: how open do you think they are to learning more about military customs, mission, etc. so they can help move the discussions along on their respective sides?"

Wolfe looked at McLeod to indicate his part in the negotiations. "You can thank Tucker for any additional openness on the part of Oberon, Ambassador," she said. "We took a break as things were getting heated, and they had a very," she looked at McLeod slyly, "can I say 'intimate' conversation, Tucker?"

He chuckled. "Hardly, Raina. But I would say that just talking with her and getting to know her a bit better seemed to relax her tremendously."

"Well done, Captain," said Redstar. "What did you speak with her about?"

McLeod thought for a moment. "Actually, about military cooperation," McLeod said. His companions seemed confused. "Let me start again. They didn't seem to have any idea of the challenges in working more cooperatively, or certainly in combining their forces. Not that cooperating is a bad thing, but it isn't simply a matter of passing out new uniforms." Everyone at the table nodded. "So, I spoke with her about military cooperation between the Alliance and the Federation and how, while we've been doing it for decades, it still isn't as smooth as it could be. I also spoke to her about how closely Raina and I have worked together and told them how rare that is in our forces."

Masters snorted. "It's unique, Tucker, and you know it."

"But in any case," McLeod continued, "I think that bit of self-disclosure and talking about how we're still trying to get it right led her to be more comfortable asking questions, and being open to the answers."

"Whatever works," said Ambassador Redstar. She added with a twinkle in her eye: "Are you both exhausted?"

Tucker and Wolfe laughed. "We were just speaking about that," said McLeod. "We think it's something we have to get accustomed to."

"Speak for yourself, Tucker. I have a starship to command soon," Wolfe jested.

"Understood," said Fleet Marshall Masters. "And I do believe you've both earned a good night's rest. Let's see what your group comes up with tomorrow." He stood.

"My recommendation is for you both to have a nice meal and put all of this out of your mind."

"Do you need any of our notes?" asked McLeod.

Masters nodded. "Whatever you want to give us -- we already have the gist of it through this oral report, which was very lucid, by the way."

"Agreed," said Redstar. "I don't even have any questions about your interchange with their staff. Well done."

"Thank you, Ma'am," said Wolfe. McLeod nodded his agreement as well.

"Then," Masters said, "We'll see you both tomorrow."

All four left the conference room, with McLeod and Wolfe going together in one direction, and the Fleet Marshall and Ambassador going in another. McLeod looked to Wolfe as they walked. "So, shall we have a really nice meal as a reward?"

Raina smiled. "Sure, so long as we commit ourselves to the gym tomorrow morning."

"You know my habits," he said. "That was going to happen anyway."

"Then yes, and I think I know the place we should go to."

McLeod seemed surprised. "Oh, so when should we meet?" he asked.

Wolfe creased her eyebrows in surprise. "You agreed to this pretty quickly."

"Well, you had obviously thought it through," he said. "Where did you want to go?"

"There's a restaurant with a chef who used to work in the Andoran system, the Outer World Cantina. I thought since we both like Andoran food -- and I haven't had it done by a really good chef in about two years, that it might be a treat," Wolfe said.

McLeod looked at her uncertainly. "And what if I wanted something else?" he asked playfully.

Wolfe rolled her eyes. "Says the man who ate three helpings of roasted roundar at the graduation banquet for the Alliance/ Federation War College."

McLeod smiled at the memory. "Fine. Back to the original question. What time?"

After checking her chron and thinking, Raina said. "1900?"

"See you then." Since he had almost two hours before their meeting time, McLeod returned to his quarters, briefly meditated, then went through martial arts forms slowly as a way of unwinding and maintaining his muscle tone. As usual, he didn't think much while doing this, but every once in a while between forms, he thought about how he could move the discussion forward the following day, and also what instructions Oberon and Ed'ards might receive from their committee members.

After his exercises, McLeod showered and dressed again and arrived shortly before 1900 at Wolfe's quarters. As Wolfe opened the door, McLeod was taken aback. While he had seen his friend in many different styles of dress over the years, including with none at all, he was a bit stunned to see that she was wearing a form fitting and somewhat revealing jumper.

She smiled as she saw his reaction. "Hey," she said, "I decided if we were going out to a nice dinner, we should be dressed for it." Looking him over, she added, "You look rather good yourself."

He shook his head, disagreeing. "Not half as good as you do."

Wolfe had already determined the best way to get to the restaurant, which was located in a quiet corner of the station. When they arrived, McLeod look wary. He was quite comfortable patronizing casual or less than pristine places in familiar areas, but was somewhat anxious when he saw the entrance. He needn't have worried. The inside of the establishment while small, was very inviting and cheerful. And he truly enjoyed the familiar smells of food from the Andoran system and, he thought, from the Twin Worlds. He was a bit surprised to sense that unusual combination. Once they were seated, Wolfe probed to learn more about the chef.

Their smiling attendant answered them quickly. "We get that question a lot. He's from Herai, but served briefly in the military and stayed in the Andoran system for years before coming home. He's really been making this place popular." Wolfe and McLeod ordered, with McLeod resisting the desire for more roasted roundar. Once the waiter left, Wolfe continued their private conversation.

"So, was your first full day as a diplomat all you thought it would be?" asked Wolfe.

"Hardly a day of real diplomacy, I think," said McLeod.

"I disagree. Just getting those two to see beyond their preconceived notions required diplomacy, said Wolfe. "And whatever you did to get Lane to open up more, keep doing it."

McLeod shook his head. "That woman makes me a little uncomfortable."

Wolfe laughed. "Oh, please," she said. "When you were talking to her, she couldn't have been more than fifty centimeters away from you." McLeod frowned, as Wolfe continued. "And she kept hanging on your every word so, let's just say that she's not at all uncomfortable with *you*."

McLeod rolled his eyes before responding. Well, in any case, I'll do what I can," he said. "I guess the real test is how they start tomorrow." He thought for a moment. "But perhaps they will come out swinging again, to see if we back off or stay the course."

Wolfe laughed. "Just like normal political posturing," she said.

Just then their pre-entrée arrived, and they both began to enjoy their food. They had ordered a vegetable dip with bread points, and a cocktail of a Hemodian shellfish. Their entrees arrived at just the right time, and they ate in companionable silence, with occasional conversations as they ate. The meal was excellent, and McLeod asked if he could speak with and meet the chef. Before he could come to their table, Wolfe excused herself. When the chef arrived, he introduced himself as Jurgan Towns, a long time expatriate from Herai, who had finally come home.

"I have to admit, I've enjoyed being back more than I thought I would," the chef told McLeod.

"It's good to meet you, Chef." McLeod rose. "My name is Tucker McLeod, and I happen to…."

"I know you, Captain," said the chef. "I was on Andora Prime when you were in temporary command of the *Valiant*."

"Oh." McLeod fell flat.

"And, I am one of the many who felt you did the right thing," the chef assured him.

"Please don't tell that to my companion. We've been friends for years and it took her awhile to forgive me -- she's from Andora Prime."

"Understood," he said.

"And before she comes back, do you happen to have blue coddle on the menu for dessert? It's her favorite."

"Unfortunately, no, Captain, but I could make some and get it to you, depending on how long you'll be here at the Twin Worlds."

McLeod smiled at the chef. "That would be tremendous." McLeod took out a card and wrote down his contact information, giving it to the chef. McLeod was excited. "This would be a great surprise to her." Looking up, he saw Wolfe returning to the table.

"Raina, this is Chef Jurgan Towns, the chef from Herai and formerly from Andora Prime." Wolfe and the chef greeted each other and chatted briefly before he return to the kitchen. After he left, McLeod and Wolfe decided to forgo dessert -- no blue coddle on the menu, she noted -- and had coffee and tea instead.

After a short while, Wolfe consulted her chron. "Early day tomorrow."

McLeod agreed.

"Shall we?" Wolfe asked.

"Let's."

Chapter Seventeen

Twin Worlds Space Station Alpha, Conference Room C

McLeod arose early and met up with Wolfe at the gym, though they didn't work out together. After exercising, they returned to their respective quarters, showered and dressed, then met for a light breakfast. They walked down to the committee conference room and set themselves up at their table. As other committee members entered the room, they seemed to McLeod to be very quiet and giving him rather furtive looks. He was about to call that to Wolfe's attention when she asked,

"What's going on here?"

"I was about to ask you the same question." McLeod caught the eye of Ambassador Redstar, indicating that he wanted to see her outside the conference room. She excused herself from the other committee members, and stepped outside, while McLeod joined her.

"You don't know what's going on, do you?" Redstar asked. McLeod shook his head. Redstar moved closer to him and lowered her voice.

"You probably don't listen to the morning vids from Herai or Hemod." It was a statement, rather than a question. "Not surprising, but you should start doing it. There was a report this morning on the negotiations, and they specifically noted that the man who almost destroyed an entire homeworld is a staff member for the committee." With that statement, McLeod sighed.

"Now, this may or may not be an issue for committee members or for the negotiating teams," Redstar continued, "because we already knew your background. The challenge is if forces on the Twin Worlds begin objecting and putting pressure on the negotiating teams to distance themselves from you," she added.

"What would happen then?" McLeod asked. "Would you just remove me from the staff?" McLeod was disappointed, but also concerned about fulfillment of the mission for the Alliance and Federation negotiating teams.

"Not at this time, no," Redstar replied. "It might change the dynamics of the discussions, though." She looked serious at McLeod. "As you've described your discussions with the other staff members, it doesn't seem as though you were strong-arming anyone, and that will play well. Let's just play it by ear, and" she looked at him seriously, "you maintain your composure."

McLeod nodded, then added, "Yes, Ma'am."

McLeod and Redstar reentered the conference room and took their places. As he entered, McLeod signaled to a puzzled Wolfe that they would talk later. Redstar did not call attention to her conversation with McLeod, but convened the meeting to discuss the progress they had made and to ask for any new comments from committee members. As they began, Captain Malvo stood up quickly to get the attention of the co-chairs.

"Field Marshall Masters; Ambassador Redstar." He paused to ensure all eyes were on him. "And to all of you. We've all heard some very pointed and negative comments being directed at one of the staff people for this committee." He paused again for effect. "The tone of the objections about Captain McLeod suggest that he is unfit for this responsibility because of his actions in the Andora System over twelve standard years ago. As a former naval officer, I know that all our actions are subject to review, be they by our superiors, or by the general public many years later, and it is very easy to second guess a decision made in the height of tensions from the comfort of our salons twelve years later. I just wanted to say that the delegation of Herai is neither questioning Captain McLeod's qualifications nor his suitability to serve as staff from the Star Alliance on this committee. And I, for one, do not intend to listen to or have my opinion swayed by these attacks on the character of a highly decorated military officer." He sat down. The silence was broken by the rise of Admiral Nereze, who received a nod from Vice Chair Patt'son.

"Well said, Captain," Nereze said. "Being second-guessed comes with the territory for military officers as we both know. We from the Hemodian delegation also voice our support for Captain McLeod." She looked at McLeod squarely. "Now, while we in this room may not respond to public opinion, others on our home planet may. However, we believe you can serve positively with this committee and don't intend for our part to allow these attacks to deter us from making progress on the important issues before us." Nereze sat down with a flourish.

Field Marshal Masters cleared his throat. "Thank you Admiral, Captain. The Star Alliance and Central Federation knew what they were doing when they appointed all of us including Captain McLeod to this committee, so we also support him." He paused and looked around the room. "And I believe the best way to ensure that these proceedings are successful is to focus our energies, talent, and perhaps sweat to a successful outcome, regardless of who serves on our team. So, shall we begin?"

McLeod felt better about his situation given the support he received from the committee members. At the same time, he understood Admiral Nereze's statement -- with enough political pressure, he might be forced to remove himself from the proceedings. The realization jarred him.

The committee meeting began, still with some posturing, but free of animosity. It seemed to McLeod that people were really trying to identify areas of agreement and difference in a respectful manner, and trying to work toward solutions. During the broader discussions, he occasionally glanced at Wolfe, and by reading her facial expressions, felt her evaluation matched his own. However, there were still concerns about weapons that the committee members seemed to ignore, yet consensus on these issues was essential to building a successful overall agreement. It puzzled him that neither Admiral Nereze nor Captain Malvo forced that issue one way or the other: both supported stronger cooperation, and while Nereze wanted the Federation to take over the combined force, and Malvo simply wanted a closer working relationship between the two forces -- perhaps by combining them -- neither spoke specifically to the utility or *futility* of phase weapons. McLeod believed their opinions would carry a great deal of weight.

When the committee took its natural break prior to the noon hour, McLeod asked the other staff members if they wanted to dine together to continue their discussions, or to work following lunch instead. To his surprise, everyone wanted to continue meeting through lunch. To his additional surprise, Lane took care of ordering lunches for them all, and they chatted casually waiting for their food to arrive. As the food arrived, Wolfe signaled to McLeod and they briefly excused themselves to meet in the hallway. Wolfe set her piercing gaze on McLeod.

"Where did all that come from?" Wolfe asked. McLeod filled her in on the vid that many committee members and others had viewed that morning. He also reinforced Ambassador Redstar's directive that they view the vids every day to keep informed on what is happening planet-side. Wolfe nodded in understanding. She also understood Admiral Nereze's concerns, and felt they needed to keep at least moderate pressure on the committee staff to keep the discussion moving.

As they finished their lunches, Wolfe asked, "Can either of you tell us where your committee members are simply *not* going to move?" Before continuing she paused, raising her hand slightly. "I'm not asking you to reveal some deep secrets of your negotiating positions unless you really want to," she said, "and we already know the general positions and areas of conflict. On the other hand," she continued, "I don't want to spin my wheels pushing to find agreement if it just isn't going to be there." Wolfe and McLeod continued to attend to them with neutral expressions.

Finally, Ed'ards spoke. "To be honest, our absolute position is a moving target," he said. "I know that Vice Chair Patt'son is very concerned about budget: everyone on every side of this is. And every one of us wants greater cooperation with Herai. And it's pretty clear that he will have to be brought to the Federation kicking and screaming. If that is still on the table, he's going to have a tough time agreeing. Of course, if he could find a way to join the

Federation with reduced costs or without having Hemodian serve in the Federation military, he might go for it."

McLeod faced Ed'ards and paused before he spoke. "Do you believe," McLeod began, "that Admiral Nereze would be willing to support greater cooperation, perhaps even a combined force *without* affiliation with the Federation *or* having the Federation be the primary force?"

Ed'ards looked pained as he considered this. "That's part of our problem," Ed'ards said. "We really aren't agreed regarding the Federation. Admiral Nereze wants it in some form, yet Vice Chair Patt'son is at best very wary of it."

Wolfe smiled. "Tough to be you, isn't it, Owen?" Wolfe said it with humor, and Owen smiled back. Wolfe looked to Oberon. "Lane, how about you?" Wolfe asked. "I know that Captain Malvo supports greater cooperation with Hemod, yet isn't particularly big on Federation membership, isn't that right?"

Oberon nodded her agreement. "I'm not sure he's really *against* Federation membership," Oberon said. "What I do believe is that he thinks closer military cooperation between the two worlds, and significant levels of cross training is far more important than Federation membership." She paused and looked up before continuing. "It's almost as though he wants us to work on creating a combined force for a few years." She paused again before looking directly at McLeod. "You talked yesterday about military culture, is that the right word?"

"Well, culture and traditions -- they vary a lot from unit to unit or military force to military force," McLeod said.

Oberon nodded, becoming more animated. "I think," Oberon began, "that Captain Malvo wants to create that new military culture with a combined or mostly combined force, then once that is established, we might look to Federation membership as a way to ensure greater security."

"There is a certain logic in that," McLeod said.

Oberon continued. "Obviously, Secretary Kayne wants greater cooperation too, but she is trying to reduce the size and maybe mission of forces overall. I've thought about that a lot, and I just don't think that's going to work." Oberon sighed as she said that, her voice dropping. McLeod signaled for her to continue.

"Well, if some of us are stuck on the issue of phase weapons," Oberon looked quickly at Ed'ards, "hear me out, on this, Owen, but if we're stuck on that issue, that suggests that we're *not* moving to reduce our military spending or presence, rather the opposite." The group was silent until Wolfe spoke.

"I agree," said Wolfe. "And yet Secretary Kayne still clings to the idea of reducing forces." Turning to Oberon directly, she added, "How open do you think she is to learning more about the military?" She chuckled as she added, "if she is bound and determined to reduce forces, I can imagine that really annoying Captain Malvo."

Oberon smiled as she responded "I'm not going to speak out of turn Raina, except to say that we have some very *lively* discussions."

"What is her hang up with the size of the military?" McLeod asked, frustrated. "Is she only concerned about money, or does she believe the military isn't doing the job they are supposed to do?"

"Or that they don't need a military force of this size to get the job done, Tucker," Wolfe replied. She turned to Oberon. "Lane, have you ever discussed the particular size of the military force, I mean has Malvo said to her point blank that the military of Herai isn't large by modern standards." Before allowing Oberon to answer, she turned to McLeod. "Tucker, what's the size of the planetary defense force for Herai, the one we've been talking about?"

McLeod replied, "It's about 1.75 million out of the planetary population of 3.5 billion." He turned to Ed'ards and Oberon. "That's about in line with most planets, perhaps a little low. You just can't get the job of planetary defense done with much less than that."

"And to think you could reduce this by any significant amount is just not realistic," Wolfe added.

"What about phase weapons?" McLeod asked. "The first time they came up in conversation, I saw Patt'son start to gnash his teeth and I wonder if any attention we pay to phase weapons might lead to an impasse in the negotiations so that we don't accomplish anything. Does that make sense?" There was a brief silence.

"Can't see how that would help any," said Wolfe. "It is a genuine area of disagreement," she paused again before turning to Oberon and Ed'ards, adding, "How much are people on the Twin Worlds concerned about limits on or expanding phase weapons?" The question seemed to confuse Oberon and Ed'ards.

Wolfe continued. "I know that these are the priorities of the committee, I just wonder how strongly the governing councils feel about phase weapons. Would that be a deal breaker?"

"Honestly, I don't know," Oberon said. "The common person planet-side wants to be secure, and obviously in our case we're concerned about radiation, and long term damage, though *how* people are protected doesn't particularly matter to the general public. It's simply not a topic I've heard discussed in the council much except while looking at budgetary expenses."

Ed'ards disagreed with his colleague. "It's actually on the minds of our people pretty much all the time," Ed'ards said. "Not among the common people planet-side, on that I agree with you, Lane. But in the Hemodian governing council, sovereignty and the ability to use weapons that don't take a lot of our resources is an everyday conversation." He added, "And that was happening long before we began talking more seriously about Federation membership."

"Then," Wolfe said, "perhaps we ought to get back to discussing phase weapons."

Chapter Eighteen

Twin Worlds Space Station Alpha, Gymnasium

Their discussion of phase weapons didn't go much better the second time around than the first time. It was clear to McLeod and Wolfe however, that the two staff members from the Twin Worlds were frustrated with their inability to encourage their committee members to compromise. After three hours, the staff had developed a list of questions for each committee member, and also a way to solicit questions from the committee members to ask the other side: questions from the Heraians to ask the Hemodians and the reverse. The staff members thought it was a good strategy, because it would allow the committee members to retain control of the discussion, but this time it was the staff members putting on the pressure. McLeod was quietly pleased Wolfe had made the suggestion and he hoped it would work.

He and Wolfe were able to spar for about an hour and half after completing their staff meeting. Just as they were leaving the rec, they saw a special report from Hemod on the vid.

"Government forces have confirmed that the security at the home of Coordinating Council Vice Chair Griffin Patt'son has been breached. At this time, reports indicate that his daughter Moriah is missing and may have been abducted. A splinter group from the Unionist forces on Herai has claimed responsibility for the attack, saying that the motives of Vice Chair Patt'son make him unfit for service in the ongoing negotiations with Herai." The vid showed the face of a thickly built man, unshaven and looking rather mean. "The leader of this splinter group is Anton Jurgan, who has been active in several attacks on Hemodian forces and holdings on Herai. Based on the severity of this attack, a directive for his arrest has been issued by Hemodian forces. We will continue to keep you informed about this incident." McLeod and Wolfe looked at each other. They had just completed a brisk workout after which they usually both felt energized; after watching the vid, their postures slumped as they shook their heads.

"What do you think this will mean for the negotiations?" McLeod asked.

"Good question," Wolfe said. "Obviously, it will not be good." She looked up in frustration. "And I really thought once we got the questions clarified, we might get some things to happen." She checked her chron. "Do you think we can go like this," she indicated their wet clothing, " to speak with Redstar and Masters?"

McLeod thought for a moment. "We may as well: they may already be looking for us anyway," McLeod said. Wolfe agreed and they left the gym, going to the corridor where all the official Federation and Alliance committee chairs had their quarters. They approached Fleet Marshall Master's suite and requested entry, but before they heard a response from within, they heard a familiar voice from down the hall.

"Captains! Great timing!" They looked to their left to see Vice Chancellor Noregan. He waved them over quickly. "We were going to contact you once we saw the vid -- apparently you had the same idea. We're all meeting in my quarters." McLeod and Wolfe quickly entered the room, and saw that they weren't the only people who had been engaged in other activities during their breaks. They took seats in the large salon and waited. Vice Chancellor Noregan continued, facing McLeod, "For once, Captain," he began, "the news *wasn't* concerning you." He chuckled before turning back to the group. "I know we've all met each other at some time, so let's not waste time here," he said. "We do have a crisis, and we need to determine what we can salvage at this point, what perhaps we should give up on, and whether we ought to declare a cooling off period in sympathy with Vice Chair Patt'son." Noregan looked around the room. "We may also wish to suspend the activities of the military cooperation committee only -- if that's something the Hemodians would support -- and continue with the other committees. What's the status of the military cooperation committee?"

Masters glanced briefly at Redstar, who quickly spoke in response. "Going reasonably, Pel," she said. "We're still trying to find a closer common ground on what military cooperation looks like, but I believe that is surmountable. A larger issue looming in the background is phase weapons -- there doesn't seem to be any movement on that issue at this time."

McLeod looked up and got the attention of the Vice Chancellor. "Vice Chancellor," McLeod began. "Captain Wolfe and I developed a series of questions with our colleagues to ask the committee members from the Twin Worlds that might help us make a bit more progress. We also agreed on a framework to solicit questions from the committee members. Our objective was to get to the heart of matters and perhaps find small cracks that might lead us toward closer agreement."

Redstar smiled at McLeod. "And you said you never did this before, Captain?" McLeod smiled in response.

"A good strategy, Captains," said Noregan. "Would any of you -- particularly you four --" indicating the general direction of the military cooperation committee, " hazard a guess as to whether Patt'son will want to continue?"

"I think that's the wrong question, Pel," said Masters. "He'll need to leave the negotiations to see about his family. The question we may wish to ask is whether we need to suspend all negotiations, or just those for the military cooperation committee. And we also need to issue our support for him."

"Already happening, Paulo," said Minister Long, who had up to that time been quiet. "We sent in the support vid a few minutes before you arrived." She looked at Redstar and Masters. "I assume you will not want to continue in the short term without Patt'son?"

Masters shook his head vigorously. "Definitely not, Demeter," he said. "The dynamics are predicated on their full participation, and while there is some trust built up, it wouldn't survive Patt'son's absence."

"Understood," Long said. McLeod reflected briefly on the level of trust that seemed to exist for the staff members on the committee, and wondered if it was typical for staff members to become closer

and more trusting in these negotiations than the principals. With
nothing else to guide him, he believed it was.

"Very well," said Long. "Then for the time being, we will suspend
the military cooperation committee in support of Vice Chair
Patt'son." Turning again to McLeod and Wolfe, she asked, "Are
there some clarifications we can still secure from the staff, or do you
believe they have supplied all they can at this time?"

McLeod and Wolfe looked at each other. "Not sure, Minister," said
Wolfe. "We would be willing to speak with them again to get
clarification; I believe we have that level of trust built up."

"Agreed, Minister," said McLeod. "We can speak to them as soon
after this meeting as you like."

Minister Long nodded. "You do that, Captains," Long said. "But
afterwards, see if you can get them to agree to review a position
paper that the two of you prepare summarizing the points of
agreement, and points of disagreement and the next course of action
to bridge the gap. While they can always object to parts of the
document, having something written and in the record is always
preferable to waiting until Vice Chair Patt'son can give the
committee his full attention."

"Yes Ma'am," said both Wolfe and McLeod.

McLeod added, "Once that is completed, Ma'am, what else do you
want us to do? I assume not go on vacation."

Councilor Trent, who had been silent throughout the exchange,
laughed. "Tired of diplomatic already, Captain?"

McLeod smiled. "No, Councilor, I just want to know how else I can
be useful."

"Understood," said Trent.

Minister Long again took command. "So, Susan and Paulo, can you receive any documents from Captains McLeod and Wolfe and forward them as appropriate to Pel and me?" she asked.

"Absolutely, Demeter," said Redstar. She looked at McLeod and Wolfe. "If you would get to that…."

"Yes Ma'am," in unison from McLeod and Wolfe. They left the conference room and returned to the corridor containing their quarters. Wolfe agreed to make contact with Ed'ards and Oberon and get back to McLeod. McLeod returned to his quarters, showered and dressed, and not waiting for Wolfe's call, returned to her quarters. When he rang, she ushered him in. He was surprised to see she was still wet from the shower and dressed only in a large towel.

"I came back too early?" McLeod asked, sheepishly. Wolfe looked confused, then smiled.

"Depends, but in this case, not too early. We're to meet Lane and Owen in the conference room for a working dinner in about thirty."

"That sounds good," McLeod said. "Did you get any sense of their thinking while you talked to them?"

Wolfe looked down quickly at her towel before replying, "Clothing first, talk later."

After dressing, Wolfe joined McLeod and walked back to their conference room. The mood there was somber, and it was clear that both Oberon and Ed'ards were shaken. "They're not military or people who are used to being threatened," McLeod thought. "They're not used to this being so close to home."

"Lane. Owen," McLeod said. "First of all, Owen, we're sorry that this tragedy has hit so close to home. This must be a tough time for everyone, but I imagine a bit more on Hemod."

Ed'ards nodded. "It is, Tucker," Ed'ards said. "This is not something you encounter when you work in a planning office." He tried to muster a smile, but clearly, his heart wasn't in it.

"Understood," McLeod said. He looked and saw the same sober expression on Oberon's face before beginning. "What Minister Long and Vice Chancellor Noregan have asked us to do is give them a summary of where we are with the negotiations at this point. Obviously, we are uncomfortable with continuing the negotiations at this time *without* Vice Chair Patt'son."

They all nodded, before Ed'ards added, "He asked us, that is the other members of the Hemodian delegation, to continue the negotiations, but our delegation head said that would not happen -- which I believe was the right course of action."

"Well, I think everyone is agreed on that," said Wolfe, "though at the same time no one wants kidnappers to direct the course of the Twin Worlds' futures." She paused before continuing. "But what we would like to do now is to clarify our areas of agreement, in addition to anything else you two may have learned from your committee members. Our hope is to be very clear about areas of agreement and disagreement and the next steps to bring Herai and Hemod closer together. So," she continued "who wants to start?"

For the next hour and a half, McLeod and Wolfe listened and asked clarifying questions of their staff colleagues. Perhaps fueled by the urgency of finding agreement, both Oberon and Ed'ards were quite talkative, and revealed some of the infighting occurring between members of their own delegations. Oberon, for example, noted particularly nasty exchanges between Captain Malvo and Secretary Kayne, with Kayne flatly refusing to consider the increases in military spending necessary to build a stronger alliance with Hemod. It wasn't much different within the Hemodian delegation, since Admiral Nereze so strongly supported Federation membership and formal unification with the Heraian military, and Patt'son opposed both. But, both Oberon and Ed'ards believed that aiming for a formal cooperative agreement with both militaries including training, service on the other's vessels and a moratorium on new phase weapons was possible. Wolfe was somewhat surprised by the potential for agreement on phase weapons given their previous discussions. She also realized that Minister Long was wise to direct that she and McLeod have this meeting with Oberon and Ed'ards; apparently, Minister Long believed this formal meeting staff to staff would help identify new areas where progress could be made. Wolfe smiled in spite of herself.

The four staff members had a very cordial and cooperative meeting that McLeod and Wolfe knew would be helpful in the overall negotiations. As they completed their task, McLeod and Wolfe committed to recording all of the information into a single document, and sharing it with Oberon and Ed'ards the following day by noon. Wolfe also suggested that they have lunch to review what they had written. Oberon and Ed'ards thanked McLeod and Wolfe for taking the lead, and left the conference room. As they left, McLeod and Wolfe sighed, then gathered their things to go to McLeod's quarters and begin working on the document.

"Can we divide this up, maybe with you noting the disagreements and me the agreements and next steps?" Wolfe asked.

"We can do that," McLeod agreed, "But why can't *I* do the agreements?" Wolfe rolled her eyes and didn't answer.

Wolfe made coffee and tea, and returned to find McLeod already working. They were quiet as they worked on their separate sections, and were surprised when they heard the door chime. McLeod rose and went to the door. He creased his brow and opened the door to reveal Jurgan Towns from the Outer World Cantina. He smiled as he entered, carrying a tray. McLeod smiled when he saw the tray and waved Towns to his small galley. Wolfe greeted Towns, but remained puzzled.

"Raina, I knew you were disappointed when the café didn't have blue coddle yesterday, so Mr. Towns agreed that he would make some for us." He turned to Towns, who revealed a large serving bowl of the sticky, Andoran dessert.

Wolfe smiled with her entire face. "This is worth the extra work for tonight," she said. She looked to McLeod. "Thank you for thinking of this." She turned to Towns, "And thank you for making it. It's my favorite, and I've missed it."

Towns smiled at Wolfe. "So I was told."

Wolfe took the serving spoon and secured three bowls from McLeod's galley.

"Yes; you both have to have some," she said. "Blue coddle is meant to be shared." According to custom, blue coddle was indeed to be shared, and both McLeod and Towns were happy to oblige. As they sat down to eat, McLeod noticed something off about Towns' mood.

"If you don't mind my asking, Mr. Towns, you seem a bit off today, maybe distracted - or perhaps just tired."

Towns nodded slowly. "A bit of everything, Captain," he said. He noted the openness of both McLeod and Wolfe, and decided to continue. "Actually, I did want to talk to you two." At this, McLeod and Wolfe gave him their full attention.

"I know you have heard about the home invasion and kidnapping on Hemod." They nodded. "Do you remember the name of the leader of the splinter group who was supposed to have taken that man's daughter?" As he asked, McLeod remembered the name.

"Jurgan."

"Yes, Jurgan -- Anton Jurgan -- is in fact, my cousin," said Towns. He paused to gain his composure. "Anton's mother called me very upset at what happened, and asked me to help. Anton has always been a somewhat volatile person, often in little bits of trouble, yet he's become very committed to political reform of late. Unfortunately, he hasn't always promoted change peacefully." He looked up, pained. "But he's never hurt anyone. He's bombed a few things, but only areas far away from people, and he's never done anything violent where people might lose their jobs over something. That's not what he does. He just tried to embarrass people or hurt the rich people economically." He looked directly at McLeod and Wolfe.

"He would never do this, yet he is very poorly regarded on the Twin Worlds, and I worry that if he is ever captured, he will never get a fair hearing." McLeod and Wolfe could feel the request coming.

"Can you please help us?"

Chapter Nineteen

Twin Worlds Space Station Alpha, Captain T. McLeod's Quarters

McLeod and Wolfe were quiet. They certainly hadn't expected to be asked to do anything outside of the committee meetings while on the Twin Worlds.

It was Wolfe who broke the ice. "And what do you mean by our 'help,' Jurgan?

Towns paused before answering. "Just for you to find out the truth, Captain," he said. "I know Anton wouldn't do this, he just wouldn't."

McLeod consulted silently with Wolfe. After a short while, he spoke. "Jurgan, I really don't know what we can do to help you." He paused looking up again. "I know we *want* to help, but we're outsiders on the Twin Worlds. So,..."

"And that's exactly why it *has* to be you," Jurgan interrupted. "You don't have any bias toward either of our worlds, and you both are known for being fair." Wolfe frowned.

"Yes, Captain I know about *both* of you." Jurgan faced McLeod again. "We know your reputations -- your complete reputations, for both of you. Everyone -- even those people who complained about you Captain McLeod know you are fair and just. We know you may be the only people who can really help us."

"And who is 'we,' Jurgan?" Wolfe asked.

Jurgan sighed sadly. "We are just his family, and people who have been trying to help Anton become more responsible and get him what he truly needs." He noticed a skeptical look on Wolfe's face. "We have no other purpose, Captain," Towns added. "Anton is my cousin. I don't believe he did this terrible thing, and we simply want someone to help us who won't try to kill Anton as their first response." He looked up. "Is that so wrong to ask for?"

McLeod pondered a moment before answering. "No, Jurgan it isn't," he said. "At the same time, we have no formal role of any kind in these negotiations, let alone on the Twin Worlds. What kind of ability would we have to even find him?" He noticed Jurgan sit up and prepare to respond, but McLeod raised his hand and interrupted him. "To say nothing of the fact that we are bound by our oaths as officers and representatives of the Star Alliance and Central Federation -- we certainly can't do anything that violates that."

Wolfe nodded vigorously. "He's right, Jurgan," she said. "We can only act if given sanction by our superiors, Vice Chancellor Noregan and Minister Long. To do otherwise would be a gross dereliction of duty, and would throw everything here into flux." Jurgan's posture slumped even further.

"We can," Wolfe glanced briefly at McLeod, who nodded, "*request* leave to help you, but we truly need some sanction to act. Once we have that -- even tacitly -- we can help you." Wolfe realized she was committing McLeod more than she probably should, but she knew him well enough to know he was likely as willing to help as she was. Of course, the possibility that they would receive sanction to act from the Federation and Alliance delegation heads was highly unlikely, so perhaps her promise to Towns was empty.

They waited in silence for a few minutes -- Jurgan somberly, McLeod and Wolfe expectantly. Finally, Jurgan spoke. "Well, that is all I can hope for then." He straightened his back. "When do you think you will have final word from your leaders?"

"We can ask them tomorrow morning," said McLeod. "What they choose to approve is of course their choice, but we will impress upon them the drive for fairness in finding out who really kidnapped Vice Chair Patt'son's daughter, and offer our informal assistance as members of the Federation and the Alliance. Also, you may not know this, but our committee work is suspended anyway."

Again, Jurgan nodded. "Well, I thank you," Jurgan said as he rose. He smiled at Wolfe. "I hope you enjoy your blue coddle -- it is my favorite, as well. Perhaps I should add it to the café's menu permanently." Wolfe smiled and rose; McLeod rose as well.

"Thank you, Jurgan," Wolfe said. She turned to McLeod. "We promise to be in touch with you soon, no matter the outcome."

"Agreed," McLeod said. "Take care, Jurgan." McLeod escorted Towns to the door and let him out. He returned to face Wolfe. She was frowning.

"What?" McLeod asked.

Wolfe sighed. "I wonder if we were getting his hopes up for nothing."

McLeod's mouth set in a grim line. "Perhaps," he said, "But I would like to help him if I could."

"Doesn't matter," Wolfe answered. "We can't and you know it." She stood. "I'm not happy, Tucker. We can't do this."

McLeod again became defensive. "Are you saying that you wouldn't do it even with permission?"

"No, I'm not saying that, but…."

"Well then," McLeod said. "Let's just see what the powers that be say tomorrow." He looked toward his table. "If your doc is loaded up, send it to me and I'll combine it into a single document."

Wolfe sighed, knowing that the issue between them was far from resolved. "Sure," she said. "When do you want to meet to give it to them?"

"Why don't you make contact with them and let me know?"

He smiled and nodded toward the dessert. "And please take the blue coddle with you -- you know I have no willpower with that stuff."

Rolling her eyes, Wolfe said, "Right, so it goes right to my hips?"

McLeod raised his eyebrow and chuckled. "No comment, but better you than me," he said. Wolfe sighed again, took up her dessert and left McLeod's quarters. As she left, McLeod knew she was right on all counts, as she usually is. But he also believed that their checking out Towns' assumption was worth their time, particularly since they wouldn't be meeting with their committee or fellow staff members for a while anyway.

He arose at his normal time for his morning workout, then went to breakfast alone. While drinking his coffee, he looked up and noticed Councilor Trent entering the café. He thought briefly, then stood so Councilor Trent would notice him. Trent smiled, and walked over.

"Captain," Trent said, "How are you?"

"Good, Councilor, good -- well, not *perfect* given the dynamics of our committee. I hope yours is going better than ours." Trent smiled.

"Well, perhaps better but by no means great," Trent said. "There are some difficult dynamics within our group as well." He learned forward. "Now, I know your committee isn't meeting now, so what are you engaged in?" McLeod filled Councilor Trent in on the report he and Wolfe had prepared for the Fleet Marshall and Ambassador. Trent listened intently and asked some clarifying questions as McLeod spoke. Then, taking a chance, McLeod mentioned the visit by Jurgan Towns the night before. To this, Trent listened equally closely. As McLeod finished, Trent held up his hand.

"This can be an opportunity for all of us, Captain," he said. "I believe your general way of handling it has merit, but I believe you may want to consider speaking with just Fleet Marshal Masters and Ambassador Redstar." McLeod frowned. "Let me continue, Captain, "he said. "I believe the task is a worthy one, and by helping to address this important issue within the Twin Worlds, we would gain significantly in terms of our credibility; that would give us greater momentum throughout all of the negotiations." He leaned forward again. "And since this is not a publicly directed task, the challenge would be to allow Vice Chancellor Noregan and Minister Long plausible deniability, do you see?"

McLeod did, yet didn't know if it would be adequate in this situation. "To be honest, Councilor, I do." McLeod paused, then continued. "Perhaps once we speak with Fleet Marshall Masters and Ambassador Redstar, we can determine what we really *can* do in this situation." Trent agreed, and offered to attend McLeod's meeting with the Fleet Marshall and the Ambassador. McLeod agreed to contact Wolfe to let her know, and they parted.

An hour later, McLeod, Wolfe and Trent sat with Fleet Marshall Masters and Ambassador Redstar. The committee chairs were happy to accommodate Trent's presence, probably owing to his status within the Alliance, and as a negotiator. After McLeod and Wolfe completed their committee report and answered all questions to the satisfaction of Masters and Redstar, Trent spoke.

"Paulo. Susan," he began. "We have another matter we would like to bring to your attention, and I would ask that you let Captains McLeod and Wolfe give their complete description of the matter before you ask questions." Masters and Redstar looked puzzled; Wolfe was a bit puzzled and annoyed, as McLeod had not given her full notice of this. However, she knew what McLeod would be speaking about.

McLeod began cautiously. "Fleet Marshall. Ambassador. We -- that is Raina and I -- have come into some information regarding the recent kidnapping on Hemod." Masters and Redstar sat up straighter. "Let me give you the background," he said, and he described how they met Jurgan Towns, and their subsequent meeting with him after the vid reports. McLeod had thoroughly researched Anton Jurgan's background, and found that what they had been told by his cousin was correct: Jurgan had never been connected in any way to violence against people, and certainly not through direct contact such as a kidnapping. This added credibility to Towns' assertion, and for his call for help. McLeod said that he would like to find a way to help Towns, and perhaps in some way aid the negotiations on the Twin Worlds.

His original assessment of Master's and Redstar's reactions was correct -- both he and Wolfe were told rather quickly that any action taken as part of the Star Alliance or Central Federation would be inappropriate, illegal, and in many ways unethical. It was at this point that Councilor Trent stepped in again.

"Hear me out, Susan; Paulo. While I agree with the basic content of what you're saying, I believe we have a greater good to serve here, again in ways that can serve our negotiations and the ultimate outcome on behalf of the Twin Worlds. What is the real harm in having a person or two visit planet-side, and ask a few questions so long as it is done in a way that does not reflect negatively on the Alliance or the Federation?"

Redstar shook her head in annoyance. "There are rules of engagement in diplomatic circles, Elias, you know that," Redstar said. "To suggest that we completely throw these out at this critical juncture, is quite honestly irresponsible." Fleet Marshall Masters was silent.

Trent responded to Redstar quickly. "I respectfully disagree, Susan, and let me tell you why. We are at a critical juncture in these negotiations, as we all agree. At the same time, the military cooperation committee seemed to be making progress, which would be severely compromised if we can't get Patt'son back to the table, and there seems to be no move on the part of the Hemodian government to force him back or find someone to take his place, which is understandable." Trent could see agreement on the faces of both Masters and Redstar. Continuing, he said, "We are at a similar place with our other committees. If in fact this Anton Jurgan is the person responsible, he will be found out; but if he is not and we can find additional information to give to the Heraian and Hemodian Authorities, it may serve to bring us back to the table quicker." He sat back in his chair, then added carefully. "And to accomplish this, I would never suggest an official enquiry done by either the Star Alliance or by the Central Federation." Redstar and Masters frowned.

"Are you suggesting a covert operation?" asked Masters.

"*Very* covert," said Trent. "In fact, what I'm really suggesting is a simple fact finding mission, in the guise of a well-deserved weekend off for Captain McLeod."

Masters thought for a moment, then said, "There is merit to what you say, Elias," he said. "However, a covert operation without some kind of sanction from a higher authority is highly irregular and could put all of us in a very challenging situation."

Redstar was quick to agree. "Exactly one of my concerns, Paulo." Turning to McLeod, she asked, "And do you have any *experience* in covert operations, Captain?"

Before McLeod could answer, Wolfe stepped in. "No, but *I* have." McLeod started to speak again, but was interrupted by Trent.

"Here is what I am proposing," Trent countered. "Captains Wolfe and McLeod," he looked to both of them to receive confirmation. Receiving it, he continued, "Captains Wolfe and McLeod travel planet-side to Herai, ostensibly on a brief vacation. Captain McLeod speaks Ketchuan, so they'll have no difficulty getting around, or asking questions. It will be up to them to secure contacts from this cousin of Anton Jurgan and finding out what they can without causing any undue pressure or notoriety. After a day or so, they simply return and give any information back to us and we feed it to the Hemodian and Heraian authorities." He paused for effect.

Redstar said, cautiously, "Elias, I'm certainly familiar with covert operations, but I have never authorized one myself." Looking to Masters, she asked, "Paulo?" Masters shook his head. She returned her famous gaze to Trent. "And yet you ask us to authorize one now?"

Trent smiled. "No, Susan, I do not." He said. His companions were all puzzled. Trent continued. "What I am asking is for your permissions to let Captains Wolfe and McLeod go planet-side to get away from the stressful environment of these negotiations. They should only be gone for two days -- I hope that is okay."

Sensing their hesitation, Trent added, "Surely as their direct supervisors, you can allow them a little free time? And since their precise activities are neither authorized nor specifically directed, you have some plausible deniability, and Vice Chancellor Noregan and Minister Long have complete plausible deniability." Trent smiled before adding, "And isn't plausible deniability the hallmark of a truly covert operation?"

Redstar wasn't convinced. "You're still asking a lot, Elias," she said. Looking up at both McLeod and Wolfe, she added "and perhaps the way to do this, is to have the discussion with three of us exclusively, if you don't mind, Captains?"

McLeod and Wolfe rose, with McLeod saying, "Not at all, Ambassador. We'll be in Captain Wolfe's quarters if you need us." McLeod and Wolfe walked toward the door, then McLeod turned again to the table before exiting the room. "Thank you for your consideration."

As they walked, McLeod noticed that Wolfe was walking with more purpose and a bit faster than usual, and he knew she would be the one talking once they arrived at her quarters. She opened the door, and ushered him in.

"What the hell were you thinking?" she shouted. "If you think I'm going to jeopardize my appointment so you can play spy, you have another thing coming."

McLeod stepped back, putting up his palms. "Never," he said. "I've wanted to see you in that chair for too many years to mess it up now. I have no intention of you going planet-side with me."

Wolfe looked confused. "But you don't have any covert experience."

"I'll get it," he said, surprised at his calm. "Raina, this is going to be a little vacation: ask some people some questions, find out some things and pass it along. If I don't find out anything, I give up and come back."

Wolfe snorted. "You've never been known for giving up, Tucker," she said.

"No, but I have been known for making strategic retreats, and that's what I may have to do depending on what I find out." McLeod paused "Raina, I don't want you to go, though I certainly don't want you this angry at me, either."

Wolfe smiled at him. "Not angry, just exasperated," she said.

McLeod returned her smile, "So, business as usual, right?"

Wolfe rolled her eyes and sighed. "I'm making tea. Coffee?" McLeod nodded.

Wolfe began making the coffee, when she asked, "Just how do you propose going about this mission?"

McLeod nodded, as if he had been formulating the plan and waiting for her question. "I think we should ask Jurgan Towns for people we might talk to; people close to his cousin and involved in the same movement. While they would certainly want to alibi him or say that he's not involved, I want to understand more about him and more about the kidnapping. Do they know who might be involved, or who operates in ways consistent with a kidnapping?" McLeod started to pace. "From my understanding, this just doesn't seem like the kind of thing that this group would do, if they are very unionist related. Sure, Patt'son likely has Caprist leanings, but Unionists generally attack at the ballot box or with strike or trade sanctions, not through kidnappings."

Wolfe was fascinated watching McLeod as he talked. She also reflected on what McLeod said and had to agree. People with strong professional and union support, many of whom are affiliated with Unionists planets and systems expend most of their energy ensuring favorable trade, wages and working conditions for professional and working class people: kidnapping isn't their style. Even when dealing with people with strong laissez-faire beliefs like the Caprists of Hemod, Unionists seldom stoop to this kind of targeted and individual attack. But, Wolfe also knew that times of crisis often led to desperate measures.

Finally, she spoke. "I agree with you, Tucker." Pausing, she added, "So, do you really want to do this?"

McLeod laughed, then responded. "I've really enjoyed our work so far, and it has really been energizing in a way. This task planet-side, it just feels right to me." He looked up to his friend. "So yes, I want to do it -- and I may need your advice and counsel to strategize before I go." She nodded her agreement. They sat in silence for a while as they sipped their drinks, until her door chime rang.

"Come!" Wolfe said, and came face to face with a messenger from Fleet Marshall Masters.

"Captains?" the messenger began. "Fleet Marshall Masters and Ambassador Redstar would like to see you. They have a proposition for you."

Chapter Twenty

Twin Worlds Space Station Alpha, Cantina

"I have a bad feeling about this," said Wolfe, shaking her head. She and McLeod were walking the last few blocks to the cantina where Jurgan Towns worked. Both of them were surprised that they had been given tacit permission to travel planet-side to investigate the kidnapping. They spotted the cantina, checked their chrons, and opened the door. After entering, their eyes quickly adjusted to the darkness and they were ushered into a more casual eating area than the one they had dined in a few nights earlier. They picked up menus, and McLeod casually asked if Jurgan Towns was working.

"No, sir." said the young attendant. "He will be coming in to work in about," he looked up to the wall behind the bar, "about 40 minutes." He turned back to McLeod. "He is a wonderful chef, sir. And he's given me a new appreciation for Andoran food." He looked a little sheepish as he added, "I've only been across the sky to Hemod in my life." McLeod and Wolfe smiled at him.

"We'll just take a look at the menu and call you when we're ready," said Wolfe. The attendant smiled and withdrew. "Enthusiastic, isn't he?" she asked.

McLeod nodded asking, "Still concerned?"

Wolfe shuddered slightly. "A bit more than concerned, Tucker." Wolfe shook her head. "I think we've both lost our minds, especially me for going along with it. If it weren't for the assurances of Fleet Marshall Masters -- which means a lot to me -- I would never go along with this," she said.

McLeod placed his hand lightly on hers. "I know you wouldn't... *and* I know you still wouldn't do it if you didn't always have my back."

Wolfe rolled her eyes, then smiled. "That's been mutual for a while, Tucker."

McLeod only smiled at her and she continued.

"So, what's the plan?"

"Hey, you're the big tough covert operator," McLeod countered

"You're not even supposed to know that," Wolfe said. McLeod's smile widened. "And to tell you the truth, Tucker, you can figure out a way to plan this as well as I can."

"I doubt that," he said.

Wolfe allowed herself a small smile. "I'll remind you of that later," she said, then she glanced at her menu.

"I'm actually hungry."

"So am I," McLeod said. "Shall we go with homeworld cuisine or Andoran?" Just then, McLeod looked up and saw Jurgan Towns approaching their table. While the man didn't seem as dejected as he had in McLeod's quarters, it still looked as if he carried the whole world on his shoulders. His mood lightened as he approached the table and noticed the open faces of the two captains. McLeod and Wolfe rose as he approached.

Towns extended his hand. "Captain; Captain," he said, nodding to McLeod and Wolfe in turn. McLeod waved him to a chair.

"I sense this is not a social call," said Towns.

"It's not," said McLeod. "In truth, Captain Wolfe and I are taking a brief vacation planet-side on Herai for a few days." Towns' expression was neutral as McLeod continued. "And we thought we might be able to ask a few 'targeted' questions on the surface to find out what really happened on Hemod two days ago."

Towns vaulted out of his chair as his eyes misted over. "Do you mean it? I was so sure that this would never happen." Towns couldn't contain his excitement. "When are you going? Shall I go with you? I…I don't know how you do these things. How can I help?"

Wolfe smiled and gently pulled him back down to his chair. "Jurgan. Jurgan," she said, patting his arm. "It's alright. Leave this in our hands." Wolfe looked up at McLeod. "Tucker and I have done these kinds of things before." She turned to look at Towns, continuing, "There is never a guaranteed result, Jurgan. But we will do our best to find the truth."

Towns studied their faces for a moment, then said, "I know you both will. Thank you."

"Now," said McLeod. "We need to know how we can proceed." He turned to look at Towns, all business. "Jurgan, who can we contact planet-side to begin our questioning? Are there people who can help us learn as much as we can as quickly as we can about the Unionist group that Anton headed?"

Towns was silent for a moment, then said. "Actually, Captain, we have been talking about that for the past day."

Towns shook his head slightly, then looked at Wolfe. "The 'we' in this case is some family members, and other associates of Anton. In fact, we wondered what they might be able to find out for themselves without additional help." He sat up straighter. "You see, we aren't military people or police - anything like that. I am a cook, one of my good friends is a miner. We are normal people. My friend is going to be your contact on Herai and will arrange for others to help you." His voice trailed off.

McLeod leaned forward to speak more quietly.

"Jurgan, another question, and it's an important one. You said that Anton does not promote violence, but am I right in assuming that this group may sometimes be involved in activities that skirt the edge of the law?"

Towns had a pained look on his face again. "Yes, Captain," he began, then grew a bit defiant. "But sometimes the edge of the law is moved to make the activities of honest strikers and activists seem like it is breaking the law."

McLeod raised his palms slightly. "Understood, Jurgan," McLeod said, then glanced briefly at Wolfe before continuing. "I ask because we want to be sure that if we meet with certain people that we won't immediately be arrested, and that is *not* an exaggeration."

"He's right, Jurgan," said Wolfe. "How easily we are able to slip in and out of meeting places to meet with people and learn what we can is essential. We can't do that if we're constantly looking over our shoulders." Wolfe continued, more confident since she had the most covert experience. "We want to find out where Anton might be, meet with him if we can, and learn everything we can in the shortest possible time, and be able to bring back what we learned to the negotiations. Can your friends help us with that?" Towns nodded.

"Then that's all we need to know right now," Wolfe said. "But we're going to need meeting places, introductions, and ways to contact them as soon as you can." Looking at McLeod, she added "We can take care of the arrangements to get planet-side ourselves." McLeod nodded.

Towns smiled again, more relaxed.

"Captains, I am a part owner of this cantina. I can take whatever time I need to make the arrangements you described. Would after dinner tonight be alright?" McLeod was going to answer, but Wolfe stepped in again.

"That would be ideal, Jurgan, but we want it done right -- if you need more time, please take it," she said. Towns nodded his agreement.

"I am working with existing long term contacts, Captains," he said. "I believe I can put things together by tonight, and if not, I will let you know what additional time I need."

"Good enough," McLeod said. Then he smiled. "Does that mean we can order lunch now?" Towns and Wolfe returned his smile, and

the captains ordered their meal. McLeod and Wolfe ate while
Towns outlined proposed meeting times and locations that he would
share with his planet-side contacts. Before they left, he told McLeod
and Wolfe that he should be able to meet them later that night or
early in the morning with the information, including meeting times
and places.

* * *

Captain R. Wolfe's Quarters, Space Station Alpha, Twin Worlds

Following their visit with Jurgan Towns, McLeod visited the
transportation desk on the station and arranged for transport planet-
side to the Heraian capitol city of Segow for noon the following day.
In the meantime, he and Wolfe packed clothing and other items for
their trip. They had both packed some civilian clothing prior to
leaving, and had worn very little of it thus far. Wolfe looked at her
clothing options and seemed puzzled.

"What's wrong?" McLeod asked.

"We need to blend in planet-side and I haven't researched that.
Usually I have a lot more time to prepare for an operation even as
simple as this one"

McLeod moved toward her pile of clothes and began lifting them
one by one. "This, this and… this are good," he said, tossing items
into her bag. "This and… this are not," and he tossed the offending
items onto a chair. Wolfe put her hand on his arm and stopped him.

"Whoa," Wolfe said. "Since when are you such an expert on
fashion?"

McLeod was not to be deterred. Pointing to a pair of her slacks, he
said, "These are perfect." Finally answering her, he added, "Since I
studied clothing and customs on the Twin Worlds a week or so ago.
There is also a strong connection of clothing to language, so what
you might wear on a planet with lots of Ketchuan speakers will be
pretty similar to what you would wear on other planets with lots of

Ketchuan speakers. Just think slightly looser and not revealing, and you've pretty much got it.

Wolfe looked at her friend skeptically. "Is there anything else you haven't told me about the Twin Worlds and how we should act?"

"Not much," McLeod said. "Language wise, we'll be fine, there are plenty of people whose primary language is related to Andoran, plus with my background in Ketchuan, we'll be good. We already know about food customs, and I expect or at least I *hope* Jurgan will give us more." McLeod placed a few more clothing items haphazardly in Wolfe's bag, then moved to her vid. There, he called up a detailed map of the capitol city. After sorting through more clothing items, Wolfe joined him.

"What are you looking at?" she asked.

McLeod squinted as he absent-mindedly stroked his finger on the map.

"I'm trying to see the general layout of Segow -- how it's organized." He looked up at Wolfe. "It's an industrial town, built originally to service the old mines that don't operate anymore. One thing I was noticing while doing my research is the presence of tunnels and a whole underground economy around Segow. Ah, here." McLeod pointed toward what looked like a tunnel entrance near the primary transport station in the south of the city. "My sense is that if we were to meet somewhere near these old tunnels -- at least to regroup -- that would be a good thing."

Wolfe was unconvinced. "That would make sense if we really knew where we were going and more about the conditions in that part of the city."

McLeod nodded. "Absolutely -- I'm just trying to identify a place that on paper would make sense because it's a place I surmise would be full of people of all backgrounds, and where locals don't pay much attention to strange people." turning to Wolfe, he added, "That would be us."

Wolfe looked at the area and the close up map, studying locations and directions. "What else do you know about Herai?"

"Well, it's an interesting paradox, at least to me," McLeod said. "Herai has more natural resources than Hemod, so a significant amount of manufacturing takes place there, so it can often remind you of a heavily industrialized city, with air pollution, lots of noise, things, like that. The contrast is when you leave those industrial areas you think you're in the middle of the tropics -- it's lush and green and very inviting."

"That does seem like a paradox," Wolfe replied.

"And from what I've gathered," McLeod continued, "many of the people live toward the edges of the factory districts as close to nature as they can, but that's not always possible. Still, the people of Herai really value and revere nature and even though their factory districts are really dirty, the government puts lots of resources behind containing that pollution. Hemod, on the other hand, has gleaming cities carved out of the desert which covers much of the planet."

Wolfe nodded her understanding. "Let me focus for a bit on Herai."

"Okay."

"I wonder," Wolfe continued, "In the absence of direct local information -- like from Jurgan's people -- it probably makes sense to meet near those tunnels you mentioned." She turned to McLeod. "Did you plan to ask Jurgan about that specifically?"

"Yes, but I'm going to suggest that we go anywhere they tell us to go, given their local knowledge," McLeod said. He checked his chron. "I haven't collected my clothes yet. Why don't I head to my quarters and take care of that? Then we can head out to dinner." Stopping, he asked. "Should we assume that Jurgan is going to come to us, or head to his restaurant?"

"Don't know," Wolfe said. "I'm not in the mood for a really formal dinner, so why don't we both go to the cantina? Jurgan may not know where my quarters are, and that way we'll both be together."

McLeod looked around. "Need more time?"

Wolfe seemed unsure. "15 minutes?"

"Okay. I'll bring the maps as well, so you can study them," McLeod said

"Good idea." Once Wolfe had finished packing, they returned to McLeod's quarters, and Wolfe provided some input into the clothing that McLeod would take planet-side, then arranged their credentials for the transport. According to McLeod, the travel time from the station to Herai should be about two hours owing to the normally high level of traffic to Segow. They also added water purifying screens to allow them to adjust quickly to the different water composition on the Twin Worlds.

Just as they were deciding they were getting hungry, the door chime rang, and McLeod ushered Towns into the room. He entered with food containers, and the smells indicated something very tasty.

Towns smiled as he placed the containers on the galley table. "I have all the information about people, meetings and locations," Towns began. "Shall we discuss them before, during or after our meal?"

McLeod knew himself and he knew his friend. "I think we can meet while we eat." He turned to Wolfe. "Raina?"

"I agree." McLeod took out utensils and placed them on the galley counter, where both Jurgan and Wolfe filed their plates. As they began eating, McLeod was surprised to see how hungry he was. He was also surprised to see a special Terran dessert prepared by Jurgan. McLeod reveled in it.

As they took their first break, Jurgan began sharing additional information. "I've notified two people about your arrival who I have worked with or my cousin has worked with for years: I have complete confidence in them." He connected his pad to the vid and called up pictures and profiles of McLeod's and Wolfe's contacts planet-side. Towns stood and approached the vid. The first picture was of a dark haired man probably in his fifties who appeared to be of medium height. He seemed muscular. "This is Lou Sligo," said Towns. "He is a miner and leader of the formal trade union. Anton has worked for him for years, and Sligo is the one who first impressed on Anton the importance of civil disobedience *without* violence." Towns turned from the screen. "He is a rough man, but a good one. He has tremendous credibility on Herai, though not surprisingly, less so on Hemod."

"This," Towns continued, changing the picture, "is Benno Zavery, a mechanical engineer." The picture showed a very tall man, thin with light colored hair. He was stoop shouldered, and seemed rather bookish. "Benno is a genius who has been helping to organize office professionals in support of the unionist movement. He and Anton met at a bar somewhere, and he's been helping ever since." Towns looked up. "I've known his family for years, and trust him as well." He sat down.

"Both Lou and Benno are convinced that Anton is not behind this terrible crime, and want to help you prove it." Sensing some objection, he continued. "And I've told them that they are to answer all your questions and take you wherever you want to go so that you can come to your own conclusions. You will find them very helpful."

"What have you told them about us?" McLeod asked.

"Just the truth, Captain," Towns said. "I couldn't really lie to them given your status -- and yours Captain," he said to Wolfe. "They know you are taking a brief vacation which is the overall story, and not unusual for this time of year on Herai."

"Understood," said McLeod. "Meeting location?" he added.

Towns changed the vid again, bringing up a map similar to the one McLeod and Wolfe had studied earlier.

Towns pointed to the map. "Either Lou or Benno will meet you at the transport station: they'll find a way to signal you." Towns handed McLeod and Wolfe a document. "All we have to do is to give my friends a time for your arrival and we can arrange the meeting. Does that give you enough to get started?" McLeod and Wolfe paged through the documents Towns had given them.

"I think so," Wolfe said. "We'll look these over tonight, and develop other questions you can send to them prior to our arrival. Once we complete that, I think we'll be ready. Is there anything else we need to know?"

Towns paused before answering.

"No, just that the mood planet-side is tense, so you may feel that from my colleagues. Please know that it is not directed at you, but the situation is becoming more challenging by the minute." Wolfe and McLeod nodded.

McLeod turned and looked at his long-time friend. "What do you think, Raina?" he asked, "Business as usual for us?

Chapter Twenty One

Twin Worlds Space Station Alpha, Heraian Transport Shuttle

As they sat on the scheduled transport, McLeod and Wolfe looked over some of the material Jurgan had sent to their pads. They were in an open but relatively empty compartment. Scheduled transports are used regularly by employees living planet-side and working on the station, so a middle of the day shuttle is frequently empty. Wolfe and McLeod appreciated the privacy. They studied the biographies of the people they were meeting carefully. As she began to become fatigued, Wolfe looked up at McLeod. "Any impressions?"

McLeod shrugged. "Of our contacts?" he asked.

Wolfe nodded.

"None at this time," he said. "They seem like decent people and the sketches give me some sense of them." He looked skeptically and rubbed his eyes. "What I can't get an idea of is what makes them tick."

"Exactly," Wolfe said, gesturing with her hands. "I don't have the sense of what drives them; even though there is *some* of that" she indicated her pad with her hand, "it just isn't enough for me."

McLeod was silent for a moment. "Well," he began, "I do have a sense of trust with Jurgan, so my hope is that his friends will turn out to be trustworthy as well."

"I hope so, too." Wolfe said. "But I won't have the confidence as we start this that I'd like to have." McLeod looked carefully at his friend. He was as anxious as she was, but knew that her anxiety was a result of her extensive background in covert operations, something he didn't have. And given her background, there was no way McLeod could allay her concerns until they were planet-side. He resolved to follow her lead so he wouldn't make a costly mistake.

"I hear you," McLeod said. "Since we can't do anything about it now, why don't we just relax until we're planet-side?"

"Right," Wolfe replied. Then she sat back and closed her eyes. McLeod knew enough to leave her alone.

He continued to examine his pad, trying to draw clearer and more defined pictures in his mind of the people he was to meet, and to help outline the questions he planned to ask them. He needed to know where Anton Jurgan might go, the people he might meet, and how and why he might be blamed for the kidnapping on Hemod. McLeod also knew their investigation should probably focus on Hemod instead of Herai but also knew they didn't have sufficient contacts to start the investigation there. Feeling fatigued and a bit overwhelmed, McLeod decided to nap as well, and by the time the transport finally docked at the central station at Segow, he felt rested. Wolfe was alert and ready as well.

Walking out onto the station, they gathered their bags and walked forward, looking casual but always alert to their surroundings. As they followed the small group exiting the transport, they noticed a man they believed to be Benno Zavery glance in their direction, then disappear around a corner. Without a word, they moved confidently toward Zavery. They passed the corner, and noticed that he was perhaps ten steps in front of them, turning in the direction of a public cab stand -- at least according to the street sign. When McLeod and Wolfe finally reached him, instead of speaking, he stepped toward a small cab, and opened the rear hatch. Finally turning to face McLeod and Wolfe, he beckoned with his hand, and they placed their bags inside. He closed the hatch, then opened the rear passenger door of the cab, and ushered them in. He followed right behind them, then finally spoke to the cab's nav and directional control.

"Waverly Museum," he said. The cab bells indicated that the direction had been received, and it started. Zavery held up his hand to prevent conversation, then took out a small box with a red light on top of it. He held it in his hand for a moment or two, saw that the light did not change color, then finally turned to face McLeod and Wolfe.

"Can't be too careful." Then he smiled and extended his hand. "Benno Zavery. Welcome to Herai." McLeod and Wolfe both shook his hand in turn.

McLeod inclined his head toward the small box. "Communications block?"

"No, rather, a detector and jammer, if necessary," replied Zavery. "I didn't think it would be a problem now, but didn't want to take any chances. How was your trip?"

"Uneventful," Wolfe said. She peered at the street as they traveled. "Just how far from the Museum are we going?"

"Not far, but our little office location is about five blocks away from the Waverly; and we'll be backtracking to get to it. Just another precaution."

"Which seems to indicate that more people know about this than should," Wolfe said.

"Not at all, Captain," Zavery said. "The simple truth is we're always cautious like this with visitors. There are people in the government who simply believe that the union needs to be either feared or protected, and it's just become common practice to circle around the location -- which is quite public, by the way." He shook his head, "You have to be Heraian to understand that, I guess."

Wolfe's eyebrows creased. "And you?"

Zavery seemed surprised.

"Actually, I'm Hemodian, but I went to school here on Herai, and found more opportunities here directly after my training. I've worked on Hemod as well, though once I became drawn to the plight of workers and technical professionals, I found myself more and more comfortable on Herai than at home." He inclined himself more toward Wolfe, continuing. "You have to understand, Captain. The Twin Worlds are similar in so many ways: language and family structure to name just two. At the same time, economics, class and politics drive so many wedges between and among us that people can find their allegiances shifting at times daily." He smiled. "You almost need a scorecard on your own planet to know who your friends are from day to day."

McLeod shared his smile. "Not atypical in many places, I have to say."

"Agreed," Zavery said. He looked out the window and thought for a moment. "I think we should be there in about ten minutes, so let me give you a few items before we gather all five of us together." He sat up straighter. "First of all, you know Lou's background and mine. We're strong Unionists, whose concerns regarding the Twin Worlds revolve around just compensation and working conditions for working people and professionals. We also have grave concerns for what would happen on the Twin Worlds if we gain membership in the Central Federation." He paused, then quickly added "or the Star Alliance." He gathered his thoughts again before continuing. "On the other hand, we believe membership in either organization might force the wealthy people on Hemod -- many though not all of whom are formally Caprists -- to share the wealth, so to speak. So, we are torn between these two competing parts of our identity, yet most of us will say that we identify proudly as part of the Twin Worlds." He looked resigned. "In some ways, you simply have to experience it to understand." Both McLeod and Wolfe nodded their understanding, so Zavery continued.

"I should probably tell you that Lou is… how can I say it ... a *challenging* person to deal with." Wolfe raised her eyebrows slightly and tilted her head at Zavery.

Zavery quickly recovered.

"What I mean to say is that he is a good man, very committed to the cause, and sometimes he forgets that not everyone is as committed as he is. In fact, he often makes that clear as he speaks with all of us, including me." Zavery seemed to be choosing his words carefully. "So, he sometimes questions people's motives, and comes off as very brusque, perhaps even rude." Zavery smiled. "I would like to say that it is not directed at you, but is simply his personality, but in some ways, it *will* be directed at you, since you are both fairly well known. Lou is always able it seems, to find something about anyone that he can become annoyed about." Zavery meant it partly in fun, and both McLeod and Wolfe laughed. Facing McLeod, he added, "And with the recent report on your involvement in the negotiations, he will probably try to press you on something from *your* past, Captain."

McLeod waved the concern way. "I've been down that road before, Benno, and please call me Tucker."

"And please call me Raina," Wolfe said.

Zavery smiled. "That would be easier," he said. He looked up and saw they were nearing the museum. He reached into a pocket, and scanned a card over the back seat payment sensor. It made a small sound as the cab stopped, then the doors opened automatically. The three left the cab, retrieved McLeod's and Wolfe's bags, and started to walk back the way they had come. After a few blocks in silence, Zavery turned to them. "I know of your love for coffee, and" he faced Wolfe, "Tea?" She nodded. "I was going to get some for Lou and me anyway. Why don't we stop along the way and grab an urn?"

Zavery took Wolfe and McLeod to a small, and rather plain-looking establishment emitting incredible smells into the air. McLeod and Wolfe looked to him to order for them, and shortly afterward, they left with an insulated coffee package, pastries, and tea. They walked in silence and soon approached a cluster of buildings located close to the inactive mine tunnels. As they walked, the area became more and more working class, Wolfe reflected. Soon, Zavery turned into a building entrance, and walked down a hallway. As Zavery walked, Wolfe felt, rather than saw that Zavery was becoming more tense. Maybe he's girding for the explosion when we finally encounter Sligo. She received her answer quickly.

"Benno!" they heard. "What's keeping you?"

Surveillance? Wolfe thought. She hadn't seen an obvious signs of that, but….

"On the way, Lou!" said Zavery. He look at both McLeod and Wolfe, looking rather sheepish.

McLeod waved him on. "Not our first time, Benno," McLeod said. "Lead the way." At this point, Zavery led them through a doorway, and once through, they faced a squat, powerfully built man, who turned from his desk to face the door.

The man snorted when he saw Zavery, McLeod and Wolfe. "About time," he said. "Maybe we can get some things done now." The man -- presumably Lou Sligo -- rose and moved toward a table, motioning everyone to follow him. "Sit, please," he said, not angry, but still assertive. The man did not offer his hand to either of them. Wolfe felt that part of the bluster was for show.

"Lou," Zavery said. "You certainly know of Captains McLeod and Wolfe?" Zavery placed the coffee, pastries and tea on the table. Sligo was wary and set his jaw as he faced the captains.

"I do, but I honestly don't know why we're talking now. This is not your battle."

"You're right," McLeod said, surprising Sligo. "It's not our battle, but it *is* a battle for someone we've come to know, and we want to help him."

Sligo made a dismissive wave with his hand. "Jurgan Towns is not one of us, either," he said. "He left the Twin Worlds to go cook around the galaxy, leaving the rest of us to do the hard work."

Wolfe decided to push back. "You ever spend time in a hot kitchen, Sligo? It *is* hard work."

Sligo laughed. "She *does* speak," he said.

"Yep," Wolfe said, smiling broadly. "I bite, too."

McLeod chuckled. "I'm going to drink my coffee, and let you two flex your muscles," said McLeod. He turned to Sligo. "And her bite is really nasty, Sligo." Turning to Wolfe, McLeod added, "When you two are finished, let me know, because I'm not going to save the cakes for either of you."

"I'll play nice if I get to eat cake," said Wolfe. Sligo laughed again as he nodded. If this had been a test, apparently McLeod and Wolfe had passed, or at least hadn't yet failed.

Sligo's posture relaxed. "I don't want you to eat my cake, so I will play nice, too," he said. And please call me Lou."

"We're Tucker and Raina," McLeod said.

Sligo reached into the pastry container and opened the pastries. Looking them over, he pointed. "You may wish to try these two -- they are the specialties of the café." He reached in and took out small papers on which to set the pastries, and offered the container first to Wolfe, then to McLeod. They chose the recommended pastries, and sampled them. All four ate in silence. Finally, Sligo called them back together again. "I have to tell you," he began, "that Anton is a friend, and a good one. At the same time, I think he has a troubled past, so much so that he decided the only way to move our demands forward was through violence and terror." He looked squarely at the two captains. "I don't know what you know about me or our Unionist movement here on Herai, but it has a history of first using a violent, then a non-violent," he paused searching for a word, 'approach' to problem solving. I am not known as a weak man -- quite the contrary -- yet I am also committed to getting what we want peacefully." He shook his head trying to collect his thoughts.

Sligo took a sip of coffee and continued. "What I am trying to do is to get the two sides of our movement together, and I can only do that by being very strong both within the movement, and outwardly as we deal with the rich and powerful who don't care very much about the working man or woman. By being strong and seeming to be uncompromising, I can keep the more violent members of our movement placated, yet still move us forward non-violently. Do you see?"

"I believe so," said McLeod. "Jurgan Towns said that you had persuaded Anton to focus his efforts on peaceful means, rather than what might be called terrorist acts." McLeod noticed Sligo bristle at the hearing the word 'terrorist', but to his credit, Sligo remained silent. "But what Jurgan emphasized most was that even in his earlier years, Anton would never engage in an act such as a home invasion or a kidnapping." Turning directly to Sligo, he asked, "What's your opinion?"

Sligo was quick to answer. "I agree," he said. "Destroying bridges, ground transports -- those are things directed at property and at corporations, but never at individuals, and no people were ever harmed in the acts directed or committed by Anton. It is just not his way." Sligo sat back in his chair, frustrated. "Now that the report has come out about the kidnapping and alleging his involvement, he has gone underground, and even *we* don't know where he is."

Wolfe watched the interchange between McLeod and Sligo, trying to gauge how truthful Sligo was. She picked up nothing but sincerity in Sligo, but acknowledged to herself that this might be wishful thinking on her part. "Who might know where he is?" she asked.

Sligo looked puzzled. "I do not know," Sligo said. "Because the person who worked closest with him for many years was killed in a ground accident a few months ago. Anton, to my knowledge, had no other lieutenant, and I tend to believe the few people who were associated with him when they tell me that they don't know where he is. We have spoken to all of those people and examined some of their former locations, with no luck."

"Who do you have left to question?" McLeod asked.

Sligo threw up his hands and shrugged. "No one. We have a network large enough to have questioned everyone." he said. "That's one reason we weren't particularly pleased to have you visit us -- we don't know what you could possibly do to help us or Anton."

"Thanks for being honest about that, Lou," said Wolfe. "So, I guess the next question to ask would be who benefits from this happening, or who has the most to gain either from the kidnapping itself or with the suspension of the negotiations?

Sligo frowned. "Who has the most to gain?" he asked. "That could be a long list."

"Well, perhaps we ought to start compiling it now," said Wolfe.

Chapter Twenty Two

Segow, Herai, Unionist Central Headquarters, Main Conference Room

"So," Wolfe said, looking at the list, "Are these all the people and groups that have a lot to gain by framing Anton Jurgan?" Before Sligo could answer, she added, "or people who may have an issue with Griffin Patt'son?"

"Yes. We believe so," Sligo said. "You have to understand though, Captain, that these are only people we know of ourselves -- there are probably many more people who have it in for Patt'son."

"Meaning?" Wolfe asked.

Sligo sighed. "Meaning, that Griffin Patt'son is just another example of a privileged rich man who gets what he wants regardless of the pain it causes anyone else." Sligo paused and exhaled slowly. "And there are lots of people on both planets who would love to give him a dressing down, though taking action against his daughter -- I just don't see it." His eyebrow furrowed and he looked up again at McLeod and Wolfe. "And in terms of moral values on the Twin Worlds, you don't mess with a man's or woman's family when you have a beef with them. It is the height of cowardice."

"I agree," said Zavery. "I think even some people close to Patt'son would like to strike against him, but striking against innocent family members is just not part of what we do on either of our planets."

"Do you think it's possible that someone from beyond the Twin Worlds is behind this then?"

Sligo and Zavery shot glances at each other, before Sligo spoke. "That has crossed my mind, Captain, though I don't have any specific evidence of it."

"Just a feeling?" asked Wolfe.

Sligo nodded. "Exactly," he said. "And I don't know what to do with that feeling."

The group was momentarily silent, until McLeod turned his attention again to the list produced by Sligo. "It occurs to me," he said, "That there are very few people on this list from Hemod." He turned to Sligo. "Could someone from the Unionist movement other than Anton be responsible?"

Sligo shook his head. "I would sincerely doubt it," he said. "I will give you the names of people in our movement on Hemod. Perhaps they can identify someone who might be trying to discredit our movement through this violence."

"Alright," McLeod countered. "Why don't we ask a different question: who or what organizations on Herai or Hemod do engage in violent tactics, including possibly kidnapping?"

Sligo seemed confused. "I think I know what you mean, Captain," he began. "But to be honest with you, violent tactics don't usually work for any kind of movement for change. The closest any of us gets is loud civil disobedience, in ways that...."

Noticing Sligo's pause, Wolfe asked, "What? Did you think of someone?"

"Not exactly, Captain," Sligo replied. "But I can tell you that another strong movement on the Twin Worlds are the environmentalists. They primarily work to reduce environmental damage due to industrialization and so forth. We are often allied when it comes to worker safety for those who work with dangerous substances."

McLeod frowned. "Something tells me there's more to it than that, Lou," he said.

Sligo shrugged. "Perhaps," he said. "And their movement has become more and more violent in recent years. I've heard rumblings that they oppose the negotiations because of what they see as a record of environmental damage they attribute to the Federation."

"*Excuse* me?" asked Wolfe.

Sligo held up his hands. "It's a little more circuitous than that, Captain," he said. "They associate the Federation, and the Alliance, I suppose, with increased industrialization and defense manufacturing, which often involves environmentally dangerous substances and processes." Sligo paused. "As I said, it's a circuitous route, but one that our 'colleagues' in that movement can travel quite quickly."

McLeod rubbed his temples briefly. He looked up, asking, "how could we determine if the environmental movement here or on Hemod might be behind the kidnapping?"

Sligo and Zavery looked at each other, both scratching their heads. "I honestly wouldn't know," said Zavery. "We can contact someone within their movement here, but you know, they are much more active here on Herai. If they were going to kidnap someone to halt the negotiations, they would have kidnapped somebody here." Turning to Sligo, he added, "Who could we contact about that, Lou?"

Sligo placed his head on his fist. "The leader of PlanetSafe has an office near here." Sligo checked his chron. "And he hardly every leaves his office except when directing operations. He's bound to be in." Sligo sat still.

Wolfe noticed McLeod begin to drum his fingers as they waited on Sligo. "Lou, can we call him, or better yet, could you do something?" Wolfe asked. "We're not getting anything done sitting here.

Sligo sat up and smiled slightly. "Oh, I can do that," he said. "It's just that if I give him even the hint of an accusation, he'll explode."

"I think this is worth the risk," McLeod said.

Sligo nodded. "I agree: I suppose if I can dish it out, I should be able to take it as well."

* * *

Sligo turned to face the group after speaking with PlanetSafe's leader, Sandio Milan. "Sandio is just as crusty as always, "Sligo said. "But he agreed to meet with me in about an hour, which doesn't give us much time to think through what I should be asking him."

"Any chance either Tucker or I could accompany you, Lou?" Wolfe asked. "There might be things that we will may want to ask given our backgrounds that might not occur to you -- no offense."

Sligo shook his head. "None taken, though I believe taking both of you would be a mistake," he said. "But Sandio has something of an eye for the ladies, so I hope you will excuse me if I suggest that you come with me?"

In answer, Wolfe looked directly at McLeod. "Not a word from you."

McLeod pulled back. "Nothing from me, Raina."

"I would be happy to accompany you, Lou," Wolfe said. "But I don't intend on wearing anything more revealing than this."

"Fair enough," said Sligo. Turning to Zavery he added, "And perhaps you and Captain McLeod can visit some of Anton's usual haunts here on Herai. And since we will probably need to head to Hemod soon as well," he noticed nods from both Wolfe and McLeod, "maybe you can complete arrangements for our trip there."

"On it," said Zavery.

Segow, Herai, PlanetSafe Headquarters

Sligo and Wolfe entered the plain looking office door of PlanetSafe headquarters, approaching a young man behind a reception desk. He scrunched his eyes when he saw Sligo, but quickly recovered.

"How may I help you?"

"We have an appointment to see Sandio," Sligo said in response. "Lou Sligo and Raina Wolfe -- we spoke to him about an hour ago."

"*That's* who you are!" the young man said. "I knew your face was familiar. I'll go see if Mr. Milan is ready for you." He exited the reception desk and knocked on a door at the end of a short hallway. Returning, the young man beckoned to Sligo and Wolfe. "He said to come on in," he said. Sligo and Wolfe followed the man into the corner office, and waved them in.

Sitting behind the desk was a man of massive proportions, Wolfe thought. The man's eyes widened when he first noticed Wolfe entering the office, then returned to their normal size. He addressed Sligo. "You had better have a good reason for interrupting me today, Lou," Milan said.

"I do," said Sligo. "I wanted to take a walk and find a place to rest before I went back home. You got a problem with that?"

Milan laughed. "You know I just hate your guts, right?"

"Yep," agreed Sligo. "It's mutual -- and I love you like a brother, too."

Milan shook his head, becoming serious. "So I know you must be here for something important," he said. "Why don't you introduce me, then have a seat." Wolfe and Sligo took chairs in front of Milan's desk.

"This is Captain Raina Wolfe, of the Central Federation, Sandio," Sligo began, "and while she knows your feelings about the Federation, we wouldn't be here if it wasn't important."

"Good to meet you, Captain," said Milan, without a trace of emotion. "Lou is correct in my general opinion of the Federation, but I also acknowledge the good done by them. Welcome." Turning his attention once again to Sligo, he added, "So what can I do for you?"

Sligo took a deep breath. "Well, you've seen the vid reports of the kidnapping of Griffin Patt'son's daughter on Hemod, Sandio." Milan nodded. "Well then," Sligo continued, "you also know that Anton Jurgan of our movement, has been accused of the kidnapping."

"No," Milan said.

"What?" asked Sligo.

"Jurgan has *not* been accused," Milan said. "He's been convicted without evidence and practically hanged by the news and vid sources with the help of our government, so *no*, accused doesn't quite sum up the situation."

Smiling to himself, Sligo replied, "I agree, Sandio. However, that is our current situation."

"And a preposterous situation it is," Milan responded. "Even at his most violent, Anton Jurgan never took physical action against any individual, especially someone he probably didn't even know," he snapped. "So again, what is it you want from me, a testimonial?"

"Not at all, Sandio," said Sligo. "However, Captain Wolfe here was asked by Anton's cousin to learn what she could about the situation and report back to her people. As we were talking, her companion asked if there were other movements on planet that are known for radical and disruptive action, and that led me to you."

Milan raised and lowered his massive chest in a sigh. "If it wasn't far too much work to get out of this chair, I would come there and smack you for that thinly veiled accusation, Lou," he said. Sligo sat silently in his chair. After about ten seconds, Milan looked at Wolfe. "Captain," he began, "protecting the natural environment of Herai is my only focus. I have no family, no other interests, no other friends.

All I have is the ground, the water, the air, and the other people who care about it as much as I do. And I can tell you that I can get pretty radical in my efforts to preserve this planet." He sat back in this chair and looked briefly out of the window.

"But you see," Milan continued, "the people I work with -- my real family, if you will-- they *do* have families, and the last thing I want to do is to place them in danger or hurt those they care about. Our actions, as radical as they may be, are directed to disrupt operations and activities that damage our environment, so they are directed at companies and rarely at government entities, but never to individual people."

"I understand that, Mr. Milan," said Wolfe. "But think with me for a minute. What if someone affiliated with PlanetSafe might have a more violent streak, perhaps not hold the same values as you, would you know who he or she might be?"

Milan shook his head. "I thought of that while I was speaking, Captain, and no one comes to mind. Our movement is large, but very centrally controlled so that we can maintain the proper public stance. Something like a kidnapping is completely out of the realm of what we or people like us tend to do. And," he continued looking directly at Wolfe, "this kind of operation directed against the family of an individual -- this may sound trite to you -- but we just don't do that on the Twin Worlds, which is perhaps why the reaction against Anton has been so incredibly strong." Turning to Sligo, he added, "I don't believe Anton is behind this, Lou, but that's where the reaction is directed."

Softly, Wolfe asked. "If someone from your movement were to go rogue and be really opposed to these negotiations, is Patt'son the person they would try to get to?"

Milan frowned. "I hadn't thought of that exactly, Captain," he said. "Though I have to tell you our movement is much stronger here on Herai, and the few names of people involved in the negotiations that I know of are well thought of within our movement. And while Patt'son is pretty well known on the Twin Worlds, organizing that kind of operation would be extremely difficult for someone generally so focused on Herai.

"So, we're right back where we started?" asked Wolfe.

"Let me continue to think, Captain," said Milan. "If anything comes to mind that may help you, I'll let Lou know. If nothing else," he added, "I am quite sure Anton is innocent, so if there is anything I can do to help clear him, please let me know."

"We appreciate it, Sandio," said Sligo. He and Wolfe rose. "And I already know that I owe you one, so don't bother to say it," he said with a smile.

"Good," said Milan. "So long as you know it, too."

* * *

Segow, Herai, Unionist Central Headquarters, Main Conference Room

Wolfe and Sligo returned to Unionist headquarters to find McLeod and Zavery casually drinking coffee.

"Please tell me you did more than drink coffee for the last two hours," Wolfe said.

McLeod chuckled. "Of course, Raina," he said defensively. "We've been very busy, haven't we, Benno?" Zavery nodded, but Wolfe just stood, arms folded. Smiling, McLeod said, "Have a seat, and we'll go over it with you?"

Wolfe and Sligo sat at the table, as McLeod and Zavery looked over their notes.

"First," Zavery began," we reviewed the locations where Anton has worked in the past, most of which, of course, are here on Herai." Turning to Sligo, he added, "I made a few more calls Lou, to people we hadn't talk to before?" Sligo nodded. "We didn't get anywhere, Lou. The people who've usually worked with Anton -- both before and after he renounced violence deny any knowledge of what happened and frankly, I believe them."

"We happened to run into one of them at the coffee shop," McLeod added. "And he seemed genuinely concerned about Anton being railroaded. Obviously, we don't have any acquaintance with these people, but I just sensed that they were telling the truth -- I just hope my gut feeling is accurate in this case," he said almost apologetically.

"We didn't get any farther, either," said Sligo. "I've known Sandio Milan for many years, and I tend to believe him. He also raised the point we discussed before -- that any action his movement would take would have been centered on Herai rather than Hemod."

"Which brings us back to Hemod," Wolfe said. "When can we get there?"

Zavery raised his hand in triumph. "Well, there I can help you," he said. Looking at Sligo he said, "Templeton is prepared for an early morning departure, Lou -- he can't do anything until then."

Wolfe winced involuntarily, which Sligo noticed. "I don't think that can be helped, Raina," he said. "I would prefer to arrive fully prepared, than to get there earlier with little to do."

Wolfe sighed. "Agreed."

"So Benno," continued Sligo, "were you able to confirm with our partners on Hemod?"

"Yes," said Zavery. "Miranda will meet us tomorrow when we arrive, along with two other union officials."

"Who?"

Zavery consulted his notes. "Sofia Black, a surgical nurse and Tad Ryder. Tad is her communications director."

"I know of Sofia, but not Ryder," said Sligo. "No matter." He turned again to Wolfe and McLeod. "Why don't we get a meal so we're ready for tomorrow?" he said. "You can both bunk in our guests rooms here for the night."

"Works for me," said McLeod

Chapter Twenty Three

"I have mixed feelings about this," said Wolfe to McLeod. They were in their shared quarters that night, preparing for their trip to Hemod.

"I hear you, "McLeod said.

Wolfe looked at McLeod, even more serious than usual. "What I really don't know yet," she began, "is how much we can trust Lou and Zavery, and of course we haven't even met their other contacts on Hemod yet."

"True," McLeod responded. "Though I also don't have enough information *not* to trust them."

"Agreed," Wolfe replied. "But we're just so far out of our element here, I don't have nearly as much to go on, and that's what bugs me."

They were quiet for a moment, then McLeod asked, "So what can we do to get past that feeling or to better prepare ourselves?"

"That's the problem, Tucker," Wolfe said. "We really can't. We have to just let things play out, and if I were on a mission that I had the chance to plan, that would be fine." Wolfe shook her head in annoyance. "Perhaps it's just the lack of control that's bothering me."

"Well, that I understand, McLeod said. "Uncertainty is much easier to accept when you have a bigger part in planning your options than we've had." He sat up. "Which reminds me, is there anything we ought to report and if so, to whom before we head to Hemod?"

Wolfe searched on the ceiling for an answer. "I would say no," she said. "We can't be very specific at this point, and we don't know how much of what we're saying is going to people we don't know outside this circle, *or* if we're being watched."

McLeod hadn't thought of that. "So since we're sort of at their mercy, I guess the primary thing we need to do is to rely on each other first and foremost."

"In other words, business as usual," Wolfe said, smiling. She turned to her friend. "You'll get the hang of this covert stuff in no time."

Tired, they prepared their racks and went to sleep.

* * *

As they arose the next morning, McLeod was repacking his gear for the trip to Hemod, not knowing if would need all he carried from the station or not.

"Do you have everything you need?" he asked.

"If you mean everything," Wolfe replied "the answer is pretty much yes. What I don't know at this point is how we'll be received on Hemod."

McLeod nodded slowly. "I know what you mean," he said. He turned to his friend. "I can't say I'm too anxious, though there are more unknowns now than a couple of days ago."

"Exactly." Wolfe paused then added, "Do you think things might get… challenging?" McLeod answered by reaching into the side pocket of his gear bag, and pulling out a small wooden tool, straight, about 6 inches in length with rounded expanded ends.

McLeod held it up. "Did you bring yours?"

Wolfe gave him a smirk, and reached into her pocket producing what at first glance seemed to be a heavy-looking pen.

"A little more stylized than yours, but effective," she said. "Plus, I have more little innocuous items like this."

"You and me both," McLeod said.

"So," Wolfe continued, "for close quarter and hand to hand -- if it comes to that, we're covered." She closed her bag, and moved toward the door.

"Coming?"

They walked down the short hallway to the conference room to find Zavery and Sligo already seated, eating breakfast. They were sitting with another man: young, with very short light colored hair, and languid.

Sligo rose as they entered the room. "Captains," he said. "Good morning." Turning to their new companion, Sligo said, "This is Decker Templeton. He will be taking us to Hemod today."

"Great," said Wolfe.

McLeod quickly extended his hand to Templeton. "Pilot?" he said to Templeton.

The younger man nodded. "I am, Captain," he said.

"Tucker."

"Deck." Templeton turned toward Wolfe, who was still unsure. "Though I know you're a pilot of some renown, Captain. I just may have a bit more local knowledge around the Twin Worlds."

"Understood, Wolfe said. "And it's good to meet you. My name is Raina." She shook his hand again. The tension lowered, Sligo and Templeton sat down, allowing McLeod, Wolfe, and Zavery to get food.

Once they were seated with food and drink, Sligo spoke again, facing Wolfe. "Again, Captains, I can assure you that our contacts on Hemod should be very helpful to our cause," Sligo said. "And they fully understand the need for discretion."

"I appreciate that, Lou," said Wolfe. "Thank you."

McLeod then turned to Templeton. "Where's your ship?"

"She is only a few mets from here at the south terminal, Captain," he said. "I usually haul freight and supplies throughout the Twin Worlds, including at the nexus station: I don't go as far as the junction though, since my range is too small."

"Capacity? asked Wolfe.

"200,000 gara-tons, so, not big but not the smallest." Templeton said.

"So, 4 and 2?" Wolfe asked.

"Actually, 4, 2 and 1, but you probably assumed that." Wolfe smiled at him. "Fortunately, I seldom have to use the upper thruster," Templeton added.

Templeton and McLeod could see Wolfe configuring the ship in her mind. McLeod smiled as he realized she could probably determine engine locations, thrust ratios, and even the quirks of flying it without ever seeing the vessel itself.

"Sounds good," Wolfe said, at last. "So, what are you telling your crew?"

"A good point," interrupted Sligo. "Deck and I have agreed that we will simply accompany him as interested observers and passengers on one of his supply runs for a small manufacturing plant near Su'gan. That makes the whole process much easier, and prevents us doing something out of place to draw attention to ourselves." Wolfe and McLeod nodded their approval and understanding.

They returned their attention to Sligo. "What is the overall plan, then?" McLeod asked.

Sligo responded quickly. "Decker's scheduled departure is in three hours, which gives us plenty of time for discussion. Once we lift off, we should be on the ground in another," Sligo looked to Templeton, " three hours?" Templeton nodded, so Sligo continued. "I contacted

Miranda Fisher, and she will meet us once we arrive. She's an old friend, and has also worked in the past with Anton. Since she knows of my work with him, I believe she can figure out the true reason I contacted her..." He paused "She also knows I am bringing companions, but not who." He smiled. "I am sure she will be surprised to see two starship captains with us." McLeod raised his eyebrows. Sligo was quick to respond to McLeod's silent question. "But I am equally sure she will not object," he said. "Miranda is pretty easy going, in my experience."

"So," said McLeod, "What can you tell me about unionist activity on Hemod from your perspective, Deck? And, what kind of work did you do with Anton Jurgan?"

Templeton was somewhat surprised at the question. "Oh," he said. "I wasn't… Actually, I haven't worked with him much at all. I have worked some with Miranda Fisher, and participated in some demonstrations, but I've been pretty low key." He seemed to be getting more comfortable as he spoke.

McLeod continued. "What is the sense on the ground on Hemod about the kidnapping -- again, from your having been there recently?"

Templeton shook his head as he answered. "I haven't heard much of anything at all, probably because the authorities just assume they already know the guilty person."

Wolfe leaned forward, "And how responsive and organized will our contacts be once we arrive?" she asked. "Where can we go, how will we get there, all those logistics?"

Sligo was quick to answer. "I've charged Miranda with helping to make that happen," he said. Continuing quickly, he added. "I trust Miranda with making the right contacts to the right people at the right time, so we should have…" he paused, "…minimal exposure and danger." He noticed some hesitation on both McLeod's and Wolfe's faces. "Captains" he asked, How can we allay more of your concerns?"

Templeton stood as Sligo finished speaking. "If you will all excuse me," he said. "I need to get back to the ship." Smiling at each in turn, he added, "see you then."

Following Templeton's departure, McLeod responded to Sligo's question. "Every day or hour we delay will make it harder and harder for us to get the information we're seeking," said McLeod. "I think we all agreed on that last night. Why don't we take advantage of the time we have now to edit our questions, so we don't waste any time on Hemod?"

McLeod noticed Wolfe's general approval. "Before you answer, Lou, I definitely agree with Tucker's approach," Wolfe said. "What I'm anxious about is who we're going to be meeting, to see if we are in danger of being targeted." She looked around the table. "I don't know any of their backgrounds, and where you have all the advantage over Tucker and me is local knowledge and familiarity with the people we're likely to be talking to, or at least coordinating with. However, as someone who has worked behind the scenes on covert operations in the past, we really have to know the right details to make this kind of operation work, especially in the extremely short time available." As she spoke, she saw both Sligo and Zavery nodding.

"Good," Sligo said. "Let's use our time wisely here."

Chapter Twenty Four

McLeod, Wolfe, Sligo and Zavery carried their bags down to the street in front of the Unionist offices.   They left the building, and then took a second elevator to an underground level. Sligo led them down a short passageway to a small groundcar. Keying in his code, he opened the rear hatch, and McLeod loaded their bags. Sligo then closed the hatch and followed Wolfe and Sligo into the groundcar. Sligo keyed in the destination, and the groundcar came to life. McLeod looked around him at the vehicle's appointments.

"Rather impressive, having your own groundcar -- especially for a union boss," said McLeod.

Sligo chuckled. "I always thought so too -- until I became a union boss and needed to come and go far more frequently than I could waiting for cabs." Sligo turned to McLeod. "Apparently, this is what we're *supposed* to do." He returned his gaze to the road ahead.

"I should tell you both that Decker is a reliable and very smart pilot." Something in his tone alerted both McLeod and Wolfe.

"And...?" asked Wolfe.

Sligo sighed. "And...Deck is a bit of a rogue. He has been known to take on jobs without asking many questions." He turned to McLeod and Wolfe, looking serious. "But I do trust him, and that's why he was the one I called." Sligo's manner and confidence was convincing.

"Fair enough," Wolfe said. They sat in silence as they continued to the station. They saw some directional signs as they neared the station, and Sligo turned down a smaller street to stow his groundcar. For a moment, McLeod wondered why he didn't use an area closer to the station, but realized that Sligo probably didn't want anyone planet-side knowing that he was traveling. McLeod also noticed that Sligo had taken some pains to dress very simply and in a somewhat rumpled manner, which it also occurred to McLeod, may be truly reflective of his style, given his long career in the mines. Perhaps the union leader persona is less of who Lou Sligo really is than a strong, proud miner.

They stowed the groundcar, removed their bags, and walked the few blocks to the employee entrance for the private terminal. They were not challenged as they entered, despite the presence of security personnel. Once inside, they walked directly to an outside elevator that took ships crews to the loading areas. Sligo checked signs on a few of the passageways, then turned right. They passed three other vessels being loaded or docked before they saw Decker Templeton. He smiled as he saw Sligo approach.

"Lou," he said, extending his hand. Sligo took it, then Templeton greeted McLeod, Wolfe and Zavery. He turned toward the hatch to his left.

"Here she is," Templeton said. *Siren.*" His pride was obvious. Returning his gaze to the group, he added, "Let me show you around." Templeton led the way through the hatch, and through a large passageway that McLeod thought might be used for loading certain kinds of cargo. He wondered where larger items might be loaded, but shook that off as he followed Templeton, Sligo, Zavery and Wolfe onto the ship. He felt rather than saw the relative size of the ship. He thought it would likely be equivalent in size to an Excursion class Alliance vessel, which for their purposes would have a base crew of about 40-50. McLeod reflected that if you were primarily hauling freight, and don't have to worry about defensive weapons stores and significant life support, a vessel like *Siren* could be crewed by far fewer personnel. As he walked, McLeod could tell that Wolfe was evaluating the ship much as he was. "Can't take the captain out of the woman or the man," he thought to himself.

Templeton stopped and as he did, McLeod noticed a small crew lounge aft of a bulkhead.

"Home sweet home," Templeton said.

After quickly examining their cabin, McLeod turned to Templeton, "Where's the nearest head?" he asked. Templeton pulled him aside and pointed down a different passageway. "Right down there on

your right; I was going to let everyone know about them but you
beat me to it. Ladies is down that way as well.

"Great," McLeod said. "Should I wait to go until you orient us?"

Templeton laughed. "Since you've already figured out half the ship
by yourself, Tucker, you don't have to wait for me." McLeod
smiled and went down the passageway. He turned into the head,
thinking to himself that it was just as utilitarian as he thought it
would be and once he washed and dried his hands he left, but heard a
sound from the opposite direction. Ever curious, he followed the
sound to a small door that was ajar and flapping back and forth
hitting the latch. He took hold of the door to close it, but first looked
inside. His eyes widened, as he saw a large cache of hand held
weapons. His examination of the small storage area took perhaps
three or four seconds, and he was closing the door when he heard a
sound behind him.

"Looking for something?" The voice was dark and sounded mean.

McLeod put on his most cordial face, as he turned to face the man
attached to the voice. "Nope. Just latching a door," he said. The
man in front of him was a few inches taller than McLeod, and
obviously very powerful. "Those kinds of sounds just drive me
crazy, you know? I'm Tucker McLeod," he said, as he extended his
hand.

"I know who you are," the man said. He gestured with his head
toward the crew area where McLeod's companions were
congregating. "I think your friends are looking for you," the man
said, and he stood fixed to the spot as McLeod nodded and smiling,
returned to the lounge. Once there, he mixed cordially with his
colleagues, occasionally glancing toward Wolfe and raising his
eyebrows indicating that he had something to tell her.

"Deck, what's the plan for loading and taking off toward Hemod?"
McLeod asked.

"We have about another half hour of checks before we're in the queue, Templeton said quickly. "We've been loaded for about an hour and a half."

McLeod nodded. "And our seats?"

"Two cabins forward of here," Templeton indicated the direction with his thumb. I'll have one of the crew take you there when it's time -- it's a lot less comfortable than this lounge, though."

"Thanks," said McLeod, looking around. "And you're probably right."

"So," said Templeton. "If there is anything you need, feel free to use the com, and ask." He left to a chorus of thank yous from the group and returned to his duties. McLeod rejoined the other team members in the lounge, sitting toward the edge of the room next to Wolfe, who only looked at him expectantly.

McLeod was relaxed as he turned to her. "Weapons," he said quietly. Wolfe's eyes widened briefly before she regained control.

She was quite cool as she asked. "Where, and what?"

"What I saw were a cache of A-9s and plasma rifles -- perhaps twenty of each," McLeod said casually. He glanced over at this companions, who were all occupied before returning his attention to Wolfe. "They're in a storage bin aft of the men's head." He pointed with his head in the proper direction.

Wolfe nodded. "More?"

"I wouldn't be surprised," McLeod answered. "I haven't quite figured out..." He turned to Wolfe. "Best guess -- how big is the crew on this ship?"

Wolfe frowned, then thought for moment. "Well," she began, "I was thinking this is about the size of a Luwen Class Federation vessel or an Excursion class..." she stopped when she noticed McLeod smiling.

"What?" she asked.

"Nothing," he said. "Kind of a 'great minds' thing. Go on."

"Well, given that they have freight where we would have stores, weapons, etc., I would guess maybe twelve to fifteen crew."

McLeod had been thinking more, but deferred to her superior knowledge. "So maybe no more hand weapons, but they would need a lot more ammunition than I saw." He leaned closer to Wolfe.

"You know, I'm not exactly worried about the weapons, given what Lou said about Templeton," McLeod said, "but I met up with a mountain of a man who saw me close the door of the cache, and he didn't look very savory to me.

"Smuggling, or worse?" Wolfe asked.

McLeod shrugged. "Can't say. Let's just be on our guard."

Wolfe looked at their companions and got a chill. She indicated them with a flick of her head. "Think they're up to it?"

"I certainly hope so," McLeod answered. They broke from their private conversion, and reengaged with Sligo and Zavery.

Soon the man who McLeod had encountered earlier -- with a slightly more approachable demeanor -- came to the lounge to escort the team to their seats for lift off. As they were secured in their seats, McLeod saw the faces of his companions and smiled slightly. He reflected that few if any of them were accustomed to vessels like this where no one cared about creature comforts. Yet they soldiered on, which impressed McLeod. Apparently, they were ready for the next phase of their operation and McLeod, with some growing concerns was hoping he was, too.

Chapter Twenty Five

Su'gan, Hemod, Primary Space Docs, Freight Entry Station

The flight itself was uneventful and McLeod was impressed with Templeton's helmsman. Upon arriving, *Siren* first had to go through customs and inspections before having their cargo unloaded. It was during the unloading process that the team grabbed their gear and disembarked. Templeton led the way, leaving his staff in charge.

As on Herai, they were in the freight and employee area of the station. Templeton briefly conferred with Sligo, and led the way to a small crew ready area. Once they entered, Sligo took the lead and walked straight up to a smiling woman of about fifty with auburn hair.

Sligo embraced her. "Miranda," he said, "It's been a while.

"It has," Fisher replied. She turned to look at the rest of the group. "I've met Benno before but please introduce me to your team."

Sligo smiled as he turned to his companions, pointing to each. "Captain Raina Wolfe of the Central Federation, and Captain Tucker McLeod of the Star Alliance." Sligo indicated each person with his hand, and they each nodded to Miranda Fisher in turn. Sligo turned to Templeton. "And do you know Decker Templeton?"

Fisher greeted each person in turn briefly, then introduced her companion. "This is Tad Ryder. Tad works in communications for the union here on Hemod. He used to be an investigative reporter, so he still has lots of contacts both with the police and among vid and news people." A smart choice, McLeod thought. Ryder was a man of average height, with longish dark hair and the air of someone with tremendous creativity and energy. "And this is Sofia Black, from our med union: she's a surgical nurse," Fisher continued. "Sofia worked with Anton for a short while in their efforts to organize more medical workers. We have a ground transport waiting to take us to our offices where we can talk." She noticed that people already had their luggage and added, "Does anyone need to stop before we go?" No one did, and they started toward the ground transport exits.

McLeod and Wolfe walked toward the rear of the group, quietly assessing their surroundings.

Wolfe spoke first. "Anything?"

McLeod shook his head. "No, or should I say not yet?" McLeod was often quite comfortable on different planets because of his extensive travel and interest in cultures. In this case, however, that interest had a sharp edge to it, and he sensed he was more wary than usual.

"I hear you," said Wolfe. McLeod and Wolfe followed Fisher, Ryder and Black out of the rather simple terminal, and Fisher first looked around, then pointed to a groundvan approaching the door.

"That's it," she said. Looking at the group, she asked, "Ready?"

Zavery responded by approaching Fisher, holding his stomach and looking rather distressed.
"Hey, Miranda?" he began, "If I could just head inside, it would be a good thing."

Fisher smiled. "Sure, the men's is near where we first met and to," she turned her body to face the incoming docks then pointed, "the right. And don't worry, we have time."

Zavery mumbled out an embarrassed, "Thanks," then quickly made his way to the men's. The rest of the group smiled, but said nothing, understanding that it could be them having discomfort on their return flight. They brought their bags to the rear of the groundcar and McLeod turned back to survey the entire building. As his eyes lowered from the roof, he peered inside and saw Zavery standing close to the man who caught McLeod looking at the weapons. He saw Zavery point toward the groundvan, and the man nod. Then they split up. McLeod frowned, and wondered if what he saw was innocent or not, something he would discuss with Wolfe when he could. Soon, Zavery returned, and the groundvan began moving toward the Unionist offices.

"So," asked McLeod, "how close to Su'gan are we going?"

"The offices are on the outskirts of Su'gan, so we can be close to the manufacturing and business areas where we tend to organize most of our workers," Fisher said. "We have satellite offices in other areas of the planet and in all major cities, but on Hemod, the action is almost always in Su'gan."

McLeod nodded. "Miranda has an incredible organization," said Sligo. "While we are much stronger on Herai by heritage and longevity, Miranda has made tremendous strides in organizing workers and professionals on Hemod. I truly believe the Unionist cause is just beginning to blossom on Hemod due to her leadership."

Fisher smiled. "Thank you, Lou -- I learned from the best." The implication that "the best" was Sligo was understood. They soon entered a metropolitan area that McLeod assumed was Su'gan. He was rather enjoying looking at the buildings and groups of people, when the groundvan stopped at a squat row of gray buildings. Fisher and Ryder left the groundvan first, opening the rear hatch so the group could retrieve their luggage. They then led the way into the building and past the security personnel. Wolfe caught McLeod's eyes as she saw the number of surveillance cams in front of them. He allowed his eyebrows to raise just enough to show that he understood her reaction.

Fisher led them into the formal offices, and introduced them to her assistant, Latifa Stew'art, a woman of about average height who immediately locked eyes with Templeton. Templeton responded in kind, though subtly enough that no one not looking for it would have noticed. McLeod rolled his eyes for Wolfe to see and she smiled. Fisher led them into a conference room, and after asking her assistant if she would help them with coffee and tea, she turned more serious.

"Tad has been speaking with his vid and news sources trying to get more information on what the authorities know, think they know, or want everyone to know." All nodded. Fisher got quiet for a moment, then turned to the group and said, "but before we get started, I'd like to show you something."

Fisher led the way down the hallway to her office, and opened the door, turning to face the group to see their reaction. She was not disappointed. As she looked again into her office, she was struck anew by the disarray left by the Hemodian authorities. "This is simply the last office to be cleaned up," Fisher began. "All of our offices looked like this two days ago." She turned without a word and walked back to the conference room. After everyone was seated, she said, "and the truly appalling thing is that this entire search -- supposedly to find information about Anton -- was perfunctory. They didn't spend much time looking, just making a mess to show that they could." The anger in her voice was clear.

"Which means?" asked McLeod.

"Do you really need to ask that, Captain?" asked Ryder.

"Please," said McLeod. "I'm just as happy to go with first names."

"Fine with me," Ryder replied with a smile. "To continue, I think the authorities were putting on a show for the news services. If not, they would have looked far more thoroughly for information." Ryder looked up defiantly. "And even their questioning of us didn't take more than thirty minutes."

"Because they already know the answers?" McLeod asked, then added, "or do you think the Hemodian authorities are themselves behind the whole mess?"

Fisher sat back in her chair as though confused. She slowly shook her head. "I don't think so, Captain," she said. "While the authorities are not our friend, this kind of action is simply not their style. Plus, what would be the government's motive?"

"To discredit the movement!" shouted Black, who had until then been quiet.

"Do you really think they would go that far," asked Wolfe. "I mean, is kidnapping something the government has ever done before?"

She was surprised when Black turned on her with a glare. "You have no idea what they're capable of!" she said. "But I suppose I shouldn't expect any more understanding from you."

As her voice trailed off, Wolfe's eyes narrowed, then with an effort, she relaxed her voice and face. "So," she began quietly, "what evidence does the union have of this possible conspiracy?"

Quickly, Fisher said, "None, Captain. And to be honest, the jury is out on whether the government is doing this or not." Fisher sighed. "We only know that their examination of our offices probably yielded nothing, and very little of what we've heard from the news and vid sources is helpful either."

"I may be out of the loop on this, Miranda," said Sligo. "but have they been able to identify more connections to Anton to strengthen their case?"

To this, Ryder chuckled. "Hardly," he said. "Kind of difficult to find something that isn't there after all."

Sligo shook his head sadly. "Not in my experience," he said.

Just then, Stew'art reentered the conference room with their refreshments.

"Let me change this for a bit," said Zavery. "Has anybody checked out any of Anton's haunts here on Hemod? I mean, do we know that he's not in hiding somewhere? If we could get to him, maybe we could begin unravelling this mess."

"If only we could," said Fisher. "Those few places Anton was known to frequent have been checked out by everybody: the authorities, us, some of our informants -- there's no one left."

"That doesn't leave us much in the way of starting points," McLeod said.

Sligo frowned. "Unless we can look into other groups that might have it in for either Patt'son or the negotiations."

At this Fisher sat forward again. "Yes, Lou, you said something about that earlier. What do you mean exactly?"

Sligo took a deep breath, and began recounting the discussion on Herai regarding radical groups other than the union which might have kidnapped Patt'son's daughter, whether they opposed the Twin Worlds negotiations or Patt'son himself.

As he repeated his conversation the previous day with Sandio Milan, Black bristled again. "Their whole movement is suspect, and you just believed everything he said to you?" she said. "Do you really trust him that much?"

Sligo turned his gaze sharply to Black. "I do, and that trust comes from knowing him for over twenty years. You, on the other hand, I met an hour and a half ago." Without waiting for answer, or in fact allowing one, Sligo continued. "We also have to take into account that the environmental movement isn't nearly as active here on Hemod -- they just don't have the personnel to pull something like this off."

"To say nothing of the fact," added Fisher, "that they are no more likely to use this kind of violence than we are, Sofia." She softened her gaze on the younger woman. "We should guard against jumping so quickly to attack movements other than our own." She turned her attention to Ryder. "Tad, maybe you should review what we have discovered during our own investigation.

Ryder clear this throat. "What I think we know is that very little specific information has been given to news and vid sources," he began. "What the authorities have been saying is that they have forensic evidence at the crime scene that points directly to Anton. They've said things such as 'links to past crimes,' and 'forensic indicators,' and lots of stuff like that which they usually talk about with all crimes, but they're not giving any specifics on what they've found. So, while it sounds like they have an easy and clear case, they're not doing what they usually do." He noticed movement in the group, and quickly added "And when pressed on that by a number of my friends, they were told that to reveal any of those specifics could put additional people in danger. So, very hush-hush, and they're putting out the sense that they are not revealing things to prevent additional acts like this from happening." Ryder chuckled. "And that, despite the excellent work my boss has done, is exactly what the average Hemodian believes."

"How about among your sources," Wolfe asked. "You mentioned your informants -- are they buying it?"

Ryder shrugged. "Most are not, but they don't have much else to go on," Ryder said. "Some have asked questions, mostly of us, but since they can't reconcile anything or investigate any threads, most have gone on to other stories."

"Where does that leave us," McLeod asked. "Do we have anything to go on that your friends haven't yet looked into?"

"What *we* have a better understanding of is how Anton actually works, and the kinds of things he does regularly," Fisher said. "Plus we believe him to be innocent, though pretty much no one agrees with us. I frankly don't know where else we can look for answers."

Wolfe sat back in her chair, obviously lost in thought. She looked up and was surprised to notice that the conversation has stopped. "Sorry," she said. "It just seems like we're spinning our wheels, here -- through no fault of our own, I might add."

Ryder opened his hands. "I'm open to anything else you'd suggest, Captain," he said.

"Raina," Wolfe replied with a smile.

"Right. Raina," Ryder repeated. "But I certainly don't have any new ideas."

"Wait," McLeod said. "Let me try this," he said as he leaned forward. "We've been focusing more on who has it in for Patt'son, or what he stands for. What we've spent less time on is on identifying people or organizations that oppose the current Twin Worlds negotiations." McLeod looked around the table. "Tell me honestly," he said, "what is your general feeling about these negotiations -- do you support them oppose them, what?" He looked to several of the group in turn hoping to provoke a reaction.

"You're not going to like my answer," said Sligo. McLeod shrugged slightly. "My personal view," continued Sligo," is that we as Twin Worlds need to focus on our own problems without involving the Central Federation or the Star Alliance, and I certainly don't support membership in the Federation."

"Why is that?" asked Wolfe. Seeing Sligo's reaction, she added, "really Lou: what is it about joining the Federation that you oppose?"

"Well, just one factor is that if we were to join the Federation, we might have to conscript young people into their military to fight in worlds far from home -- that just doesn't sit well with me. I only support a purely voluntary military force. And let's be honest, it wouldn't be the children of the rich and powerful serving on Federation starships -- it would only be the families of the working class."

"I can understand that," said McLeod. "Any other reasons?"

"That's easy," said Black. "The more money we need to spend to join your Federation club, the less we have to provide a living wage for workers on planet. I doubt you'll find any working families that fully support Federation membership."

Wolfe thought for a moment. "And let me suggest that the environmental groups like PlanetSafe might oppose the negotiations or Federation membership, since that's what we keep talking about -- because any increase in production to fund a growing military would harm the environment; does that sound about right to you all?"

"It sounds about right to me," Ryder replied. He looked to his Unionist colleagues and saw general agreement. Ryder turned around toward Wolfe, but McLeod spoke instead.

"All this tells us that your two movements oppose either the general negotiations, or" he glanced at Wolfe, "that dreaded Federation membership." He sighed. "What this doesn't tell us is other people or groups that opposed the negotiations."

"Such as?" asked Fisher.

"Oh, I don't know," McLeod replied. "Maybe business groups, professional organizations, maybe the news and vid services themselves. Maybe it's the military of one or both of the planets. Does any of this sound plausible to you?" He looked around the table impatiently.

"Well?" he prompted.

"It's not that we object, Captain," Fisher responded.

"Just Tucker is fine, Miranda," McLeod replied.

"Well, Tucker," Fisher continued. "We, or at least I, haven't thought about it from that angle before. Though having said that, I still don't know who or what group would kidnap someone over a negotiation."

Sligo humphed. "It's a little bit more than that, Miranda," he said. "These negotiations could change life on the Twin Worlds significantly, and any person or group opposed to radical change might be upset by the negotiations."

Wolfe glanced at McLeod, and sensing his frustration, said, "Here's a question: what kind of violence or direct action has been taken against the government for anything in the last year? Think about yourselves, environmentalists, maybe youth groups, ethnic issues…"

Fisher let out a breath. "The Caprist Alliance," she said, quietly. Sligo, Ryder and Black turned immediately to her.

"Exactly," said Ryder.

"You've lost me," said McLeod.

To this, Sligo chuckled. "It is the ultimate irony, Captain," he said. "That virtually anything that gives additional support to the environment, or to the working man or woman spawns a backlash among the most radical Caprists on the Twin Worlds." He shook his head. "The Hemodian Council proposed a new health plan a year or so ago which would have strengthened coverage for younger people, and the reaction among these people was explosive."

"It was a crime," Black said. "The entire proposal was for the health of young people, but these people called for all kinds of action against the councilors, and since no one knows exactly who they are, the councilors backed down -- they were afraid of being targeted."

McLeod sighed and drummed his fingers. "And none of you thought to mention this group to us until *now*?"

Sligo spread his arms. "To be honest, Captain," he said, "we have been so focused on Anton and defending our movement, that we did not think of them."

McLeod nodded, saying, "I suppose I can understand, that Lou. But can we try to think outside of this box now?" McLeod extended his hand, to soften his statement. "Our time is running out, and I think we need to pull out all the stops right here and now."

Sligo glanced at Fisher, who said, "A good approach, Tucker. Who wants to start?

* * *

"So," began Wolfe, "what can you tell us about these militant Caprists?"

Fisher looked to her colleagues, then sighed and began. "Captains, Caprist philosophy, that of profit and free market at all costs, is often at odds with our concerns for workers and their safety and prosperity."

Black snarled. "That's an understatement. They try to undo even the smallest advances we've been able to make, and they are as violent as the authorities say we are, yet nothing seems to be able to stop them."

"Perhaps because whoever they are, they have the wealth to target those who oppose them," offered Ryder."

"Who have they opposed?" asked McLeod.

Black closed her hands into fists. "When the health plan was proposed, they spoke out against the head of the governing council. And after they warned him, they set fire to one of his business buildings. The fire was big enough that not only his building, but three others were destroyed." She looked up." And that put a lot of people out of work."

"I remember that," added Zavery. "I think some other members of the council asked for a second reading of the proposal, and it was put on indefinite hold." He smirked. "That got the head of the council off the hook so he could save face, but it was pretty clear what happened. These guys seem to be untouchable."

"And nobody knows who they are?" asked Wolfe.

"No," Ryder replied. "Though I can tell you that if any government folks get ahold of one of them it won't be pretty; the reaction against them would likely be incredibly nasty."

"And these Caprists wouldn't take revenge against them for that?" Wolfe asked.

"Probably," said Zavery, "though I think the council is so ticked that they'll shoot first and ask questions later."

"And they don't usually take direct action against people or their families; I mean, they don't attack or shoot people?"

Sligo shook his head. "I know you've heard it before, Tucker, but we just don't do that on the Twin Worlds, and they haven't either."

McLeod scratched his head. "So why would the Caprists -- militant or otherwise -- feel the need to oppose the negotiations? If the Twin words were to develop stronger ties, is there some reason to believe that would hurt the free market on either planet?"

"Caprists on the Twin Worlds are very conservative, Captain," Ryder said. "They would say that any significant change in government can cause instability in financial markets, which leads potentially to lower profits."

"And is that what they've been saying?" asked Wolfe.

Ryder squinted. "They haven't been saying anything about this," he said. "I can only tell you that if they were to speak out against the talks, a lot of government officials would get nervous.

"Including Patt'son?" asked McLeod.

"Sure," said Ryder. "I mean, Patt'son is a Caprist himself, but none of the moderate guys is safe from the militants."

Black shook her head. "We shouldn't assume they wouldn't hurt Patt'son just because of that; they've done violent things before and maybe they just decided to cross the line this time."

Curious, Wolfe asked, "and why would they do it now?"

"You just don't know what these people are capable of Captain," Black replied. Her tone was confrontational, but Wolfe ignored her."

Fisher looked uncomfortable. "I don't think we'll find much here," she said slowly. "I'm confident that neither Patt'son nor his family would be targeted by the more militant Caprists."

"That wasn't the question, Miranda," countered McLeod. "With all due respect." He faced her with a genial smile. "Regardless of our personal feelings about the militant Caprists -- which I'm sure are justified by the way -- many people on the Twin Worlds identify as Caprists, but I'm sure very few are engaging in violence."

Sligo nodded. "I would agree with that," he said. He laughed. "I even have coffee regularly with a number of friendly Caprists, and they would never countenance violence, by them or by us."

"Exactly," McLeod replied. "So it's not Caprists per se that we are opposing, it's these militants." He noted general agreement around the table. "So, just who the hell are they?"

The silence around the table seemed to grow in intensity, until Wolfe couldn't stand it. "Anyone?" she asked. "Doesn't anyone know, and do we think these people would take this action against "Patt'son?"

"Well, there are rumors," Fisher replied.

Wolfe stood up. "I'm afraid rumors aren't going to help us find Jurgan or Patt'son's daughter," she said, sharply. "Can we get past rumors and to hard facts? Or are we just wasting our time talking about Caprists?"

"I believe we should move on," Fisher said, rather quickly.

McLeod frowned, and shot a quick glance at Wolfe before speaking. "I'm all for moving forward with another plan to pursue if we think the Caprist angle won't work." He paused. "But I have to ask, Miranda, why you're so sure there's nothing to follow up on here." He looked kindly, but assertively at Fisher.

Fisher looked down, then put her head into her hands. The group watched her with some concern, waiting until she was ready to speak. Finally, she raised her head and looked wistful. "I probably should have mentioned this earlier, " she said. "But I am confident that the Caprists we're talking about wouldn't attack Patt'son or his family because…" she sighed. "Because he's one of them."

"One of…" Sligo began.

After looking down, Fisher said, "he's one of the militant Caprists, though he doesn't engage in some of their more outrageous acts."

"What *is* it with you people?" McLeod asked before thinking. Controlling himself, he added, "we're all trying to do the right thing here by clearing Anton if possible and doing what we can to help Patt'son's daughter. Can we please put all our cards on the table here?"

Sligo, still surprised by Fisher's statements, asked for calm. "I think Tucker is justified here, Miranda," he said. "And you seem very confident about Patt'son. How is it you know so much?"

"We tapped into some of his communications," Fisher said with an embarrassed smile. "We were concerned about some proposals he had made within the Twin Worlds Coordinating Council and decided we needed to know more about him."

Sligo grunted. "Can't say I blame you, Miranda," he offered. "Though it is rather hard to support the same techniques the authorities use against us.

"We're trying to help people," said Black. "I think that's a real difference between us and them.

"Be that as it may," said McLeod, "Can we *please* stop holding things back? We may not have a great deal of time…."

Just then, Latifa Stew'art opened the conference room door. "Turn on the vid, Miranda," she said "Channel 7: you need to see this."

Fisher turned on her vid, and turned to Channel 7. "… have offered no explanation for the kidnapping other than their demands that the negotiations between our government and Herai's be suspended indefinitely. Authorities have made the return of Moriah Patt'son their top priority, and are asking anyone with information to come forward."

"The authorities have released a redacted recording of the ransom telephone call. What you will hear now is the voice that the authorities say is Anton Jurgan." A picture of Jurgan -- probably from a police station -- was shown on the screen as the very scratchy voice began. "We can no longer stand by while rich politicians give away the birthright of the working man and woman to a safe and prosperous planet. Griffin Patt'son is the embodiment of this level of privilege within our upper classes, and we have no conflict with his daughter. We will be happy to return her safely once the Twin Worlds negotiations have been terminated. This is truly in the hands of Hemodian authorities; we hope they make the right decision. You have forty-eight hours to comply." The voice terminated.

McLeod turned to the Unionists. "Could that have been Anton?"

Sligo turned his head slowly and shrugged. "It's possible, Tucker, but I'm not sure."

Fisher shook herself and turned to Ryder. "Tad, could you contact some of your sources to see if they have any additional information beyond what we just saw on the vid?"

"Sure Miranda," he said. "What are you looking for?"

"I really don't know, Tad," she began. "maybe things like how they received the ransom vid, timing, anything that wasn't just presented to the general public.

Ryder stood, energized. "I'm on it," he said as he approached the door. Looking back over his shoulder, he added, "and if there's anything else you want me to look into, just call me."

After he left, Zavery turned to Sligo. "To be honest, Lou," he said. "It did really sound like Anton."

"It did," Sligo said with a sigh. "Though I am shocked and saddened to admit it."

"Sad or otherwise," McLeod said. "If the Caprist angle isn't the right one, we don't have a lot of time to find another one."

* * *

"Tucker," Wolfe began, "if this is so focused on the negotiations, maybe that's where we ought to start."

McLeod had been thinking the same thing. "Alright then," he said. He turned to face the group. "As you know, Raina and I are serving as staff members for one of the committees for the negotiations, specifically, the committee on military cooperation. That's also the committee Patt'son is serving on. We came planet-side to help get Moriah Patt'son back and to clear Anton Jurgan if he was innocent."

"Our ultimate goal was to help get the negotiations back on track," added Wolfe. "Jurgan Towns, Anton's cousin asked us to help."

"We're saying this," McLeod continued, "so that you know how we came to be here. And since calling off the negotiations seems to be the motivation for whoever kidnapped Moriah, there may be something about the negotiations or maybe about our committee that has sparked the kidnapping."

Wolfe looked grim. "And regardless of who the kidnappers are, we don't have a lot of time to spin our wheels."

"Agreed," said Sligo. "What can we do now?"

"Let's get back to basics," said McLeod. "Who is behind the kidnappers, meaning who benefits from calling off the negotiations, either just for the military cooperation committee, or for the entire negotiation?" He turned back to Wolfe. "Raina, as you think about this, and about the issues our committee was handling, who had more to gain from a stalemate or failure?"

Wolfe paused before answering. "Well, if one of the ultimate goals was full affiliation with the Federation," she began, "that would seem to eliminate Nereze, since she wants greater cooperation between Hemod and Herai *and* Federation membership. Stopping the negotiations would result in neither."

"Zara Nereze?" asked Sligo. Wolfe nodded.

"I would tend to agree with you," Sligo said. "She is strong, honest and very … blunt? No, I believe if she opposed the negotiations, she would do so directly."

Wolfe chuckled. "Yes, blunt might describe her, though my assessment of her matches yours," she said. She turned to the rest of the group. "What we're working on in the committee is finding ways for greater military cooperation between the two planets, including things such as training exercises, maneuvers, and mutual defense. We're also talking about the ways in which Federation worlds support Federation military forces and some of the guidelines for Federation membership as it relates to the military."

"Hah!" said Sligo. "I can just imagine those conversations!"

Wolfe laughed. "Let's just say they were challenging -- and leave it at that, Lou," she said.

"We know that's a lot to understand quickly," said McLeod. "Members of the committee are an interesting mix of military types and bureaucrats who don't have any military background."

Continuing, Wolfe added, "Committee members other than Zereze -- well *all* of them want greater cooperation between Hemodian and Heraian forces in some form. Two seem to want the forces to be combined and two don't but cooperation is supported by everyone: having the negotiations stop now wouldn't serve their needs." She looked up at McLeod, thought for a moment, then spoke. "What about weapons issues?"

McLeod caught her meaning. "A good question." McLeod turned to Sligo and Zavery, "One of the issues we have been struggling with is the insistence of the Hemodian forces on the use of phase weapons, which of course pose a greater danger to the environment because of radiation. You may not know that the Federation strongly discourages the use of phase weapons among its members. Are there people who have a strong interest in the creation of phase weapons on Hemod?" He shook his head to clear it. "No, wrong question. Try this: can you think of someone who has a connection to the manufacture of phase weapons on Hemod who may have been public about their opposition to the negotiations?" From the expression on the faces of both Sligo and Zavery, it was evident to McLeod and Wolfe that their colleagues weren't particularly familiar with phase weapons.

McLeod looked again to Wolfe before returning his gaze to Sligo and Zavery.

"I think we know some of the weapon manufacturers on Hemod, Sligo conceded. "But we," he looked briefly to Zavery for confirmation, "have no idea how involved or vocal they may have been before or during the negotiations."

Wolfe consulted her pad, as both Sligo and Zavery looked at each other and began to mention the names of people and companies within the defense industry on Hemod. Zavery began a news and vid search to see which of the manufacturers had been opposing the negotiations.

"Okay," Zavery began, "We *think* we're interested in companies that produce phase weapons, is that right?" Turning to Wolfe, he added, "do we know which companies on-planet do that?" Wolfe's brow furrowed. She checked her pad, searching through company and individual names.

"One name is Verinox Limited," she said. "It says here that they are authorized to handle all kinds of radiation in their manufacturing, including cells for phase weapons. What I don't know is how invested they are in phase weapons."

"What do you mean by invested?" McLeod asked.

"Invested as in how big a part of their business involves manufacturing phase weapons." Wolfe looked up at Sligo and asked, "Do you know what else they do besides defense?"

"I don't know much about them as a company, or what they do," Sligo said. "We've never done anything with or *to* them if that's what you're implying."

"No, no," Wolfe said. I'm just trying to understand more about their business. If defense is only 10% of their business, say, and phase weapons are only 10% percent of that, then they don't have much incentive to scuttle the military cooperation talks."

Sligo nodded his agreement. "That does make sense," he conceded. "but I still don't have anything to tell you."

McLeod began a second search. "Well, a simple way is to match up corporate directors with the lists we already have of individuals who might benefit from hurting Anton's or the movement's reputations," he said. He was quiet for a moment as his pad conducted the search. While waiting, he turned again to Zavery and Sligo. "Let's get back to the Hemodian connection," McLeod continued. "Since the attack and kidnapping occurred on Hemod, if we were to focus on activities solely on that planet, where would you start?"

"As Lou said before, Captain," Zavery began, "we don't have anyone within the movement who would do such a thing, either on Herai or on Hemod."

McLeod grew impatient. "Benno, that's a given," he said. "What I'm asking you is not would *you*, but who would? What person or company on Hemod would or might be so inclined?" A small light flashed on McLeod's pad. Wolfe reached for it, examined the results, then passed it over the McLeod. After looking at it, he frowned.

"I don't see any familiar names there, McLeod said. "though some have very common Twin Worlds surnames, so that makes it more difficult."

Sligo learned in toward McLeod. "What surnames are you talking about?" he asked.

McLeod shifted his pad so Sligo could see it. He pointed to the screen. "Like here, we have a Ryen, a Grippin, a Ward'on." He scrolled down. "And here are a couple of Ja'fars, and a Vandren - I mean, the last thing we want to do, I think, is to assume that every Vandren is related to this one, and therefore a potential criminal."

Sligo agreed. "You have done your research, Captain," he said. "To know that these are indeed common surnames on the Twin Worlds means you have studied us far more than I thought you did." He bowed ever so slightly. "I am impressed."

"I'd rather that we were making actual progress, rather than puffing Tucker up any more," Wolfe said.

Sligo picked up on Wolfe's tone. "Of course, Captain," he said, "And I agree with you."

McLeod turned to Sligo again. "So what do any of us know about some of these names from Verinox Limited?"

I've accessed the annual report of Verinox," Wolfe said, "and it says they are the leading manufacturer of phase weapons technology and materiel for Hemod, Herai, and another planetary system."

"I imagine that would be Savien, said Sligo.

"Correct," said Wolfe. "And it looks as though phase weapons represent 35% of their overall business.

McLeod whistled. "That does sound like a substantial portion of their business," he said. "How many other companies produce phase weapons on Hemod or Herai?" He assumed she would have to search before answering, but instead she responded immediately.

"Five others," Wolfe said. "And while they each have smaller pieces of the overall pie, phase weapons represent a major part of all their businesses."

"Do you have the names of some of their directors?"

Wolfe nodded and quickly responded, "And some of the names sound like the ones from before."

"Not the same people?" Zavery asked.

"I doubt it, but some of the surnames are similar, though they may be just common names on the Twin Worlds." Wolfe sat back in her chair. "I think all of us need to search these names to determine what their individual interests are, or perhaps their connection with other movements, such as the governmental council on Hemod."

"Raina, I agree," said Sligo. "Can you send the names to all of us? Perhaps each of us can take one company and dig enough to uncover any connections."

"That's one way," said McLeod. "But we may need to go over these together, since it's possible we'll ignore a connection if we don't collaborate on it."

Without speaking, Fisher pressed a button on the table. A large vid screen lowered on the far wall and began to twinkle.

"We can put the information from all our pads in separate sectors of the vid," said Fisher. "That way, we may be able to see some of the connections."

"A good idea," said Wolfe. "I'll send each of you data on one of the companies. I'll retain data on all five to see what I can find from that level, and look at vid archives about the companies."

"Good," said McLeod. "Let's get started." Within minutes, data streamed to each of their pads and the five began their work in earnest. McLeod and Wolfe sat next to each other, working silently. Eventually, McLeod looked up and touched Wolfe's arm. He moved his eyes furtively around the room, indicating their companions, then raised his eyebrows.

Wolfe was quiet in her response. "Some very odd dynamics," she said. "We can talk later."

"Yes."

About an hour later, and after a few isolated questions and answers around the room, Wolfe asked how far people had come in learning more about the companies.

"What do we think we have?" she asked. She saw a slight resentment in Black's face but chose to ignore it.

"Hard to say, Raina," said McLeod. "It does seem as though each of these companies has a strong vested interest in at least maintaining their production level of phase weapons."

Agreed," said Zavery. "But are there any connections, perhaps through the news vids that tie these together? It seems to me that there are no connections or reasons strong enough to lead to a major crime like this. I mean, as companies of this size, couldn't they just put pressure on their council representatives like they always do? Why do it this way?"

"Perhaps, Benno, times have changed enough that they think they can't always get what they want with their wealth," said Sligo. He waited for what he thought would be an objection from either McLeod or Wolfe, and seeing none, continued. "Times have changed and continue to change. Bringing in the Federation would be such a large change that perhaps the companies were reluctant to take any chances." The room was silent for a moment.

"Another question," said McLeod, breaking the silence. "How much of a presence do these companies have on Herai? Since they are all based on Hemod, and that's where the kidnapping took place, we may need to travel there."

"Okay," said Wolfe. "Let's see where these companies are located." She strode to the vid. "I can plot the locations of all the companies and their plants, and they tend to be in the same area," she turned from the screen, "probably due to the natural resources there. But the Vice Chair's residence is in Su'gan, the capitol city, perhaps -- it looks like...."

"About ninety mets away," said Zavery.

Wolfe frowned. "Are there any tunnels on Hemod like the ones on Herai?" she asked.

"Some," Zavery said. "They serve much the same purpose, except they are better regulated and there are fewer of them. Your point?"

"Don't have one yet," Wolfe said, "Except I can see how having a network of tunnels -- some active, some not -- would be a great place to hide someone. And since the tunnels are near the companies, if they are the ones behind this kidnapping, wouldn't they likely be using that space?"

"That seems like a leap to me, Captain," Black said.

"It is," Wolfe agreed. "But I'm trying to determine where we can make those leaps -- our answers may not always come to us in a straight line." Turning to Fisher, she asked. "Other than your offices, where would you say your stronghold would be on Hemod?"

"That would be," Fisher began, touching her pad, "about here." The icon lit up on the vid.

"So," said Wolfe, "about 40 mets to the south of the city. Why there?"

"That's where the majority of manufacturing plants and professional areas are located: between there and Su'gan," Fisher said. "We always locate where we can organize our workers most effectively."

As Fisher spoke, Wolfe nodded while McLeod frowned, still struggling to find an answer. "Let's recap," Wolfe said. "One major company that benefits from the ending of negotiations is Verinox -- the leading manufacturer of phase weapons on Hemod. The question I would pose is: might Verinox want to protect their business enough to have someone disrupt the negotiations through a kidnapping, and blame it on the Unionists on planet?" She looked around the table. "That is what we were thinking, correct?" A chorus of yesses.

Fisher raised her head, her eyes squinting. "I agree with you in principle," she said. "Verinox fights our efforts like everyone else, but they haven't been particularly nasty or more difficult than any of these huge corporations -- and I certainly can't think of anything they do that might have involved Anton."

"It doesn't have to involve Anton," McLeod countered. "He just may be a convenient person to point the finger at. If someone else had a more violent past -- yourself, for example, that's the person who would be implicated." More nods around the table.

"So, given that," continued McLeod, "who can we talk to or where can we go to investigate the possible Verinox connection?" He turned to Fisher for the answer.

"That would be me -- or at least I started the discussions and organizing," Fisher said. In all honesty, many of us were involved in that, I mean didn't you attend one of the meetings, Benno?"

"Yep," Zavery said. "That was the initial meeting where we laid out what the law allows us to do so we could at least be sure Verinox knew our rights, but what six, or seven of us attended that meeting?" Fisher nodded. "That's the only one I attended, but who was following up?"

"I don't remember," Fisher said. "Let me see if Latifa can find that information." She left the room to consult with her assistant. She returned in a few minutes with a coffee and tea tray.

"She's working on it now, but I thought we could use this in the meantime." The group reached forward and served themselves while engaging in small talk. McLeod and Wolfe spoke together quietly, each hoping that investigating Verinox would give them the information they needed to clear Anton, or at least get the Twin Worlds negotiations back on track. After about five minutes, "Stew'art returned, indicating that she had sent the requested information to Fisher's pad.

"Thank you, Latifa," Fisher said. "Can you sit with us for a moment as we go through this?" Stew'art nodded and sat next to McLeod, which surprised him until he realized that he was sitting directly across from Templeton. Ryder entered the office right after Stew'art, but chose not to interrupt the proceedings.

Fisher scanned the information sent to her by Stew'art and frowned. "On this list, there are seven people as Benno mentioned. Besides the two of us, there were," she paused. "In all honesty, the usual suspects: for defense companies, the lead is always Elliott Underwood, and he most often works with two others, Davis Harr'gan and Lee Ba'ker. Besides them, our previous communications person attended, as did our general counsel, Kendl Throne." She looked up briefly. "Kendl died a couple of months ago, but he'd been sick for a while. And our communications person Kaitee Lowe took another job -- it's a revolving door job, people tend to move around a lot here."

"That's true," Ryder said. "Lots of us are out there moving from company or organization to another, and then we might get back into news or vid companies. It's very fluid. Oh, and just so you know," he added. "I've got calls out to some of my contacts, but no information as yet."

"Thanks, Tad," said Fisher.

"Getting back to Lowe, was it? How long would you say she worked for you -- could there be any connection she had with Verinox?" Wolfe asked.

"Actually, Kaitee moved back to Herai a few months later, as I recall," said Sligo. "I know her family and I think they had a family crisis, which prompted her job change."

"I do remember that now," said Fisher. "So it looks like our sources closer to Verinox would be Underwood, Harr'gan and Ba'ker." She looked up. "I can contact them now, if you wish."

"I think that would be helpful, Miranda," said Sligo.

Before she could direct Latifa to make any calls, McLeod spoke. "Also, could you tell me the prime contact or contacts at Verinox that you spoke to?"

"That may be a question better posed to Elliott as lead at Verinox, Captain."

McLeod nodded. "Then perhaps I'd better let you make those calls," he said.

Chapter Twenty Six

Su'gan, Hemod Unionist Headquarters, Main Conference Room,

After several calls, Fisher was able to arrange a meeting for that evening with Underwood, Harr'gan and Ba'ker. By that time, the group had enjoyed a working lunch, with the team from Herai laying out their assumptions and speculations and what they had learned through their research. They also shared the information they learned about several of the defense companies, not just Verinox. There was general agreement that the course of action being taken was wise, and that Verinox might yield valuable information regarding Anton or the kidnapping.

"So, where is it we're going this evening?" Sligo asked.

Facing the entire group, Fisher replied, "To a rather quiet restaurant with a conference room. It's commonly known as a gathering place for the union, and we eat and meet there often. So, I think it will be a good place to meet." She looked to both McLeod and Wolfe. "And I think you'll enjoy the food."

Wolfe rolled her eyes, and inclined her head toward McLeod. "That won't be a problem for him," she said. "He finds food he likes in the most unlikely places."

McLeod chuckled. "She's right, so I know I'll enjoy it." He looked up. "Time?"

Fisher quickly checked with Stew'art. Turning back, she said, "1900 hours, which is" she consulted her chron, "about two hours from now. We can take you to our lodge to rest a bit and to freshen up if you wish."

"Sounds great," said both Black and Wolfe.

The group gathered their things and Fisher took them in the groundvan to an inn run by the union. There, they were able to wash up, unwind, and prepare for their dinner meeting. McLeod and

Wolfe were placed in the same quarters, which surprised but didn't bother them. Having shared small spaces on several occasions, they were very comfortable with each other.

"I'm hoping that we will finally get some answers from these conversations, "McLeod said.

Wolfe shrugged. "That's assuming that this entire line of reasoning is correct."

"True," McLeod said. "And I'm certainly hoping it is." He looked toward her. "Any read on the people we met today?"

Wolfe paused before answering. "I sense that Fisher is pretty genuine, as is Ryder," she said. "I didn't get any strange feelings or vibes."

"Me neither," said McLeod. "Though I was a little amused by the antics of Templeton today."

Wolfe laughed. "Rogue was an apt description of him, though in all honesty, I didn't see Stew'art as particularly difficult to approach, if you know what I mean."

"I agree." McLeod said.

* * *

The trip to the restaurant was quick being only a few blocks away from the lodge. Stew'art had come along as a staff resource for Fisher, which seemed to please Templeton no end. They had already been seated when Elliott Underwood, chief union organizer for defense companies arrived, accompanied by Davis Harr'gan and Lee Ba'ker. Underwood was barrel chested, -- obviously a working man. Harr'gan on the other hand, looked like the accountant that they later learned he had been. Ba'ker was a substantial woman, no nonsense but with a wicked sense of humor.

Once they were seated, Underwood played host. "I'm very pleased to meet you, Captain McLeod and Captain Wolfe," said Underwood.

McLeod and Wolfe nodded and smiled. "And welcome to our little hole in the wall but very fine restaurant." He turned to Decker Templeton. "And you, Captain Templeton, this is a rare pleasure. I've heard of you before, but have never had the pleasure."

"Thanks," Templeton said.

Underwood turned to face the entire group again. "We have taken the liberty of ordering a number of traditional Hemodian dishes for tonight so that we can have a productive conversation. I hope that will be okay." Seeing assent all around, Underwood continued. "Miranda, can you give me a sense of what we might accomplish here tonight?"

Fisher nodded and faced the group at the table. "Elliott, we are obviously very concerned about Anton, his reputation and ours, and I believe I can speak for all of us here when I say that we do not believe Anton to be guilty of this kidnapping, and want to find any information that might shift the attention away from him, and frankly from all of us." McLeod wondered who Fisher meant by "all of us," but remained silent.

Underwood gave a small smile as he listened to Fisher. "I don't think we will ever have the attention completely away from us, Miranda," he said, "but your point is well taken. Obviously, you believe that Verinox has something to do with his whole situation, but frankly, I don't see it." He looked this time at Sligo, "How did you come to this conclusion in the first place?"

Before Sligo could answer, Wolfe interrupted. "Lou, may I?"

Sligo nodded.

"Elliott, Tucker and I have been serving as staff to the military cooperation committee for the negotiations taking place between Herai and Hemod, though we serve separately for the Central Federation and the Star Alliance. One of the significant issues that has arisen is phase weapons and how much Hemod would be able to use them in the event of greater cooperation between the planets or if they were to attain Federation membership." Underwood scrunched his face slightly, so Wolfe quickly continued. "There are restrictions on phase weapons that the Federation wants for all its affiliated worlds because of radiation concerns, yet Hemod's military uses them extensively."

"And Verinox is a huge producer of phase weapons," interjected Harr'gan.

"Correct," said Wolfe.

"Kind of a stretch, don't you think?" asked Underwood. His tone was truly questioning, rather than accusatory, so Wolfe responded in kind.

"Hard to say, Elliott," Wolfe said, "We were trying to determine what other motivations there could be for the suspension of negotiations separate from the Unionist movement. For our committee, the biggest sticking point on that committee was phase weapons, which led us to Verinox. So, yes, it *is* a stretch, but it is a thread we felt we had to investigate."

Underwood had listened respectfully, and nodded. "I can see that." His eyebrow furrowed. "What I don't know is what I can tell you. Verinox wasn't any harder or easier to work with when trying to organize workers, and I certainly didn't feel anything extra they put on behind the usual corporate bluster. Davis, Lee?"

Ba'ker who had been listening intently, responded. "I didn't sense anything," she said. "I mean, they're a big corporation, and they want us as far away from their workers as possible, but that's the same with every big company we deal with."

Harr'gan nodded his agreement. "I agree. They were just like everyone else." The table was quiet.

"Let me try to change our tactic here," said McLeod. Let's think not about Verinox by itself, but about the negotiations. What have you all learned from news and vid services about the negotiations?" The question seemed to stump the union leaders, who looked back and forth to each other before Underwood ventured.

"Well, I've heard that the usual differences between the planets is impacting the negotiations." Confusion around the table. "Let me explain," Underwood said. Looking at McLeod and Wolfe, he continued, "You know that Hemod tends to have the larger corporate headquarters and entrepreneurs, and some manufacturing, while the heavier industries including the vast majority of mining and resources are on Herai." Nods around the table. Those differences are reflected in the negotiations: Heraians are concerned about environmental damage and exploitation by Hemod, but also by the Federation. On the other hand, Hemodians are concerned about resources and environmental security and economic expansion possibilities. These are not really in conflict, but given our very long histories, they seem to be." He thought for a moment. "I guess I haven't heard much about military cooperation, except that people are concerned what form it will take and whether either planet would lose elements of its sovereignty - things like that. As for the kinds of weapons either side would have, I'm afraid if I heard what weapons *were* being talked about, it would go in one ear and out the other."

"Understood," said McLeod.

Wolfe had opened and scanned her pad. "What about these other companies?"

"What other companies?" asked Underwood.

Wolfe looked up. "Oh. Sorry. We identified four other companies that produce phase weapons though they are not as large as Verinox. We wondered if you could tell us anything about them.

"If they're defense companies, we should probably know about them." Underwood said.

"The companies," Wolfe began, "are CamaStar, Tamas Holdings, Genesis II, and G3." She looked up and saw Underwood, Harr'gan and Ba'ker stifling smiles.

"What?" Wolfe asked.

"It's nothing, Captain, just a case of 'small man syndrome,'"
Underwood said. Seeing her reaction, he added, "The owner and
CEO of Genesis II is a man by the name of Reb Hollander. He's a
small man in stature, but he's got a lot of bluster. I would even say
he got close to threatening us when we went to visit him to outline
some of the legal issues involved in organizing."

Harr'gan and Ba'ker nodded. "Boy, did he," added Harr'gan. "Kept
saying that no union was going to ruin his business or take his
workers away. We've heard it all before, but this guy seemed really
primed."

Wolfe quickly scanned her pad before asking. "I see that phase
weapons technology accounts for about 20% of his business; did you
get the impression he was looking to expand that?"

"He was looking to expand everything, Captain," said Baker. "My
sense is that this guy wants to be a much larger defense company,
and it doesn't much matter how he gets there. As Elliott said, we
don't really have backgrounds specifically in phase weapons or any
kind of weapons, we just try to organize workers who are in heavy
industry or areas with lots of dangerous exposure; the actual
percentage of certain kinds of weapons isn't something we know
much about."

"Would you think this Hollander is the kind of person who might
actually go so far as to kidnap someone to protect his business?"
asked Sligo.

Underwood looked dubious. "Lou, I've met a lot of ruthless people
in this job, but I don't know anyone I think would commit criminal
acts like this," he said. "Mind you, they are committing criminal
acts with their working conditions, but a kidnapping is very different
from that."

McLeod was direct. "But, if you were to guess, is this Hollander one
of the more ruthless?" he asked.

Again, Elliott pondered before answering. "I would say he is pretty
nasty, and his company means everything to him. I would certainly

say he is one of the most driven and company oriented people I've met, and he would probably do a lot more than some of the others to get what he wants. I don't know if that translates as ruthless, though."

"We should also remember that phase weapons aren't a huge part of his business," said Benno Zavery, who had until then been silent.

"Meaning?" asked McLeod.

"Oh," Zavery began, "Just meaning that we should be careful about going down this new road so quickly. He is still a lot smaller than Verinox; they really have the most to lose."

"That's true," Wolfe admitted. "In the case of a reduction in phase weapons, Hollander and his company would have fewer opportunities to grow: Verinox might lose a core of their business. Yes, it's a very good point." Just then, the first course of food was served, and the group held off further conversation. As the meal came to an end, Fisher took time to summarize where they were.

"Why don't we for the moment focus primarily on these two companies -- Verinox and Genesis II to investigate further?" Fisher asked. All around the table nodded. "So, how should we proceed?"

"I believe we need additional information on both companies through news and vids," Wolfe said. "We're going to need to know their latest transactions, where they may be growing, etc., some things we can't just do at a distance." She looked up at Underwood. "Any possibility we could get in to see some people who wouldn't be too concerned about a visit from a small team of people from the union or the Federation?"

Underwood thought for a moment. "I think so," he began, as he silently consulted his colleagues. "We actually have pretty good relations with many of the people there." He looked to his colleagues. "Davis, can you call your contact in HR at Verinox to chat with her?" Harr'gan nodded. Underwood turned to Ba'ker. "Lee, I think we ought to tread carefully at Genesis II. Who do you think we could talk to who wouldn't be a challenge?"

Ba'ker thought for a moment, but it was Ryder who answered.

"Ordinarily that would be tough, Elliott," Ryder began. "But you may remember I went to school with their new PR coordinator -- my sense is that if a very small group goes to speak with them we'll at least get in the door without causing any undue concerns."

"Tad, can you call her in the morning, then?" asked Underwood. "Maybe get a meeting for the afternoon?"

"Sure," Ryder said, then added "well, then Miranda, will that do for tonight?"

"I think so," Fished replied. "Everyone?" She looked around the table to general nods of agreement. "Great then. Thank you Elliott."

"Don't thank me until we have a result," Underwood said, and smiled.

"Point taken," Fisher said.

Chapter Twenty Seven

Su'gan, Hemod Union Memorial Inn

McLeod and Wolfe returned to their quarters in the lodge by groundvan, maintaining a contemplative silence all the way. As they entered the building, they noticed Templeton on a com.

When he glanced at them, he looked up and smiled. "I have a breakfast date tomorrow with Latifa," he said. Wolfe suppressed the desire to ask if that would be after an all-night tryst. "Right now, I have to get back to my ship to look over the next order for transport," Templeton continued.

Where are you going next?" asked McLeod.

"The same route I usually take -- back and forth between the Twin Worlds. I usually don't go off world except for maybe three or four times a year -- other than to the station of course. It's a good thing I don't get bored easily."

"And your cargo?" Wolfe asked.

Templeton waved his hand as if bored. "Not sure, but I'm pretty sure it will be some finished goods and some heavy equipment that has to go back there -- don't ask -- I never can figure why things don't just stay on-planet." Templeton smiled. " So, when do you believe you'll be going tomorrow?

"Can't say," said McLeod. "I do know that Tad Ryder has to make contact with his friend at Genesis II, probably by early tomorrow. With any luck we might be there," he looked to Wolfe.
"What do you think, Raina -- by around noon?"

Wolfe shrugged. "That seems about right," she said.

Templeton nodded then took up his bag. "Well, I think the right place for me to be is on the ship, so I may see you tomorrow."

As he left, McLeod held up us hand. "You know, this really isn't your battle, Deck," he said.

"I know," Templeton began. "But I don't always get food as good as I had tonight -- I'm happy to spend as much time with you guys as possible regardless of the reason."

Wolfe laughed. "Seldom a home cooked meal?"

Decker shook his head and smiled. "Right. I'm off."

"See you tomorrow, Deck, " said McLeod. Wolfe waved goodbye and Templeton left the lodge with a small bag.

McLeod looked at Wolfe. "Two to one he's…"

"Don't bother, Tucker," said Wolfe. "He obviously wouldn't need to take a bag to head back to his own ship."

"You're probably right," he said.

Wolfe looked up at McLeod. "Do you think we're on the right track?"

McLeod shrugged. "I certainly hope so," he said. "There's an awful lot here to take into account." He checked his chron. "In any case, we can't do anything more tonight, so I'm going to bed."

Wolfe nodded her agreement, and they entered the lodge.

Both McLeod and Wolfe awoke early and each went through separate regimens of quiet dynamic exercise -- enough to wake them up completely and to become limber and ready for the day. After quick showers, they joined the others for a light breakfast in the inn's small private kitchen.

Once they were seated, Ryder came in brimming with excitement. "I arranged for us to meet at 11:00 this morning at Genesis II with the PR Director, Rachelle Pace," he said. "She said she would be happy to meet with us, and I sort of mentioned that you two would be there," he added, indicating both McLeod and Wolfe."

Wolfe smiled. "That doesn't happen to *me* very often," she said.

McLeod snorted. "Don't let her fool you --yes, it does, particularly in both Federation and Alliance worlds," McLeod said. Turning more serious, he asked, "What did you tell your friend about our visit?"

"Well, Tucker," Ryder said, "I mentioned that you were doing research because of the negotiations, and since the two of you were more expert in weapons systems than the staff you were working with, you came to the Twin Worlds to learn more about the defense industry first hand." McLeod considered this, and looked to Wolfe for her assessment. She tilted her head and made a slight face.

"Hard to know what else we could have told her, Tucker," Wolfe said. With that, McLeod was satisfied.

Just then, Zavery came into the kitchen, looking a little pale -- much the same way he did the day before after the flight from Herai. "Good morning," he said, with very little enthusiasm.

"Something tells me you are not a morning person, Benno," joked McLeod.

Zavery could only smile. "No, I'm not, though I wish that was my only problem this morning."

"Something stronger?" asked Sofia Black. "I can probably get something for you. What are your symptoms?" She spoke as she worked her way to her small med bag.

Zavery raised his hand. "Oh no," he began. "I don't think I need anything, perhaps just another couple of hours sleep."

With her hand already in her med bag, Black replied. "Are you sure? It's really no trouble, and I have plenty for stomach upset, headache or both."

Zavery shook his head. "No, I think I'll be alright." He smiled weakly. "Don't want to take too many meds, you know."

Black shrugged. "Suit yourself."

Fisher had entered the room and overheard the interchange between Black and Zavery. "Do you want to sit out the visit to Genesis II, Benno?" she asked. "I believe our plan is to try to speak with someone at Verinox this afternoon, so maybe you can join us then."

Zavery nodded. "Yes, I think that would be a better idea," he said. "In fact," he said, looking around and turning away from the food. "Maybe I should just go back to bed now." He rose from the table, said his goodbyes and left the kitchen.

After he left, Fisher continued. "I haven't heard yet from Elliott, but I know he will be calling his contacts at Verinox this morning and setting up a time for us to meet there. We thought it would be fine for Tad to set up and lead the meeting this morning at Genesis II because of his close personal connection with the PR Director." Everyone seemed to agree with the approach, so Fisher continued. "But what we should probably do is to work out some of the questions we want to start with so it is coordinated."

"I agree," McLeod said. "And Raina and I have already developed some questions that are relevant to the discussion; many of which seem to fit with what Tad told his friend -- about weapons systems as they relate to the negotiations."

"Right," said Wolfe. "And what I hope to get from Tad's contact is some idea of the other people and players we should investigate. But what I most want to be sure of is that we don't spook her - I think this should be as casual a meeting as possible."

"Agreed," said Fisher. "In fact, I wonder if we ought to have fewer of us at the meeting than we had originally planned." She looked around. "Obviously, we need Tad, and Captains McLeod and Wolfe. Sofia, do you feel the need to be there?" Black shrugged, but also clearly was annoyed at the possibility of being excluded.

Turning to Sligo, Tad asked. "Lou, do you mind sitting out the meeting at Genesis II?"

Sligo humphed. "Not at all," he said. "I've got plenty I can do in the groundvan while you're in the meeting. Miranda and I can also prepare for our afternoon meeting with Verinox." Fisher nodded her agreement.

"Great," said Ryder.

"That's good then -- and good logic all around," Fisher said. Now," looking at McLeod and Wolfe, "Can you send us the questions you've already developed? Maybe we can add others you haven't thought of."

At 1030 hours, the group assembled in the groundvan and Ryder keyed in the destination.

I think you'll like Rachelle," he said. "We've been friends for years.

"You said she does Public Relations for Genesis, right?" Asked McLeod.

"Right. So her job essentially is to promote the company and keep them out of news and vid trouble."

McLeod shrugged. "Doesn't sound like the easiest position, given what we've heard about her CEO."

"Maybe," Ryder said. "But I certainly don't think Rachelle would do anything wrong, -- certainly not something like this. And we don't even know that the company has done anything wrong, either."

"That's true," McLeod admitted, "so I guess we shouldn't get ahead of ourselves."

Ryder smiled and looked slyly at McLeod. "And I thought I might be able to snag a date with her -- we haven't seen each other for a while, and she implied when I called her that she doesn't have much of a social life."

"Nice to accomplish two things with the same phone call, huh?"

"Yep." Within about fifteen minutes, the groundvan stopped in front of a small building attached to a larger industrial building, probably a manufacturing facility. They got out and secured the groundvan, then consulted briefly with Fisher and Sligo.

"Remember folks," began Fisher, "It's probably best for Tad to take the lead, and go into your more searching questions more gradually, and over time. My hope is that you get an invitation to a formal lunch off site, then try to seat," she looked at Ryder, "Pace, right?" Ryder nodded. "Pace with Tucker and Raina for a more focused conversation. Everybody on board?" All members of the group nodded their agreement.

"Alright. Good luck," Fisher said.

Ryder, McLeod and Wolfe entered the facility, and with their names already at the security point, they were directed down a hallway to the last door on the right. As they turned toward the door, they saw a blonde woman of about Ryder's age looking out at them, and she quickly approached the door.

"Tad!" she cried, embracing him. "Where have you been and what have you been doing?"

Ryder smiled as he returned the embrace. "Just trying to make a living, as always, 'Chell." He turned to indicate McLeod and Wolfe. "Let me introduce Captain Raina Wolfe of the Central Federation and Captain Tucker McLeod, of the Star Alliance."

"Hello, Ms. Pace," Wolfe said as she extended her hand."

"Oh, please, it's Rachelle," Pace said, as she took Wolfe's hand.

"Great, I'm Raina." Wolfe turned toward her colleague, "and he's Tucker."

Before she could perform more introductions, Pace said, "Let's go to the conference room rather than talk in the hallway. She turned toward the inner office area. "And I took the liberty of ordering coffee and tea for us. Come this way." Pace and Ryder led the way toward the conference room. She seemed very open and friendly which, Wolfe thought, were good qualities for a Public Relations Director for any kind of company, but especially for a defense one. The group got settled and poured their drinks as they chatted amiably.

As the murmur of conversation died down, Ryder addressed Pace. "'Chell, let me tell you why we came today, and thanks again for making time for us." Pace smiled and nodded as Ryder continued. "You probably know that the negotiations going on with the Federation and between the Twin Worlds are not going as well as they could, and one of the reasons is the terrible kidnapping of Vice Chair Patt'son's daughter."

Pace's eyes squinted, but after a few seconds, Ryder continued. "Well, Captains McLeod and Wolfe are serving as staff on the military cooperation committee for the negotiations, and thought while they had a few days off, that they would do some research."

Pace frowned. "I'm not sure I follow you, Tad." Her body language indicated some discomfort, but not too much.

Ryder continued. "Here's the thing, 'Chell. One of the sticking points within the committee they're working with is weapons agreements, and the two sides don't seem to be able to get close on that issue. It's very complicated, far more complicated than I could explain." Ryder turned to McLeod and Wolfe. "You see, Tucker and Raina thought if they could learn more about the defense industry on Hemod and Herai, they would be able to serve the committee better."

"Yes, Rachelle," said Wolfe. "And the fact is," she lowered her voice and leaned forward, "the two staff members from Hemod and Herai are budget people, and don't know much about defense. So, besides staffing the committee, we're also educating them so the more we learn, the better we'll be able to help the committee at least try to come to some kind of agreement that benefits the Twin Worlds."

While Wolfe spoke, Pace seem to visibly relax as the full explanation was revealed. Then her eyebrows creased. She turned to look squarely at Ryder. "What's the union's part in this?" she asked.

"Well 'Chell," began Ryder, "there isn't really a union angle to this at all. The fact is that Tucker and Raina didn't have any contacts on-planet to help them. They happened to meet up with a Heraian chef on the space station and he knew my boss. So, we're really just providing contacts for them."

"That makes sense," said Pace. "Though I don't know how much I can help you, given my own knowledge base."

Ryder was quick to respond. "And we understand that, 'Chell. We just wanted to start somewhere, and I knew you better than anyone else in the defense industry. Anything you can tell us would be more than Tucker and Raina know now."

Thus soothed, Pace turned to McLeod and Wolfe. "So, what can I tell you?" she asked.

Chapter Twenty Eight

For the next forty minutes, Wolfe and McLeod asked Pace mildly focused questions about the defense industry on Hemod, and specifically about Genesis II's place in the defense industry. Pace certainly knew enough about the general workings of Genesis to provide simple answers. However, while she was informative and open, it became clear early on that some of the nuances of how weapons best worked and the ways to deploy or not deploy them was lost on Pace. She didn't really understand how phase weapons work, for example, nor some of the long term concerns about using them that were part of Federation and Alliance military culture. Pace was also unaware of any actions being taken at Genesis II regarding phase weapons. She did mention, however, that she'd heard that her CEO believed that the negotiations were a waste of time, and that Hemod should simply go about the task of defending itself.

Wolfe and McLeod were careful not to push any area so strongly as to raise Pace's suspicions, but they believed they were dangerously close to doing so.

McLeod decided to call for a break. "This has been very helpful, Rachelle, but could I be directed to the men's?" That question was the signal for Ryder to engage Pace in more casual conversation about their pasts and to let them bond (and for Ryder to secure a date), thus reducing Pace's anxiety. It was also a signal that McLeod thought they had gone about as far as he thought they could at this particular meeting.

"Of course, Capt. ... Tucker," Pace said. "You just turn to go out the front door and it's in the first alcove on the right."

"Thank you," said McLeod. As he started toward the door, he heard loud shouting coming from the corridor, and stepped back from the door just in time. The door flung open and a small snarling man entered and glared at everyone, before settling first on McLeod, then Pace.

"Ms. Pace, you need to return to your office *now*," the man said. "And I'll deal with you later." His tone was menacing, and Pace, at first startled, rushed to comply, offering quiet apologies on the way out. Hollander, or at least that's who everyone thought he was -- returned his glance to McLeod. "I'm not in the habit of harboring wanted criminals in my company, *Captain* McLeod," Hollander began," but fortunately, I won't have to worry about that for much longer."

McLeod, after first falling back from the explosion that was Reb Hollander, stepped forward, unfazed. "Well, I've been criticized for things in the past but never for being a wanted criminal," he said coolly. "I presume I have the pleasure of addressing Reb Hollander, CEO of this company?"

Hollander frowned. "I know who *and* what you are, McLeod," Hollander said, "and no amount of nice talk is going to save you this time." There was a gleam in his eye that was unsettling to McLeod, despite his ability to appear cool.

"Mr. Hollander," Ryder said. "If there is something we've done to upset you, you may certainly feel free to let us know. Is this attack the way you want us to remember Genesis II?" He said it as a mild threat, but Hollander didn't flinch.

"Well if you're in the company of this criminal, maybe I'll get rid of the union and McLeod at the same time." Hollander reared back on his heels. "Hah!"

"And I hardly think that serving in the Star Alliance makes someone a wanted criminal," Ryder continued, his tone testy.

Hollander smiled. "Well, on your way out, feel free to check the public vids." He checked his chron. "And you'd better do it soon, as the authorities should be here very soon."

Ryder looked as though he wanted to respond again, but it was McLeod who spoke. "Well, we've certainly no reason to stay where we're not wanted, everyone," he said. "Shall we go?" As McLeod began making his way toward the door, he noticed Hollander inching toward him, either to block his exit, or to provoke him. Wolfe saw it as well, and she moved quickly between the two men so McLeod could exit. Outside in the hallway, the group got their bearings, and still puzzled, moved quickly to the building exits.

They could hear Hollander calling after them. "Better hurry, Captain!" he shouted with a laugh. "You don't have much time!" Hollander was clearly gloating.

Still unaware of what was happening, the group exited the building and began moving even more quickly toward their groundvan. As they left the security area, they heard,

"Stop! We are authorized to detain you!"

"You cannot detain citizens without authorization," Ryder said. "This cannot stand!"

Wolfe brusquely took his arm. "Tad, something else is going on here," she said. "We don't have the time to argue citizen's rights!" Reluctantly, Ryder allowed himself to be pulled toward the groundvan. Other security personnel came out from the building and near the street as the group neared the vehicle. The security personnel numbered four now. McLeod, Wolfe and the others remained confused, but also extremely tense.

"Tucker McLeod," said the main security person, "We are authorized to detain you on behalf of the authorities! Stand down!"

McLeod had had enough.

"For what!?"

"For the murder of Benno Zavery and Raina Wolfe! Stand down!"

Wolfe exploded. "What!?" She was about to say more, but McLeod interrupted her, touching her hand so she could see the number of people around them.

He turned to Ryder. "Tad, get in the van and be ready to go."

"But…"

"Go!" McLeod shouted, then turned, and calming himself, glanced briefly at Wolfe.

"Something tells me the guns they're carrying" he pointed to the sidearms on the guards "aren't regulation, and I'm not inclined to surrender to them."

Wolfe didn't hesitate. "Be ready, Tad," Wolfe said. McLeod and Wolfe noticed Sligo and Fisher getting out of the groundvan looking confused as Ryder approached them.

Wolfe turned back to the security men. "You do realize," she began, facing the officer, "That *I* am Raina Wolfe, and I am certainly not dead yet." The head security man smiled menacingly.

McLeod shot a glance at Wolfe, then returned his gaze to the security officer. "I guess this is where we surrender to you." He and Wolfe stayed close together, hands loosely at their sides, and waited. The head security man hesitated, then motioned with his head for his staff to secure McLeod and Wolfe. As they approached, McLeod and Wolfe slowly shifted their positions so they could maintain their positions relative to each other. The entire circle of the security men around McLeod and Wolfe could not have been more than five meters in diameter. As the guards continued approaching, Wolfe glanced down quickly and noticed that McLeod had his kongou stick in his right palm. She smiled and slightly squeezed the ornate pen in her hand. Given that they were not threatening in any way, only the head security man kept them covered with his sidearm while the others approached them. As the largest security man reached for McLeod's left arm to turn him around, McLeod swung his right arm in an leftward arc, catching the man in the side of his left temple, shocking him and sending him to the ground in pain and barely conscious. A second guard, ready to restrain Wolfe, was momentarily immobile as his colleague hit the ground and he hesitated a bit too long. Wolfe chambered her leg into a hard thrust kick that caught him in the floating ribs. She heard a satisfying muffled crack as he went down, heaving.

The lead security man, unfamiliar with close order combat, raised his sidearm, aiming it directly at McLeod's chest.

"You… you stop right there!" he shouted. He looked to his only standing colleague and said,

"Get him in cuffs!" The fourth man lunged to secure McLeod before he got away. McLeod stepped slightly to his left, then brought his right arm with the kongou straight forward, hitting the man in his solar plexus. After contact, he kept the arc of his arm going, swinging it around the man's back then bringing the stick and fist down hard on the back of his neck. His back turned, McLeod prepared to face the head security man again when he heard the crack of a sidearm and felt a searing pain in his left shoulder. He turned in rage, ready to attack or at least avoid a second shot, when a knife flew into the man's right shoulder. He dropped his sidearm, and, before he could remove the knife, Wolfe calmly walked over to him and kicked him in the head. Not bothering to check on McLeod, she first removed the knife, and wiped it on her jacket before replacing it in her ankle holster.

"I'll be damned if I'm going to lose my favorite knife to that son of a bitch." Wolfe said, angrily. Turning, she went straight to McLeod. "I am forever saving your sorry butt, Tucker, she said.

"Help me up," McLeod said. They started walking when he said, "Get some of those weapons -- we may need them." Wolfe nodded and picked up three of the sidearms, and ran to the car. She returned to pick up additional magazines and continue helping McLeod get into the groundvan. As they started walking, McLeod heard a moan. Leaving Wolfe, he walked to the man he'd originally attacked, shifted his weight, and kicked him in the side of the head. Then, McLeod and Wolfe quickly returned to the groundvan and took off.

Chapter Twenty Nine

Su'Gan, Hemod Groundvan, Public Streets

"What the hell is going on?" Sligo asked as the groundvan sped through the streets of Su'gan hurtling toward…

"And just where are we going?" asked McLeod. His voice was thin and showed the strain.

"Short term or long term?" Ryder asked, then added "We're going to the tunnels on the west side of the city. They go underground all the way to the transport station. The tunnels aren't used very much, and we should be safe there."

"This is not your fight, Tad," Wolfe said. "There is no *we* that has to include you."

Fisher interrupted. "I'm not so sure of that, Raina," she said. "We were able to catch a short part of a vid broadcast."

"And?" McLeod asked.

Fisher sighed. "And they said they identified the bodies as Raina and Benno Zavery, and" she paused, "that Tucker was last in the company of all of us from the union. They're saying that we may all be involved."

"Not exactly," said Sligo, "But they want us all for questioning, which given how the authorities feel about our movement, doesn't bode well for us." Sligo's voice was somber.

"So, where are we going again?" asked Wolfe.

Ryder was distracted as he answered, and very tense. "We're going to the tunnels, but I've keyed in two more destinations afterwards, in hopes they won't know where we really went."

"But people," Wolfe said with authority, "You're bound to be safer on your own than with the two of us."

McLeod stirred. "You don't have to do this either, Raina; they're not after you; after all you're dead," he said.

Wolfe shook her head. "No," Wolfe began. "If they find out I'm alive, I *will* be dead." She turned to Fisher. "And just why did they think I was dead anyway? What's the whole story here?"

Fisher looked bewildered. "We missed that part of the vid, so we don't know," she said. Then she started. "What about Benno?" Wolfe looked at everyone in turn. "If Raina isn't dead, what about him?"

"Yes," said McLeod. "What *about* him?" They rode in silence through the streets, and heard another vid report.

"...in the garden district identified as Captain Raina Wolfe of the Central Federation and Benno Zavery, of the Unionist movement's Heraian Central Office. McLeod was last in the company of Miranda Fisher, Sofia Black and Tad Ryder of the Unionist movements Hemodian Office, and Lou Sligo, a union organizer from Herai. They are wanted for questioning as material witnesses. Anyone who encounters McLeod is urged to contact authorities immediately..." The vid was silent for a while until the face of Elias Trent appeared on the vid. "We are very concerned and saddened by this brutal crime at the hands of one of the Alliance's officers. I feared that Captain McLeod would be unsuitable for this kind of assignment, and perhaps his true nature has come out in this attack on an officer of the Central Federation and the good people of the Twin Worlds." The vid was silent for a moment again, then continued. "We have received confirmation that the Star Alliance will be activating Captain McLeod's ID chip so that he can be more readily located so that this crisis can come to a swift conclusion." The vid changed to another story, and Fisher turned it off.

McLeod sat in pain for a while, before turning to Wolfe. "What is it, Raina -- twenty three years?" McLeod shook his head. "Twenty three years and this is what I'm worth?" He sighed. They were silent for a moment, before he continued, his voice stronger and more resolute.

"You each have to decide what you want to do, and whether you're going to go with Raina and me."

Wolfe smiled as she held a cloth to his shoulder.

"Try to decide before we get to the tunnels," McLeod said.

"I'm going with you," said Black, quietly. "I don't think there's anything for me here." She sounded sad.

"I think you are right, Sofia," said Sligo. "We are not particularly safe anywhere, and I for one would rather chance it in the tunnels than with the Hemodian authorities."

"I agree," said Fisher. "There is much more here than we understand as yet, and I want to get to the bottom of it." They were silent, until they all looked at Ryder. He finally realized they were staring at him.

"Well, don't look at me," he said with a smile. "I'm staying. I kind of like the tunnels."

* * *

The group arrived at a street a few blocks from union headquarters, and a few blocks in a different direction from a tunnel entrance. After helping McLeod out of the groundvan and taking all they could carry, they started for the tunnel entrance. The groundvan delayed for a moment, then sped off to its next destination.

"How many more destinations are keyed in?" asked Wolfe.

"Three more," said Ryder. "I hope that at least gives us some time to get away."

"We can only hope," said Wolfe. The group moved as quickly as they could considering they needed to help McLeod who was bleeding and in a great deal of pain.

Once inside the tunnel entrance, Fisher looked around at the passageways and turned to Ryder. "From here, which way do we go?" she asked. Ryder looked at the passageways briefly then pointed toward his left.

"There are two ways, the most direct way is the far left," Ryder said. "But the other tunnel next to it gets there too, only it would take longer."

"Well, if the authorities are after us, and find this tunnel entrance," said Sligo, "Would it make more sense to take the way that is less direct -- I mean to misdirect them?"

"I'm not convinced they'd be that ignorant, Lou," said Wolfe, adding, "though your logic is sound, and I would agree than we should take the second passageway." She shifted her weight to support McLeod more effectively. "But we have to get him stabilized as quickly as we can." She turned again to Ryder. "Is there a place inside where we can stop to take care of that quickly?"

Ryder thought for a moment, then said, "I think so. Follow me." With that, Ryder led the way down the passageway, with all following him. Wolfe and Sligo walked in the rear with McLeod. After a few minutes, Wolfe left Sligo to speak with Black.

"Sofia," Wolfe began, "We're going to need your help."

Black's eyebrows furrowed. "*My* help?" she said. "I don't have a clue right now. What can *I* do?"

"But you do have a clue about how to patch up Tucker's shoulder, and..." Wolfe looked away, very tense.

"And?" Black said.

Wolfe shook herself, then turned to face Black squarely. "We need you to remove Tucker's ID chip."

Black stopped in her tracks, her eyes widening. "Me!? I can't do that! I'm not a doctor, I'm…"

Wolfe interrupted, calmer now. "What you are is the only person who can do *any* of this, Sofia." Wolfe peered directly at Black, saying, "We need you, and only you. Please -- for all of us."

Black remained stunned and shaking her head. "I've never … I mean," she paused, biting her lip. "This is hard."

Wolfe chuckled to ease her own tension. "Sofia, you know more than you think you do. And we'll all help you as best we can."

"But," Black countered. "Do you know he even wants me to remove his chip? What little I know about those things, the can be very hard to remove." Black looked away.

"Trust me," said Wolfe. "He wants the chip removed, because otherwise everyone else will be in danger. Even" her voice became quiet "at the possible cost of his own life. It's kind of what Tucker does." She shook her head again. "Look, let's try to get ourselves away from the entrance so we can set up a place to take care of this." She glanced at Black's hand. "I see you have your med kit." Black only nodded, still numb.

A few minutes later, Ryder stopped the group by a large hole in the wall. "Raina," he said, and he waved his hands to get her attention.

"What do you have, Tad?" she asked.

Ryder seemed proud of himself. "You said you wanted to get Tucker stabilized." Ryder stepped aside to let Wolfe see the room within the walls. It looked as though it had at one time been finished, perhaps a break room or supply area. "Will this do?" he asked.

"I think so, but we need to do a bit more than get him stabilized."

"His chip?" asked Fisher.

Wolfe nodded her head. "I've already asked Sofia to do it. Tucker will ask her anyway -- I just decided to save time."

Fisher nodded, gravely. "High risk right?"

"Very," Wolfe said. "But there really is no choice."

Fisher squared her shoulders. "Whatever you need me or us to do," she said.

Wolfe smiled, saying, "Make that same offer to Sofia -- *she* needs the boost of confidence now."

Fisher frowned, but nodded.

Just then Sligo entered, supporting a weary looking McLeod, and Sligo directed him toward a very old, but still sturdy low table near the corner of the room. McLeod was directed to sit so that his clothes could be taken off of him in the easiest and quickest way possible. Sofia Black took a look at McLeod and the area she would be working with. She also examined the supplies she had in her med bag and tried to visualize what she needed to accomplish. She got Wolfe's attention as she got started.

"My first inclination, " Black said, "is to cut off his clothes, but I don't want him to be without anything especially if it gets cold. I also haven't seen the shoulder wound yet to know what I'm working with." She looked down at McLeod, suddenly more nervous. "Do you know the exact location of your chip?" McLeod nodded, and raised his right hand to touch a spot on the left side of his neck toward the back. He looked at her and beckoned her to touch the same spot. She touched it carefully, then felt methodically to get a better sense of location and how much the surrounding tissue had grown around it. Her eyebrows furrowed.

"I don't feel a lot of scar tissue here."

"Right," McLeod said. "The chip was originally in another location but had to be removed because of an injury."

"That may be a good thing.'" Black said. "That means you have a lot less tissue growth around it, so taking it out should be less of a problem."

McLeod was quiet. "Whatever works, Sofia," he said.

"Alright then," she said." "Let's try to get the clothes off and see what we're working with." Very slowly, Wolfe, Black, Sligo and Fisher carefully manipulated McLeod's arms and trunk to expose the wound on his left shoulder. Happily, it seemed to be a flesh wound, with a bullet simply taking a small hunk out of his shoulder. While very painful and resulting in loss of blood, Black didn't have to worry about digging out a bullet before dressing the wound. She paused for a while, long enough for Wolfe to ask what she was thinking about.

Black pressed her lips together. "I'm not sure I have enough anesthesia."

"I didn't know you had *any*," Wolfe replied.

Black shook her head. "No, I have some but very little, and looking at this wound and … taking the chip out, I don't think I can spare any for the shoulder." She looked as if she wanted to cry.

"You know I can hear you, don't you?" asked McLeod.

Black jumped when she heard McLeod's voice. "Of course, I was just… just…."

"You were just going over the options, Sofia, and we appreciate that, don't we Tucker?" said Wolfe.

"Sure." McLeod admitted. He closed his eyes briefly, then added. "Just take care of the shoulder without anesthesia."

Black's mouth was set in a grim line. "I appreciate that, Tucker, but taking out the chip will still require a lot more than I have." Black took a deep breath before continuing. "I don't know what to do."

"Let Raina and I take care of that," McLeod said. He turned to Wolfe. "You need to help me get into a deep healing trance for the chip. It's not hard, just help me stay focused so I can meditate and get under enough to stand the procedure."

Wolfe was skeptical. "I've never done that with you before."

"But, you've seen me in other states like that, right?" Wolfe nodded. "This is the same, only it has to be a lot deeper," he said. "If I was doing it for fun, I wouldn't need your help, but I have too many distractions here with the pain and after the shoulder procedure." He frowned before continuing. "Maybe we should do the chip first so any meditative state I'm under will help with the shoulder." McLeod became more excited. "Because if we do the shoulder first, the pain will make it harder for me to meditate, and," he whispered, "time is really important here." Wolfe nodded and looked at Black.

"Sofia, slight change in plan," Wolfe said. She approached Black, and placed a hand on her shoulder. "We have to do the chip first with whatever anesthesia you have, *then* we do the shoulder." Black frowned.

"I don't understand." Black said, her shoulders dropping ever so slightly.

Wolfe smiled at her. "I only understand part of it myself, Sofia," Wolfe said. "But Tucker is a master of several martial arts styles and some of them have very strong healing components. I've seen him withstand incredible amounts of pain or discomfort, and he tends to heal muscle and tendon injures extremely quickly." She paused. "Yeah, kind of like a superpower that way. Anyway, he's going to go into as deep a trance as he can, and you will use as much of the anesthesia on his neck as you need to. You'll perform the chip removal, and assuming he lives, *then* you tackle the shoulder."

Black was silent for a moment before asking, "Do you really think that will work?"

"Tucker does," Wolfe said, adding, "and I'm willing to try it." She stood straighter, then said. "Just tell all of us what you need us to do -- or *not* do, and we'll do it. The clock is ticking, Sofia." Black nodded her head, then took a few deep breaths. She removed several items in sterile wrapping from her med bag, and organized them on her jacket spread down on the floor. Then, she called Miranda Fisher over.

"Miranda," Black said. "I need you to hold this jacket in your arms so I can take the tools off of it when I need them. "You don't need to give me anything, just make sure nothing falls on the floor." Fisher nodded.

Black then looked to Lou Sligo. "Lou, I don't know if Tucker is going to try to move while I'm operating, but he can't. Can you hold him down."

Sligo nodded. "Just tell me how -- I'll do anything." Sligo said.

Black then looked again to Wolfe. "Can you start this trance thing?" she asked her.

"I'm still *here*," said McLeod.

Wolfe rolled her eyes. To Black, she said, "Yes, he *is* insufferable." Then she turned her attention back to McLeod. "This had better work." She looked into his eyes. "What do we do?"

McLeod took a long slow breath. "I'm going to take a number of long slow breaths like that one," McLeod said. "I need to do that to help my heartbeat slow a little. While I do that, I need you to do something."

"Something?"

McLeod breathed again. "It doesn't matter what, just so it's the same thing the same way, like stroke my arm or hand; try that."

Wolfe hesitated.

"You were worried about time, Raina," McLeod reminded her. Wolfe closed, then opened her eyes, then started slowly stroking the back of his right hand, up and down… up and down…. McLeod's breathing continued in much the same way: slow breath in, slow breath out, and Wolfe could see in a few minutes how his breathing, once a little strained, became smoother and smoother. She noticed the tension gradually leave his chest and neck muscles and his arm relax. This continued for a time -- she truly couldn't say for how long. He had never looked so vulnerable to her, and she was shocked to feel her eyes fill. She blinked the tears away, choosing to focus instead on stroking his hand ... up and down … up and down. A few minutes later, she nodded to Black, who took her own deep breath and began.

Throughout the two procedures, McLeod was relatively calm: his body reacted a few times to tugs and cuts, but Sligo's firm yet gentle touch prevented any mishap. Black was surprised at how easily she was able to free the chip from McLeod, and remarked again that having the chip reimplanted so recently was very fortunate. The shoulder injury was also a matter of some suture, and dressing, and she found she had sufficient flush in the med bag to perform at least a basic cleaning of the wound. She also had enough dressing for both wounds.

Finally, after less than an hour of work, she stood up, almost surprised that she was done. She nodded to Sligo and Fisher, who relaxed. Black turned to Wolfe and said, "I think we're done."

Wolfe was startled and seemed to come out of her own trance at the same time. "Oh," she said. "Okay. What do we do now?"

Black pursed her lips. "I don't exactly know. Half the time our worry during recovery with patients is because we have to wake them up from the anesthesia. But Tucker's had very little and it was localized. I suppose it's possible that he could wake up and be feeling pretty good almost immediately."

Wolfe considered this. She took a breath first. "We should probably move him a lot earlier than we want to. In the meantime, I'm" Wolfe glanced briefly toward her other companions,"just going to stay here with him a little longer."

Black smiled and nodded. "I understand."

"Oh, and Sofia," Wolfe continued, "have Tad take that ID chip, smash the living daylights out of it and maybe take it to another tunnel away from this one in case it's still working, okay?"

"Will do," Black said, and she left Wolfe and McLeod alone.

Wolfe turned her attention back to McLeod. "We have to stop doing this to ourselves, Tucker," she said, then she smiled. "Neither of us is invincible, you know." She stayed with him for a while, and stopped stroking his hand, believing that might help him come out of the trance. Gradually, she began to see signs of movement; his breathing took on a more active tempo, and she could feel his heartrate climbing. She turned to the rest of the group, who had been watching her.

"I think he may be out of it, soon, and we'll have to see if he can move and how far," Wolfe said. "I would like to be as far away from the tunnel entrance as we can as soon as we can." She turned to Ryder. "Tad, did you destroy the chip?"

He nodded. "As much as I could, and I scattered the components in a couple of different tunnels."

"Good. Let's get everything ready to move as soon as Tucker wakes up..." she could feel McLeod move.

"Noisy in here," he whispered.

Wolfe rolled her eyes. "We'll try to be more quiet," she said.

McLeod opened his eyes into slits, then took another deep breath. "Surgery over?" he asked.

"Yep. Sofia did a great job."

Black had been moving toward McLeod as soon as she noticed him moving. "First of all," she said, "don't touch anything." Black's more assertive manner both surprised and amused McLeod, who smiled.

"Yes, Ma'am," he said.

"Oh. Sorry." Black said. "How are you feeling?"

McLeod thought for a moment, then said. "Actually, pretty good. I can feel a lot of soreness in my shoulder and a little in my neck, though I guess I'll feel a lot more in my neck after a while."

Black checked McLeod's chron. "Probably, but maybe not," she said, "since the anesthetic I used would have worn off by now."

"That's good news, then." McLeod looked at Wolfe. "I think in a little while, maybe thirty minutes, I'll be ready to move somewhere else. I don't know how far, but we need to get farther from the entrance."

Everyone looked at Wolfe. "Thirty sounds good to me," she said. She looked at McLeod. "And I know you're not going to leave before you're able, are you?" McLeod only smiled. The group settled back in and discussed their intent once they arrived at the transport station. Their hope was to secure passage back to either Herai or the station without notifying the authorities. Sligo mentioned that he had access to funds and credits to secure passage that was neither tied to his legal name nor to the union. Wolfe's eyes widened when he said that, but given the mood toward the union she'd seen in the past few days, she didn't question it. They had just about completed their discussion when they heard a voice behind them.

"So," said McLeod. "Are we going?"

Chapter Thirty

Su'gan, Hemod Western Tunnels

The group had been walking quickly and carefully down the passageway for about 15 minutes seeking a safe place to stop and get their bearings. Turning after a few minutes, Wolfe looked back and realized that McLeod was nowhere in sight.

"Stop!" she said, holding up her hand.

"Are you crazy?" said Sligo. "We have to get out of here before they find us!"

"Tucker's not with us." Wolfe said to him. "We have to go back."

Sligo's face first showed shock, then his mouth set in a determined line, and he nodded. He looked to Fisher, Ryder and Black. "We have to go back," Sligo said. Wolfe led them back and within minutes, they saw McLeod bent over and obviously breathing with difficulty.

Black went to him immediately and examined his shoulder. "You've started bleeding again," she said. "I'm sorry-- I'm not a doctor -- I should never..."

McLeod could see that she was fighting tears. "You did a great job, Sofia," McLeod said.   "And we know we asked you to do a lot more than you are accustomed to. Please don't worry about it." He looked up and saw Wolfe looking concerned. He smiled at her. "Not as easy as I thought it would be."

Wolfe could hear the strain in his voice. "Never is," she said. She looked him directly in the eye. "What should we do now?"

McLeod smiled again. "You get me to a safer hole in the wall or hidden passage somewhere so I can recover, then you get yourselves out of here before you're captured."

Black was distraught. "We can't *leave* you! You're hurt. We can't!" She was openly crying now. McLeod looked up and caught Sligo's eye.

"Sofia," Sligo said. "Please come here. They have to talk." Sofia turned toward Sligo, and he led her away.

Once they were out of earshot, Wolfe turned again to McLeod. "How bad are you?" she asked.

McLeod considered for an instant being coy or funny, but knew that wouldn't be appropriate, so he said, "Maybe 60% -- more or less -- nowhere near enough to be of help. I think I need to get somewhere and get myself into a healing trance -- enough to slow everything down, so my body can recover." He looked toward Black. "I think if Sofia can stop the bleeding, I'll be much better in a few hours or a day."

Wolfe continued to study his face, then lowering her eyes, said, "Okay." She turned to the group and changed her demeanor again. "Change of plan," she said. "We need to find a safe place for Tucker to stay, get him stabilized again, then get on our way. " She looked to Ryder and Fisher. "If we were to change direction, to avoid being found, is there a passageway we could take that would still take us to the station, but in a more roundabout way?"

"We were almost there when we turned around," Ryder said. "We can go a little farther this way, then turn left." He thought again before continuing. "I don't know about safe places there, but I would assume there would be some somewhere."

Wolfe was resolute. "Good. You lead the way." Turning to Sligo, she said, "Lou, you and Sofia help Tucker -- the sooner we get him safe, the sooner we can go to plan B or C or wherever we are at the moment." Not waiting for a response, she added, "Let's go."

Sligo and Black cradled McLeod carefully and began the slow walk to the passage as Ryder led the way. As they walked, Fisher got into step next to Wolfe. She could see the strain on Wolfe's face.

"This is becoming more difficult," Fisher said quietly. "I don't mind telling you that I'm afraid right now."

"Nothing wrong with that, Miranda," Wolfe said. She turned to Fisher. "We have a plan now, we just need to stick to it."

Fisher looked into Wolfe's eyes briefly and then away. "I'd have thought you would be more upset, given your relationship...." Fisher's voice trailed off, and Wolfe allowed herself a small chuckle.

"There's inside upset and outside upset Miranda," she said. "Tucker and I have been in a lot of scrapes over the years; this is just another one. A big one, mind you, but we'll get through it."

Fisher shook her head. "I don't know where you get your confidence from," she said.

"Part of it is an awful lot of experience, and the other," Wolfe indicated with her head behind her, "is the man behind us." She looked up and noticed that Ryder had stopped. "Is this the passage?"

Ryder nodded. "It's not very big, but I know it goes all the way through to the station."

"How much longer will it take us to reach the station if we go this way?" Wolfe asked.

Ryder looked up briefly as he calculated the answer. "Maybe a couple of hours longer, maybe more. But I think it is a better way to go -- there would be no reason to go this way, plus they are really only focused on Captain McLeod's chip, and they think he killed you, so there would be no reason to track you, right?"

Wolfe nodded, then turned back to the rest, pointing. "Down this way. Tad, let's find a place for Tucker before he drops." Ryder continued down the passageway, which could only hold a maximum of three people abreast which made it slower going for McLeod, Black and Sligo. Ten minutes into the tunnel, Ryder stopped and entered a side passage. He held up his hand as he started going in, but Wolfe said, "I'm going with you."

Without turning to the rest of the group, she said, "Wait here." She and Ryder entered the passage way and within a minute came into a large open area which was relatively cool, probably at a constant temperature given its underground location. Wolfe could also hear the sound of water, and after following the sound, found a small stream toward the corner of the room. She looked up at Ryder. "I think this will do." Ryder nodded his agreement.

"Get everyone else in here so we can get him settled" Wolfe said. Ryder left the room, and Wolfe allowed herself to collapse a little on herself with concern and a little genuine worry. Yes, she had gotten a lot of confidence from McLeod on several occasions in the past, but it had always been when they were together -- each helping and supporting the other: the situation today was unique. Soon, she heard the group enter the room bringing McLeod with them. He looked worn and a little pale.

Wolfe turned to consult with Black. "Sofia, where should we put him?"

Black looked around then said, "I think… resting over here," she said. "there's a bit of back support here that will help with blood flow." She continued to look around. "Some of this ground is soft. We should bring it together and make a softer spot so he'll be more comfortable." Turning back to Sligo and McLeod she said, "Put him down here while we get things together, Lou." Sligo complied, and Black, more confident now, directed the others on what to do. She quickly returned to McLeod, and examined his shoulder and neck. "It's something of a miracle that your neck is actually in better shape that your shoulder. I thought removing that chip would do you in."

McLeod chuckled "Of course, no one shot a bullet into my neck either."

Black allowed herself to smile. "No, just an unqualified nurse with a throwing knife," she said,

"Which I'm very happy Raina kept sharpened," McLeod said. He looked up again at Black. "Has my shoulder stopped bleeding?"

Black nodded. "Yes. I think so, and since we don't have anything else to dress it with, I'm not going to touch it, since it's going to at least partially scab over." She looked at him again. "There is the definite possibility of infection, but I think we should risk that, rather than having you bleed out." Looking again at the others and at the stream, she added "and I'm going to have us gather some way of getting you some water, too." she looked around the room. "The temperature in here is a good thing. Water won't evaporate as quickly, so maybe we'll soak some clothes that you can suck on."

"That doesn't sound very appetizing," McLeod said. Black smiled, then turned when she heard her name called.

"Sofia," said Wolfe. Wolfe pointed to a slight mound of soft ground. "Will this do?"

"Yes," Black said. We can move him very carefully there and get him settled. As she turned toward McLeod, Sligo and Ryder came to McLeod and lifting low on this body to avoid his shoulder, helped him toward the mound and got him settled.

McLeod wiggled his bottom as he got into position. "This actually feels good," he said, more for the benefit of Black and the others than for himself. He looked up and saw that Wolfe was still somewhat strained.

"What can we leave to place over him that will keep him comfortable?" Black asked. "And do we have anything that can hold water?" Black was clearly far more comfortable and in her element now. Sligo had an inner garment that he could sacrifice for McLeod, but no one else could spare clothing given that they had left the hostel so quickly. McLeod was grateful for the inner garment, which he draped over himself. Once settled again, he looked up at Wolfe. "Give me a little time to relax and get myself settled so I can help my body heal," he said, "Maybe… fifteen minutes?" Wolfe nodded. The others sat to rest and drink from the stream, which was surprisingly refreshing.

Wolfe rose and addressed the group. "In about ten minutes, we're going to leave, with Tad in the lead," Wolfe said. "We'll need to move carefully." Turning to Ryder, she added. "Can we make it to another safe spot prior to getting to the station?"

Ryder's brow creased. "Yes, but I thought we wanted to get off planet as soon as we can?"

"We do, but given the time, there's no way we'll be able to commandeer a vessel by the time we get there." Ryder checked his chron, and his face fell.

"Oh."

Wolfe was dismissive. "Not to worry," she said. "We can make great progress until then and perhaps be in hiding close to the station by early light. Then we can get out of here."

"Can't we just stay here with Tucker?" asked Fisher.

"No," Wolfe said. "We need to get closer to our objective before we stop," Wolfe said. "If we try that from here in the morning, we stand a greater chance of being captured." Her voice sounded harsh even to her, and she heard a sharp intake of breath from Black. Wolfe sighed. "There really is no other way." They sat in silence, no one wanting to be the first one to speak or respond, until Wolfe checked her chron and said, "We need to go." The group arose, said brief goodbyes to McLeod, and started toward the passageway.

"I'll be right out," Wolfe said. As the group left, she checked on her friend, and noticed his breathing seemed relaxed. "I don't want to do this," she said quietly. "But I don't know any other way to get us out of here alive and safe."

McLeod opened his eyes. "And you don't know how much I wish I could disagree with you," he began, "But you're right." Shifting his eyes toward the passageway, he added, "Take care of them: they're good people." Wolfe nodded, and McLeod noticed the tear trickling down her face.

He got emotional himself. "No tears, not now," he said, feeling his own eyes get moist. "Happy tears when we're all through this." Wolfe nodded and wiped the tear from her eye. With a small smile, she said,

"Looks like we may have something to talk about when this is all over…."

"Looks like," he said.

"Don't you dare die on me," she whispered.

"Thought never crossed my mind," McLeod replied. Wolfe rolled her eyes, smiled, then squared her shoulders and left.

Chapter Thirty One

Su'gan, Hemod Western Tunnels

Leaving McLeod behind, Wolfe, Sligo, Fisher, Black and Ryder made their way toward the transport station. They walked for about two hours until Ryder asked them to stop.

Wolfe went right to him. "What's up, Tad?" she asked.

"I think -- in fact I *know* -- that we're not too far from the transport station. And like you said before, we don't want to get there at night when everything is closed."

Wolfe nodded. "About how close do you think we are?" she asked.

Ryder scrunched up his face for a moment, before saying, "I'd say about a 15 minute walk."

"Okay," Wolfe said. She turned toward the rest of the group. "Okay, Tad's going to help us find a place to stay for the night," Wolfe said. "Anybody who wants to help, have at it." As she slowed down and began looking for a convenient place -- preferably one with potable water, Wolfe finally began to feel fatigue from all the stress and challenge of the last twenty four hours. "Hard to imagine that a couple of days ago, we were having a leisurely dinner, and now I'm dead, Tucker's a criminal, and we're all in hiding," she thought.

"Found a place!" Black shouted. "Come see if this will do, Raina." The entire group followed Black's voice and agreed that the space was good as a temporary spot they could rest in. They entered, noticed the fresh water, and all drank enough to stave off dehydration. Finally, they sat down on the floor, silently. As Wolfe looked at their faces, she saw the same fatigue and stress on their faces that she knew was on hers. She searched for a way to reduce the stress and offer them some comfort, but came up blank.

"We don't know who is around or following us," Wolfe said, quietly, "So we should probably have two people on watch at all times. I'm thinking two hour watches with rotating people for continuity." Seeing blank looks on their faces, she explained. "So, the first watch might be Tad and me, then Sofia and me, then Sofia and Miranda, etc. That way, one of us will always know what happened the watch before. To be honest, I don't think we'll have much to do, but I just don't want us to be surprised." Nods all around.

"I think that makes sense," said Sligo. "Do you believe we'll be safe here?"

Wolfe looked around to her companions. "There's really no way to know, Lou. Let's just try to make it as best we can."

Sligo nodded. "Agreed," he said. The group settled in again and grew quiet again. Troubled by the way things were going, Wolfe decided to speak to her colleagues.

"Look, folks," she began, "I wanted to let you know that I know this is not your fight. And I know that we've got you into much more trouble than you ought to be in." Sligo started to object, but Wolfe pressed on. "And I also know that I've not been elected to be in charge here, and if anything I've done has offended you, I apologize. I know I don't have the right to impose this on you." She laughed. "Tucker and I are just so accustomed to leading that it's hard for either of us *not* to be in charge."

Sligo and Fisher both laughed as well. "We're thankful that you *are* in charge, Raina," said Sligo. "I have plenty of resources, but this," he waved his hand around indicating the room and the people within, "is beyond me. I wouldn't know the first thing to do."

"I agree, Raina," said Fisher. "And to be honest, this situation is far bigger than Tucker or you." She shook her head in annoyance. "No, there is a something going on here and we have to get to the bottom of it." Ryder and Black nodded their agreement and understanding, for which Wolfe was grateful.

"Thank you" Wolfe said. "Thank you all." She stood. "Now, how about Tad and I take the first watch, until about," she checked her chron, "about 1100, then I'll stay on with Sofia." She turned to Sofia. "You can pick your second partner. In the meantime, I'm going to start our watch, and please rest when you're not on watch, because when it's my time to rest, I'll be sleeping." Ryder and Wolfe stationed themselves near the entrance to the room, which was fortunately hidden by an overhang.

They sat in silence for a while, before Ryder spoke. "This is all new for me too, you know," he said. "I've done a lot of this, but trying to escape from the police is a new one."

Wolfe smiled. "It's new for me, too," she said. "In fact, usually I'm part of the authorities, rather than being hunted by them." She turned to Ryder. "And I can't say I like it this way."

Ryder was silent again. When he spoke, his voice was much smaller than before. "Do you think we'll be able to get off planet?"

Wolfe, reacting to his voice, became more confident. "I *do* think so," she said. "We just need to keep our wits about us, and focus." She smiled. "I know this is tough for all of you, Tad. I mean, I can imagine that Lou's been in tough situations before given his background, but not anybody else."

Ryder chuckled. "Right, I'm just a PR guy who's worked in offices his whole life, such as it is. So, the idea of running around like this just doesn't compute. But my family members are all members of the union: I thought this would be my dream job." He grew serious again. "I hope 'Chell is going to be okay."

"You can't worry about her, Tad," Wolfe countered, "because you can't do anything to help her anyway. It's clear that Hollander was involved in this situation -- he was gloating a little too much. And if he was involved anyway, I can't see him doing anything to hurt someone who wasn't responsible for anything. Plus, he's got what he wants, right?" Ryder nodded. "So, let just focus on ourselves, and let Rachelle take care of herself. Plus when we get out of here, we can check on her then."

Ryder nodded again, then looked at Wolfe quizzically. "How did you get here?" he asked. "I mean, I know you're a ship's captain, but why did you choose to do that?"

Wolfe laughed again. "I didn't have much choice," she said. "It's the family business." Seeing Ryder's reaction, she continued.

"I'm third generation in the Central Federation military services. My parents -- actually my adoptive parents -- served as did their parents before them." She shrugged "I guess in theory I had a choice, but it was the only one I really knew." She looked up. "But that's okay, I've enjoyed my time in the service."

"But as for being a ship's captain," she continued, "that's only recent. I was appointed commander of FV/*Axon* last month. Tucker, on the other hand, has already had two commands."

Ryder frowned. "Somehow, I thought you had been in the service for the same number of years."

"We have -- almost exactly," Wolfe said. "But the Central Federation doesn't count service on Star Alliance vessels as time in rank: the Alliance does." Ryder seemed puzzled. "You see, it's possible for Federation personnel to serve on Alliance vessels and vice versa."

Ryder nodded. "I think I knew about that."

"Right, Wolfe continued. "Except that when I served on Alliance vessels -- twice -- the Federation didn't count that as time in grade. So people who graduated from the academy with me have already had their first commands. Tucker got his first command seven years ago, because the Alliance counted his service on two Federation vessels as time in grade."

Ryder shook his head slowly.

"It doesn't have to make any sense Tad," Wolfe said. "Andora Prime, my home, is one of the charter members of the Central

Federation, so I have no reason to change, and the Federation has been good to me and my family." She leaned forward and spoke more quietly. "And I have to tell you, my father practically disowned me when I told him I was accepting an appointment to an Alliance vessel, actually where I first met Tucker." Ryder frowned, but Wolfe continued.

"The Federation and the Alliance have been allies for years, but there are still differences between the two groups, and some bad blood. My father just didn't take it well." She turned to him again. "But he's come around, and now he's proud of me, and proud that I decided to work so closely with the Alliance."

"It sounds pretty complicated," Ryder said.

Wolfe laughed again. "That it is," she said, "And you probably need a guidebook to figure it all out." They sat in silence for a while, then engaged sporadically in idle conversation until Wolfe told Ryder to get some sleep, and asked him to send Black over to her. Minutes later, Sofia Black sat down.

"Have you ever fired a weapon like this before?" Wolfe asked, holding the sidearm out to Black.

Black shook her head. "I'm just a nurse."

"You're not *just anything*, Sofia," said Wolfe. Then she stopped, and reached out her hand to touch Black's arm. "Please stop saying that. You are tougher than you think you are - you've already proven that. So stop putting yourself down." Black nodded. Wolfe held up the sidearm again.

"All you have to do is point and squeeze the trigger; it's easy." She paused. "I know that can be hard to even think about, but this is not a time to be afraid and not a time to give up." Black studied Wolfe's face for a moment, then nodded. "Good," Wolfe said. "Let's sit."

They sat in companionable silence for a while, then Black said, "I … need to apologize."

Wolfe frowned. "For?"

"For," Black began, "for treating you so horribly when I first met you."

Wolfe shook her head. "It's not a problem, Sofia," she said, but Black would not be deterred.

"No, it *is* a problem, Raina. I don't know what I was thinking, or why I seemed to resent you." She hesitated. "Actually, I do know." She looked up again at Wolfe. "We've all heard here on the Twin Worlds about the Federation and the Alliance, and frankly they're kind of scary to most of us. I suppose I didn't want to have to do what someone from the Federation or the Alliance told me to do, and…." Wolfe waited.

"And I also think I was envious, because you're doing what I think I always dreamed of doing."

Wolfe chuckled. "Well, it ain't all it's cracked up to be, Sister, but thank you for your apology. I do think I understand."

Black smiled. "You seem to be happy," Black said.

Wolfe smirked. "You mean, right now? This is not how I would describe happy."

"No. I mean in the Central Federation -- as an officer," Black said.

"Well, it's what my family has done for generations, but even putting that aside, I guess you could say I'm happy."

"And Captain McLeod seems happy."

"He is: this is all he's ever wanted to do, too."

"Then why would he want to leave?" Black asked. Wolfe frowned. Black continued. "I overheard someone talking about it, that Captain McLeod wanted to leave the Star Alliance."

Wolfe considered, then said. "That's a good question, and I don't really have the complete answer to it, but as he told me, he's grown tired of shooting when he can find a way to talk his way out of conflict instead."

"But he obviously *can* fight," Black asked.

"Oh yes," said Wolfe with a smile. "Tucker is the best."

"But not at Genesis II."

"Well, I didn't say he was the *only* good fighter," Wolfe said with a laugh.

Black searched Wolfe's face. "You care for him, don't you?" she asked.

Wolfe raised her eyebrows. "I do," she said. "In lots of ways. He's probably my best friend. I don't know if he knows that, but he is. We haven't always been that way: when he served on *SAV/ Valiant*, he almost destroyed my home world: that didn't bring us any closer. But, we've served together lots of times since then, and we've come to know and understand each other and to trust each other completely."

Black looked back to the group and considered their situation. "Was this always your choice," Black asked, "to fight along with him?"

Wolfe laughed. "Wouldn't have it any other way. He knows it and I know it." She checked her chron. "Why don't you get your watch partner up and I'll rest for a bit," Wolfe said.

Black rose. "And Sofia?" Wolfe added. "Thank you for taking care of Tucker."

Chapter Thirty Two

Su'gan, Hemod Western Tunnels

Breathe in, breathe, out. Breathe in, breathe out. McLeod soon found himself awake and relatively refreshed. He looked around the room, and remembered where he was and why he was there. Instinctively, his right arm went to his left shoulder. He moved the left shoulder ever so slightly, and while he felt tightness and soreness when he moved it, there was no underlying throbbing pain. He also seemed to have a good range of motion, which surprised him. He was more cautious about moving his neck given that he had had major surgery on it. He moved his neck from side to side, then up and down, and found that, like his shoulder, he had some pain when he moved, but no underlying discomfort. "Maybe that will come as I start moving," he thought.

McLeod decided to stay relatively still for a while as he assessed his body and wait until he was ready to move to a full sitting position, and then stand. He took his time, both assessing his readiness to move and thinking about where Wolfe and the others might be. He was hoping they had been able to make progress toward the transport station. He checked his chron which read 0500 hours: he had rested and healed for about 14 hours. "They may have already arrived at the transport station and secured passage to Herai or the space station by now," he thought. I suppose all I can do is move toward the transport station and stay hidden."

Finally, he felt he was ready to stand, and he did so slowly. He was steady on his feet, and lifted his left foot forward slightly and then his right foot, walking forward and then backward a bit, before engaging his hips for lateral movement. He knew that he needed to do a full body assessment, so he slowly, then with greater speed, balance and confidence, performed two forms from his strongest style, Ryanjin Kenpo. The forms helped him see how each part of his body was working, his ability to attend to sounds, ability to turn his body for defense, his level of flexibility and his ability to commit to strikes and kicks in his own defense. As he completed the forms, he was a little tired -- not uncommon for someone who puts everything into his forms, and found that he had healed sufficiently to continue to the transport station. He recalled telling Wolfe that he was at about 60% -- at best -- the day before. Now, he felt he could easily be between 80% and 90% competent. He only hoped that he would continue to improve over the day rather than deteriorate.

McLeod looked down and realized that his companions had left him a sidearm and two additional magazines of ammunition. He silently cursed them for giving him so much ammunition when they had so little to spare. He walked to the entrance of the room and looked out. He remembered that Ryder had told the group they would be going to the right, so McLeod turned right and cautiously made his way through the tunnels.

* * *

The final watch team was Tad Ryder and Miranda Fisher. As their watch came to an end, they awoke Lou Sligo and Sofia Black -- Wolfe had awakened on her own just prior to the end of the watch. Wolfe greeted each of her companions, then took a deep breath and smiled. "Well, I really did sleep last night," she said. "I hope you all got a decent rest, too." She looked to each of them in turn. "Are we ready?"

"You lead, and we'll follow, Raina," said Sligo.

"Thank you, Lou," she said. Turning to Ryder, she added, "Can you show us the way out of here, Tad?"

"Sure," he said. He started toward the doorway, then turned back asking, "What about Tucker?"

Wolfe turned to face him and said stoically, "We have to go on or none of us will get off-planet, Tad. Tucker has gotten himself out of much tougher scrapes than this one. We just need to go on." As she finished, she smiled again to Ryder, and gave him a slight nod.

"Okay," he said. "Follow me."

* * *

McLeod continued at a steady pace for over an hour. He was right in that moving did cause some discomfort. Fortunately, he was still able to move effectively and consistently. He paused once, just to rest, and to examine his sidearm. "Not bad," he thought. It was unfamiliar to him, but he determined that it was essentially a point and shoot, so he found a way to secure it under his belt so he could keep both of his hands ready in case of an attack. He didn't know how long he still had to go, and he knew he wouldn't get much better as he walked: he only hoped he would be able to handle himself when he got there. Shaking it off, he breathed in deeply, squared his shoulders and started off again.

* * *

A little more than twenty minutes into their walk, the group began to hear distinct sounds ahead.

Ryder stopped to think, and Wolfe approached him. "I know you don't have a map of this tunnel, Tad, but what do you think is ahead?" she asked.

Ryder looked around, and thought. "I think we go ahead and" he thought again, then started. "We can either go straight, or to the right toward the end. I think the right fork takes us to the freight area." He looked up at Wolfe. "Is that where you want to go?"

Wolfe called over the group. "Tad said the fork to the right takes us to the freight transport area, which implies," she consulted briefly with Ryder, "that going straight takes us to a passenger and private area. I don't think we want that."

"I agree," said Sligo. There is a great deal more security at passenger areas -- at least there *usually* is." His tone caused a reaction among the others.

"Usually?" asked Fisher.

Sligo nodded. "Yes. I just have a feeling," he began, "that security will be heightened everywhere, including the freight areas. But I really don't think we have any choice. Plus, the freight area is where the private vessels that aren't used very often are stored -- assuming we could actually get access to them."

"Alright, then," said Wolfe. "I think that's the best plan we have." She turned again to Ryder, "Up to you, Tad." He nodded and began walking again. Five minutes later, Ryder turned right. The group could hear more and more sounds, some loud, some regular and in the background. Ryder began moving more cautiously as he got closer and closer to the exit. Once he could see light, he stopped. Wolfe joined him at the front.

"I think this is it," Ryder said.

Wolfe nodded, then turned to him, seriously. "You're going to have to go out there and check things out."

"But I don't know what to look for, I mean what...."

"You can do this," Wolfe countered. "I'd go myself, but I don't know what kind of alerts are out on me."

Ryder frowned. "There are no alerts on you -- you're dead."

Wolfe considered this, then said, "Well, I suppose we could go together at least part of the way," she said. "Let's report to the others." They returned to consult with Sligo, Fisher and Black. "We need to go on ahead to check on the transport station and see how we might be able to get off-planet," Wolfe said.

Sligo was unconvinced. "Seems risky," he said.

Wolfe shrugged. "Story of my life," she said.

"Maybe if Tad and I...." Sligo began.

"Thought about that," Wolfe said, "but Tad was right -- he wouldn't know what to look for in terms of ships, access -- this is not something either of you can do alone. Plus, you and Miranda are probably even more well-known on Hemod than we are. Once you're spotted, it's all over." She turned to Ryder with a smirk. "Plus Tad has already reminded me that I'm already dead. I don't think people would be expecting me to appear anywhere."

"Even if your pic has been on the vid?" asked Black.

Wolfe shook her head. "Basic psychology," she said. "Since people already know I'm dead, they won't consider that I actually might not be." She could see confusion on Black's face. "Don't over think it, Sofia." Turning her attention to the entire group again, Wolfe said, "Any questions?" Seeing none, she turned her attention again to Ryder. "We're on, Tad." He nodded and they crept slowly toward the transport station.

Around forty meters ahead, they saw more light, and moved even more slowly toward it, with Wolfe taking the lead. She quietly told Ryder, "Keep your sidearm handy, but not exposed if you can help it." Ryder nodded, and Wolfe could sense the tension rising within him. She only hoped he could hold it together long enough. Wolfe moved forward again, finally seeing a number of ships. She checked her chron and noticed that it was still a bit early for passenger flight - - she didn't have any idea how commercial flights were scheduled on Hemod. She continued to survey ships, looking at their size, and assessing how complicated all of them would be to fly. As she turned her attention back to the left, she saw *Siren*. This could be perfect, she thought. If anything, Decker would know somehow that she's alive and understand what really happened.

"*Siren* is right there." Seeing confusion on Ryder's face, she continued. "*Siren* is the ship we travelled on from Herai -- it's Decker's ship."

Ryder's mood brightened. "That's great," Ryder said. "Should we go get the others?"

"Let's wait until after we speak to Decker," she said. They moved carefully toward *Siren*. As they neared her, they saw the mountain of a man who was Templeton's chief of staff by the door speaking with another crew member. Something in his manner bothered

Wolfe; she pulled Ryder aside in the shadows next to another ship. They inched close enough to overhear the mountain.

"…the loading of the cargo. The rest of the men will be back by then, so it shouldn't take too long to get cleared." The man he was talking to nodded.

"What about Decker? We haven't seen him yet. When is he going to get here?"

The big man towered over his colleague and snarled. "Don't you worry about Templeton," he said. "For now, I'm going to be your boss."

The smaller man stepped back and nodded his head. "Okay, okay," he said. "I got it."

Wolfe rolled her eyes, but the situation also bothered her. Decker may be a rogue, but he impressed her as someone who would never abandon his ship. The gnawing concern she'd had for over a day grew, and she touched Ryder briefly, saying "We can go back now. We've got some things to do." Ryder followed her quickly back to the tunnels. As they rejoined their group, Wolfe explained the situation, and that *Siren* was one of the ships in the commercial transport area. She noticed that the others were as puzzled as she was about Templeton's absence. Wolfe was reasonably confident she could fly the vessel, and she had seen during their trip to Hemod that the ship had some minimal defensive weapons just in case. Once she had fully explained the situation, she turned to Fisher. "This may seem out of the blue, Miranda, but where does Latifa Stew'art live?"

Fisher was confused. "*My* Latifa?"

"Yes. Where?"

Fisher thought for a moment, then said. "She lives on 17th St., south of downtown. It's a nice little apartment close to one of the new shopping areas…"

Wolfe interrupted. "Is there a name for that part of the city?"

Fisher's eyes widened, and she collapsed, shaking. "I… it's…"

Wolfe put her hand on Fisher's arm, comforting her. "The garden district." Wolfe said. It was a statement rather than a question. Fisher nodded, to the shock of the others. "Which helps a lot of other things fall into place," Wolfe said. She looked up. "I think," she looked to Fisher - "*we* think that the two people who were killed weren't Benno Zavery and me, but Decker Templeton and Latifa Stew'art." Sligo, Black and Ryder were stunned. Wolfe continued. "And the fact that Zavery hasn't come forward means he may have been involved in this entire conspiracy."

Sligo was not convinced. "Benno came to us highly recommended," he began. "I have no reason to doubt him or his background."

Wolfe raised her hands ever so slightly, seeking to mollify him. "I get it, Lou," she said. "On the other hand, if you remember, he tried to discourage our going to Genesis II at our planning dinner, and he was the only one who didn't go with us. Mind you, he may have been sick yesterday, but I have real doubts about him given that our visit to Genesis II was definitely a set up: Hollander is a snake, and he was fully prepared for us."

Fisher nodded her head slowly. "It does makes sense when you look at the whole picture, Lou," she said to her mentor. "We don't have to accept that now, but I never could explain why they would think that Raina would be killed and with *Benno* of all people, I mean how could the authorities get that so wrong without at least someone around to confirm it?" Sligo opened his mouth, but wasn't quick enough.

"It would explain a lot, Lou," Black said. "And if Benno isn't involved, then why hasn't he come forward to say that he's alive? I mean, what would he have been doing in the garden district, anyway?"

Sligo sensed he was outnumbered. "Well, he may have lived there when he lived on Hemod years ago; did you ever think of that?"

asked Sligo. "Look, I don't know much of anything right now. The last twenty four hours have been very difficult for me. But I'm not ready to write off Benno; after all, they think he's dead. And who would want to kill him?"

"Who would want to kill *me*, Lou?" Wolfe countered. "And my ID data is easily available from Federation sources: there's no way they could identify the dead body as mine if they really checked." She frowned. "Something is going on, and I want to know what it is." She sensed that she was adding to the tension rather than relieving it, so she took another deep breath. "Right now, what we need to do to is onto that ship and find a way back to either the station or to Herai. I think the *Siren* is the easiest for us to take because I'm pretty sure I can fly it. Also, they don't have a full crew, so there aren't that many people to overpower." She looked at everyone squarely. "So, can we get going on this?"

Wolfe first confirmed that those with weapons knew how to use them and were ready to do so. Wolfe took the lead this time, working her way toward *Siren*. Sligo was second in line, followed by Fisher, Black and Ryder in the rear. They approached *Siren* and could overhear talking from the mountain.

"...about four hours," they heard. "We've already refueled and filed the plan. When will you get here? Ha! Alright, you just make sure to make the transfer. I'm not going to be somebody's second forever." He checked his chron, "Half an hour? Good." He closed the connection.

"I suppose we could wait half an hour to see what's going on." Wolfe said.

"What?" the mountain asked, but he grew silent when he felt the barrel at his neck.

"You know," Wolfe said, "I never liked you -- *please* just give me a reason...." The big man sat down.

"Tad -- you and Miranda go through the ship looking for other crew members. "I don't know what the plan is or what's going on, but we can't trust anybody to be on our side with this." Ryder and Fisher nodded and began going through the ship.

To Black and Sligo, Wolfe said. "We need to close all the hatches except the main and get ready for the arrival of our benefactor -- or I guess, *his* benefactor. The main controls are in the cockpit."

"On it," Black said.

Sligo rolled his eyes. "Youth," he said. They started toward the cockpit, leaving Wolfe alone with the mountain.

"I'm not afraid of you," the mountain said.

Wolfe smiled. "The feeling is mutual." Wolfe backed off to get distance and be able to respond if the mountain tried to take her. "And I have no doubt that I've killed more people than you have. So, like I said, *please* give me a reason."

Fisher and Ryder soon returned, with two loud crew members in tow. "Muth!" one cried. "Who are these people? What's going on?" Ryder poked them with his weapon, and they grew silent.

"These are the only two we found, Raina," Fisher said.

"Thank you, Miranda," Wolfe said. "The others are probably still to arrive, so I guess now we just wait." To the crew members, she said, "You can sit down over there."

Ryder was confused. "But if we have the ship, why don't we just go now?" he asked.

"We could, Tad," Wolfe admitted, "But we need to know more about what's happening behind the scenes so we can fix it." She turned to the mountain. "Unless you -- Muth, was it? want to just tell us now; it would save us a whole lot of time." He folded his arms and turned away. "Yeah, that's what I thought, Wolfe said. To Fisher and Ryder, she said, "We wait -- at least until Lou and Sofia get back."

A few minutes later, Sligo and Black returned. "We got the hatches closed except for the main, as you requested.

"Good," Wolfe said. "Now, I need you to stay here while I head down toward that crew lounge. Sofia, come with me." Black and Wolfe traveled to the crew area and to the area near the heads where the weapons were stored. Wolfe checked the door, and after a short while, was able to open the closet. Peering inside, she thought back to what McLeod had said to her. "Did he say twenty pulse rifles and twenty A9's?" If so, at least five of each were missing. She took three more of each with extra ammunition clips and canisters along with a long coil of wire, and reclosed the door, but only after damaging the closet so it couldn't be reopened.

Wolfe and Black returned to Sligo, Ryder and the prisoners. Holding out the weapons, Wolfe said, "Just in case there are more crew members here." She gave them to Sligo. "In the meantime, we need to get these idiots tied, placed in a secure area, and get ourselves ready to leave." Wolfe quickly and efficiently used the wire to secure the hands of all three prisoners, then she rose and wiped her hands. After leading everyone to the cockpit, she turned to face her companions again.

"Now," she said. "We wait."

Chapter Thirty Three

Su'gan, Hemod Main Spacedocks, Cockpit, Siren

Less than twenty minutes later, a light on the main panel indicated that one of the hatches was opening.

"What is that?" asked Fisher.

Wolfe squinted, then rose. "It's one of the hatches; the one aft and to port -- it's opening."

"What does that mean?" asked Fisher.

"It means either we missed a crew member on the ship, or someone is entering from the outside." Wolfe looked around. "We have to investigate." She pressed two pads on the panel, then looking at Sligo, she added, "Lou, can you go with me?"

"Of course," Sligo said. He grabbed a pulse rifle, checked that it was primed, then followed her out of the cockpit. Wolfe turned back as she left. "Guard Muth and the other two and if they try anything stupid, just shoot them."

Wolfe and Sligo crept carefully down the passageway toward the open hatch. They passed the crew lounge and the armory and were passing the bulkhead marking the forward most storage tank when they heard a sound to their right. Sligo turned to investigate while Wolfe continued straight. She had only gone around twenty meters when she heard Sligo.

"Ahh!" Sligo shouted and Wolfe heard him hit the deck.

"Lou!" She continued moving swiftly but carefully. As she turned down the area he had traveled, she saw Benno Zavery standing over the prone form of Lou Sligo. Zavery was pointing a sidearm at Sligo's head.

Wolfe kept her weapon pointing at both of them, unwavering. She spoke calmly. "Right on time, Benno," she said. "Muth said you were on your way."

Zavery's mouth set in a grim line. "He's a bigger fool than I thought he was."

"Well, big certainly describes him," Wolfe said. "We were tempted to leave earlier, but I wanted to get you here first, so people could see that *both* of us were still alive."

Zavery laughed. "It won't help you," he said. "McLeod is still finished."

It was Wolfe who laughed this time. "Lots of people have counted Tucker out -- people a lot better than you, in fact." She seemed to relax a bit. "So tell me Benno, what was in it for you? Power in the union? Money? You must have gotten something out of it to kill two people."

"No one was supposed to be killed like that," Zavery said angrily. "You forced my hand!"

"Right," Wolfe said. "That's what *all* the super criminals say." She grew more serious. "They never did anything to you; if you wanted to fight somebody, why didn't you fight Tucker or me? But Decker and Latifa... they will get you for those, Benno."

Zavery breathed out. "They were convenient, and it let us get you out of the way. You didn't give us any choice. If you'd just gone to Verinox like we directed you to, they never would have died. Their blood is on *your* hands."

Wolfe maintained her cool as she examined the area trying to see what her fighting options would be. "Which just confirms that Hollander is involved," she said. "That suggests it's money." Wolfe shook her head. "Doesn't surprise me at all -- he's a pretty nasty man, just like you. So, what's happened to Anton Jurgan?"

"Anton is a decent enough guy," said Zavery. "But he is a zealot. He could have had enough to retire in the nicest resorts of the Twin Worlds, but all he cared about was the damn union."

"Right, such a bad guy."

"No," Zavery countered, "Just an idiot."

"So, you may as well tell me about Patt'son's daughter and Anton. Are they both alive?"

Zavery exhaled. "Yes," he said, "But Anton's going to be killed when they rescue her. His tone changed. "I'm kinda sorry about him."

"But not sorry enough to let him live -- yeah, that's pretty sorry," said Wolfe. "So," she added. "How are we going to resolve this? You have a weapon, and I have a weapon…."

"And you have that pesky Federation honor -- I don't have that problem. You won't let someone else die," he looked at his feet, "like Lou here." Wolfe remained relaxed, hoping that he would flinch as she saw his arm begin to tense. But before he could squeeze the trigger, he wrenched, screamed and grabbed his leg, then collapsed. As he fell, Wolfe could see Tucker McLeod standing ten meters behind Zavery. Wolfe quickly advanced to Zavery to take his weapon and only then did she see the knife sticking out of his thigh. Wolfe faced McLeod.

"You're not the only person who can throw a knife, Raina," he said.

"You could have done that earlier," Wolfe said, as she removed Zavery's sidearm and checked him for more weapons.

"Hey, I was just following your lead," McLeod said. "You were the one who kept asking all the questions."

Wolfe looked at him and smiled. "It's good to see you, Tucker.

McLeod squeezed Wolfe's arm. "Good to see you too." he said. "So, was this one of those 'get the super criminal to talk' things?"

"Something like that." She reached into her pocket and took out wire to secure Zavery while patting her pocket. "Plus, it's all been recorded, so he can't deny it later." She looked at Zavery's thigh. "You gonna take that?"

McLeod answered by reaching down and pulling his throwing knife from Zavery.

"Ahh! You didn't have to …."

"Shut up!" McLeod and Wolfe said in unison. They finished securing Zavery, then saw to Sligo, whose injury seemed minor.

Wolfe looked to McLeod. "Alright. Let's get off this sorry planet." Sligo could walk -- slowly -- and McLeod and Wolfe were able to drag Zavery to the cockpit. As they entered, Muth's eyes widened. Ryder, Black and Fisher were happy to see McLeod.

"Tucker!" Black cried. "You're okay!"

McLeod smiled. "Yes, thanks to you, Sofia." Black was smiling from ear to ear, then went to examine Sligo.

Wolfe brought them back to reality. "Watch both of these people," she said, indicating Muth and Zavery. "And if you have to shoot them, try not to kill them -- we want them alive when we arrive at the station." After examining the cockpit, she added, "This is large enough for us all to stay here. Get everyone properly secured and strap in." McLeod nodded his agreement. Wolfe returned her gaze to Black. "And Sofia, take care of Lou." Black nodded. "Now, we can finally get out of here."

Once they seated a snarling but immobilized Muth into his seat, McLeod and Wolfe settled into the helm, with McLeod noticing how different it looked from any Alliance or Federation controls. Wolfe examined the controls carefully.

McLeod turned toward her. "Are you sure you can fly this?"

Wolfe turned to him and glared, then rolled her eyes as she returned to the controls. "I'm going to forget you said that," she said. She refocused. "I need you to check the headings so we can get out of here." She glanced at him and pointed at the display. "Do you see it there?"

"Aye." Wolfe glanced over and quickly realized that McLeod was taking his supportive role seriously. She pressed several controls to start the engines, and ran the required checks.

"Whatever you want me to do, let me know." said McLeod.

Wolfe nodded, then flipped the com switch. She was all business.

"*Siren* to AC." A few seconds silence.

"Air Control."

"*Siren* engaging flight plan; requesting release and airway assignment."

"Original flight plan was for 1100 hours," *Siren*. You're early. Acknowledge."

"Acknowledged," said Wolfe. "Change of plan, AC."

"Standby, *Siren*."

While they waited, McLeod asked. "Is it going to be a hassle keying in the course and destination?"

Wolfe shook her head. "I've got it."

"AC; *Siren*."

"*Siren*."

"You're cleared for Airway 2. Acknowledge."

"Acknowledged. Thank you AC. *Siren* out." Wolfe keyed in the display again, and saw a map of the airways. She was able to maneuver the vessel toward the airway, and prepare for departure. She called over her shoulder.

"Secure positions," she called, indicating that the team should be properly seated.

"Time to go home," Wolfe said. And *Siren* rose into the sky.

Chapter Thirty Four

Cockpit, Siren

Once safely beyond the Hemodian atmosphere, McLeod turned to Wolfe.

"You really can fly *anything*, can't you?"

"Told you that before, Tucker."

"Any reason to be worried about the Hemodian defense forces on our way to the station?" McLeod asked. She shook her head.

"I doubt it," said Wolfe. "There should be no one on planet to scream -- with the possible exception of Hollander -- and I don't think he'll find out for a while." Wolfe stood. "No. I think we're fine until we have to talk our way onto the station."

McLeod inclined his head toward the aft bulkhead of the cockpit. "Does that mean we can spend a little more time talking to Benno?" McLeod tried to stand, but Wolfe waved him off.

"No," she said "You're still not 100%. Just watch the helm." She left the helm and rejoined the team at the bulkhead.

"Somebody drag that sorry piece of humanity up close where I can see him," she said. Sligo roughly dragged his former friend toward the helm, taking little care to Zavery's obvious discomfort. Sligo leaned Zavery against a wall, stared at him until Zavery looked away, then returned aft. Wolfe knelt by Zavery to examine the wrap around his thigh. "I don't imagine you'll have any trouble with that thigh, though I wouldn't take up running anytime soon."

Zavery scowled at her. "I don't have to say anything to you."

"Not a problem," McLeod said, as he turned from the helm. "All you have to do is listen." He looked up at Wolfe. "Do you want to go first?"

She shook her head. "Nope. Senior Captains first," she said.

McLeod gave a small smile to Zavery. "So, when did you first hear from Councilor Trent?" Zavery's eyes widened ever so slightly, his nostrils flared a bit and then he glanced away before returning his attention to McLeod.

"I don't know what you're talking about," Zavery said.

"Did you see that?" Wolfe asked. "That eye reaction?"

McLeod nodded. "And I saw the nostrils, too."

"Ooh, I may have missed that." Wolfe turned again to Zavery. "You have a lot of tells, Benno; you should really work on that. Of course, you'll have a lot of time to reflect on that while you're in prison on Hemod." Zavery huffed.

"We already know about Hollander, we know about the kidnapping, Anton's abduction and possible murder, and about the murders of Templeton and Stew'art," said McLeod. "We really don't need any more confirmation from you, but I thought you might like to, you know, clear the air. I mean, do you really want to share the blame with just Hollander? Don't you at least want to implicate Trent?"

"*You're* going to be implicated in the murders on Hemod -- I don't have anything to worry about," Zavery shouted.

"Except your recorded confession," said Wolfe. "Forgot about that, didn't you?" Zavery's face blanched. "Yes. You *need* to worry, Benno. Templeton and Stew'art were decent people -- a little flaky, but decent people. And I know that Miranda Fisher will push this pretty hard. And if they don't, I can assure you that a threat to a Federation senior officer will place you in Federation custody. And that, I can make sure of." Zavery looked less confident. "And I wonder how you got the authorities on Hemod in your pocket to falsely identify two dead bodies." Wolfe stared harder at Zavery. "How did you do that, Benno?"

"Also gonna be hard to explain why you didn't come forward when everybody said you were dead," said McLeod.

"And it's going to be just as hard for Trent to explain how he so quickly jumped to the conclusion that I was dead and Tucker was a murderer, before demanding a check on the evidence," Wolfe said. She turned again and smiled at Zavery as she continued. "And this has got to be the first time that a Star Alliance diplomat has so quickly requested that the ID chip of a senior Alliance officer be activated before any evidence is identified or analyzed."

McLeod locked his eyes again on Zavery. "And requesting something as big as that would require *hours* of lead time. So, Trent had to have formulated the request before he was officially notified of the crime by the authorities. All that would take was a simple time stamp on the official request."

"The simple truth is that Trent is going down, too. So, no -- you don't have to say a thing to me or to Tucker," Wolfe said. "Except that if you did, it would guarantee that Trent doesn't get away before we arrive at the space station. Up to you, Benno."

Wolfe and McLeod turned toward the helm. "You can have him back, Lou," Wolfe said. "Just don't rough him up too much."

They flew in relative silence until a location about 25 clicks from the space station. At that point they noticed a short distance fighter and were hailed by the station.

"Station Alpha Control to *Siren*."

"*Siren*," said Wolfe.

"Records of flight plan show you significantly earlier than your filed plan. Acknowledge."

Wolfe frowned and looked at McLeod, whose eyebrow were furrowed.

"Acknowledged."

"Explanation?" The voice Control was clipped.

"Early start," Wolfe replied. Brief silence.

"Control to *Siren*."

"*Siren*."

"We need a better explanation than that. We have information that there is a wanted criminal on board."

"Oh?" said Wolfe. "And who is this criminal?"

"The identified criminal is Tucker McLeod, Senior Captain in the Star Alliance, wanted for two murders." Wolfe smiled so wide, it probably could have been heard through the com.

"That individual is indeed on the ship, Control, and is under my direct supervision," she said. "I am bringing him in to the authorities, though ..."

"Negative, Siren. He is to be taken directly to the authorities on Hemod. This is a directive from the Twin Worlds authorities on this station."

Wolfe rolled her eyes. "Control, this is Captain Raina Wolfe of the Central Federation, and I can certainly vouch that Captain McLeod is under my complete control, and further that the second person who is supposed to have been killed by Captain McLeod -- Benno Zavery -- is here as well, though somewhat the worse for wear." There was silence for almost a minute.

"*Siren* Captain. Confirm your identity."

Wolfe sighed. "Captain Raina Wolfe, ID Delta Alpha 774 669, of the Central Federation." Silence again.

"*Siren*. Captain Raina Wolfe is dead. Can you confirm your identity?"

"You mean besides my ID?"

"Affirmative."

"I'll be happy to show you that when we dock."

"Negative. Clearance is denied, *Siren*."

Wolfe turned off the com and turned to McLeod. "These people are really starting to piss me off," she said. As she spoke, another fighter appeared on the screen.

McLeod pointed. "Second fighter," he said.

Wolfe checked the vid and sensors. She let out a long slow breath while shaking her head.

"Not exactly what I was hoping for," she said.

"Your maneuver," McLeod said. Wolfe frowned. "Your maneuver," he repeated. "The one you used in your wing on the *Reese*? Aren't they still showing that at both academies?"

Wolfe slowly nodded. "These aren't Federation or Alliance fighters."

"No, but there are plenty of them in Control, and this is probably their only entertainment. Just key it in."

Wolfe's fingers began gliding over the controls.

"*Siren*. Acknowledge."

"Acknowledge what?" she asked McLeod. He shrugged.

"Acknowledge what?" Wolfe asked Control.

"Acknowledge your return to Hemod."

Wolfe sighed. "Negative, Control. We have a murderer on board as well as other personnel seeking Central Federation asylum." Silence.

"*Siren* repeat."

Wolfe continued keying in the maneuver. "Control, we have a murderer on board as well as other personnel seeking Central Federation asylum. Acknowledge clearance to land." Wolfe completed keying in her maneuver and noticed a third fighter near the other two.

She turned to McLeod, "Bring Muth up here."

"Muth?"

"The mountain."

"Oh," said McLeod. He left his station and brought Muth to the helm.

Wolfe turned to Muth. "Look, I don't have time for silent or stupid right now," she said. "Those Hemodian fighters are just itching to take us down and I need to key into their com channel." Her request sounded quite calm, yet her intensity made a clear impact on Muth.

Before Muth could answer, McLeod added, "And we know that you can do that, since there's no other way you could smuggle weapons around here without being able to listen in to all the planetary forces." McLeod leaned forward, "And I'm really not in the mood to be without ears out here." He pointed to the vid, "These guys aren't going to be easy to beat if we can't hear what they're doing, got it?"

Muth first frowned, then seem to deflate before eyeing the control panel. "Hit the button under the com switch and go to '431.' That's their usual working channel," he said.

"Thank you," Wolfe said, as she followed Muth's instructions. Immediately after heading to 431, they could hear the chatter.

"Orders, Ma'am?"

"Standard maneuver, Smits," the commander said. "We should be able to bring this little bucket in easily. Seven-seven on my mark. Stand by."

"Standing by," came two voices over the com, almost simultaneously.

As he listened, McLeod noticed Wolfe reading changing measurements showing the position of the three fighters.

"Tracking?" he asked.

Wolfe nodded. "Yep," she began. "It looks like they're planning to use a squeeze maneuver -- kind of like the first maneuver taught to rookie Alliance pilots."

"That should be easy to avoid," McLeod said.

"In theory," Wolfe replied. She thought for a moment, then switched on her com again.

"*Siren*, Control."

"Control."

"Control," Wolfe began, "please acknowledge Central Federation and Star Alliance personnel within Station Alpha Air Control." After a brief silence, Wolfe heard,

"*Siren* repeat."

Wolfe continued keying in the maneuver. "Control. Acknowledge Federation and Alliance personnel within Station Alpha Air Control."

"*Siren*. Federation and Alliance personnel are in control. Confirm reason...."

"Just wanted them to have a ringside seat," Wolfe said with a light chuckle.

She turned to McLeod, "Ready?"

"Aye," said McLeod.

Wolfe turned for the last time to her companions, saying, "Hold on, people." She turned back to the controls, and with little effort at all, thrust Siren forward and down, quickly threading itself between two of the fighters.

"What the…" came the cry from one of the fighters.

"Stay in formation," said the commander. "She is one against three. Stay in formation seven-seven!"

Wolfe's eyes shifted quickly from vid to monitors to the controls, before keying in her second maneuver. *Siren* looped quickly around until she was directly behind the pursuit fighter to the right.

"She's on me!" cried the fighter.

"Abbott," said the commander. "My wing. Go to four-four."

"Aye," came the muffled voice of Abbott, as he moved to provide support to his team members.

"Red Team," came the voice of Control. "Status?"

"Control, Siren has executed evasive maneuvers…"

"Red Team, we need this ship subdued now."

"Yes, sir," came the annoyed voice of the squad commander. The commander watched as Siren inched closer to the first fighter.

"Impressive," McLeod said.

Wolfe snorted. "Hey, you study fashion on new planets, I study fighting formations."

"Of Twin Worlds military?" McLeod asked, incredulously.

"Yep," Wolfe replied, not taking her eyes off the helm.

"I didn't think this ship could move so well," McLeod said, after shaking his head.

Wolfe shook her head dismissively. "Remember when I was talking to Templeton about the ship configuration, the '4 and 2?'"

"Ah," said McLeod. "The '4 and 2,' but also the '1', right? The extra drive."

"Exactly," replied Wolfe. "The '1' is the key to everything."

McLeod looked at ship positions on the vid and asked, "Any indication of weapons being charged?"

Wolfe quickly scanned a few of the gauges and shook her head.

"No," she said. "I think this is an operation to contain us rather than to attack."

McLeod was silent again before he asked, "Your maneuver?"

"Not yet," Wolfe replied. "They aren't ready for it yet." She looked again at the progress of the fighters, her eyebrows furrowing.

"We need to hit the other side of the station," she said.

"Under-over?" McLeod asked.

Wolfe looked at him and smirked. "No. Better way," she said. "On my mark; I need to time this carefully." Wolfe noticed the two fighters pursuing her gaining, and trying to pin her between them and the fighter in front of her.

"In position," said the squad commander.

"Aye, Ma'am…" came the response.

Their response was cut off by *Siren* seeming to drop vertically, then flip upside down and shoot off to the other side of the space station.

"Ma'am…?"

"Red Team, high-low!" came the shout from the commander.

"High-low, aye!"

Wolfe noticed the split in the fighter squad, making quick mental calculations as she considered the possibilities. McLeod, anxious to speak yet also cognizant of Wolfe's need to concentrate, remained silent. As they appeared on the other side of the station, McLeod felt rather than saw Wolfe shift direction to move toward the far starboard tip of the station, near one of the observation towers.

"Position shift, Ma'am!"

"Acknowledged. Regroup in standard."

The squadron appeared on the side of the station, and regrouped before beginning a smooth, coordinated movement directly toward *Siren*.

Wolfe and McLeod watched calmly until McLeod turned to his friend. "Should I have brought the snacks?"

Wolfe rolled her eyes. "Pay attention please, Tucker." She returned her attention to the vid.

"Almost…. almost…"

Then without word, *Siren* turned hard to port, then fired across open space before spinning on its axis to a position aft of all three fighters. Because of the way in which the maneuver was engaged, *Siren* momentarily appeared to be both forward and aft of the fighters.

Wolfe and McLeod heard muffled cries from their team as they weren't prepared for the maneuver.

"Sorry about that, people," Wolfe said.

*"Who **is** that guy?" cried one of the pilots.*

"Stand ready," said the commander.

"Ma'am?"

"Stand ready!" she repeated. Then she contacted Control.

"Red Team leader, Control"

"Control."

"Control, just who is this pilot supposed to be?"

"Stand by." Mere seconds later, control responded.

"Control, Red Team.

"Red Team."

"Pilot is rumored to be Capt. Raina Wolfe of the Central Federation. The pilot iden..."

"Control, that has to be her; no one else can fly like that." Silence for a moment.

"Stand by, Red team."

"Aye." The squad commander drummed her fingers on her panel as she waited.

"Red Team, Control."

"Control."

"Awaiting instructions, Control."

"Red Team, based on the observation of the pilot by Federation personnel, there is sufficient evidence that she is Capt. Raina Wolfe."

"Meaning?" asked the commander, impatiently.

"Meaning, you are now an escort rather than a pursuit squadron."

"Aye."

After hearing this exchange, Wolfe waited for about a half minute, then keyed in.

"*Siren.* Control."

"Control."

"Anything you have to tell me?" Silence.

"Cleared to dock, Captain Wolfe."

Chapter Thirty Five

Twin Worlds Space Station Alpha, Main Docks, Siren

Wolfe turned to the team to caution them about their arrival at the station.

"Now, we already know what we have to do," she began. "There's no telling who is going to meet us and how they're going to receive us. We need to have Muth, followed by me with the sidearm, then Zavery and the other crew who are followed by Lou. Tucker is next, who is followed by Tad, Sofia and Miranda." She turned to Ryder. "Tad, you need to have a weapon while you're behind Tucker so it looks like he is in custody. So long as Federation or Alliance personnel take him he's good. What I don't want is someone from the Twin Worlds." Then she added, "Present company excluded, of course."

"So, are we ready?"

"Sure," said McLeod. "Let's go. I have to use the head."

Wolfe shook her head, and held up her hand. "We may all need that sense of humor before this is all over, people." Then she turned to Muth. "Up," Wolfe said. "You're first out of the ship, and first in case they have weapons." They surveyed the people outside then opened the main hatch, walking slowly down the ramp. They faced several soldiers from Hemod and Herai, in addition to a Federation prolate.

A Hemodian officer who was obviously in charge said, "Weapons down!"

Wolfe raised her hand slowly to stop the team's movement. "We have five in custody here," she said. "It wouldn't do to have any of them get away."

The man shook his head. "Custody is *our* job, not yours captain," the man said. "Weapons down!"

Wolfe calmly faced the Federation prolate. "Prolate, As a Su-Captain of the Central Federation, I offer myself to you for review and protective custody, and the same for the people under my charge. There are ten of us." The prolate started a bit, then relaxed.

"Prolate," Wolfe continued. "Is there any doubt that I am who I say I am?"

To this, the prolate was quick. "No, Ma'am, she said.

"I didn't think so. Now, according to Code 661 subsection 9, any Federation officer and those under their charge or command may surrender himself or herself to another Federation officer for review and protective custody. Therefore, we surrender ourselves to you."

The prolate stiffened, the let out a slow breath as she faced the Hemodian officer. "Commander," she said. "That is a Federation regulation, and I am bound to follow it." As the Hemodian's faced showed rage, she continued, "And they certainly can't get away from you on this little station."

The Hemodian officer took in a slow breath, and said, "Stand down," thus relaxing his soldiers.

At this, Wolfe turned her head slightly to her team. "Lower your weapons," she said. And they did. The young prolate approached Wolfe, and she continued.

"The people in custody are Muth, here, for attempted murder, Benno Zavery for murder, attempted mur...."

"Zavery!" the Hemodian commander cried. "But he's dead, and..."

"Just like me," Wolfe responded. "Or didn't you remember that I was supposed to be dead, too?" The commander shook his head, confused. "To continue," Wolfe said, "Zavery is being held for murder, attempted murder, kidnapping and conspiracy. We also have Senior Captain Tucker McLeod of the Star Alliance who was falsely charged with murder of, in fact, Zavery and me. But we

thought, just in case, we should have him in custody, too." Wolfe
turned to the prolate. "You won't need any restraints on McLeod."
She offered her weapon to the prolate, and it was accepted.

Wolfe continued, "The other two with us have been injured: Zavery
with a knife wound, and Muth was just roughed up a bit.
Fortunately, we had a surgical nurse tend to their wounds. McLeod
was also shot in the left shoulder." Wolfe looked at the prolate
again. "Prolate, don't you think you ought to get more Federation
officers or NCOs here to help you?"

"I can take care of that," the Hemodian Commander said. And he
directed a member of his staff to the com to make the request.

"Prolate," Wolfe said.

"Ma'am."

"I need you to communicate with Vice Chancellor Noregan and
Minister Long and have them summon Councilor Trent to the central
conference room, preferably with guards." The prolate stared.

"Perhaps you ought to record or write this down, Prolate," Wolfe
said.

The prolate nodded. "Ma'am," she said as she clicked her recorder.
Wolfe repeated the request. Shortly afterwards, a fire team of
personnel from the Central Federation arrived, and took them all into
custody.

* * *

Wolfe insisted on having the entire group together to begin the
review. Muth and Zavery were taken to a dispensary for treatment
of their injuries, but were under constant Federation and Twin
Worlds guard. McLeod was permitted to stay with the team. They
sat in a large conference room, and were told to be silent until called
for. To Wolfe, McLeod seemed to be in a sort of trance, probably
hoping to continue healing from his surgery. An hour later, Wolfe
was summoned for her individual review. She rose, but asked for

the prolate who had originally taken them into custody to be assigned to guard the remainder of the group. There was some objection, since Federation officers are not usually sent to guard, but the prolate was assigned along with another NCO.

Before Wolfe left, she took the prolate aside and asked, "Of these two sergeants, who do you trust the most?" The prolate seemed puzzled. Wolfe continued. "Or the one who best thinks for himself?" The prolate smiled and indicated one with her head.

"I'd like him to take me, please," said Wolfe.

The prolate nodded. "Works for me, Ma'am." she said.

"And Prolate," Wolfe said. "Don't let anyone pull you away from this room. These people" she indicated the team with her hand, "are under your control and custody only. Do not let anyone other than one of your direct superiors *who you know* take them. Understood?"

The prolate nodded and seemed to understand. "Yes, Ma'am," then added, "I made a point of reviewing Code 661 subsection 9, so I know the rights and obligations well."

"Well done, Prolate," Wolfe said. "And just so you know, you may be pressed on that."

The prolate stood straight. "Ma'am," she said. Wolfe was led away by the sergeant two corridors down to a conference room. She was directed to sit down, and was shortly joined by a Hemodian officer, who dismissed the sergeant. "Sir, I cannot leave this individual without Federation supervision."

"You can, and…."

"Then, I will have to return her to Federation control, sir," said the sergeant. To Wolfe, he said, "Let's go." Wolfe arose, before the Hemodian officer stopped them.

"Wait," he said. He shook his head. "I'm not used to this, but it doesn't really matter. Just sit down. He looked directly at Wolfe this time. "I assume you want a Federation officer present during questioning."

Wolfe nodded. "Yes, and I made a request to both Vice Chancellor Noregan and Minister Long that they summon Councilor Trent, and…

"Well, *that* I can say has already happened," the commander remarked. "And I don't think Councilor Trent was very happy about it." Wolfe looked to the Federation sergeant, who nodded. Then, for the first time in days, Wolfe relaxed.

"Captain," the Hemodian officer said. "Are you alright?"

Wolfe smiled. "More alright than I have been for a while, Commander." Just then, a Federation Commander and staff sergeant entered the room.

They spoke with the Hemodian Commander. "Hey, Silas."

"John." The Hemodian commander pointed at Wolfe. "There she is."

The Federation Commander smiled. "Present circumstances aside, I'm honored to meet you, Captain. Seeing your maneuver in action -- that was the best," he gushed.

Wolfe smiled. "Glad to know it was still impressive, Commander."

Wolfe turned to the Hemodian. "Are the Ambassador…" she began, but the commander held up his hand.

"On the way, Captain," he said. "We communicated with both Ambassador Redstar and Fleet Marshall Masters as soon as you were cleared to land." He smiled as he leaned forward. "And they were very happy to learn that you were safe."

Wolfe rolled her eyes and returned the smile. "As safe as I can be after a rather harrowing night on Hemod, Commander," she said. As she finished speaking, she heard the door open and Ambassador

Susan Redstar burst into the room, followed by Fleet Marshall Masters.

"Captain," Redstar said as she took Wolfe's hands in hers. "It's good to have you back."

Wolfe squeezed Redstar's hands in turn. "Thank you, Ambassador," Wolfe replied. She glanced at Masters and started to rise, but Masters stopped her.

"Captain. Raina," he said. "Please don't get up. Let's just sit and talk." Masters gave Wolfe a look that said he was proud of her.

Wolfe exhaled and relaxed. "Fleet Marshall. Ambassador," she began. "I'm ready to get started, and," she continued holding up a recording chip, "this may be of value in evaluating my story."

Masters took the chip, then looked to her and simply said,

"What can you tell me, Captain?" he asked. "What really happened planet-side?" With that, Wolfe began her tale.

* * *

McLeod was being held in a small room, with two rather lifeless looking Hemodian guards, and a Federation corporal, who was clearly in charge. McLeod was waiting patiently, relaxing, and hoping to allow his body to continue healing. He had been waiting for about fifteen minutes, when an alarm sounded with both red and orange lights alternating. The Hemodian guards, understanding the seriousness of the alert, immediately left the room.

The Federation corporal turned to McLeod, and said, "Boy, that was…." he lurched, then fell to the floor. As he fell, the angry figure of Elias Trent was revealed.

McLeod glanced toward him, then said, "Took you long enough," he said.

Trent, though angry, played along. "Worrisome delays, Captain."

McLeod shrugged. "I understand that, Councilor -- assuming you are still a councilor."

"For now," Trent said. "Though that may not be the case later if I do not get off this station."

"Don't stay here on my account," McLeod said. "I certainly don't think hanging with me is worth your position -- or your life."

Trent nodded his head slowly. "Perhaps," he said. "I just didn't want to leave without a parting gift, Captain. You must realize that you are the cause of all of this."

McLeod, sighed, noticing his tremendous fatigue. "Right," he said. "All I ever wanted to do was be a good officer and make a difference in the galaxy." His voice grew quieter and he shook his head slowly. "I just don't understand people like you, Councilor. You were successful, doing the things you said you wanted to do; you had everything."

Trent laughed. "Not everything, Captain," he said. There is no real wealth, no real power in these governing councils within either the Alliance or the Federation. I only hoped to have the chance at a more -- *comfortable* retirement."

"Something tells me you were not involved in the murders," McLeod said quietly.

Trent shuddered. "Hollander is a *vile* man," he said. "I don't even think Zavery knew what he was made of. When Benno told me that those people were killed, I knew it was the beginning of the end."

"Which didn't stop you from accusing me, I noticed."

"It did not," Trent said. "That was, I'm afraid, part of the plan all along." He looked up. "Your presence was the catalyst for all the bad things that happened, and you were to take the blame. Eventually, we would find both Patt'son's daughter and the body of Jurgan and while that would have nothing to do with you, by that time, the negotiations would have been cancelled, thus ensuring Genesis II's continued success. We clearly did not count on you or Captain Wolfe."

"And *everyone else*," McLeod corrected. Every member of that team, save Zavery of course, was crucial." Trent bowed his head in acknowledgement.

"And just how did Zavery get picked to be on the Unionist team anyway?" asked McLeod.

"He volunteered," said Trent, "and did it so consistently and so loudly, that given his background, he was the obvious choice."

"So," McLeod began, "did you come to kill me?"

Trent sighed. "I thought about it," he said. "But there really is no out for me, so it's not worth it. And I have to admit, whether you are in some area of the diplomatic corps or on a starship, you have tremendous value to the future of the galaxy. And I suppose I've realized, a bit too late I grant you, that I don't have the right to take that away." He looked at the scar on McLeod's neck. "Oh, and I'm sorry about your chip. I really hadn't gotten approval from the Alliance -- I made the official request and wanted to let the Hemodian authorities know that we supported them."

McLeod fingered his neck as Trent spoke, then indicated the corporal with his eyes. "And the corporal?"

"A mild shock," Trent said. It shouldn't last more than another minute or so. Oh, and the location for Moriah Patt'son and Anton Jurgan has been given to the authorities: I'm sure they'll be released safely soon." McLeod nodded. Trent crossed to the table across from McLeod and laid a small device on it, then moved a chair over to sit close to McLeod.

"Since I have nowhere else to go, do you mind if I wait here?"

Chapter Thirty Six

Star Alliance Beta Quadrant Headquarters, Conference Room C

"This board of review is convened to review the actions of Senior Captain Tucker McLeod, past Commanding Officer of SAV/ *Endeavor*, those actions specific to participation in a diplomatic mission to the Twin Worlds of Herai and Hemod which occurred Stardate 2459.8," said Fleet Marshall North, board chair." McLeod knew the review would not be as cordial as his previous reviews, but since his actions were generally lauded by the authorities on the Twin Worlds and they aided in solving a double murder, he didn't expect to leave the review with any significant penalties. Still, a board of review can do or say anything about an officer, so he needed to be prepared.

Introductions were made of all the board members, including surprisingly, Minister Demeter Long of the Star Alliance.

"I am Fleet Marshall Morgan North, Star Alliance. Our board members will introduce themselves, starting on my right.

"Mark Santana, Senior Captain, Star Alliance."

"Theric Raju, Senior Captain, Central Federation."

"Minister Demeter Long, Star Alliance."

"Thank you, board members," said North. He looked up. "Our purpose today is to review the actions of Senior Captain Tucker McLeod during his diplomatic mission to the Twin Worlds, but solely in the context of his behavior as a Star Alliance officer. Captain McLeod had previously requested a career change to the diplomatic corps, and the opportunity to try out an assignment was suggested by former Councilor in the Beta Intercouncil, Elias Trent, and approved by Minister Demeter Long, who is serving with this board. Captain McLeod served as staff to the committee on military cooperation and weapons of the larger negotiations." North turned back to McLeod.

"Captain McLeod. Would you please recount your actions during the official negotiations, and how you sought to support those negotiations?"

McLeod squared his shoulders, noticed a small smile on the face of Long, then relaxed.

"Well, that is a large request, Fleet Marshall, and a complicated one, so I will start at the beginning." Then, he began.

McLeod's recounting of the events, particularly to the senior captains who were less aware of what had occurred, and of his severe injury was startling, in some ways even to him. He had recounted how his covert mission had the approval of his committee chairs and that because of his location on the Twin Worlds, he had been unable to seek additional guidance from his superiors. However, he spoke quite clearly of how his behavior and that of Captain Raina Wolfe of the Central Federation was consistent with the expectations of a senior captain within the Star Alliance, including his protection of human life, duty to the principles of the Alliance, and for justice. As he finished his narrative, the board was silent. After a few moments, Demeter Long faced the chair and smiled. North acknowledged her.

"Fleet Marshall North, and members of the board," Long said. "There is always the opportunity to interpret actions of individuals in light of the guiding principles and expectations they have to fulfill, which I am sure is your task here today. For the record, however, let me say two things: first, that the facts of the situation as recounted by Captain McLeod are the truth -- nothing added, and nothing left out. Second, it was the actions of Captain McLeod, Captain Wolfe and their companions which provided the spark that made the negotiations successful and rooted out a conspiracy which has rocked the Beta Quadrant Intercouncil and the Twin Worlds." Long looked briefly at all the board members. "I will let you decide how to determine conduct becoming an officer." Then, Long turned to McLeod.

"Captain," she began. "I believe you were informed that Councilor Trent has been indicted for treason."

McLeod nodded. "I have, Minister," he said. "And I must admit I still shudder when I think of his part in the whole conspiracy."

"Trent is facing a life sentence," Long responded. "It is a disappointing ending to his diplomatic career. Long smiled. "On the other hand," she continued, "I can see you have many talents, and *some* of those may be applicable to the diplomatic corps. However, the majority of what we do is not the behind-the-scenes cloak and dagger work that occurred on the Twin Worlds, but the behind-the-scenes slogging, research and persuasion that you and Captain Wolfe engaged in with your committee. You staffed that committee quite well." Long smiled again. "And if you are comfortable with doing that again *and again*, then moving to serve on the committees yourself, you may have a place in the diplomatic corps.

Then, Long changed tactics. "Consider though, your strong and extensive experience as a ship's captain serving both the Star Alliance and the Central Federation. You have good skills and instincts for diplomatic activities, yet you are one of the finest anywhere when it comes to commanding a starship. Further, you are one of the most highly respected officers in both the Alliance and the Federation." Many of the board members nodded their heads as she spoke. Minister Long was the most persuasive person he had ever met, thought McLeod, and he was happy she was in his corner, rather than opposing him.

After a short silence, Feel Marshall North continued. "Captain McLeod has completed his informal report," said North. He looked around the conference table. "What questions do you have?" There followed questions from all of the board members none of which, reflected McLeod, really probed much. He answered them politely, and actually enjoyed the back and forth with his fellow officers, all of whom he had encountered in the past. As the questions died down, the chair again called the board meeting to order.

"Captain," North began, "I think we have enough from you at this time. Have you anything else to add?

McLeod did not. "No, Sir." McLeod said. "Thank you for the opportunity." McLeod rose, was properly dismissed, and was leaving the conference room when the board chair stopped him.

"Tucker?"

"Sir?"

Wait outside, if you would."

McLeod nodded. "Sir."

Ten minutes later, Morgan North himself opened the conference room door and beckoned McLeod inside. McLeod took two steps into the room where he noticed a familiar friend and mentor.

"Fleet Marshall Sinclair!" he cried, smiling widely.

Sinclair rose. "Let's greet each other as friends, Tucker." They advanced and embraced each other.

McLeod was surprised. "What are you doing here?"

Sinclair chuckled, and waved everyone to seats, everyone consisting of Fleet Marshall North, Demeter Long, McLeod and himself. As the formal head of the Central Federation Space Service, every military person there was his subordinate: yet Sinclair had always been more of a mentor and guide to McLeod than task master.

"What am I doing here," Sinclair repeated. "I am here to perhaps talk an old friend out of leaving the Star Alliance force he has served so well. They tell me Tucker, that you are considering moving to the diplomatic corps." Sinclair gave a small shudder as he said "diplomatic" to the amused delight of Long. "Is that correct?"

McLeod smiled. "It is, Fleet Marshall," said McLeod. Sinclair nodded, which McLeod knew meant "keep going."

"I've enjoyed and been honored to serve in our military, and I want to continue to serve the Alliance in some capacity," McLeod said. "Having said that, I believe too often our first reaction is to threaten or fire rather than to listen, and persuade. If I've learned anything from these last two weeks, it is that persuasion is still the best way."

"Did you enjoy the assignment -- the official part, I mean?"

McLeod nodded. "I did -- especially working so closely with Captain Wolfe again. Working with the other committee and staff members gave me a glimpse into their culture and what was important to them, and I believe we worked well together as a team. I could certainly see myself doing that again in a similar assignment."

Sinclair smiled. "How about the unofficial part of the assignment?"

McLeod laughed. "There *was* no unofficial part of the assignment, sir."

Sinclair nodded again, and McLeod continued.

"Well, except for being shot and undergoing warfare surgery," McLeod began to their smiles, "I rather enjoyed it. We were able to investigate and resolve a very difficult situation, with no loss of life on our part. That certainly couldn't be guaranteed, but I'm proud of it none the less. So, yes, I did find it enjoyable and a positive accomplishment."

Sinclair looked at his colleagues, before raising his chin to North.

"Captain McLeod," began North, "I have been authorized, to again offer you command of SAV/ *Valiant* for its next tour, with your serving as Fleet Captain for Beta Quadrant." Before McLeod could speak, Long broke in.

"And I have been authorized to offer you a position as a staff member with the diplomatic academy, to both train and serve as a member of diplomatic missions on behalf of the Star Alliance."

McLeod was speechless, but before he could acknowledge either offer, Sinclair spoke again.

"And I have been authorized to suggest a third option to you."

Chapter Thirty Seven

Star Alliance Beta Quadrant Headquarters Conference Room C

"Tucker," began Sinclair, "You've mentioned previously about your dedication to the Star Alliance, and of course also to the Central Federation as a former executive officer. Can you expand on that?"

McLeod was confused, but started. "Fleet Marshall, the Star Alliance and the Central Federation are important forces for good in the galaxy. I entered the service hoping to make people's lives better, help keep them safe, and help people cooperate for the common good. I believe I've done that in both the Alliance and the Federation." He had become more animated now. "It's one of the reasons I want to make the shift to diplomatic. I believe that if more worlds were voluntarily aligned with the Alliance or the Federation, we would have a stronger and better framework for lasting peace and prosperity in the galaxy. It's also one of the sadder parts of my experience on the Twin Worlds, because I realize that while they may be able to settle their internal challenges for now, they are unlikely to continue to pursue Federation membership at least in the short term." McLeod raised his eyes and smiled. "But that's what self-determination is all about." Sinclair nodded, but this time, McLeod knew the fleet marshall wasn't asking him to continue. "How does he do that?" McLeod mused.

"Thank you, Tucker," Sinclair said. "I believe we all knew of those feelings, but we needed to hear them again." He sat back in his chair. "We asked you here Tucker, to see if you might be willing to consider, as I said before, a third option, which we believe would help you to continue to do what you say you want to do within the galaxy." Sinclair turned his attention toward the wall to his right. "Take a look at this vid screen," he said. McLeod looked to the large vid screen, and quickly, a ship appeared on it. He looked at it briefly, then turned to Sinclair.

Sinclair continued, "What do you think, Tucker? How would you describe this vessel?" McLeod looked at it briefly again, then rose from his seat to look at the vessel more closely. He was nodding his head, and evaluating when the fleet marshall interrupted his thoughts.

"General description?"

"Well, Sir, I would say it is in the same general class as a Luwen or Excursion class vessel from the Federation or Alliance, though not either one of those -- quite similar , though."

"If configured for battle, what would you say the complement would be?"

"About the same as for a Luwen or Excursion Class vessel," he said. "Somewhere between 40 and 60." Nod from the fleet marshall.

"What about weapons?" the fleet marshall inquired.

"That's harder to say, "said McLeod. "Part of evaluating the weapons that might be employed depends on configuration." Sinclair nodded again. "But, if I were pressed, I would say several torpedo bays, plasma missiles, and some projectile cannon." He paused again to think, and turned to the fleet marshall. "Maximums might be around 200 torpedoes, 150 plasma missiles, and perhaps 500-1000 projectiles, but that would depend on size and type. Obviously, depending on date of manufacture, it may also have phase weapons."

Sinclair turned to his colleague. "Morgan?" North had been smiling, and he nodded his head before adding, "That sounds about right, Tucker. Now," he turned and pointed to the vid screen again as the picture changed. "What about *this* one?" The ship on the vid screen was of similar size, but was obviously a fresh ship.

McLeod frowned briefly before answering. "I would say it was a transport ship --a freighter. In fact," he squinted again, "it reminds me of a ship from the Toshino shipyards -- you know, very big, reliable, not particularly quick but not designed to be."

"What about weapons?" asked North.

McLeod shook his head. "Not many, and purely defensive," he said. "So, most likely projectile cannon and some torpedoes." He shook his head again. "No, if the ship was traveling by itself, the kinds of things they would be transporting wouldn't warrant more weapons. And if they were transporting cargo that would make them more open to piracy, they would have private escorts with more powerful weapons."

North nodded his head, and turned to Sinclair. "I would have thought the same, Xavier."

Sinclair smiled. "I would agree, Morgan," Sinclair said. Then he turned to McLeod.

"What if I were to tell you, Tucker," he began, his eyes Twinkling, "that those two ships" he pointed to the vid screen, "are one and the same?"

* * *

Central Federation Beta Quadrant Headquarters, Temporary Officers Quarters

McLeod walked confidently down the passageway with his holo pack, and stopped in front of the door. He touched the door chime and waited.

"Come!" Wolfe said. Her door slid noiselessly to the side as she moved to greet her visitor. She smiled, stepped aside to let him in, and motioned toward an empty chair.

"So," she began, "Are you still employed?"

McLeod smiled back. "Yes, it actually went rather well, considering."

Wolfe frowned. "Considering what?"

"Considering the three choices I was given. That doesn't happen very often." McLeod continued to smile, and Wolfe was cautious.

"Alright, I'll play," she said. "Are you gonna tell me the three choices?"

"Sure," McLeod said. "One is to take command of *Valiant* -- they're holding it for me for two more weeks."

"That's the one you should take," Wolfe interjected.

McLeod stared at her. *"Continuing,"* he said sternly, "Option two is a position at the diplomatic academy, and following that with assignments on committees and teams like the one we just served on." He turned to Wolfe. "Minister Long seems to think I have a flair for this sort of thing." Wolfe was silent as she rolled her eyes.

"But then, they explained option number three, and that got me thinking." Something in McLeod's face interested her.

Wolfe sat up straighter. "Who is 'they?'"

"Well, for one thing, it included Fleet Marshall Sinclair…."

"Fleet Marshall Sinclair!" Wolfe found herself suppressing the urge to rise and stand at attention.

"In the flesh," said McLeod. "You can imagine how I responded to that."

"Wow."

"Exactly. So, I'm here to make an appeal to you."

Wolfe frowned. "Regarding this third option?"

"Yep."

Wolfe made a "come on, gesture." McLeod laughed, and turned on the holo pack. The pack projected a 3-dimensional version of the first ship he had been shown in the conference room, turning on an axis. "Here it is," he said. "You know, I respect and love *Valiant* -- but this" he gestured toward the holo -- "has really turned my head."

Wolfe frowned again. "It's … little," she said. Then she saw the ship morph.

"Whoa!"

"Exactly," said McLeod. He faced his friend. "It's primarily Federation technology, and according to Fleet Marshall Sinclair, Minister Long and Fleet Marshall North of the Gamma Quadrant, this ship is not for regular travel."

"What's it for?"

McLeod hesitated before continuing. "Think Kenya System. We orbited that world for weeks trying to work with their internal politicians…"

"The local Shans," said Wolfe.

McLeod shook his head. "Not really -- I would say it was more like radical Independents. Anyway, they were bombing trade access points and causing havoc." McLeod could see a metaphorical light bulb turn on in his friend's head.

"So you went planet-side and removed all the mines," Wolfe said. "I remember after that: the military and civilian forces of the homeworld were able to bring order and stability back to the planet." She turned to McLeod. "You did that."

McLeod looked up, still recalling the incident. "Well, we, but yes, I was involved in that, and it was strangely satisfying, helping a world knock down barriers to the Federation. And I remember doing the same things with a couple of worlds seeking Alliance membership. Now, that wasn't diplomatic, per se, and it wasn't purely military, but it made a difference in both the diplomatic and military fronts there." His energy rose again as he spoke.

"This new ship's basic task is to continue work like that in any region or quadrant where we can advance military cooperation, diplomatic work, and both Alliance and Federation membership and scope within the galaxy. So, using this lens, our work on Hemod and Herai *was* kind of diplomatic."

Wolfe remained confused, but intrigued. "So," she said, "that's your new mission?"

"It's the mission of *Raven*," McLeod said, pointing to the ship. "Fleet Marshall Sinclair indicated that it is an Experimental Revopod Vessel from the Nova 9 shipyards; the letters were RVEN, so *Raven*."

Wolfe pointed. "This is *Raven*?"

"Right."

"But you said it's primarily Federation technology."

"Yep." Just then the holo changed to a very different configuration.

Wolfe's eyes widened again. "How many configurations does this ship have?" she asked.

"Five," McLeod said. "And it has seven different and cloaked ID beacons. It's only going to appear to be what we *want* it to be."

Wolfe continued to shake her head. "Wow," she repeated. Then she squinted, "But if this is primarily Federation technology, does this mean you'll be the first Alliance captain of a Federation vessel?" Before he could answer, she added, "or does this mean that you're finally going to cross over to our team for good?"

"Well," McLeod said, "There are those who would say if anyone was going to be the first Alliance Captain of a Federation vessel, it would *have* to be me."

"I'd certainly agree with that," Wolfe said. "So, what is the plan for *Raven*?"

"The plan is to have a joint Alliance and Federation crew, with two captains: one Alliance and one Federation, like the *Galatea* years ago."

Wolfe shuddered. "Not the best example, but then, they're not you," she said.

"Or *you*," McLeod said. Wolfe's and McLeod's eyes locked.

"Wait a minute," Wolfe began, "there's…."

McLeod help up his hand. "There's nothing that would compromise your taking over FV/ *Axon* as scheduled. But who else in the Federation is better qualified for this kind of role than you? Just as there is really no one in the Alliance better qualified for this role than me."

Wolfe shook her head. "This is asking a lot, Tucker."

McLeod nodded his agreement. "Well, they've been working on *Raven* for over seven years, and during half of that time they've been trying to find the inaugural commanders who can turn their vision into reality. And, it is the preference of Fleet Marshall Sinclair that we be the inaugural team." McLeod smiled.

"No pressure, right?" Wolfe asked.

"Not from the Fleet Marshall: I can't promise that for me."

Wolfe sighed. "How many worlds would you be traveling to? Notice that I said '*you*.'"

McLeod was excited nonetheless. "Oh, that's the best part," he said, then grew a bit somber. "Remember our defeat at Canbera Prime?"

Wolfe blew out a breath. "The *Chilko* and the *Scimitar* practically destroyed each other because…"

"Because they didn't understand each other," McLeod said. "They couldn't communicate, they had no real knowledge of tactics or strategy, weapons configuration, or just the basics of working together. It was just a disaster." Wolfe nodded gravely.

McLeod continued. "Well," he said, "That has to change. Do you realize there are only 9 active officers in the Alliance or the Federation who have ever served full tours on the opposite organization's vessels?" Wolfe squinted, trying to name all the officers, but shook her head and conceded the point.

"Well," McLeod continued. "Someone has to teach these tactics to our officers and senior NCOs-- the ways of collaborating that have become second nature to you and me."

"I can already see where this is heading, Tucker, and I'm not sure I like it."

McLeod chose to ignore her point. "When they offered me *Raven*, they told me they needed a Federation captain and co-director of the new training academy who would share command of *Raven* with me." He smiled. "My only question was would I have any input into the choice of the Federation captain. Fleet Marshall Sinclair looked at me and said,

"Why don't you just go and ask Raina yourself, Tucker?"

"So before you sock me, here's the proposal: you have eighteen to twenty standard months of refit of *Axon* ahead of you. If nothing else, we really need your experience in curriculum and training to get the academy started and to train someone else to take over when you assume active control of *Axon*." McLeod looked at Wolfe more seriously, "The Federation needs you and needs *Axon*, especially in the Beta Quadrant, but there is no one other than you who can really do with this *Raven*." So, how about two months here and one month there to supervise *Axon* and continue with crew selection, and most especially with selection of the next Federation captain for the academy and *Raven*?"

Wolfe looked at him before responding. "You know I need to be successful on *Axon*. It may be my only Federation command."

McLeod huffed. "That's their problem, not yours -- you should have had command years ago."

"I'm not getting into that. But I really need to think this offer through."

"Raina, know that anything you choose to do will be alright, and also know that you are the person I want to work with on this."

Wolfe smiled. "Again, no pressure, right?"

"Call it medium pressure," McLeod said. "And if you decide the answer is no, I'll need your help in identifying someone else from the Federation; unfortunately, that is a very short list."

There was a twinkle in Wolfe's eyes. "So, do you think we could attract a couple from that short list for this team?"

"If that's consent," began McLeod, "the answer is 'yes.'"

"Let me give you my final answer after speaking with Fleet Marshall Wyndham." Wolfe looked up. "Does he already know?"

"I'm not sure, though I bet he's been given a pre-notice."

"So," Wolfe began, her head indicating the holo, "Can you show me some more of those configurations?"

The end

If you liked this book, review it at fjtalley.com or by using this QR Code:

Feedback is sincerely appreciated.

Thank you,

F. J. T.